Pha..er wrists
and blir...his eyes
filled he.. fingertips acro...here disappear. ....uld not
resist ar.............

Go ....into his
chest. H..ger kept
him san..s much
havoc o..hen and
he push...forced a
weak cr..Phaedra
could fe.....

WILD RAVENS

ALTONYA WASHINGTON

Genesis Press Inc.

Indigo Love Stories

An imprint of Genesis Press Inc.
Publishing Company

Genesis Press, Inc.
P.O. Box 101
Columbus, MS 39703

ISBN: 1-58571-164-0
Manufactured in the United States of America

First Edition

Visit us at www.genesis-press.com
or call at 1-888-Indigo-1

DEDICATION

To everyone who always believed my dreams would come true.

ACKNOWLEDGMENTS

I thank and praise God for the gift of writing.
I thank all the readers and book clubs who have made writing such a joy.
Deatri and Angelique: my wonderful editors. Thanks ladies.

PROLOGUE

Throbbing drums resound with a haunting rhythm. They announce the Voodoo ceremony.

Haiti 1860

"Duvalier! Dammit, man, keep up with me for Christ's sake!" Fredericks Toussaint's low voice shook with anger when he glanced back to see his brother-in-law lagging behind.

Duvalier Adolfe brushed at the sweat beaded on his forehead and sighed. His brown eyes were blurred by the smoke in the air. The foreboding black cloud made it difficult to follow Fredericks' hurried stride.

Fredericks' handsome face twisted into a murderous frown. He couldn't believe he was out in a darkened field in the middle of the night. Unfortunately, he was a protective older brother and could not sleep knowing his sister was somewhere out there.

"Fredericks!" Duvalier called, his voice hushed from fear, "I think I hear something."

"So do I." Fredericks confirmed, a grim smirk tightening his lips.

The two young men pushed on. They drew closer to what sounded like hundreds of footsteps moving in a syncopated fashion. Fredericks' onyx eyes widened, as he spied the orange fire dancing high above the tall grass.

"Damn you, Lucia." He growled, knowing he would find his twin sister in the group gathered around the dazzling flame.

"Fredericks, perhaps we should get help from the others." Duvalier suggested in a hopeful tone. Although it was his own wife—the mother of his three children—frolicking in the field, he had no desire to be her rescuer.

Fredericks shook his head, grimacing as his long cloak caught in the thick stalks of grass. "You know damn well we can't do that. Now shut up and move!"

Duvalier's eyes closed briefly as regret settled within his bones. His heart pounded at the sight of the fire. The monstrous flame seemed to come alive against the black sky.

"Lucia, this time you've done it my girl," Fredericks silently chanted. He could imagine how their elder siblings would react if they discovered the girl had taken part in this sort of ritual. Of course, this was not the first time Fredericks' twin had ventured out to one of the forbidden ceremonies against their wishes. Moreover, it was not the first time Fredericks himself had set out to bring her back. He could only hope to return his sister home without alerting their older brothers and sisters. He knew they would surely whip Lucia if they discovered she had been party to the same evil they believed had taken the lives of their parents.

Fredericks and Duvalier pressed on until they reached a clearing in the center of the field. Fredericks ducked low in the high grass, pulling a dumbstruck Duvalier down with him.

The clearing covered a vast area of land within the field. People were chanting and dancing with feverish intensity. The drums provided the thundering melody that aroused the spirit and moved the feet. The age of the crowd ranged from the most elderly to the youngest members of the village. Upon first glance, it appeared that the group was simply in the midst of a great celebration.

Unfortunately, Fredericks and his family had seen the "dark side" of the religion, and they had no desire to be part of it.

"We have to get Lucia out of here," Fredericks whispered and focused on the mesmerizing scene before him. "We must join the ritual."

Duvalier, who had closed his eyes for a moment of prayer, gasped at the suggestion. "What?"

"It's the only way to get Lucia out of here without being noticed," Fredericks reasoned, pulling the hood of his black cloak over his head.

Duvalier followed his brother-in-law, pulling his cloak hood over his thick bush of hair. Taking a deep breath, he ran out behind Fredericks and joined the dance.

The two blended into the sea of bodies. They mimicked the wild, uninhibited movements around the scorching flame. Fredericks' stare remained alert, and soon he glimpsed his sister through the popping flames and thick smoke.

Lucia Toussaint-Adolfe threw her head back and ran her slender fingers through her long, thick braided hair. Her arms began to flail fiercely in the air as she repeated the chanting of the other participants. She was so carried away by the euphoric emotions surging through her, she did not notice her twin brother dancing in her direction.

Fredericks managed to grab Lucia. He gave a silent prayer of thanks that he had gotten her. She was so taken by the spirit of the moment that she did not realize she was being "abducted." She didn't scream, and Fredericks was confident they could leave without ever being noticed.

However, things were not meant to move quite so smoothly. Lucia looked around and saw her brother's sinfully handsome face, her eyes narrowed. A piercing scream ripped from her throat, and she instantly began to struggle in his arms.

Fredericks' hold around his sister's waist immediately tightened, and he wound his free hand into her hair. "Shut up, Lucia, unless you want to arrive home unconscious." He warned.

"You black bastard! Get the hell away from me!"

"Lucia—"

"You let me go this instant, Fredericks! I mean it!"

Fredericks gave a sharp tug on the braids, urging Lucia's head back. "I will not let you remain here another instant. Do you understand me?" He sneered, his eyes seeming to shoot daggers right through her.

"You will not let me?" Lucia repeated, her expression just as murderous. "You stinking bastard, I am as old as you are. I curse your bloody soul to hell!"

Fredericks let go of Lucia's hair as he laid a harsh blow to the side of her face. "Shut your filthy mouth! I am taking you home."

Lucia's body bucked wildly as she tried to escape her brother's embrace. "I'm not a child, you horse's ass!"

"Speaking of children, you have three at home crying for you, witch!" Fredericks growled, cupping his sister's chin in his hand.

The mention of her sons sent Lucia into an even wilder rage. Duvalier held back, hoping Fredericks could control her. When he saw that she appeared to be even more outraged, he rushed over to help calm her.

Unfortunately, Lucia was beyond taming. It seemed that she possessed more than her usual strength that night. Fighting against Fredericks, she reared back and her elbow connected with Duvalier's throat as he approached.

"Lucia," Duvalier gasped in shock. The breath was knocked from him, and he fell back into the raging fire.

Duvalier's tortured screams reached their ears. Fredericks and Lucia ceased their fighting. Incredibly, the chanting around them grew louder. It drained the man's cries for help. Fredericks pushed his sister aside and rushed to rescue his friend from the searing flames. The scorching mass engulfed the Duvalier's body, turning it charred and bloody at once. Miraculously, the crowd didn't seem horrified by the event. Instead, they grew more frenzied as though celebrating the fact that one of their members was so overcome by the spirits that he actually sacrificed himself to the yellow orange inferno.

Fredericks could not believe his eyes, which widened at the terrifying scene. The fire incenerated Duvalier's body. The greedy flames devoured everything they touched. Lucia's screaming finally broke through Fredericks' entranced mind.

"You bloody bastard," Lucia breathed, hatred making her high-pitched voice sound raspy.

Fredericks ignored the words and hoisted Lucia across his shoulder. With his burden, he ran from the scene which was still at its peak.

"Get your filthy hands off me you son of a bitch! You murdered my husband, damn you!" Lucia's screams and curses filled the air and showed no signs of abating. "Your soul will rot for this Fredericks! I'll make you pay. I swear it! I swear it!"

Fredericks grimaced. His sister's foul words grew louder the closer they came to their home. He had hoped to sneak her inside without anyone's knowledge. Of course, that would not be possible after all that had happened.

Fortunately, Lucia was almost unconscious from delirium when her brother's heavy boots bounded upon the wooden steps.

"I'll make you pay for this, Fredericks. I swear it. You will pay, you will…" Lucia's words had lost their volume, but not their intensity. She lay like a limp sack across her brother's shoulder and sighed words of revenge.

No sooner than Fredericks reached the top step of the house, did the front door open. The family—consisting of five brothers, three sisters and their spouses—rushed out to the small porch.

"Oh my Sweet Lord!" Lisette Moreau screamed when she saw the white paint on her younger sister's face.

"Christ, Fredericks, what went on here?" Chapel Toussaint, the eldest, demanded.

The excitement of the evening took more of a toll on Fredericks than he realized. His long legs almost buckled beneath him, and the family relieved him of Lucia. Tunel and Briggs, two of the brothers, helped Fredericks into the house.

"What the hell happened tonight, Ric?" Chapel demanded once again. He braced his hands on the other either side of the chair Fredericks occupied.

Fredericks sighed, resting his head back against the chair. "I followed her to a gathering out in the fields."

"Shit," Chapel whispered, as did the other men in the room. "Damn her. She gave you a good fight, I take it?" He asked, glancing back at his sister, who laid in Lisette's arms.

Fredericks' gaze was hooded as it slid over to his twin. The girl was unable to move, but still murmured words of hate.

"She did at that," Fredericks confirmed. He waited a moment then

5

looked into his brother's onyx eyes. "But, it was Duvalier who received the most punishment."

Topol Toussaint, the next eldest brother, looked out the spotless glass windows. "Where the devil is he?" he asked, frowning into the night.

Fredericks' eyes closed, and he inhaled a deep, shaking breath. "He tried to stop Lucia and me from fighting. One of her blows caught him in the throat. He fell into the fire—a monstrous flame. Duvalier is dead."

The men were silent. Soft sobs could be heard from the women in the room.

"Duvalier...Duvalier..." Lucia groaned in her partially conscious state. Her lashes finally fluttered open, and her eyes focused on Fredericks. "You son of a bitch." She sneered. "I hate you. With everything in me, I hate you. You will pay for this shit, Fredericks."

Chapel frowned and looked at his youngest brother. "What the hell is she rambling about, Ric?"

"She blames me for his death. I think she has blocked out what really happened out there tonight."

"I have blocked nothing out, you filthy black bastard!"

"Shut your mouth, Lucia!" Topol ordered.

"Blast you, Topol. Blast all of you!" the girl screamed as she fought viciously to escape her sister's arms.

As the woman struggled to hold Lucia down, Chapel grimaced and stormed over to them. With one swift blow from his fist, he knocked Lucia unconscious.

"Now listen everyone," Chapel ordered his silenced family, "we have no choice but to leave this place."

"Leave?" someone asked.

Chapel nodded. "Before the same evil that destroyed our parents destroys us. Duvalier's dead, Lucia's mind is in shambles. We can not remain here."

"But, Chapel, are you sure about this?" Tunel asked, stepping closer to his brother. "To take everything and go? Just leave?"

"We have no choice. Look at what has happened this night. Not to mention all the nights before," Chapel replied, his expression a mixture of sadness and anger.

Though everyone in the room agreed with Chapel, none of them wanted to leave. They had all been born and raised in Haiti. For all the evil that had infiltrated their lives, there had been just as much good.

The Voodoo religion, like many other religions, involved acts of piety. Healing of sickness, love and protection of home, land and family were just as important in the Voodoo religion as they were in other beliefs.

It was, however, the "dark side" that the family feared. There were those who practiced what was called the "work of the left hand." Secret societies, those who believed in zombies and other wicked acts—such as human sacrifice—were to be avoided at all costs. The majority of the Toussaint clan believed that this particular evil had taken over their village.

"Fredericks? Fredericks!" a frantic, female voice called.

Marguerite Levieux Toussaint rushed into the sitting room. Her exquisite hazel eyes searched the room for her husband.

Fredericks stood and opened his arms to his pregnant wife. He buried his handsome face into her thick, wavy hair and inhaled the fresh scent it always carried.

Marguerite hugged him tightly, closing her eyes as she breathed a sigh of relief. "I was so worried," she whispered.

"Shh…it's alright. Everything is alright," Fredericks soothed.

Suddenly, Ibo—husband to Saeeda, the eldest sister—cleared his throat and stepped forward. "If we can't see the need to leave for all our sakes, then we must for the sake of the children," he solemnly declared, his look soft as he looked toward Marguerite's swollen belly.

"My husband is right," Saeeda agreed, coming to take her husband's arm. "It'll be best for us all if we leave this place."

Everyone focused on Marguerite and Fredericks. Soon, they were all nodding in agreement.

Mandel Toussaint, the middle brother, stepped to the center of the room. "Lisette, you and Saeeda take Lucia upstairs and help her pack."

"I'll help," Marguerite offered, and the other wives followed suit. In Fredericks' arms, she turned and pressed a tender kiss to his lips. "I love you," she whispered.

"And I you," he whispered back. His onyx stare was intense as it traced every inch of her lovely, brown, oval face.

The women adjourned upstairs to pack the family's belongings. Meanwhile, the men made arrangements for their voyage out of Haiti.

"I'll take everything from him. I swear it," Lucia promised. She had recovered from Chapel's blow to her face and was cursing her twin with renewed fervor.

Sadly, Lucia vented her hatred and anger in the presence of her three, small children. The boys—Marquis, Carlos and Dante—stood, watching their enraged mother. They were in tears as Lucia told them her version of their father's death.

Young and impressionable, the children were easily influenced by their mother's words. Instantly, the uncle they adored became the man they would hate.

Seeing the tears filling her son's eyes, Lucia pulled the boys close to her. "Do not worry, my loves." She sighed, pressing kisses to their hair. "Fredericks will pay. Every one of them will pay."

Marguerite found her husband on the porch later that night. She watched him for a moment before joining him on the top step.

"Careful, Love," Fredericks cautioned as his wife eased herself onto the step. He turned to help her down then pulled her close. "What are you doing out here?" he asked.

"That's what I came to ask you," Marguerite replied, her wide bright eyes searching Fredericks', narrowed ones.

"I wanted to get some air."

"You must be tired after all that has happened?" Marguerite noted, smoothing her small hand over her husband's cheek. "You should try resting before we leave."

Fredericks kissed Marguerite's hand. "I'll rest when we are far away from here."

"So, you agree with Chapel that we should leave?"

"I've never been in more agreement with anything."

Marguerite sighed and looked up at the star-filled sky. "This is the only home we have ever known. There has been so much happiness."

"And so much pain," Fredericks reminded her. "Now we are to have a child. I don't want any of that to touch our girl."

"Listen to you." Marguerite laughed. "I'm the one with the gift of sight."

Fredericks kissed her cheek. "Well, you say we are having a girl so often that I now believe it. I only want you and our child to be safe."

Marguerite threw her arms around Fredericks' neck and hugged him tightly. "If you think it will be good for us, then so do I."

"I do, love. I truly do."

CHAPTER 1

~Dominica 1879~

"You are the image of her."

"So you often tell me."

Fredericks Toussaint covered his daughter's hand where it rested against his stomach. "It's true." He assured the striking, raven-haired young woman at his bedside. She would be so proud of you. She would be as proud as I am."

"Papa…" Phaedra Toussaint whispered, leaning close to kiss her father's hair-roughened cheek. "You always make me feel as though I could slay dragons," she teased.

Despite his weakened state, Fredericks managed to laugh. "My dear beauty, I have no doubt you could, should the need ever arise."

Phaedra's striking eyes twinkled with the love she felt for her father. "There don't appear to be many dragons in existence these days."

"On the contrary, love," Fredericks replied, his voice harboring a solemn tone. "There are still a few left to slay."

"I don't understand, Papa."

Fredericks brought Phaedra's hand to his mouth. "Keeping Toussaints together may prove to be quite a battle."

Phaedra's eyes narrowed. "Toussaints?"

"Phaedra, you know that I am dying."

"Papa don't—"

"Hear me now," he softly urged, squeezing her hand. "I'm the last of the eldest remaining on this plantation. When I go, it'll be up to you and your cousins to keep Toussaints thriving. It's your heritage."

Phaedra kissed her father's temple. "I know that, Papa. But you should rest—"

"Listen to me, Phaedra. I know that you and your cousins have had your differences, but it is imperative that you make peace with them."

"Why, Papa?" Phaedra asked, fire coming to her eyes. "Those three have certainly never sought my friendship."

"You must be above that!" Fredericks snapped, the fire in his eyes clearly outmatching his daughter's. "You must get along with them. They will need…someone to love them, care for them when I am gone. I know they pretend to be callous and untouchable, but that is because they have had a very rough time of living with the scandal surrounding their father's death."

Phaedra was clearly unconvinced. "They have lived in luxury since the day they came to Toussaints. Love appears to be the last thing they want or need."

"My sweet, no one else in our family has ever given my twin sister's sons a chance. They were three innocent boys, living in the shadow of a tragedy. They will live under their mother's sins forever."

"Alright, Papa, I'll make the effort…for you," Phaedra soothed, smoothing her hands across the bed covers. "I want you to rest now," she urged, then kissed his cheek and left the bedchamber.

Out in the hallway, she folded her arms at her waist and thought about her father's words. She strolled the red carpet lining the corridor and prayed for the strength to do as he had asked. She hated the trio of brothers as much as anyone in the family. Perhaps, her hatred ran more deeply, since she had practically grown up in their shadow. As most of the family moved on over the years, she had been a witness to their transformation from spoiled boys to pompous men.

Phaedra passed the open door of her father's study with little more than a quick glance in the room. Still, it was long enough to catch sight of her cousins there.

"What are you three doing in here?" she spat, watching Marquis, Carlos and Dante Toussaint whirl around to face her.

Carlos stepped forward. "Phaedra, calm yourself."

"Calm myself? Calm myself when I've just come from my father's bedside, where he's fighting for his life, to find you three rifling through his private things?!"

"Rifling, Phaedra?" Dante challenged, pushing his hands into the small pockets of his waistcoat. "An unfair choice of words, don't you think? We are, after all, Uncle Fredericks' business assistants."

"Hmph. Assistants in spending his money, you mean?"

"You little—"

"Get out of here and spend some time at your uncle's bedside instead of sniffing around like a pack of dogs scrapping for meat!" she ordered, realizing it would be impossible for her to offer a friendly hand to her cousins. With those words, she turned and left the study. The folds of her emerald gown flowed behind her in a cool, graceful fashion.

"That little wench!" Dante hissed once he and his brothers were alone.

The eldest of the three, Marquis Toussaint, had remained calm and silent. He listened as his brothers vented their frustrations. When they turned to him for answers, he stood.

"Once our dear uncle is dead and buried, our first order of business is to get rid of that over-confident young woman, " he said, fixing his brothers with a firm look. "In spite of the fact that she is a woman and has no real head for business, that won't stop our uncle from leaving this place to her when he dies. I won't allow that. I want this land, and I intend to have it."

One month later

Serenity mingled with the cool sea air like a tangible thing. Though the day was slightly overcast, the skies above the lovely island had remained calm. As the foamy waves crashed against the rocks along the bank, a strong wind stirred. Heavy banana tree branches swayed in the invigorating breeze, their leaves dancing merrily. A young woman sat high atop the cliffs overlooking the Caribbean Sea.

Phaedra Toussaint closed her eyes and inhaled the clear sea air. She heard a bird call and her long lashes fluttered open to locate the direction of the cry. The brisk breeze lifted tendrils of her thick, waistlength hair and she had the look of an angel in flight as the wavy locks whipped around her , oval face.

Phaedra's expression was solemn as she watched the breathtaking view. She couldn't believe how much her beloved home had changed. The peacefulness that would have relaxed most, only reminded her of how deserted the land was. It seemed that only a few short years ago, sounds of life and laughter had filled the air.

The Toussaint clan had settled on the small island of Dominica in 1860. It was a struggle that would have discouraged many, but the Toussaints were a determined clan. The group restored the inherited plantation to its former glory. They cultivated the land which produced the most splendid fruits. The crops yielded unimagined profits and brought the family wealth they never expected or dreamed of. Hardwork, dedication and sacrifice paid off in the best way. The family settled the vast area at the tip of the island and flourished. They thrived abundantly, in addition to the lush fruits, vegetables and healthy animals that inhabited the frequently rainy land.

Phaedra sighed as she snatched a long stalk of grass from the ground and chewed it absently. Yes, she thought, family had once thrived here. Unfortunately, that all changed, and, now, even her father was gone.

A lone tear blurred her vision for a brief second then slid down the flawless skin of her cheek. Two hands settled upon her shoulders. Thankful for the interruption before her emotions could get the better of her, she looked up.

"Kwesi," she sighed, smiling at the sight of her father's great friend and advisor.

Kwesi Berekua was named for a small village on the other side of Toussaints. His family had settled on the land and was a great help to the Toussaint clan when they arrived in Dominica from Haiti.

Kwesi pushed the front of his green cloak from his shoulders and knelt beside Phaedra. He pressed a soft kiss to her cheek then pulled her close. "My love, I give you my apologies for not being here to pay my respects to your father."

Phaedra closed her eyes briefly. "There's no need for apologies. I know you would have been here, if possible."

Kwesi bowed his head, acknowledging Phaedra's kind words. "I'll visit Fredericks before I leave," he promised, referring to the burial site where his friend had been lain to rest a week earlier.

"He'd appreciate that," Phaedra said, patting the older man's hand.

Kwesi's eyes crinkled at the corners.. "The place has changed," he noted, appraising the lush greenery that painted the landscape. "Not so much in a physical sense, but…a mood. Do you know what I mean?" he asked, turning to face her.

Phaedra studied Kwesi's brown face in amazement. "I was just thinking that same thing."

"Were you?"

Phaedra nodded at his surprise then returned her solemn stare to the sea. "I was remembering the family and how they filled the place with such…laughter and love. It was a wonderful way to grow up, and then they were gone. Almost as if something…made them all leave."

The surprise on Kwesi's face changed to one of concern. "Are you alright, my love?"

Phaedra ran both hands through her thick mane then buried her face in her palms. "I've just had my mind on home a lot lately," she explained. Her clear, melodic voice muffled.

Kwesi placed his arms around her shoulders and pulled her close. "I can understand that. We both agree that the place has changed."

Phaedra rested her head against his shoulder and sighed. "I've been thinking a lot about Haiti," she clarified.

"Love, Dominica is the only home you've ever known."

"But my roots, Kwesi. My roots are in Haiti. It was the home of my parents."

"A home your parents fled. Remember that," Kwesi advised, standing.

"But why? What could've been so terrible? Terrible enough to make them leave. Take everyone and leave?"

Kwesi shook his head, watching Phaedra; who watched him wide-eyed and expectant. Jesus, she has so much of Fredericks and Marguerite in her, he thought. "My girl, don't torture yourself with this. Your father would not approve."

Phaedra's eyes lowered to the ground. "I know," she admitted in a child-like voice. "I just can't help but feel some sort of attachment to that place, even though I've never been there. I haven't even told anyone about the dream."

"What dream?"

"The same each night. It's as though a message is trying to be delivered, but a fog clouds my view. Whatever it is, I believe it would open my eyes to everything."

Kwesi pressed his fingers to the bridge of his nose. "Phaedra, you shouldn't be thinking of such things."

"But, I can't help it!" she snapped, closing her eyes against the worry on Kwesi's face. "But that is enough about me anyway…what's going on with you?"

A knowing look tugged at Kwesi's full lips as he helped Phaedra to her feet. "Your father left some things that he needed you to be informed of after his passing."

"What things?" Phaedra asked, brushing grass and leaves from the crisp material of her dark blue riding dress.

Kwesi took her hands in his. "It has to do with your inheritance and its terms."

"Mmm hmm," was Phaedra's response as she fell in step next to Kwesi.

"Since Fredericks was left in charge of the land when the family…went their seperate ways, it became his property. As his only child, you are therefore his sole heir. Of course, your father would have left it to you anyway. He had the utmost confidence in your ability to run this estate." Kwesi told Phaedra, watching the pride sparkle in her eyes. "Anyway, this will all be yours on your twentieth birthday."

Phaedra stopped walking and turned. "What happens until then?"

Kwesi propped one hand on his hip and stroked his thick gray beard with the other. "Well, once you're in charge, it will be your responsibility to keep your cousins…comfortable. Until that time, Marquis, Carlos and Dante will be the overseers of the land and the money."

"Hmph. That should make them very happy," Phaedra predicted.

"Hmph. They were at that," Kwesi acknowledged, remembering the happiness on each man's face when he read Fredericks' wishes to them. "Of course, I'll be there to oversee the bulk of their dealings. I think Ric wanted them to ease into the idea of you taking charge," he pondered. "Phaedra, I want you to do something for me."

"Of course," she said, her lovely eyes searching his face intently.

"Just be careful," Kwesi said in his lightest tone. His eyes, however, relayed an urgency in the message.

Phaedra leaned back to give him an inquisitive look. "Now who's sounding strange?"

"Listen to me," Kwesi firmly ordered, bringing his hands down over her shoulders. "You are to be a very wealthy young woman in little more than a year. There are people out here who will do anything to take that away from you. It's not common for a woman to hold such power," he cautioned, fearing that Fredericks had greatly underestimated his nephews' sense of fairness.

"Kwesi—"

"Just be careful," he repeated, kissing her cheek. He walked away, pulling the green cloak around his broad shoulders.

Phaedra's captivating stare was soft as it followed Kwesi's departing figure. It was comforting to have someone worry about her. Somehow, it enabled her to deal with her father's absense.

She wrapped her arms around her slender figure and turned back to the ocean. It drew her close, like a fish to lure. She wanted to look into its blue depths for hours. Unfortunately, the clouds made good on their promise and delivered the rain. The heavy pellets of water hit her just as she resumed her seat along the cliff.

"Midnight! Let's get out of here!" she called, racing toward the breathtaking black Arabian that frolicked in the distance.

The Stallion broke into a light gait as it raced toward its mistress.

"Good boy," she cooed, smoothing her hands over the animal's sleek, onyx mane. She easily pulled herself astride the horse's bare back, and they took off across the field.

The black Stallion and his mistress made a captivating pair as they flew amidst the pelting rain, across the lush, green land. Phaedra felt completely liberated as she thought about her father's wish to have her run the estate. Though she had always been proud of her ability to run the place as well as, or better than, any man; knowing that her father felt that way, left her ecstatic.

Of course, Phaedra had always been eager to learn how to take care of her home. Many marvelled that the tall, voluptuous beauty could have anything other than clothes and parties on her mind. Phaedra had a strong rugged demeanor. She loved the outdoors and had no problem getting her hands dirty.

This facet of her character only seemed to make her more appealing to the opposite sex. Phaedra left every man who met her thunderstruck. Her flawless cocoa complexion was as satiny as it appeared. Her dark eyes were quite mesmerizing. Her small nose and full lips enhanced the fresh, innocent quality she exuded. The only mar to her exquisite features was the small beauty mark that sat just below her earlobe. The manilla colored mark greatly contrasted against the smooth darkness of her skin. But, her most outstanding attribute was her thick mass of shiny, wavy, raven-colored hair that fell to her waist and followed her like a dark cloud.

Though she was confident in her looks and her ability, she was not conceited or snobbish. She was driven by the need to be self-sufficient and protective of her home. She would have to be, in order to survive what lay ahead.

WILD RAVENS

"A toast, brothers. To Uncle Fredericks having such a kind heart," Marquis Toussaint said as he raised his delicate, crystal goblet in the air.

"Hmph. More like a guilty heart," Dante Toussaint grumbled, setting his own wine glass to the cherry wood hutch.

Carlos Toussaint, the middle brother, reclined in a high-backed arm chair. "That is irrelevant, Dante. We have the land."

Dante rolled his eyes. "Yes, we have the land, but only until that little wench turns twenty," he reminded Carlos then turned to Marquis. "I don't care to relinquish my hold on Toussaints."

The eldest brother regarded his younger siblings with a cool look. "I agree with you both. I am determined to ensure our hold on this property."

Dante and Carlos watched him closely.

"Just what do you have in mind?" Carlos asked.

"That, I don't know." Marquis sighed, stroking the light beard that covered his jaw. "We'll have to work fast, though. I want Phaedra occupied. Too occupied to assume her responsibilities when the time comes."

"Nothing would occupy Phaedra that much," Carlos stated, defeat tinging his words.

"That's why it will have to be something that will get her off Toussaints before she turns twenty."

Dante laughed. "Brother, that girl has never been off this island. This will have to be quite a plan."

"Don't worry, little brother," Marquis advised, a wicked smirk coming to his round, face. "It will be. It will be quite a plan."

The brothers once again raised their glasses in toast. The three Toussaint men had already gained reputations on the small island for being ruthless in business, and that ideal definitely pertained to family matters. Lucia Adolfe, their mother, had changed her children's names back to Toussaint soon after their father's death. Though she hated her family passionately, she wanted her children to be privy to all the power and wealth that name would provide.

Of course, Lucia had meant for her sons to inherit all the land and money. The boys hated Fredericks and wanted to avenge their father's death, but Lucia taught them to supress their emotions. At least, for a while. It was imperative that Fredericks trust her sons above everyone else.

Once the boys grew into men, they decided to rid the land of the family. The elders of the Toussaint clan were not so difficult to manipulate. Fredericks, however, was a different matter. Though they managed to gain their uncle's favor, they could not "encourage" him to leave. Marquis, Carlos and Dante felt it was at their mother's intervention when their uncle suddenly took ill and died.

Now, Phaedra was the only family who remained on the island. She was proving to be even more difficult to sway than her father. Marquis didn't have a solid plan to get his cousin away from Toussaints. He only knew that it would have to be done by force.

"Tisha! Tisha!"

Tisha Tou looked up from the large tin tub of wet clothes and waved at Phaedra. The young woman was racing toward her on the black Stallion.

"Now I know I haven't dirtied that many pieces during these last days?" Phaedra teased, swinging off Midnight and eyeing the bundle of clothing.

The forty-one-year-old Tisha looked almost as young as the woman she had practically raised. "How much would you care to wager on that?" she asked, shaking her head.

Phaedra thought it over for a moment then sighed. "Nothing."

"That's what I thought."

"Tisha, why don't you ever use the washing bin I fashioned? I assure you it works."

She glanced over her shoulder and looked in the direction of the stable, where Phaedra's "creation" was stored. "That contraption is a bit too complex for me."

Phaedra gathered her thick hair and quickly twisted it into a long braid. "I promise you it is not as difficult as you think." She told her best friend, once she was done braiding her hair. She pitched in to help with the wash.

Tisha and Phaedra worked in silence for several minutes. After a while, Tisha removed her hands from the water and stared at the young woman next to her. "Something isn't right with you today," she softly noted.

"What?" Phaedra asked, a nervous laugh escaping her lips.

"You heard me."

"Well, I don't know what you mean."

Of course, Tisha knew Phaedra far too well to let things end at that. She watched the girl for a long while. Finally, Phaedra stopped toiling in the wash.

"Ever since things began to change around Toussaints—with the family leaving and all—I've been feeling strange."

"Sickly?" Tisha queried, her palm already pressing Phaedra's cheeks for any signs of fever.

"No, nothing like that," Phaedra assured her, kissing the woman's hand. "It's as if something's happened or is happening all around me. Something…errie," she confided then shook her head. "Listen to me…I think I'm just uneasy with my father being gone and all." She pushed the morose thoughts to the back of her mind. Forcing a dazzling smile to her lips, she kissed Tisha's cheek and walked off with Midnight at her heels.

Tisha's deep gaze followed Phaedra, until the girl had disappeared into the stable barn. She wondered if the time had arrived to have her talk with the young woman.

"You're serious about this, man?" Dubois asked, wiping the sweat from his brow.

Zephir Mfume raked one massive hand through his crop of black hair. His slanting gaze scanned the darkened landscape, and he nodded. "I'm very serious."

Dubois pushed the wide-brimmed straw hat back upon his head. "Do you believe all the talk of there being precious stones out here?"

"Those are nothing more than stories. Not one piece of this land has been sold by the Toussaints in all the years that they have owned it. Instantly, it is assumed there must be something of great value out here."

"But, you don't assume that?" Dubois asked, after a moment of silence.

Zephir's grin revealed a gorgeous set of white teeth and double dimples. The look made him appear dangerous and boyish at once. "I don't believe myths, but I can feel this. There's something out here, and I intend to have it."

The determination in Zephir's rough voice was real. For weeks, he and his most trusted crewmen had been scoping the lush Toussaint land without the family's knowledge. Although the midnight treks upon the land had not been productive, Zephir knew it was only a matter of time.

"What will you do if it is true?" Dubois asked, rubbing a hand across his brown, hair-roughened jaw.

Zephir shrugged a broad shoulder. "I'll worry about that when the time comes. Right now, I think we should begin exploring those caves we found not far from here." He called to the rest of the men and instructed them to gather everything and head out to the caves.

Zephir Mfume was a brooding young man. The son of an African slave and Cuban farmgirl, he was a natural leader and dedicated when it came to getting something he wanted. Understandably, the fact that he was a tall, confident and extremely good-looking, made obtaining his desires less difficult. Zephir possessed a thick, luscious crop of silky close cut hair. Heavy tendrils fell onto his wide forehead which often shielded his penetrating, slanting black look. The long nose and full lips further enhanced his fantastic looks. Standing well over six feet tall, his body could have been the model for a chiseled statue. His skin was so smooth and dark that it intensified the shade of his eyes and hair.

Zephir was always in the market to increase his sizeable wealth. Carmelita Castillo; Zephir's mother, had been left a small yet productive farm when her father passed away. Tumba Mfume had come to Manuel Castillo's estate as a child slave. Carmelita and Tumba became instant friends and practically grew up together. When the time came for the lovely young woman to choose a husband, there was no doubt in her mind whom that man would be. Over the years, the couple transformed the small farm into a highly productive acquisition; making it one of the most impressive estates on the island. Still, it was important for Zephir to have his own. He was not above being ruthless and would do whatever it took to get that land.

As Zephir and his crew forged ahead to the remote caves, where the promise of gold waited, no one could deny the utter beauty of the place. Zephir remembered what he had told Dubois. The Toussaint's had not sold one square inch of the land in all the years they had owned it. How? How could he make it happen?

Inside the main house on the Toussaint plantation, every room was decorated with palm-sized crystal figurines and hand-carved statues. The regal pieces of sanded wood were family possessions that dated back several generations.

Family portraits documented the clan from their coastal origins in West Africa and Haiti to the Caribbean isle of Dominica. Exquisite carpet tapestries lined the majestic corridors and sitting room walls. The tapestries depicted the imposing cliffs and rolling hills of the island. Their vibrant colors captured the ethereal allure of the coastline and exotic beauty of the people of Dominica. Porcelain lamps, engraved with colorful floral markings by a local artist, provided an illumination which had nothing to do with the firelight the lamps emitted.

The grand, mahogany staircase sat just off from the foyer. The banisters were polished to a brilliant gleam and were carved with the names of every Toussaint. The second story of the twenty bedroom domicile was no less spectacular. There were two additional sitting rooms, each located on either the east or west wing of the house. For the brothers, there were three immaculate studies, complete with mulberry desks and bookcases, containing writings on subjects ranging from law to agriculture.

Phaedra's bedchamber appeared to be in direct contrast to her personality. It was the bedroom of a lady, not the tomboy that she always tried to be. In one corner, there were three Chippendale chairs imported from the south eastern portion of America. The chairs were decorated with a red painted cotton floral print and flanked a small, round mahogany table covered by an embroidered lace cloth. A neat, plain black walnut desk-on-frame sat along one wall. The desk's myriad of small, interior drawers secured Phaedra's personal writings. The dressing glass shipped from Great Britain was mounted on a cherrywood case and was engraved with Phaedra's name. The case contained a seemingly endless array of jewels and hair accessories.

The polished maple bed had towering posts that supported the canopy, which matched the floral print on the chairs. The bedspread was, of course, the same pattern and added to the delicate appearance of the room.

Still, the serenity of the room did not help Phaedra rest any easier. She thrashed about in her sleep, tangling the heavy bed covers. Her long, hair was splayed across the stark, white pillowcases as she fought against the images in her dream.

A heavy fog clouded every corner of the vaguely familiar room. There was a large bed with white linens covering the surface. There appeared to be figures in shadow. However, it was impossible to tell if they were human bodies or pieces of furniture. From the thick fog, there appeared to be a hand moving closer. A faint, jingling sound surrounded it…

WILD RAVENS

Phaedra woke with a scream. Her eyes darted nervously around her bedchamber, and she pushed her sweat-drenched hair away from her face.

"Dear, God, what is happening to me?" she whispered into the darkness.

CHAPTER 2

Phaedra was out of bed at sunrise. As she rushed around her room, choosing her clothes for the morning, it almost appeared that she was running from something.

Once she had slipped into a long, black riding dress, she flew out of her bedchamber and raced down the stairs. She took the carpeted steps two at a time and sprinted down the long corridor toward the kitchen.

"And where are you off to in such a rush, young lady?" Tisha called, watching Phaedra run to the back door.

"I promise to be back in time for lunch." She sighed, pushing her hair away from her face.

"Phaedra—"

"Tisha, please, I have to get out of here," she snapped and hurried out of the house.

"Whoa, where are you off to in such an uproar?"

Phaedra pressed her hand against Carlos's arms as she caught her breath. "Going for a ride," she announced.

Carlos frowned, not caring for the frantic look in his cousin's eyes. "Have you eaten breakfast this morning?"

"No."

"Phaedra—"

"I'm not hungry, dammit!" she snapped, pressing a hand to her forehead.

Carlos's thick brows drew close. "What is this? What's the matter with you?"

Phaedra bowed her head and took a deep breath. "I'm sorry, Carlos," she said, although concern from Carlos or his brothers was an emotion she rarely if ever experienced.

"What's the problem?"

"Just a bad dream. I didn't sleep very well."

Carlos curled his hand around Phaedra's arm and began to walk with her. "Tell me about it."

"It's nonsense, really." She looked at the overcast skies. "It's been the same for several weeks," she sighed, at that moment desperate to talk with anyone. "I'm in a room—a strangely familiar room. I can't tell whether there are people there with me, but I do see a hand coming toward me, and there is a jingling sound…"

"Then what?" Carlos stopped in his tracks and turned her to face him.

Phaedra shrugged. "Well, that's it. I wake up shaking and sweaty and unable to get back to sleep."

"Hmm…and you have no idea what it means?" Carlos frowned as he scratched his thick black hair.

Phaedra shook her head and rubbed her hands over her arms to ward off the chill she felt. "I have no idea what these dreams mean. I don't think I want to know."

"Come here," Carlos softly ordered, pulling Phaedra close for a hug.

In spite of her vague suspicions, Phaedra thanked him for his concern anyway and ran in the direction of the stables. Carlos watched her, a worried frown clouding his smooth, face.

"You worry too much, 'Los." Dante laughed, when Carlos told him and Marquis about Phaedra's dream.

"What if she is like her mother?"

"'Los—"

"No! What if she is able to see things the way Marguerite could?"

Marquis pointed a finger in his brother's direction. "Carlos, we made a decision to never speak of that!"

Carlos's wide eyes narrowed slightly. "We cannot ignore this! Our own mother told us how powerful Marguerite's gift of la prise des yeax was. People actually sought her advice!"

"Carlos, that's enough!" Dante roared, grabbing Carlos's shirt collar and jerking the man close.

Carlos pushed Dante away with such force the man stumbled. "You listen to me, little brother. If Phaedra is capable of the sight as her mother was, she could foil our plans permanently! We could wind up penniless."

Dante raised his hand to silence Carlos. "We may wind up penniless anyway if you can't control your nerves."

"My nerves?!" Carlos thundered, shooting Dante a look of disbelief. "Marquis, surely you can understand me here?"

"Well," Marquis began when he saw Tisha pass the study where they were meeting. "Carlos, we'll speak no more of Aunt Marguerite and this supposed gift."

A devastating, white smile flashed on Zephir's molasses-toned face. He stared at the small, yellow stones in his hand then took one of them between his fingers. He bit down on the nugget then inspected it closely. Finally, his deep-set eyes rose to the group of men filling the room. As his deep chuckle sounded, the other men followed suit. Soon, the roar of male laughter filled the house.

"Are we to begin excavating now, Zephir?" Yves Fabush asked, his green eyes gleaming with anticipation.

Zephir thought on it for a moment then shook his head. "Not yet. You all should remain on the ship during the day as usual. We'll continue to dig only for an hour or so at night for the time being."

At once, the man began to question that decision. Zephir raised one hand, silencing the conversation of the crowd.

"Now listen, I want to be upstanding and honest about this."

"Up...standing?" Dubois questioned, knowing he had never heard his friend utter such words.

Zephir stood from the large, black arm chair he had occupied. "Upstanding and honest Dubois," he confirmed, slapping the man's shoulder.

Silence reigned for several moments. The crew of strong, rugged men had never heard Zephir Mfume mention words like "upstanding" and "honest." They were quite shocked.

Zephir enjoyed the confusion he saw on each man's face. After a while, he decided to ease their minds. "Yes, I think this situation calls for honesty. But only...to a certain degree," he added. The wicked gleam in his eyes put the men at ease, and another round of laughter filled the house.

Phaedra had been out riding most of the day. The noonday bell rang clearly when the meal was ready, but Phaedra just couldn't make herself go back to the house. She knew Tisha was probably beginning to worry. Unfortunately, the closer she came to her home, the more uneased she felt.

Of course, Midnight had no complaints. He loved racing through the lush, green landscape as much as his mistress. Phaedra had not realized how long she had been riding, until she found herself in a remote, unfamiliar patch of land.

The area had always looked so deserted and errie, no one in the family every spent time there. Phaedra, however, seemed to be drawn to the place. Ironically, the eerie affect of the place beckoned her. The fogged visions haunting her dreams bore striking resemblance to the desolate expanse of the land, and she could not turn away from it. She nudged Midnight onward towards the caves.

Suddenly, an imposing black-cloaked figure emerged from the mouth of the cave. Phaedra was as stunned by the existence of another human presence as she was by the power which seemed to radiate from the man who stood in her line of sight. Her eyes narrowed, and she urged Midnight closer.

"You! You there! What are you doing out here?!" she fearlessly demanded to know.

Zephir had ventured out to the caves for privacy and to plot his next move. He had been standing outside the cave for almost three minutes before tuning in to the angry voice shouting at him. When he looked up, he was…thunderstruck.

Phaedra had no idea what a delicious and inviting vision she was to the devastatingly handsome man who stood watching her. "What are you doing here?" she demanded.

Zephir was in no hurry to answer. He raked Phaedra's slender voluptuous form with roguish intent.

Phaedra tossed her head back and tried to steady herself beneath the stranger's unwavering eyes. The man began walking toward her; she sat straighter in the saddle. "You stay back!" she ordered, hating the shakiness of her voice.

Of course, Zephir ignored the slightly nervous demands of the beauty astride the black horse. He continued to walk closer, until he stood next to her.

Phaedra prayed the man who held her captive with his eyes had not heard the gasp she uttered. Her own eyes widened when she realized his height even surpassed that of the great Arabian she rode.

"He's beautiful," Zephir complimented Midnight, petting the horse's shiny mane. Once again, his eyes slid away from the animal to Phaedra. His unnerving black eyes traced her shapely legs, visible beneath the raised hem of her long skirts.

Phaedra tugged the reins, pulling Midnight away from Zephir. The Arabian sought the man's touch again; she grimaced. "Who are you?"

she whispered, her perfectly arched brows drawn close.

Zephir's trademark, wicked grin reappeared. "What right have you to ask?"

Stunned by his response, Phaedra leaned forward. "You are on my property."

"And who are you?" Zephir asked, clearly impressed.

"Phaedra Toussaint and this is my land. I'd like you to leave."

Zephir stood back on his muscular legs and regarded Phaedra cooly. His slanting, obsidian stare slid from her lovely, face, down the length of her neck to the opening of the black riding dress she wore. In her haste to dress that morning, Phaedra had not bothered to button the riding frock to the top. Of course, Zephir was not displeased. His deep-set eyes caressed the portion of cleavage that peeked out from behind the material.

"I'm afraid I cannot do that," he finally said.

Phaedra frowned and dismissed the weakness she felt from his intense appraisal. "You can't do what?"

Zephir sighed and forced his eyes away from her buxom. "You asked or ordered me to leave. I can't do that."

"And why is that?"

"Because I live here."

"On my land?"

"On my land."

"What the devil are—"

"We're neighbors," Zephir explained. The devilish smirk he wore proved that he clearly enjoyed her confusion. "My name is Zephir Mfume. I recently purchased the land connecting yours."

"Oh," Phaedra flatly replied, acting as unimpressed as Zephir had when she told him who she was. Her wide eyes scanned his massive frame once more then she pulled on Midnight's reins. "I suggest then, Mr. Mfume, that you get back to your own land and leave mine alone."

Zephir's heavy brows rose as Phaedra turned the Arabian and galloped away. The satisfied look on his face clearly stated that he was impressed by the striking beauty.

As Phaedra rode off, she could not resist the urge to look back at the man. It was as though the stranger uttered a silent command that she had to obey.

A soft chuckle escaped Zephir's wide chest when he saw Phaedra look back. He decided that it was time for a visit to the Toussaint estate.

"Are you sure about this, man?"

Zephir finished the remainder of his Brandy and savored the warmth that filtered his throat and chest. "Very sure," he told his friend.

Gaston Little was well versed in legal matters. He took a seat before Zephir and regarded him closely. "Well, what can I do for you?"

"Is the beauty…Phaedra, in charge of the land?"

"Ahh…Phaedra." Gaston sighed, completely agreeing with his friend. "Yes, she is beautiful. But…no, she is not in control of the property. From what I understand, her cousins Marquis, Carlos and Dante oversee the estate."

Zephir went back to the rear of his study. He refreshed his drink at the stout, fully-stocked clawfoot bar there. "Good."

"Why is that?"

"I met her today." Zephir sighed, taking a swallow of the Brandy. "She is very…fearless."

Gaston crossed his arms over the pristine white shirt he wore. "Hmph, that she is. But, it surprises me that you would not want to deal with her instead of her cousins," he noted, aware of how his friend loved the fairer sex.

Zephir shrugged. "Well, I know I'd have no trouble coaxing her into agreeing to my proposition," he admitted. "Unfortunately, I have no time for wooing. I want that land, and I want it fast."

Phaedra was seated at the dressing table which complimented the cherrywood dressing glass case. She held a 17th century, silver-handled brushed that had belonged to her mother. Each night, Phaedra looked forward to her nightly ritual of brushing her tresses. Using the elegantly crafted brush with its raised markings, she felt a powerful yet unspoken connection to her mother. Unfortunately, her preoccupation with the unsettling dreams prevented her from fully enjoying the small luxury.

Tisha had been stealing glances at Phaedra since she had walked into the room. As she turned down Phaedra's bed, she wondered if it was time to have their talk.

"Love? You are going to brush all the hair right off your head."

Phaedra snapped out of her trancelike state and smiled at Tisha's teasing statement. "Sorry." She sighed.

"Something wrong?"

Phaedra shook her head. "Mmm mmm."

"Is that true?"

Phaedra stared at Tisha through the mirror for a few moments then turned to face her. "I've been having dreams of…something. I don't know what they mean."

Tisha finished with the bed then walked closer to Phaedra. "What are they about?"

Taking a deep breath, Phaedra looked down at her hands. They were clasped tightly in her lap. "I'm not sure. I'm in a room, in a bed— I think. I don't know if there are other people there. But, I do see a…hand coming toward me, and I hear something jingling."

"And the dreams? Are they the same each night?"

"No…before they were…very fogged. Just recently have I been able to see the hand and hear the jingling."

Tisha knelt before Phaedra and pulled the girl's hands into her own. "Listen to me, child. You must not be frightened of this. It is who you are."

"What do you mean?" Phaedra quietly asked, not liking the set look in Tisha's brown eyes.

Tisha's full lips tightened as she searched for a way to talk to Phaedra without upsetting her. "Sweet child, the dreams have come to help you."

"Help me?" Phaedra asked, her voice flat.

"Your mother—"

"What about my mother?"

"She had what is called, *la prise des yeux*. It is the gift of second sight. Your mother was a Manbo, a priestess blessed with the gift. Of course, once she married your father, she…prayed for the strength to control it. He was greatly against her using such powers. I don't know how successful she was in trying to harness such a gift."

Phaedra laughed, standing from the cushioned seat before her dressing table. "I see why. It's completely outrageous. You are trying to tell me a silly dream is—is giving me, giving me some—some sort of message?" she asked, trying to keep her voice light. In her heart, she knew Tisha spoke the truth.

"Phaedra, dear listen to—"

"Tisha, please don't!" she ordered, in a hushed frantic tone then pressed her fingers to her lips and began to cry.

Tisha stood and rushed across the room to her. "Shh…my love. It is alright."

Phaedra turned, shaking her head wildly. "But it isn't, Tisha. It isn't," she whispered, dropping her head to the shorter woman's shoulder. "You don't know what I'm going through. I cannot sleep. I'm afraid to, too afraid for fear of what I might see."

Tisha pushed Phaedra away and watched her closely. "You must not be afraid of this, child. For your own sake, you must face it. You must face the message in your dream."

"He needs to be thouroughly cleaned, Zeke. We've been riding hard this morning." Marquis issued the orders in a curt tone and passed the horse reins to the stable man.

Zeke nodded and led Lightning, a lovely white Stallion, to the barns.

"Mr. Marquis?"

Marquis pulled off his leather riding gloves and looked up to see Melin, one of the housekeepers, rushing toward him. "Good morning, Melin," he greeted in a brisk manner.

Melin bowed her head briefly. "A message for you, sir," she breathlessly announced and handed her employer a small white package.

"Thank you." Marquis tore into the envelope and scanned the contents.

Melin's heavy fringe of lashes swept her cheeks as she bowed once more. Then, she was running back to the house, leaving Marquis alone on the front porch.

"Zephir Mfume," Marquis whispered, his heavy brows rising as a questioning look came to his face.

"Well, who is he?" Carlos asked, adding lemon to his cup of English tea.

Marquis glanced over the note again. "According to this, it seems that Mr. Mfume is our new neighbor," he informed his brothers, whom he'd summoned to his study.

"I had no idea someone bought that land," Dante said, brushing a speck of lint from his tan riding coat.

Marquis shook his head. "Neither did I. It's only ten acres or so. The land has proven to be unsuited to cultivating. Besides, it is tremendously overgrown…I'm surprised he wanted it."

"I wonder why he wants to meet with us?" Dante pondered.

Again, Marquis referred to the note. "It says here that he has a proposition he wishes to discuss."

Carlos looked up from his tea. "What sort of proposition?"

"He should arrive this evening." Marquis announced, folding the note and pushing it to the inside pocket of his tailored navy and burgundy suit coat. "I suppose we'll find out then."

Phaedra appeared at the dining table later that morning. She remained silent as she delved into the hard scrambled eggs with cheese, toasted bread with freshly churned butter and smoked beef sausage.

The brothers regarded one another with nervous lookss. "Silent" was not a word used when describing Phaedra Toussaint. Each morning, she rambled incessantly about new ideas she had for the estate.

"Phaedra? Anything wrong?" Dante finally asked, his curiosity getting the better of him.

"No…Why?" She asked, never looking up from her plate.

"You're awful quiet," Marquis noted from the head of the table.

Phaedra only shrugged. "I'm fine." She munched on a piece of crunchy toast.

"Have any more dreams?" Carlos asked.

Although Phaedra was consumed by the dreams, it didn't stop her from questioning the cousins' sudden concern for her. At the same time, she recalled one of her final conversations with her father and the promise she made to try and be civil with them. Therefore, she set her fork aside and decided to confide in them. "I had a talk with Tisha last night. She gave me some very good advice."

"Which was?" Dante questioned, idly stirring his tea.

"She told me to stop hiding and open my mind to them," Phaedra announced in a refreshed tone.

Marquis frowned. "That is strange advice."

"How so?" Phaedra asked, watching him expectantly.

"It just is," Marquis replied, returning his attention to the sausage and eggs on his plate. "I only hope you are not becoming involved with any Voodoo magic."

Phaedra's eyes pinned each of her cousins with inquisitive looks. "Marquis, I am surprised to hear you say such a thing. It was only a bad dream. Something causing interruption in my sleep, nothing more."

The brothers seemed to be content with the explanation. Phaedra, on the other hand, had become all the more suspicious.

That evening, after spending all day in the stables, Phaedra was changing into riding clothes once more. She had hoped to have supper in her room and relax in a steaming bath after her day in the field. She would not have the chance to indulge in the soothing treat. No sooner than the bedroom door closed behind her, she was informed that Midnight and Lucinda, her favorite horses, were about to become parents.

"Tisha!" Phaedra called, snatching a fresh pair of breeches and an old linen shirt off the shelf. "Tisha!"

Tisha met Phaedra on the stairs. "Good heavens, child. What is it?"

"Lucinda is about to foal. Save my supper, and I'll eat when I get back."

Tisha shook her head, a sour look on her round face. "You will waste away to nothing with the way you eat."

Phaedra gathered her thick hair in both hands and pinned it up. "I promise to eat the moment I return."

"Food loses something when it is not eaten right after being cooked," Tisha stated, her lovely smooth face clouded by a frown.

"Tisha..." Phaedra sighed. She was about to follow the woman down the hallway leading to the kitchen when a thunderous knock on the front door, stopped her cold. "Who in the world?" she whispered on her way to answer the door. Tisha continued on down the hall.

Phaedra's sharp gasp filled the foyer, when she whipped open the heavy, maple door. A man stood there covered in a heavy black cloak. She had to tilt her head back in order to look into his face. The man towered over her, filling the doorway with his massive frame. Phaedra thought he looked vaguely familiar, but could not decide where she had seen him. His silky black hair shielded his eyes from view and made him appear as dark as the night surrounding him.

"Good evening, Miss Toussaint," Zephir greeted, the devastating white grin instantly appearing.

Phaedra actually jumped at the sound of the rough, deep voice and unconsciously began to back away from the door. "You have some nerve coming here," she grated, trying to retain her strong, regal composure.

Zephir bowed his head and eased a hand through his hair. "Thank you," he replied, purposely goading her.

"What business do you have at my home?" she demanded, glaring up into his face.

Zephir did not wait for an invitation and stepped inside the house. Phaedra had no choice, but to back away. She stumbled slightly and gasped when he grabbed her.

She quickly slapped his hands away. "Thank you, but I don't need your help!" she said, regarding him with cool suspicion. "You can tell me what business you have here, though."

Zephir leaned down, so he could peer directly into her eyes with his slanting ones. "My business is with the men of the house and does not concern you."

"You jackass."

Zephir's warm hearty laughter filled the foyer. "Such language coming from that lovely mouth," he whispered, stepping closer to her.

Phaedra tossed her head back and tried to stamp down the sudden weakness that surged through her. "I'm the—the man of the house," she managed to say, when her back was against the wall. She took a moment to study the incredible size of his hand lying right next to her head along the wall. Clearing her throat, she forced her eyes to his.

The deep dimples appeared in either side of Zephir's wide mouth. My God, she is so lovely, he silently noted. His extraordinary eyes slid from the top of her touseled mane, over her breathtaking face, to her heaving buxom. With tremendous effort, he forced his gaze back to hers. "Would you explain that?"

"Explain what?" Phaedra asked in a dazed voice.

"That you're...the man of the house," he clarified, glancing once more at her chest.

Phaedra tried to shake off the strange hold Zephir's eyes cast over her. "This land is mine," she firmly informed him. "Now, in light of that, I suggest you take your business elsewhere."

"Now, isn't that interesting?" Zephir whispered, pushing one hand into the pocket of his trousers.

Phaedra tossed her head back. "How?"

"You. Trying to tell me that you run this entire place alone?"

"Well, it's true so if you would please leave—"

"Not so fast," Zephir said, his raspy voice sounding unusually soft. He thouroughly enjoyed the banter with the beauty who watched him with anger in her eyes.

Phaedra's frown deepened, and she shook her head slightly. "What the hell do you want?"

Zephir raised his hands defensively. "Easy Miss Toussaint. I am only trying to commend you."

"On what?"

Zephir scanned the foyer, gazing at the impressive, curving carpeted staircase. "You have a very lovely home here. Not to mention, an incredible amount of land. I commend you on being capable of handling such a vast estate."

The frown darkening Phaedra's face disappeared, but her eyes narrowed in suspicion. "Thank you," she managed.

"I find it even more interesting that you're all alone out here," Zephir added, moving closer to tower over Phaedra once more.

She did not like the look he gave her one bit. She cursed herself for becoming so unravelled by his looks and words. Determined to ignore it all, she fixed him with a hard expression. "I assure you, Mr. Mfume, I'm not all alone here."

Zephir shrugged. "The help does not count. You don't have a man around to…take charge."

Innocence prevented Phaedra from grasping the clearly suggestive meaning of Zephir's words. Still, she knew she did not like it. Her almond-shaped eyes scoped the fierce looking man before her. It took some effort to swallow as she scanned the breadth of his shoulders, his exceeding height, his blackberry skin, eyes and hair…Though Zephir was a sinfully handsome man, Phaedra could not get past her unease at being alone with him.

Just then, Marquis entered the foyer with Carlos and Dante. Phaedra unconsciously uttered a relieved sigh.

"Mr. Mfume?" Marquis called.

Zephir flashed Phaedra his dazzling grin yet again as he raked the length of her body once more before he turned.

Marquis offered his hand. "Marquis Toussaint," he said then glanced across his shoulder. "These are my brothers Carlos and Dante."

"Zephir Mfume. Pleasure to meet you gentlemen."

While the four men shook hands, Phaedra decided to make a hasty exit. She rushed toward the kitchen, her boots sounding noisily against the hardwood floor lining the corridor.

"Phaedra?" Marquis called, noticing her making the exit.

"I'm in a hurry, Marquis," she quickly replied, turning to look at her cousin. She could not resist glancing at Zephir as she did so. She cut her eyes from the mischievous, knowing look he sent her way and stormed off.

CHAPTER 3

"Mr. Mfume, you have most certainly intrigued us with talk of this proposition," Marquis said, as he handed his guest a stout, brass goblet filled with , fragrant Burgundy.

Zephir nodded. "Well, that sounds good, considering you all don't even know what it is," he said, joining the brothers when they all laughed. He tossed back the drink in one swallow and stood. "Gentlemen, I am interested in purchasing the land adjacent to my property."

Marquis exchanged glances with Carlos and Dante, before stepping to the center of the sitting room. "Mr. Mfume, I don't know if you are aware of this, but—"

"In all the years the Toussaints have owned this land, no part has ever been sold," Zephir cooly stated.

Marquis nodded, obviously impressed. "So, you know the history. That is good. Mr. Mfume, this family has endured many setbacks in an effort to retain control of this land. We aquired it from an uncle who worked this very plantation as a slave. Only he remained when his master died. His loyalty earned him sole ownership of the land. Upon his death, it was left to his

brother's children—the only living relatives he had. Since then, we have all fought diligently to overcome numerous hardships—including the threat of our own enslavement."

Zephir bowed his head, gnawing the inside of his jaw for a moment. "As I said, Marquis, I know the history of the land. It is an impressive story. Your family has had to fight heartily to retain possession of this land. Besides battling your own neighbors, you've been at odds with the white man in his desire to be lord and master over Toussaints and all who dwell here. You should be proud that your family has overcome such trials. Will this sentiment prevent you from selling a portion of the land to me now?"

"Mr. Mfume?" Dante called, leaning forward in an upholstered walnut armchair—one of the many that furnished the sitting room. "If I may ask, why would you want to purchase the most unattractive area of our estate?"

A knowing grin tugged at Zephir's full lips. "When I aquired my own land, I didn't realize how small it was. I'd like to add to it, if possible."

"I see." Dante sighed, crossing his long legs at the ankles.

Zephir turned toward Marquis. "Well, Mr. Toussaint, my question remains. Will your sentiment prevent you from considering my offer?"

Marquis perched his hand in the small pocket on the olive green vest he wore. "It may not prevent us from selling. It would mean that your offer would have to be...very profitable."

Zephir resumed his seat in one of the roomy armchairs. "Gentlemen, I'm an extremely wealthy man. In addition to having my own money, I'm heir to one of the most impressive estates in Cuba—where my parents live."

"Now it is our turn to be impressed," Carlos noted, as his brothers nodded in agreement.

"Does that mean we can do business?" Zephir asked, propping his elbow on the arm of the chair and resting the side of his face in his palm.

"You'll have our answer by tomorrow evening," Marquis said, offering his hand to Zephir. "If you'll join us for dinner?"

"I'll be here," Zephir promised, shaking hands with the brothers. He would eagerly anticipate the dinner. Not only would he receive an answer to his proposal, but he would have an opportunity to see the woman/child who had captivated him with her fiesty demeanor, her beauty and sensuality.

"Tisha!" Carlos called. "Please show Mr. Mfume out," he instructed the woman when she arrived in the room.

Tisha nodded toward Zephir and waited for him to cross the room.

He bowed toward her and offered his arm. Surprised by such a galant gesture, Tisha developed an instant liking for the brawny stranger.

"Where's the lady of the house?" Zephir asked, once they were strolling toward the foyer.

Tisha smiled. "One of the mares is in foal. Phaedra had to be there."

"I see," Zephir replied, disappointment at the news showing on his face.

Tisha sensed something good imbedded within the powerful, fierce-looking young man. She pressed her small hand to Zephir's massive one. "This way," she instructed, pulling him aside to the long corridor which lead to the kitchen. "She's in the stables. I'll show you."

"Do you think he'll agree to our terms?" Carlos asked, watching Marquis refill his wine glass.

Marquis laughed. "I hope so. I would hate to turn down the profit we're sure to make from what he's prepared to offer."

"He would be the perfect accomplice," Dante said, watching his brothers nod in agreement. "I wonder what his reaction will be? Will he spit in our faces or accept?"

Marquis tossed back the remainder of his drink and grimaced. "He'll accept if he knows it is the only way he will obtain that land."

Outside, Zephir followed Tisha's directions from the kitchen to the stables. The sound of hushed conversation filtered out through the tall, wooden doors. Zephir pushed one of the doors open and stepped inside. His heavy black boots fell softly against the hay, bringing him closer to the scene before the array of horse stalls.

He leaned against one of the sturdy wooden beams that supported the bar, and his black stare grew more intense. Phaedra was on her knees in the hay. She sat amidst a group of men. The rough-looking group hovered around her as she coached a gorgeous shiny black horse that was about to foal. Smoothing her hand along the sleek, silky expanse of the powerful animal, Phaedra hummed. The tune seemed to soothe the mare, in spite of the discomfort of labor.

Zephir folded his arms over his chest and looked on in amazement. Phaedra whispered into the mare's ear, coaxing the lovely horse through the delivery. The awesome animal actually rested her head in Phaedra's lap while enduring the painful contraction as the colt forced its way into the world.

"Come on, Lucinda, girl. Make Midnight a proud papa," Phaedra cooed, smiling when Lucinda's ears twitched at the sound of her voice.

"Miss Phaedra," one of the stablehands called.

"What is it?" she whispered, frowing slightly towards Cofi who had spoken. Her frown deepened when he motioned for her to come forward.

"Oh no," Phaedra whispered, seeing what had Cofi so concerned. The colt had not turned. This would not be an easy delivery. "She won't do a thing unless I coax her," Phaedra whispered, casting a worried look towards Lucinda. "I can't coax her and turn to colt at the same time," she told Cofi.

Of course, any one of the stablehands could have performed the task. Unfortunately, Lucinda was very particular and would let no one aside from Phaedra touch her. She'd just have to get over it, Phaedra decided and was about to issue orders to one of the other hands when she felt the softest touch against her shoulder. Her words smothered on a gasp when she saw Zephir.

"Can I help?" he offered, already removing the cloak from his shoulders.

Phaedra snapped from her mesmerized state and shook her head. "She won't let you. She won't let any of the other hands touch her and they see her every day."

"May I try anyway?" he requested. "There's a chance she might repond favorably to my touch."

Phaedra didn't doubt that a bit. After a brief hesitation, she finally nodded and stepped aside. The entire group was entranced by the event. Though they had seen hundreds of colts born before, Midnight and Lucinda were the favorites of the estate. The birth of their first foal was a great event. They all watched in silent amazement as Zephir whispered soothing soft words in a foreign tongue. Lucinda's ears twitched and she raised her head slightly as though giving Zephir permission. He chuckled and whispered more words, smoothing his hand across her swollen belly. Then using infinite gentleness he managed to turn the colt swiftly and efficiently.

Eventually, a shivering, shimmering black colt pushed its way into the world. The crowd grew alive with shouts of happiness. Phaedra clapped more enthusiastically than anyone. Her eyes sparkled with happy tears as she watched the colt test its new legs. After a few moments, she turned to thank Zephir, but she found that he had already moved to the other side of the stable and away from the celebration.

Determined to overcome the anxiety that affected her, she made her way across the barn. "Thank you," she said when he finished washing his hands in one of the water buckets lining the wall. "Lucinda's never been so agreeable. I commend you skills."

Zephir shrugged. "Although I'd like to take credit, I believe Miss Lucinda was behaving as any mother would. She knew her baby was in trouble. She would've made a deal with the devil to save him."

Phaedra regarded him closely. "A deal with devil, is that how you see yourself?"

"Isn't that the way *you* see me, Miss Toussaint?"

"I only want to know why you're here? Instinct tells me it's something...devilish."

Zephir's deep chuckle rose slowly as he savored the confrontation. He'd never tire of watching her. The beautiful rich chocolate tone of her skin, the loveliness of her face, her voluptuous form—the heaving, unconsciously-seductive movements of her breasts beckoned his eyes. The sound her voice was becoming music to his ears. He was actually beginning to look forward to their heated bantering.

"To hell with it," Phaedra snapped, with a quick shake of her head.

"Giving up so easily?"

Phaedra ordered herself to keep walking. Unfortunately, Zephir's deep voice, tinged with amusement, commanded her response. "It's useless trying to extract information from you about your business with my cousins. I know I'm wasting my time."

"Hmph, I never would have thought you a quitter," he called, appraising the sultry view she presented from behind.

She turned and brought her finger within inches of his chest. "Oh I never give up. I assure you of that. I'll find out what you are up to with my cousins."

Confusion registered in Zephir's striking eyes. "Up to? What an interesting choice of words! I have the feeling you think it is something…dishonest?"

"I know them," Phaedra replied with a simple shake of her head.

The taunting smirk on Zephir's face was replaced by a serious look. Phaedra had no idea how she captivated him and how infatuated he was becoming.

"Good evening, Zephir," Marquis greeted as he walked into the sitting room that next evening.

"Thank you, Dante," Zephir said as he accepted a snifter of Cognac. "Good evening, Marquis," he greeted the eldest Toussaint and shook his hand. "Well, since everyone is here, have you all come to a decision?" he asked, leaning against the tall, polished mahogany bar.

Marquis nodded toward his brothers and stepped forward. "We've agreed to sell you the land, Mr. Mfume. Our price is on this card," he said, handing Zephir the folded paper.

Zephir set his glass to the bar and scanned the figure. "It's acceptable," he said, watching the men chuckle.

"There's one condition of the sale, Mr. Mfume," Marquis cautioned as he raised one finger.

Zephir took a long swallow of the Cognac. "And that is?" He eyed each man speculatively.

"You must agree to take our cousin as well."

Zephir was a difficult man to either shock or surprise. After hearing Marquis's statement, however, he was both. The look of utter disbelief on his face was impossible to miss.

"What did you say?" he finally managed to ask. His raspy, baritone voice was barely above a whisper.

Dante set his glass to the clawfoot, mahogany coffeetable. "We want to give Phaedra to you," he clarified.

Zephir's slanting eyes narrowed further when Dante made their position clear. Turning back to the bar, he splashed more of the Cognac into his goblet. The brothers smirked at one another, watching their guest tilt the contents of the glass down his throat.

We want to give Phaedra to you. The words replayed themselves in Zephir's mind over and over again. *They can't be serious, can they?* But, what if they were? He found it loathesome that three men, entrusted to protect a young, innocent woman, would offer such a thing. He turned away from the bar and faced the brothers.

"Why?" he asked.

Marquis, Dante and Carlos exchanged uneasy looks.

"Questions, Zephir?" Dante challenged. "We thought you would jump at an offer such as this."

"That's right, Mr. Mfume," Carlos agreed. "Considering the fact that you would be acquiring such a beautiful, vivacious woman."

Zephir nodded, and eased one hand through his hair. "It would be the perfect reason to accept."

"But?" Marquis questioned.

"But, it doesn't answer my question. Why would you offer your cousin to a complete stranger?"

The brothers studied the hard, suspicion carved into Zephir's chiseled features. Their eyes met and held for several moments. Finally, they nodded in agreement.

Marquis waved toward the upholstered armchairs, urging Zephir to take a seat. "Mr. Mfume, when Phaedra turns twenty, this land will be hers. Completely hers. She will own everything. We cannot allow that to happen."

"So you're going to sell her?" Zephir asked, still unable to believe what he was hearing.

Marquis leaned forward. "The terms of the will clearly state that Phaedra must be here on Toussaints when she turns twenty in order to claim the land. The girl has never been off this property, she would never leave willingly."

"Especially when she knows what is at stake," Zephir added. "I take it she is aware of these terms?"

"If her father's advisor has spoken with her, and we are sure that he has," Marquis said, bracing his fingers against each other.

Zephir leaned back in the chair, crossing his long legs at the ankles. He appeared to be in deep concentration.

"Mr. Mfume?" Carlos called, pinning Zephir with an unwavering hazel stare. "If it will help you to know, Phaedra is not yet nineteen. Now, if you're willing to wait…that's your option. But know this: Phaedra is not of a mind to sell any of this land. I guess you should ask yourself just how badly you want it."

Zephir had been pondering that very thing. He knew he would do anything to get that piece of land. After all, he was there trying to convince the Toussaints that he was their friendly gentlemanly neighbor, when he was just the opposite. He faced the grim realization that he was left with little choice if he wanted that gold. Accepting the preposterous offer was the only way. Besides, as Carlos had alluded, what man wouldn't jump at the chance? To be lord and master over such a voluptuous, fiery, young woman could be the most rewarding part of the deal. That being the case, he knew no other man would turn down such an offer. He wanted Phaedra just as any man would and, while the proposition was preposterous, he knew he'd curse himself forever if he left her in the care of the three heartless men she trusted.

"When would this take place?" Zephir cooly inquired. He figured the brothers would already have the details planned, since Phaedra would never come with him willingly.

The brothers exchanged satisfied looks, then pulled their chairs closer to Zephir's.

"We need you to take Phaedra away. Far away from Toussaints, at least until she misses the deadline to acquire the land," Marquis whispered.

"And you believe it would be that simple?" Zephir asked, a doubtful smirk on his face.

Marquis chuckled. "Getting her away from here would be the most difficult part. Once she is on unfamiliar territory, she will cling to you because she will know there is nowhere else she can go."

Zephir couldn't believe how coldly they discussed their own cousin's fate. And he thought he was ruthless. "You'll have my answer by the end of the evening," he said, watching the brothers nod their approval.

Phaedra tied the flimsy tassles that dangled from the bodice of her dress. She rushed down the stairs, cursing herself for remaining in the stables so long. The last thing she wanted to hear that night was her cousins chastising her for not being punctual. She was still fiddling with the ties, when she rushed into the sitting room.

"I apologize for being late. I hope—"

"Phaedra, we have company, dear," Carlos called.

Phaedra's head snapped up, her hands falling away from the bodice of her gown. Instantly, her face contorted into a suspicious frown. Zephir Mfume's towering presence over her shorter cousins caused her eyes to widen. Her breathing increased to such a rapid pace that her breasts threatened to burst from the confines of the gown's low neckline.

"What the hell is he doing here?!" Phaedra demanded, storming to the center of the plush room.

"Phaedra!"

"You watch your mouth, young woman!" Dante and Marquis simultaneously chastised her.

The harsh tone of her cousin's voices did not faze her. "I can't believe you two are yelling at me for being impolite to this… this…"

"Watch it, Phaedra," Carlos warned.

"This rogue!" she bellowed.

Marquis stormed toward his angry cousin and pointed a finger in her face. "Now, that is enough. We'll not have you offending out guest!"

"To hell with him!"

"Phaedra!"

"This man is a thief and you all are inviting him into our home—"

"He is a dinner guest and our neighbor, and you will treat him with respect!"

Phaedra rolled her eyes away from Carlos and glared at Zephir. "He's probably taking stock of all our valuables while pretending to be our friendly neighbor."

Dante rushed forward and pulled Phaedra around to face him. "Girl, you will shut your mouth or you will be sent upstairs with no supper! Do I make myself clear?"

Phaedra looked to the floor. Heavy lashes brushed her cheeks and her soft mouth curved down into a pout. Meanwhile, Zephir enjoyed the scene. It was a treat seeing her so angry. He could not believe how much more beautiful the emotion made her.

Phaedra looked up again and saw Zephir watching her. In an effort to dispel the nerves twisting in her stomach, she opened her mouth to blast him once more.

"Why don't I take her into the dining room?" Zephir offered, before Phaedra could get herself into more trouble.

"That is a good idea," Marquis stiffly consented.

Phaedra tensed the moment she felt Zephir's hand curl around her upper arm. The nerves in her stomach grew more pronounced, and she actually experienced a shortness of breath. Suddenly, she stopped walking and raised her hand.

"Could I please have just a moment alone with my cousins?" she softly requested.

Zephir released her arm, but not before his fingers massaged the area at the bend of her elbow. The wicked smirk reappeared when he heard her soft gasp.

Phaedra rubbed her arm, trying to escape the tingling she felt there. Zephir nodded to the brothers and left the room. She watched him until he was out of sight.

"What's going on here?" she questioned, her almond-shaped eyes snapping with suspicion.

Marquis shrugged. "What do you mean?"

"You know damn well what I mean."

"Phaedra, save your filthy mouth for your stable hand friends. We don't want it in here."

Phaedra sent Dante a tired look. "What is he doing here? What type of business do you all have to discuss?" she asked, making her voice soft and sweet.

The three men shrugged in unison. "Mr. Mfume simply wanted advice on how to tend the land he just purchased. It's been unworked for quite some time," Carlos informed her.

"Is that right?" Phaedra added, the pointed look in her eyes telling them she wanted more of an explanation.

"Phaedra, you know better than anyone how difficult it is to plant here. Especially with such a rainy climate. Zephir had questions he hoped we could answer."

Though Phaedra's suspicion was a bit doused by Marquis's explanation, she was not completely convinced. For the time, she decided to keep that to herself.

Zephir followed Phaedra's every movement and mannerism. He sat reclined in his chair with one finger propped along the side of his smooth cheek. He studied every detail of her face, and he felt his manhood stiffen as visions of bedding her filled his mind. Yes, the brothers' offer was becoming more enticing with each passing second.

Phaedra watched the inviting plate of roasted fish, rice with greens and panbread. It was her favorite meal, and she couldn't eat a bite. It was all she could do to remain seated with Zephir focused solely on her.

"So, Mr. Mfume," Dante began, after several moments of silence, "I believe you told us earlier that you are from Cuba?"

Zephir reluctantly pulled his eyes away from Phaedra. "That's right. I was born and raised there."

"I've heard it's a very beautiful place." Carlos noted.

"You heard correctly. But, like most men, I couldn't wait to get out in the world and stake my claim."

"Hmph."

"Phaedra…" Marquis called in a warning tone when he heard his cousin's unimpressed response to Zephir's words. "So where have your travels led you?" .

Phaedra continued to pick at her food while Zephir entertained her cousins with stories of his travels. Her own ears perked at his colorful tales and at how he became a "self-made" man. Several times during the course of the meal, she stole secret glances at him. Her heart pounded fiercely beneath her breast as she scanned the size of his hands, the width of his shoulders and the expanse of his chest. Soon, she was just as entranced by his stories as her cousins were. She did not realize that she was hanging onto each word spoken in his gravel-toned voice.

Zephir caught her peeking; she quickly looked away.

"So do you like to travel, Phaedra?" he asked, very interested in knowing more about her.

Phaedra glanced around the table. "Well, I suppose I'd love it, if I'd ever done it," she shared taking pleasure in the chuckle Zephir uttered.

"Where would you go if you had the opportunity?" he asked, his eyes caressing every inch of her face.

Phaedra thought over the question. "Well, after living on an island all my life, I suppose I'd like to see the opposite. Perhaps someplace cold."

"Anywhere in particular?" Zephir inquired, focusing on the stark white tablecloth.

"A place where it snows," Phaedra replied. She was so pleased at being included in male conversation, that she missed the look exchanged between her cousins and their guest.

Though Zephir did not confirm it with Marquis, Carlos and Dante, they were certain. Phaedra had unknowingly charted her fate.

Phaedra trailed her nails across the tablecloth and thought about traveling to an icy region. Suddenly, her breath caught on a gasp as a vision came to her mind. She and Zephir were sailing out actoss the bluest ocean. She stood nestled against the unyielding wall of his chest, his arms were secure around her waist. The embrace offered a content-ment she had never known. Why would she think of something like that? Traveling alone on a romantic holiday with such a rogue? This sinfully beautiful, powerful rogue who looked at her with such prom-ises of erotic delight, her face would surely be flushed red if her com-plexion were lighter.

Stop it Phaedra! She ordered herself. Zephir Mfume was the bane of her existence, wasn't he? His words only stirred disgust and anger-not the delicious tingles of an enjoyable heated banter. He found her beautiful; that was evident in the way he looked at her. Clearly he want-ed her. She wanted him, didn't she? No! She told herself. Besides, she didn't even know what it was to want. Still, she couldn't dismiss the sensational waves that rose inside her whenever he was near.

"This is a fascinating place," Zephir complimented, later that evening.

The five of them had gone out to one of the verandas for tea. The night was cool and clear. It allowed the moonlight to touch the land with a silvery glow.

"Phaedra, why don't you give Mr. Mfume a tour of the grounds?" Marquis suggested.

Phaedra was quite certain Zephir had already seen most, if not all, of the land, but she did not comment. She had no desire to entertain Zephir by causing another scene and stood to smooth down the lovely fuschia evening gown that billowed about her.

"Mr. Mfume?" she called. Though she gracefully complied to Marquis's orders, her nerves grated at the thought of being alone with the giant stranger.

"Zephir, please," he told her, standing as well. Waving one hand before himself, he urged her to lead the way.

Phaedra tried to remain aloof, yet pleasant. She showed Zephir around the part of the property closest to the house. When she unwittingly led them to the maze of gardens, she cursed herself. Though it was one of the loveliest parts of the estate, the gardens were quite intimate. The private, romantic patch of land was the last place she wanted to be alone with Zephir Mfume.

"The uh, gardens were my mother's idea," she told him, her voice shaking. "She loved flowers," she quietly added.

Zephir agreed that the gardens were breathtaking, but his attention was more focused on Phaedra. "Was she as beautiful as you are?"

Phaedra closed her eyes and walked ahead of him. "We're here for you to compliment the flowers, not me."

"Is that right?" Zephir asked, kicking a stone with the tip of his boot. "I thought you wanted to be alone with me?"

"What?!" Phaedra snapped, whirling around to face him.

"You can admit it. There's no one out here but the two of us,"

Zephir said as he walked closer.

"You overbearing bastard! How dare you assume something like that?!" she screamed, her voice trembling out sheer frustration.

He shrugged one massive shoulder, while pushing a hand into the pocket of his tanned trousers. "Come now, Phaedra. You've been watching me—"

"Watching you?!"

"Watching me all night," He stopped a few feet in front of her. "Then, you lead me out to this intimate garden—"

"Now you wait just a damn minute!" Phaedra ordered, stomping over to him and poking her finger into his chest. "Your arrogance has caused you to poorly misjudge me, Mr. Mfume."

"Zephir, please." He insisted.

"I have not, nor will I ever, lead you anywhere intimate! I don't know what you expected, Zephir, but I'm so happy I could disappoint you!"

One of his wide hands rose to capture Phaedra's index finger that was poked into his chest. "Miss Toussaint, why do I get the feeling you don't like me?"

Phaedra snatched her hand away from his and stepped back. "Because I don't like you."

Zephir's eyes twinkling mischievously. "This is no way to treat a neighbor."

"I think you're a thief, pretending to be a neighbor!"

The thick black mane flying wildly about Phaedra's face captivated Zephir. He could actually feel himself filling his hands with it as they kissed. For the second time that night, he felt his anatomy responding to the image of her in his arms.

"Do you hear what I'm saying to you? Zephir?"

He shook away the picture of them making love in the garden. "I'm sorry. What were you talking about?" he absently replied.

Phaedra shook her head as she glared at him. "I don't trust you. My cousins are hiding something about their business with you. Be warned, I intend to find out what it is before they involve themselves in any foolish ventures with you."

"Such as?" Zephir softly inquired as he closed the distance between them.

Phaedra rambled on, even as his stalking stride brought him uncomfortably close. "I have an awful feeling," she was saying, "you want something, and I believe it is Toussaints. I can't let that happen," she told him.

Zephir stopped before Phaedra then let one finger reach out to stroke the portion of her bosom that showed above the fuschia silk bodice of her gown.

The whisper soft caress immediately silenced Phaedra. The offending finger dipped into the cleft between her breasts; she gasped, her eyes following the trail of his touch.

Zephir caught his bottom lip between his perfect teeth, an expression of awe coming to his face. His long, silky lashes closed over the intense obsidian eyes. Male satisfaction surged through his body when he discovered that her skin was actually as soft as it appeared.

Phaedra tried to control her rapid breathing, but could not. She was unknowingly driving Zephir mad as her breasts heaved quickly against his teasing fingers. From the simple touch, Zephir knew he would not be able to let her go without feeling her in his arms. His hands slid down to her waist, and he lifted her before him.

Phaedra cursed herself for putting herself in such a predicament and also for feeling so disoriented. She ordered away the uneasy twinges coursing through her and raised her eyes to his. The cool night air lifted the silky black locks of Zephir's hair. Stunned by the intense manner in which he watched her, she gasped yet again. He took full advantage of the opportunity. His head dipped, and his tongue settled deep within her mouth.

Phaedra had never been kissed that way before and could only cry out at the shocking gesture. Her eyes widened briefly, before her lashes fluttered close. The onslaught of the kiss instantly turned her legs to syrup. Her breathing came in short, ragged pants beneath the long, wet thrusts of Zephir's tongue.

Resist him, dammit!, a tiny voice ordered in the back of her mind. She tried to respond to the order as her hands curled into fists which she weakly pounded against his chest.

Zephir ignored it all. He only added more pressure to the kiss. Tasting the sweet cavern of her mouth and hearing her surprised response, he knew she had never been kissed in such a manner. The knowledge only encouraged him, and he could not get enough of her.

Phaedra could scarcely catch her breath. Zephir's lips suckled her own, before his tongue invaded her mouth and he proceeded to kiss her all over again.

"Zephir…" she whispered, hearing him utter a low growl in response. In a slow, uncertain manner, she mimicked the strong, confident, sultry movements of his tongue.

Zephir chose that moment to pull away. His knowing look caused Phaedra's anger to return full fold. She slowly slid out of his crushing embrace. The moment she felt the bottoms of her fushia slippers touch the ground, she slapped him hard and raced from the garden.

A wolfish grin spread across Zephir's face. He rubbed his hand across the tiny sting left by her blow. He knew there was no way he would refuse the Toussaint brothers' offer.

Marquis, Carlos and Dante were all smiles when Zephir returned to the veranda.

"What happened between you two?" Marquis asked, scratching his long sideburns.

Zephir frowned, even as a wicked look crossed his face. "What makes you ask?"

The brothers chuckled. "Hell, man, Phaedra ran past us like the devil was at her heels!" Dante humorously noted.

"I thought she looked ready to murder someone!" Carlos said, through his soft laughter.

Zephir joined in on the laughter, but did not quell the brothers' curiosity. "I accept your proposal. When can I collect my…merchandise?" he asked.

Marquis looked toward the double doors leading back to the sunroom, before he spoke. "Phaedra's nineteenth birthday is next month. We will be having her party that night. Some guests will be staying overnight, but many will leave that very evening. You can take her then."

Zephir frowned, stroking his clean-shaved cheek. "During a party? Isn't that a bit risky?"

Carlos shook his head. "If you take her before the gala, there will be too many questions. Too many people will miss her."

Zephir realized the man had a point and nodded. "Well then, we will do it your way."

"You're welcomed to tend the land." Marquis shook Zephir's hand. "We'll be in contact when the papers are ready."

"That's fine." Zephir shook hands with Dante and Carlos then bid them a goodnight.

Tisha met Zephir in the foyer and showed him to the door. He walked out into the night, and took Tisha's hand in his.

"Is Phaedra alright?" he asked, worried that he'd upset her too much.

She patted his arm. He had no idea how concerned he looked and sounded, she thought. "She is just fine."

Zephir glanced toward the staircase then favored Tisha with a dazzling look. Satisfied with the answer, he left the house.

"Mmm...no, no...wait...please wait."

Phaedra moaned in her sleep. She was in the midst of another disturbing dream. This time, however, there were no foggy visions or strange sounds. This dream was crystal clear and featured Zephir Mfume. She was alone with him in the garden once again. What they did in the dream went far beyond the kiss they shared. They were things Phaedra had only heard about from older cousins. The vivid images were so shamefully erotic, she actually felt as though she were experiencing the man's touch again.

Outside Phaedra's bedroom door, Tisha passed the way to her own room. She heard the gasps and jumbled words coming from the inside and knocked on the door.

"Phaedra?...Child? Are you awake?" Receiving no answer, she knocked once more then stepped inside the darkened room. Her eyes widened when she found the covers strewn across the bed and Phaedra tossing and moaning in her sleep.

"Phaedra? Child, wake up. Come now."

Slowly, Phaedra drifted out of her slumber. A lazy smirk tugged at her soft mouth when she saw Tisha. "Is something the matter?" she whispered.

Tisha sat upon the edge of the bed. "Love, you were tossing and crying out in your sleep."

Phaedra turned her face into the pillow.

"Was it another bad dream?"

Phaedra shook her head and lowered her eyes to the bedcovers. "No...no. It was...different."

"More visions?"

"Mmm mmm. This was about...Zephir Mfume."

"Oh...I see," Tisha noted in a quiet tone as she allowed a knowing look to touch her face.

Phaedra grew frustrated and sat up in the bed. "Dammit, Tisha, why am I dreaming about him? I despise him."

Tisha pushed Phaedra back down in the bed and began to tuck the covers around her. "Come now. Despise is such a strong word."

"I wish I could think of something stronger," she grumbled, pushing her long, wavy locks away from her face.

"I sense a goodness in him. Not to mention how handsome and powerful looking he is."

"Tisha!"

"Hush. It is good to see you are not immune to this one."

Phaedra sucked her teeth. "I don't trust him, and it's just a matter of time before I discover what he's up to."

CHAPTER 4

Phaedra caught herself peering in the direction of Zephir's land for the fourth time that morning. Frustrated, she pushed both hands through her hair and shook her head.

She hadn't seen much of the man during the last two weeks. His kiss had awakened feelings in her she never knew existed. Though his overwhelming self-confidence and arrogance drove her mad, she could not help but feel drawn to him. The silent admission made her grimace, and she perched a wide-brimmed straw hat atop her head as she headed toward the barn. She had decided to help the stable hands groom the horses that day. None of the workers had yet arrived, but that did not stop her. She finished two of the horses and was brushing a third.

Zephir had decided to put some space between himself and Phaedra. After the scene in the garden, he felt it best not to see her for a while. The choice was more for his benefit than hers. He had always prided himself on the ability to remain emotionally detached where the opposite sex was involved. Knowing her cousins plans for her, had instilled a sense of possessive protection within him. He had come to feel as though she was in some way his responsibility. Phaedra, however, had stirred something in him that he could not shake. Once he kissed her, he did not want to stop, and he believed his need went far beyond anything physical.

Tisha informed Zephir that Phaedra was out in the stables. He found her easily. For a while, he stood watching her. His intense expression moved from her heavy boots, across the shamefully tight cream-colored breeches, to the oversized shirt. He studied the hat she wore. *Lord,*

Chicago Public Library
Harold Washington - HWLC
4/17/2013   3:08:36 PM
-Patron Receipt-

ITEMS BORROWED:

1:
Title: Wild ravens /
Item #: R0405163865
Due Date: 5/8/2013

-Please retain for your records-

BWADE

she is so unlike the women I am used to! Strong willed and independent. Her fiery dislike for him had only managed to steadily arouse him. If Phaedra knew that, she would sure hate him more. The thought caused him to chuckle.

Phaedra heard a rumbling sound behind her and turned. Finding Zephir standing there, her heart dropped to her stomach. "What are you doing here?"

"Watching you."

"What for?"

Zephir pushed his hands into the pockets of his black trousers and stepped further into the stable. "It's interesting to see that you tend your own horses."

Phaedra was not flattered. "What's so interesting about that?"

"Well, you obviously don't have to." He leaned against one of the stable doors.

Phaedra rolled her eyes away from him and turned back to Jubilee—a stunning chestnut Hackney. "I don't believe in that. If I'm able, I help."

"How good of you to assist your…servants," Zephir cooly insulted just to get a rise our of her. In truth, he thought it was admirable that she was not above getting her hands dirty.

"What the hell is that suppose to mean?"

Zephir shrugged. "It's just nice to see you help your servants."

"You say 'servants' as though they are slaves." She shot him an accusing glare.

"Slaves, servants. One in the same, right?"

"Hell no!"

"Phaedra, I did not mean to—"

"The hell you didn't," she snapped. "How dare you walk in here and accuse me of treating my own people like slaves? They are anything but. They are well paid, treated like family and they even have days away from work."

"I see," Zephir whispered, walking closer to her. "Does that mean you're all alone out here?"

The question set Phaedra on edge as an exasperated look fell over her face. Finishing up with Jubilee, she led the horse back to its stall. "What do you want?" she finally asked.

"Are you sure you want to know?"

She secured the Hackney in her stall and turned. "I demand that you stop toying with me!"

"But, it's so much fun."

Suspicious of the determined look on his face, she quickly backed away from him. Unfortunately, she was not fast enough. In one smooth move, he caught her wrist and flung her across his shoulder.

Phaedra pounded her fists against his back. She tried to kick him, but one arm held her legs pinned next to his chest. "Get your filthy hands off me!"

"Me, filthy?" he teased, carting her to the depths of the stables. "You're the one who's been playing with horses."

"Insufferable ogre, let me go dammit! Zephir!" she raged, finding it difficult to breathe being thrown over his wide, sinewy shoulder.

In one movement he complied, letting her leave his embrace by tossing her to the mound of hay in an empty stall.

She took in gulps of air as her eyes focused on him. She wanted to slap the confident smirk from his face, but something stopped her. The look he fixed her with told her that he was toying with her, intentionally trying to anger her. She was determined to disappoint him. What more was there to do if she didn't fight him, she wondered as she grew more intrigued.

Zephir allowed his eyes to feast on the tousled luscious sight before him. Then, he too dropped to the mound of hay and trapped her beneath his considerable weight. Instinctively, she pressed her hands against his wide chest.

Zephir was tired of playing games. His need to touch her almost overwhelmed his ability to reason. His hands slid to her inner thighs, and he settled himself between her legs.

Resist him! She commanded herself. Unfortunately, her mind and her body had different agendas. He took both her wrists in one hand and held her arms above her head. Her heart lurched and she anticipated what he would do next.

Zephir dropped his full weight on her. His sensuous mouth slid down the smooth line of her neck, while his free hand ventured beneath the hemline of the shirt she wore.

A stunned cry ripped from Phaedra's throat as his palm closed over her breast. Moments later, he thrust his tongue deep into her mouth. He groaned as he felt the soft mound filling his hand. He let go of Phaedra's wrists and caressed the length of her body in a blatantly possessive manner.

She was torn between the need to fight and the urge to surrender to the unfamiliar, incredible sensations surging through her. Zephir tore his lips from hers and stopped to nibble at her earlobe, as his other hand found its way beneath the shirt.

Aching to see what he touched, Zephir lifted the material. His breathing almost stopped at the captivating beauty of her body. Her skin was flawless, her stomach flat and her breasts were full, but firm.

Phaedra closed her eyes against the determined look on Zephir's face. He lowered his head to the valley between her breasts; she gasped. His lips glided over her skin, causing goosebumps to appear on the smooth surface.

Zephir lost himself in the sweetness of her body. The rise and fall of her bosom beckoned his mouth. Phaedra's eyes widened to small moons when she felt his lips close around the tip of one breast. The persistent tingle in the most private regions of her body grew more pronounced. She couldn't help but respond to the effect of his tongue swirling around the firm nipple.

Zephir heard her soft, wanton cries, and he slowly raised his head. Though he was reluctant to call an end to the fiery scene, he knew he had no choice. As badly as he wanted Phaedra, he could not take her there on the stable floor where anyone could happen upon them. Besides, he wanted her in a way that should not be rushed—she was too special for that. Zephir cleared his throat while tugging her shirt back across her chest.

"Sorry I have to disappoint you, Phaedra, but I do need to tend to my land." He pushed himself onto his knees.

Phaedra's eyes snapped open and were instantly filled with anger. She jumped to her feet and laid a hard slap to his face. "You shameless son of a bitch! Disappointment is the last thing I feel!"

Slowly, Zephir came to his feet and brushed away the hay clinging to his black linen shirt. "I understand why you have to say that," he told her, intentionally taunting her into a fight. "Maybe we'll be able to finish what we started later."

Phaedra tossed her heavy black tresses across her shoulder. "We?" she asked, in a surprisingly cool voice.

Zephir sent her an arrogant smirk in response.

"You'll never finish anything like this with me, Mr. Mfume."

Zephir pushed one hand through his healthy locks and stepped closer to Phaedra. He rubbed a few tendrils of her hair between his thumb and index finger. He eased the silky locks away and pressed his mouth against her ear. "Don't make promises you'll have to eat, Miss Toussaint." He pressed a kiss to her earlobe.

The remote caves had proven to be so vast, Zephir and his trusted crew needed extra help. Dubois had been left with the task of finding additional labor to assist with the excavation.

Unfortunately, Dubois's choices did not sit well with Zephir. When he met the new workers, they immediately set him on edge.

"You men ever do any excavating?" he asked, receiving blank stares in response. "Yes, no?" He prompted, growing more aggravated by their silence.

The burly lot of men looked over at Dubois, who nodded.

"Have you all ever worked in any caves, doing any digging?" Zephir simplified. He rolled his eyes and turned away. "Jesus," he whispered, running a hand through his hair.

The men nodded and looked back at Zephir. They began to nod, their toothless grins appearing.

"We've done it all!" one man proudly replied.

"I'll wager that," Zephir grumbled. "A moment of your time, Dubois?" He walked away from the ragged group. When his right hand stood nearby, Zephir leaned close. "Where did you find these jackasses?"

Dubois cleared his throat and glanced behind him. "Their ship docked at Delices," he said, citing one of the villages on the island. "They were looking for work. I told them we were conducting a mining operation in the caves. We talked about their experience. They are in satisfactory shape and it is obvious they need the work."

Zephir massaged the base of his neck. "Did you tell them what they would be digging for?"

"Not exactly."

Zephir nodded and looked over at the group. "Alright, listen to me, Dubois. I trust you and your judgement. But, if these bastards take so much as a fleck of gold, I'll beat the shit from them and have you dispose of the bodies."

Dubois nodded and walked back to the group. Meanwhile, Zephir headed to the caves. The mining was proceeding rapidly and he was quite pleased. He was even more pleased by the fact that

the land belonged to him legally. The satisfaction soon faded and was replaced by a sour look. The thought of what he had agreed to with the Toussaint brothers made him feel sick.

Still, he could not deny that he wanted Phaedra. She was loud, offensive, tomboyish and rough, but he wanted her. Their encounter in the stables told him he was weakening her defenses. Though she was inexperienced in the ways of men, Zephir could feel the fire lurking beneath her innocence and that excited him. As loathesome as the brothers were for offering Phaedra to him, he found himself wishing the weeks until the party would fly by.

Phaedra Toussaint's 19th birthday gala was slated to be a day-long event. Invitations had been messengered months in advance, and the day would be complete with a breakfast celebration, lunch on the grounds and a birthday ball that evening. Horse drawn carriages began to arrive early that morning for the birthday breakfast. That breakfast had been planned especially for family and close friends. Therefore, when Zephir Mfume arrived, Phaedra had no qualms about voicing her disapproval.

"You're neither family nor friend so what the hell are you doing here?" Phaedra inquired angrily as she stepped out to the front porch.

"Phaedra..." Dante called.

Zephir had taken no offense. "It's alright, Dante."

"No it is not," Marquis argued. "Phaedra, this may be your birthday, but you'll show respect to each guest."

Phaedra's chin rose defiantly. "The hell I will."

"You little brat! This man is our neighbor."

"This man is a thief," Phaedra corrected Carlos.

Zephir turned and tapped the side of the black carriage to instruct his coachman to move on. His eyes were narrowed when he looked upon Phaedra once more. "Gentlemen, please, I take no offense to your lovely cousin," he assured the men as they all began to stroll toward the house. "Though she is nineteen, it's clear that she's still a child. We shouldn't ask too much of her," he added, masking his satisfaction when he heard Phaedra gasp.

Marquis, Carlos and Dante were nowhere near as reserved. Their hearty laughter filled the air as they ushered Zephir into the house.

"Phaedra, I do pray that you'll introduce me later."

Phaedra turned to pin her friend Marci with a stern look. "That man is unworthy of being introduced to anyone I know."

Marci Jasper's wide eyes twinkled with mischief. "Well, dear, if I must renounce our friendship to meet that man, consider us enemies."

"Marci!"

"Oh, Phaedra, stop it now. You know that man is devastating.

Beyond devastating."

"He's an arrogant, dishonest jackass."

Marci tapped a white handkerchief to her heaving bosom. "That may be true, but with that build and that face, those are only minor flaws."

Phaedra closed her eyes. "You have completely lost your mind."

"And you've lost something else," Marci countered, propping one hand to her hip. "Love, doesn't something stir inside you when he looks at you?"

"Stir?" Phaedra parotted, her expression leery.

Marci turned to face her friend more fully. "Oh don't be coy with me, Phaedra Toussaint. You're no different from me or the other fifty women here who have seen that delicious man. To have something that powerful between your legs must be tantamount to Heaven."

"Marci Jaspers!" Phaedra cried, feeling her cheeks burn in response to the woman's lurid assessment. "Please, let's just go inside."

"Sounds wonderful," Marci drawled, looking down to make sure an ample amount of cleavage showed provocatively above the bodice of her coral gown. "On second thought, I think I'd prefer introducing myself to your delectable guest. In a more private area of the house, of course."

Marci Jaspers was not alone with her interest in Zephir Mfume. To Phaedra's dismay, she could not escape a conversation with a woman without being questioned about the devilishly handsome stranger. Her friends and cousins constantly marveled at how gorgeous and virile-looking the man was. Though Phaedra had her own lusty encounters with Zephir, she was still an innocent to many things. Several times during the next few hours, she found herself shocked by the sultry comments she heard. She wondered if she was so shocked because of the comments or because she'd had some of the same thoughts. Desperate for time alone, she set out for a walk, while preparations were being made for late lunch out on the grounds.

"Running away from your guests?"

Phaedra grimaced at the deep voice filling her ears. "Only one," she called, silently cursing herself for venturing so far from the house.

Zephir sat down in the tall grass without a care for the fine fabric of his tanned breeches and matching three quarter length coat. He had not lost sight of his lovely nemesis since he had arrived.

Phaedra's eyes slid over the length of his long legs encased in the polished black boots. She tried to take a deep breath, but only managed to intake a shuddery gasp.

"Would you like my gift now or later?" he asked, his deep, rough voice carrying in the breeze.

Phaeda frowned and sent him a suspicious look. "Gift?"

"Mmm."

With a wicked look, she turned away. "I'm sure that I've seen whatever it is. Most likely it came from one of the rooms in my home."

Zephir only shook his head and handed her the square wrapped package he'd carried under his arm. "See for yourself,"

Hesitating briefly, Phaedra reached for the parcel. A hushed sound passed her lips when she unwrapped the gift and saw the exquisite painting inside.

"One of my men is an amateur artist. I told him about the birth of Midnight's colt and asked him to render a drawing," Zephir explained.

"This—this is beautiful," Phaedra breathed, taking in the detail of the piece. "Why would you do this?" she asked.

Zephir tilted his head. "It's your birthday, remember?"

He's dangerous, Phaedra, a warning voice told her. Such a thoughtful gesture would draw her to him more than she already was. She originally believed him to be cold and devious at heart and had no desire to let go of the assumption. She wouldn't lose her heart to such a man, she vowed.

"Well, I thank you then," she primly replied and covered the painting with its wrapping. "It's good to know this wasn't stolen from my walls or anyplace else."

Zephir's boisterous laughter rumbled forth. "Such vinegar on that tongue. I've never known a woman who hated me the way you do."

"Mr. Mfume, I'm sure you've never taken time to know anything about a woman except what lies beneath her skirts," she said, propping the painting against the base of a tree trunk.

Zephir's grin added something wicked to his devastating features. "Such a tongue. You can't possibly be the innocent you claim to be with a tongue like that."

Phaedra turned and slapped him, hoping his jaw stung as violently as her palm. Unfortunately, she regretted the act the moment she'd carried it out. Zephir's expression grew more wicked, and he moved closer. Her lightning reflexes were no match for his. In a split second she found herself beneath him in the towering green stalks of grass. Regardless of his desire, Zephir knew he'd never take her against her will. In spite of her family's plans for her, he couldn't fathom why he'd become so attached to a woman who held such intense dislike for him. Still, he knew that he wanted her to no end. He wanted all of her, though. That was the thought that frightened him now. Surely, his feelings hadn't grown so deeply in such a short span of time, he worried. Nothing had ever mattered, but the gratification. Now, this young woman with fiery words and fiery dislike had him in an almost desperate state of confusion. True, she'd probably hate him less if he stopped touching her. If only he could command himself to do so.

"Zephir," she spoke his name not knowing whether she wanted him to stop or to continue. "Wait," she managed.

"You want me to stop?" he taunted.

Phaedra blinked at the question. "I-I don't know," she admitted.

At that moment, Zephir seemed just as stunned by her words as she. His expression intensified then and he took her wrists and held them in a loose grip above her head. The embrace sparked memories of that day in her stables. Phaedra told herself she had no desire to be in such a wanton state ever again.

Zephir tugged at the bodice, until one breast was bare. He outlined the mound with the end of his nose then added his lips to the caress.

Phaedra focused on the luminous clouds filling the sky and forbad herself to move. She tried to convince herself that the man who held her so scandalously was having no affect on her senses, but her lashes fluttered each time his breath touched her skin. His mouth circled the dark cloud surrounding the nipple. His lips brushed the firm tip so lightly, she barely felt him there. He continued to torture her with the whisper soft caress, until she began to arch closer.

Phaedra felt Zephir release her wrists, but she was too weak to move. As he took the nipple between his lips and suckled upon it, a soft moan escaped her. She turned her face toward the tall grass and allowed herself to sample the sweet promise of ecstasy.

Zephir tugged upon the bodice until the other breast was freed. His tongue soothed one nipple, while his fingers manipulated the other. Phaedra squeezed her eyes shut tightly as thunderous waves of pleasure surged throughout her trembling body. His tongue bathed her breast unashamedly then returned to suckle the tip with maddening intensity.

He was reluctant to bring an end to his enjoyment, but he did. To take her now, would be to take advantage-he knew that. She wasn't ready. He satisfied himself with the knowledge that one day she would most certainly be his. He buried his face in the soft valley between her breasts and inhaled the faint coconut scent of her skin.

"I can't wait for this party to come to an end," he groaned, pulling away to see confusion clouding her captivating eyes. He then fixed the gown's bodice and helped her to her feet.

Phaedra couldn't look at him. She had allowed this man liberties with her body that should have only belonged to a husband. Still, in some hidden dimension of her soul, she knew it was right. Of course, that was the one thing she would never admit aloud.

"Some of the guests will be leaving shortly after dinner. We think it would be best for you to take her then."

"That's right, things will be less conspicuous in the dark."

Zephir stood and went to freshen his drink at the liquor cabinet. His mood had taken a sour turn, and listening to the Toussaint brothers explain their plans was doing nothing to improve it.

Marquis walked over to the buffet and clapped Zephir's shoulder. "Look alive, man. In a few hours you can bundle your prize into your carriage and be off to enjoy it."

Zephir tossed back the shot of whiskey and relished the burn in his gullet. Despite the payoff, the idea of snatching Phaedra away from her home sickened him. He thought about their interlude in the meadow earlier that afternoon. He found her so irresistible, so delicious and he wanted her as he had never wanted any woman. As though sensing her presence, he looked up and found her standing in the doorway of the study.

Marquis followed the line of Zephir's stare and saw his cousin. "Don't you have enough manners not to eavesdrop?!" he snapped, fearing she may have overheard their plans.

Phaedra tore her eyes away from Zephir's and fixed Marquis with a scathing look. "Your petty discussions don't interest me. Dinner's served." She walked away as silently as she had approached.

During the dinner feast, Zephir was informed that Dubois was out in the foyer. He noticed Phaedra's eyes following him as he left the dining hall and graced her with a flirtatious wink and grin. She rolled her eyes away, and he couldn't help but laugh.

"Sorry to interrupt the celebration," Dubois said, when his friend walked out into the foyer. "Problems with a few of the men."

Zephir's mood darkened for the second time that day. He didn't need descriptions to know that the "men" in question were the same ones they had hired off the island.

"What have those bastards done?"

Dubois's light green eyes flashed with unease. "Picked a fight with our men at the caves. They absconded with only a few pans of gold."

"But we both know they will be back for more?" Zephir remarked, watching Dubois nod.

"What do we do?"

"We wait, but not for long. Those fools will no doubt spread word of our find as soon as they have a few drinks inside them." Zephir decided when he saw Marquis Toussaint in the hallway. "Find Reynolds and have him bring my carriage around front."

"Is there anything the matter?" Marquis inquired as he watched Dubois leave.

"Yes, I'm afraid so," Zephir confirmed, his raspy voice sounding low and weary. "It'll affect our plans for tonight. I'll make new arrangements for Phaedra, but it may take a few days before the situation resolves itself."

Marquis was disappointed, but wasn't about to argue with the brooding giant who stood before him. He shook hands with Zephir and waved him into the night.

CHAPTER 5

The crickets performed their familiar, high-octave song in the otherwise still night. The house was deathly silent. The night was quite cool and helped everyone to sleep soundly for the first time since the party three days prior.

Sadly, Phaedra had not benefitted from the calm of the evening. Once again, her bedchamber was filled with soft whispers and frightened cries. In the midst of another haunting dream, she tossed fretfully. Her legs were caught in a tangle of bedcovers, while her long hair splayed wildly across the pillow.

Again, the disturbing dream played the familiar story. The heavy fog, so prevalent before, was now a thin mist. Phaedra could see that there was definitely a hand coming toward her. The strange jingling sounds came from a charm necklace entwined between the fingers. The haunting piece of jewelry was beautifully crafted. Charms of bamboo, onyx and strange brown pieces dangled from the mahogany beads of the necklace. The bracelet created an unnerving rhythmic tune as it dangled from the hand looming overhead.

Phaedra fought against the message in the dream. The unfamiliar, frightening images were too unsettling, and she struggled to break away. Several moments passed before Phaedra awakened. Her hair was a wild disarray, and sweat covered her skin, causing the thin white shift to cling to her shivering form.

Quickly, she tossed aside the tangled covers and bolted from the bed. She fled her bedchamber without bothering to change or cover the shift she wore. She raced down the stairway, through the house and outside. She made her way to the stables and pulled Midnight from his stall. Then, they rode off into the night covering a vast expanse of the land. The more distance placed between them and the main house, the more at ease Phaedra became. Her breathing soon returned to normal and she loosened her deathgrip on the reins.

Her long brows drew close and she took a moment to gain her bearings. Once again, she had journeyed to the remote stretch of land on the outskirts of Toussaints. Again, she was drawn to the area. It was as though something pulled her toward the caves dotting the edge of the land. For a moment, Phaedra cast a blank look toward the foreboding structures. She caught movement near the mouth of the caves; she determined that there were men moving around down there.

"They're working," Phaedra whispered in awe of what she was seeing.

Surely there was a group of men toiling away inside the caves. Intrigued, she pulled Midnight's reins, urging him onward. She stopped the stallion a few yards from the work site and jumped to the ground. She wanted to take a closer look so secured the horse within the privacy of a secluded tree. She headed to the caves, taking care not to be noticed.

She approached a mound of massive boulders and knelt behind them. From the position, she could see that the caves were lit by torches lining the walls. The men working seemed to be quite excited by their labor. Phaedra could see them transporting silver pans filled with dirt, to tables set up just outside the caves.

She left her hiding place behind the boulders and hurried to the opposite side of the cave. From her perch above, she had an overhead view of the tables. She risked taking a closer look and could spot gold flecks glistening in the black dirt.

So, that's what you're up to. Though she had not seen Zephir anywhere near the caves, she knew he was responsible. Clearly, the man was no more than a thief trying to swindle her cousins out of their property, she surmised.

The realization angered Phaedra so, that she decided to put an end to Zephir's plan. She stood from her crouching position behind the boulders and boldly headed down to the caves.

"You men there!" she called, without observing the danger of her position. "Get the hell off this property or you'll hang for trespassing!"

The burly group of men, stood motionless. Their work was forgotten as they stared at the breathtaking, scantily clad beauty. Amused, they began to walk closer.

Phaedra propped her hands on her hips and tossed her hair back. "Get the hell off this land."

The men exchanged glances then favored Phaedra with their ghastly leering. Still, she was undaunted, her fearless nature preventing her from realizing the seriousness of her predicament.

"Are you going to make us leave, pretty?" one of the men asked as he came to stand before her.

Phaedra's lovely face carried a murderous frown. "I will."

The man's lecherous eyes slid across the soft skin left bare by her shift. His stubby fingers slid over the lacy straps, pushing one from her shoulder. "Are you going to drag me off the land, pretty?" he asked, joining his cohorts in laughter.

Phaedra finally began to take note of her situation. Determined not to show fear, she tilted her chin back and tried to move away. Unfortunately, the group surrounded her. There was no escape. Before she could make another move, one of the men grabbed her from behind. His arms closed like steel bands around her body.

Phaedra struggled viciously. Her foot caught one of her attackers squarely in the groin. The the man howled in pain. A satisfied smirk crossed Phaedra's lips.

"Get this little slut on the ground!" the group's leader ordered. As his shabby companions obeyed, the man pulled a torn leather belt from around his waist.

Ever the brave soul, Phaedra continued to fight. Unfortunately, the group quickly had her pinned to the ground. Hating the feeling of defeat that washed over her, she began to scream. Her terrified cries had no effect on the group. The burly, grotesque man who appeared to be the leader, knelt over her and began to rip her dirtied shift.

Phaedra bucked wildly beneath the man and succeeded in unsettling him. Surprisingly, the man laughed.

"We got a lively one here, boys!" he shouted, lowering his mouth to her neck. "I like that," he whispered in her ear. He jerked her thighs apart with one hand while using the other to free himself. The man uttered a lusty bellow in anticipation. He was jerked away, only seconds before he could complete his brutal task.

Phaedra kept her eyes squeezed shut. Tears streamed her cheeks as she fought to still her breathing. It was hopeless, though. Her entire body shook from fear.

"Dubois, make sure she is alright!" Zephir roared, as he held onto the man he had just pulled off Phaedra.

Dubois rushed over and lifted her into his arms. He saw that the girl was so shaken and terrified that she barely responded to his touch.

Meanwhile, Zephir and the rest of his men laid into the group of attackers. A satisfied look came to Zephir's face as he pounded one man into a bloodied mass. He and his crew had assumed the group Dubois hired would return to the caves. They were already on the way to catch them in the act of swindling the gold. When Zephir found them with Phaedra, he felt a rage unlike any he had ever experienced. The men cried out as their bones were broken, teeth were smashed and their eyes blackened. Zephir threw one man against the wall of the cave and stormed over to Dubois.

"Get rid of them," he ordered, his rough voice brooking no argument.

Dubois could not mistake the underlying meaning of Zephir's words. He waited for his friend to kneel beside him so that he could place Phaedra in his arms.

"You foolish girl," Zephir whispered against her hairline, pressing soft kisses to her temple.

Phaedra was so terrified, she did not realize she was being rescued. The moment she felt herself being lifted from the ground, she began to fight. One of her blows landed against Zephir's jaw.

"Dammit," he growled. "Foolish wench, stop fighting me!" he ordered, hauling her more firmly against his chest.

The angry, deep voice from above only fueled Phaedra's fighting instincts. This man, however, felt ten times stronger than the one who held her before. Feeling defeated for the second time that night, she began to cry.

"Please stop the weeping," Zephir groaned. A grim look was cast across his magnificent features as he treaded the tall field leading to his home.

Phaedra's head snapped up, her eyes narrowing as she looked into his face. Realzing who held her, she laid a cracking slap to his smooth, jaw. "Wretched bastard, what the hell is going on?!"

"If you know what's good for you, you'll shut your mouth." He tightened his hold around her waist.

"I knew you were doing something dishonest. I just didn't know what. Until tonight."

"Mmmm…"

"You black thief! You'll die for this! If it's the last thing I do—"

"The last thing you almost did was to get yourself raped and killed!" Zephir interrupted. "Now either you shut up or I'll complete the task myself!"

Phaedra gasped, the look on Zephir's face convinced her that he meant every word. Still, knowing that he had tried to cheat her family, prevented her from remaining silent. "You'll pay for this, Zephir Mfume. Trespassing, stealing. I'll personally see to it," she threatened, her small fists pounding against his iron shoulder.

Zephir did not respond, though he silently cursed what had happened. There was no way he could risk the Toussaints discovering his plan. Undoubtedly, Phaedra would tell everything she knew the moment she returned to the main house. Suddenly, an idea so delicious, so wicked came to his mind. There was a way to keep Phaedra and the land without the brothers ever knowing of its hidden wealth.

"Where the hell are we going?" she demanded, breaking the silence.

"You'll see when we get there."

"Oooo you-you filthy devil. When I get home…"

Zephir only sighed as he listened to Phaedra's angry words and threats.

"What is this place?" She pushed her hair away from her face and saw a grim looking house in their midst.

Zephir allowed her to slide out of his embrace as they stepped onto the porch. "This is my home."

"Why are we here?" She asked, her heart slammed against her chest at the look he sent her way.

Phaedra turned and attempted to run from the porch. Zephir simply reached out and caught her by the hem of her shift then pulled her inside and took her into a dim sitting room. He set her to a forest green armchair then headed to a tall, wooden table stocked with bottles of wine and whiskey.

Phaedra's wide eyes darted from Zephir to the front door. Like a flash, she was out of the chair and running to the front. He caught her, just as her fingers brushed the tarnished doorknob. She fastened her teeth around his hand and bit down.

"Shit!" he hissed, tossing her into a chair like a sack of clothes. He braced his hands on either side of her and brought his face close to hers. "You are testing me, and I am not a man known for my patience."

Extraordinarily fearless, Phaedra kicked out at him. The heel of her foot connected with his thigh. In response, Zephir caught her bare leg. His hands caressed the silky smooth length of her calf, stopping beneath her knee.

"Would you like me to break this for you?" he asked, his voice soft, the tone polite.

Her eyes lowered to the hand covering her leg. Quickly, she shook her head.

The familiar, wicked look reappeared, and Zephir patted her bare thigh. "Good," he said, rising to his full height. "Now you sit here. Quietly." He headed toward the whiskey table once again.

Phaedra curled her legs beneath her and rubbed her hands across her arms. She took a moment to study her surroundings. The cold, drafty interior of the house reminded her of the stables after dark. Obviously, no woman occupied the place, for it had the look, smell and feel of a man.

"Drink this."

Phaedra jumped at the harsh tone of Zephir's voice. He was offering her a glass brimming with a red liquid. "What is it?" she asked.

"Drink it."

"Why? What is it?"

Zephir knelt before her and pushed the glass into her hand. "Something to calm you. You have had wine before?"

"Of course I have," she haughtily replied, her chin raised in defiance. She tilted the glass to her lips and drained the contents. "Can I go home now?"

"No."

"Why ever not?"

His piercing eyes slid from her face and tousled hair to the ripped, dirtied shift she wore. "You have just been through a rough ordeal. You need your rest."

"I can rest at home. In my own bed."

He laughed shortly. "Why, Miss Toussaint, I get the feeling you do not appreciate my hospitality."

Her mouth fell open. "Hospitality? Your men just tried to force themselves on me. Now if you think I want to stay here—"

"Those were not my men."

"Hmm…why don't I believe you?"

Zephir sighed. "They worked for me, yes. But, I didn't trust them. I gave them a chance to prove themselves."

"Ha! I'm sure they made you proud tonight!"

Zephir held his index finger inches away from Phaedra's chin. "Whatever you may think of me, I do not condone rape or thievery."

She laughed at such lunacy, but was cut short by her own yawn. "Mr. Mfume, I may be young, but I am no fool. Thievery? You say you don't condone thievery? Tell me, do my cousins know about the gold you are excavating from those caves?"

The hard glint flashing in Zephir's eye, pleased her immensely.

"I thought not," she said, standing from the arm chair. "If you will excuse me, I think I need to have a talk with my family."

Zephir made no attempt to stop her. He watched as she took a few steps then stumbled. At once, he was behind her—holding her close. "I'm taking you to bed," he whispered against her ear and lifted her into his arms.

Phaedra frowned and closed her eyes. All at once, her head was spinning madly. "What did you…give me?" she asked, her speech slurred.

Zephir shook his head. "You're right, Phaedra. You are no fool," he said, remembering the sleep tonic he had laced around the mouth of her wine glass.

Phaedra had drifted off, by the time Zephir opened the door to his bedchamber. He tucked her beneath the covers, locked the room door then headed to the Toussaint Plantation.

"I have searched this entire house and the stables! She is nowhere to be found!"

Marquis, Carlos and Dante watched Tisha in amazement. The woman had awakened them that night with news that Phaedra was missing.

"Perhaps she went for a ride," Dante suggested, walking across Marquis's study to fix himself a drink.

Tisha propped her hands over her hips. "In the middle of the night?"

Carlos rushed over to Tisha and placed his hands on her shoulders. "Come now, Tisha. You know how she is. Are any of the horses missing?"

"I don't know," Tisha whispered, covering her face with her hands.

A thundering knock against the front door brought them all from the study. Everyone watched as Melin rushed to open the door. When Zephir walked into the house, Marquis, Carlos, Dante and Tisha hurried down the staircase.

"Mr. Mfume, please tell us you have seen Phaedra?" Tisha whispered, her voice filled with worry.

Zephir looked down at the small woman, his eyes soft. "I've seen her and she's fine." He pressed a kiss against the scarf covering the woman's head. His caught the brother's attention. "May I speak with you all for a moment?"

The brothers nodded and went into the sitting room down the hall from the foyer. Zephir patted Tisha's shoulder then followed them.

"You have seen Phaedra?" Carlos asked.

Zephir nodded once. "I have."

Marquis stepped forward, his hands clasped. "Has something happened?"

Zephir's expression was grim. "She's well. However, something has happened. She…came to me earlier this evening. I'm afraid her innocence has been compromised."

Stunned amazement replaced the look of uncertainty on the brother's round faces.

"I think it best that she come with me now instead of waiting any longer. In light of what has happened, she is understandably uneasy about facing you all," Zephir stated, his voice unwavering.

Marquis beckoned his brothers, and they met in a small huddle. "My brothers, this could not have worked out better if we had planned it this way."

"You're right," Carlos agreed. "This is the perfect explanation for a sudden disappearance by our cousin. Phaedra giving herself to a practical stranger and then running away with him will be the perfect way to prove her incompetence to run this estate."

"We'll have the land in no time," Dante predicted.

The brothers turned back to Zephir, looking quite pleased.

"We think you are right, Mr. Mfume," Marquis told him.

Zephir nodded, a look of satisfaction crossing his face. "Have all of her things packed within the hour. "I'll send for them." He headed for the arched doorway of the sitting room. "Does she have any warm clothes?"

Carlos shot his brothers a confused look. "Yes…but why?"

Zephir didn't bother to look back. "She is about to see the snow she has always dreamed of."

"Oooo…" Phaedra moaned, pressing her palms against her head. Her temples pounded from the ache that lingered there, while her stomach churned and made the strangest sounds.

Slowly, her eyes opened, and she squinted against the dull light that filtered the room. She saw that she was on a bed that occupied a great deal of space. Of course, she had no idea where she was. She lay there for several moments, trying to remember what had happened to her. Unfortunately, everything appeared fuzzy, and it actually hurt to think.

Knowing she could not lie there forever, she ordered herself from the bed. It took several moments to push herself into a sitting position. Once she managed to swing her legs over the side of the high bunk, she eased her feet to the thick, gray rug covering the floor. There was a small, round window to one side of the room. Phaedra tried to make her way to the window, but found it almost impossible to dispel the nausea that overcame her with each step she took.

Her fingers finally curled around the smooth, wooden base of the window. She stood on her toes and peeked out. To her horror, she saw nothing but a sea of light blue water! Her legs weakened beneath her, and she rested her forehead against the wall. She took one more look out the window, hoping that she had been hallucinating. The water remained, shimmering and calm. She could feel the blood rushing to her head. Before she could pass out, the heavy wooden door at the front of the room burst open.

Phaedra forced her eyes open and turned to see who had entered. Zephir's imposing form loomed in the doorway of the cabin.

Overwhelmed and more frightened than she ever thought possible, she dropped to the floor.

"Dammit," Zephir muttered and slammed the door behind him. He stormed over to Phaedra and pulled her into his arms. In one effortless motion, he lifted her off the floor and carried her back to the bunk.

A small frown clouded her face as she tried to open her eyes. "What…what's happening?" she moaned.

"Shh…I can barely understand you," he whispered, his raspy voice tinged with amusement.

"Where are we going?" she questioned, her small fists pounding lightly against his chest.

"Somewhere far, far away," he called softly and placed her back into the bed.

"Mmm…" She sighed, sleep claiming her the moment her head touched the pillow.

Zephir was about to pull the heavy quilts over her partially clad form, but something stopped him. He could not resist the urge to touch her—just once. From the moment he had seen her, he imagined her completely unclothed. The sight of her luscious body bared to his view had kept him awake many nights.

He decided to put an end to his torture and gently eased the torn, dirty shift from her body. She wore no other garments and was nude beneath his sultry, pitch black look. His eyes traced every inch of her body, entranced by the rich, cocoa color of her skin. The full, firm breasts, flat stomach and the mound of glossy black curls shielding her womanhood, rendered his entire body weak.

Driven by the insistent demands of male arousal, Zephir was unable to resist touching her. His hands cupped and weighed her breasts. His thumbs brushed the nipples hardened by the coolness of the cabin. He lowered his head and took one of the firm tips between his lips. She moaned slightly beneath the touch, causing him to still the caress. She did not awaken, and Zephir tentatively stroked the hard bud with his tongue. The sweet taste of her skin forced a tortured moan from his throat, and he took more of her breast into his mouth. His hands slid across the incredible softness of her body. He cupped her hips before moving down to squeeze her full buttocks.

Zephir ordered himself away from the loveliness of her body. Cursing himself for taking advantage of her unconscious state, he pounded his fist lightly against the bed. Weakened by arousal, he left the cabin.

CHAPTER 6

Zephir spent the next hour strolling his ship—The Venus. The spacious vessel had been in his possession for several years and had sailed the world many times. This time, The Venus was headed to Wesleyville, a small township on the Newfoundland coast. There, Zephir retained a cozy chalet that was won in a chess match with Cantone Lezard.

A grim look came to his face as thoughts of his old foe filled his mind. The notorious Moor had hated Zephir Mfume from the day he had lost his beloved snowy chalet. Lezard had always vowed revenge, claiming Zephir cheated during the match. In the years since, their paths had crossed on numerous ocassions.

Zephir pulled a heavy black cloak around his shoulders and gazed out upon the calm waters. He hoped Lezard was off on an excursion that would keep him away from Wesleyville. However, if their paths were destined to cross, so be it. Zephir could only hope Lezard's vow of revenge would not affect his own plans.

Turning away from the sea, Zephir headed back to the cabins. Phaedra was sure to be awake, and he knew she would be expecting answers. He had decided to put her in his cabin for safe keeping. Though he trusted the crew with his life, he was not about to tempt them with the devastating beauty. A slow grin spread across his face at the thought as he eased a heavy key into the lock and pushed open the door. The moment he stepped inside, a loud angry cry touched his ears. Phaedra had literally jumped him from behind. Her nails dug into his neck while her shapely legs encircled his torso. She was like a wild animal, fighting frantically for her freedom.

Zephir easily turned the tables, however. In one, easy motion, he caught her arm and pulled her from his back. As though she weighed nothing, he tossed her atop the tangled bed. His expression made him appear as sinister as Lucifer. Of course, the murderous look on Zephir's face did not intimidate Phaedra. The moment she was dumped to the center of the bed, she made another lunge for him. Her slender fingers curled around the collar of the long, cloak he wore. Her knee connected with the sensitive area between his thighs, forcing him to utter a low grunt. A look of unmistakeable satisfaction brightened Phaedra's lovely face. Unfortunately for her, Zephir's discomfort only lasted a brief while. He lost complete control over his temper, shoving Phaedra back to the bed and falling on top of her.

Finding herself pinned beneath his massive weight, Phaedra struggled. It was impossible to move, and, finally, she raised her lovely, wide eyes to Zephir's face.

"Now you listen to me," he began, his rough voice sounding surprisingly calm, "from this moment on, you will do exactly as I say. No questions. No arguments. Do you understand me?"

Phaedra opened her mouth to blast him.

"The first word past those lips had better be yes," he warned.

"Yes," she replied in a sweet, simple tone.

Zephir could almost see her fire as he intentionally goaded her. "Yes, what?"

"Yes, you will regret the day you ever placed your hands on me, you rotten bastard," she promised, her low voice shaking with distaste.

Zephir could only smile. She was so incredibly brave, he thought. She had absolutely no idea how serious her situation was. As badly as he ached to tell her that her beloved family had sold her, he waited. It would be better to save that tidbit for a more opportune time.

The silence gave Phaedra a chance to become aware of her nudity. Zephir was aware of it as well. Phaedra's unclothed body affected him so, that he could not stop the bulge that rose along the muscled ridge of his thigh.

Phaedra's innocence prevented her from being shocked by the reaction of his body. It was his look that left no doubt in her mind regarding his train of thought. This prompted another bout of struggles on her part. Though she knew it was hopeless escaping him, she had to try.

"Get off me, you imbecile! You're crushing me!"

"Stop fighting me, Phaedra," he warned, nearing the end of his patience.

"Get the hell away from me, dammit!"

He took her wrists in one hand and pressed her arms high above her head. She continued to fight, her hips arching wildly beneath the powerful male above her. When her efforts barely nudged him, she let out a frustrated cry.

"You filthy Cuban mongrel! I hate you!"

Zephir had been called all sorts of names stemming from his mixed heritage. Thankfully, his parents had raised him in love and taught him to have confidence in his abilities. As a result, insults rarely, if ever, fazed him. Hearing them spew from Phaedra's lips, though, affected him differently. For the first time, the words hurt fiercely as they cut deep.

Phaedra could see how he was affected when he let go of her wrists and blinked. In spite of her frustration, the wounded look in his eyes filled her with remorse. "Zephir," she whispered, brushing her fingertips across his eyes as through attempting to make the sorrow there disappear. His long lashes shielded his gaze from view, and she could not resist arching closer to him.

Go Zephir, he said to himself, feeling her breasts crushing into his chest. He realized now why he goaded her so shamefully, her anger kept him sane and gentlemanly. Her softness and concern wreaked as much havoc on his hormones as they did his heart. His head dipped then and he pushed his tongue deeply into Phaedra's mouth. The kiss forced a weak cry from her throat. He freed her mouth after a time and Phaedra could feel her soft lips throbbing from the pressure of his.

Taking advantage of her nude state, Zephir pressed more kisses along her neck. His strong teeth nipped at her skin as his touch lowered. He suckled her breasts like a man dying of thirst. Moving on, his persuasive lips grazed her ribcage. Her fingers sank into his thick, silky locks. Zephir's hair felt so wondrous between her fingers, that she actually gasped from the sensation. Knowing that she should be refusing, her fingers curled into the black mass and she tried pulling him away.

Zephir, however, was set on continuing what he had started earlier. His tongue blazed a trail across her hips, caressing the toned line of her thighs before dipping into the valley between…

"What are you doing?" Phaedra gasped, her eyes widening at the shocking, unfamiliar caress.

Zephir's hands curved around her thighs and held them apart. Phaedra's lashes fluttered shut as her fingers loosened their hold in his hair.

"Zephir…" she moaned, as his tongue traced the outline of her womanhood.

As he delved inside, she arched off the bed. He pulled her back to the tangled bedcovers and deepened the strokes of the erotic kiss. Phaedra thought she would faint beneath the touch. Instinctively, her hips moved in slow, circular motions that brought her closer to his mouth. Zephir deepened the thrusts of his tongue. A ragged groan escaped him, when he felt her respond to the caress. He carried out the devastating act for a while longer, then barely managed to pull himself away. Phaedra unknowingly uttered a tiny sound of disappointment, that pleased him more than he realized.

"I'll have you sent some warm clothes," he told her, rising from the bed and running a hand through his hair.

Phaedra was speechless, her wide eyes following his every move. When the cabin door closed, she emitted a relieved sigh and pressed her trembling legs together. She tried to still the moisture that slid down her thighs and caused her to replay the scene that had just occurred.

"Hold it!" Zephir ordered the deck hands who carried a large, red trunk.

The men set the trunk in front of Zephir's feet. He knelt and flipped open the brass lock. His hands delved into a well of lovely feminine garments.

A knowing smirk crossed Dubois's face as he watched his friend. "She's getting to you, isn't she, my man?"

Zephir rolled his eyes toward his friend. "Never."

"Is that a fact?"

"She is a beauty, but far too brash and arrogant for my tastes." He slammed the trunk closed.

Dubois folded his arms over his chest. "Hmm...brash and arrogant? She sounds just like you."

Zephir grunted. "Exactly." He beckoned the two deck hands. "Take this to my cabin. I'll be along."

"So, why are we heading so far out?" Dubois asked, focusing on the calm shimmering waters.

"I needed to get Phaedra as far away from Dominica as possible." Zephir sighed, propping his foot against the ship's bow and staring ahead.

Dubois nodded, stroking the beard that covered his chin. "You think we may run into Lezard?"

Zephir shook his head. "I pray not. I'll have my hands full as it is with Phaedra."

"So why take her to Newfoundland?"

"It is the perfect place for her. She'll be completely unaccustomed to the climate and the terrain. I can hold her there without locking her up or watching her every waking moment." He drew his warm, black wool overcoat more tightly around his wide shoulders.

"And Lezard?"

"Lezard, is an inconvenience I'll have to deal with sooner or later. If it's meant for us to meet in Wesleyville, so be it."

"Thank you so much. I can't wait to soak in this."

The awestruck young man stood speechless in the presence of the raven-haired beauty. Christian Martell watched Phaedra tread her fingers through the tub of water he had prepared for her. "I hope it is to your liking, Miss," he said.

Phaedra looked at Christian and laughed. "Oh, it will be. Thank you for your kindness."

"Oh, 'twas no problem at all, Miss," the boy gushed.

Christian's infatuation was hard to miss. Of course, Phaedra took note of his politeness and flashed him a dazzling look. "It must be fascinating working on a ship?" she inquired as she stood and held the bed quilt more tightly around her body.

"Oh…yes, yes it is."

"Mmm…I haven't even had the chance to see more than this cabin." She sighed, gazing around the room. "I don't suppose…no, no."

Christian tilted his head to one side, a concerned look coming to his light-complexioned, oval face. "What? What is it?"

"Well," Phaedra drawled, turning away from the young man. "It would be quite a treat to see the rest of the ship…sometime."

Christian flushed a bright crimson. "Well, Miss…"

"I understand that you are very busy," Phaedra said as she whirled around to face him. "Anytime that you could spare would be greatly appreciated."

Christian cleared his throat nervously. "Um, may I um let you know, Miss?"

Phaedra heard the young man's uneasy tone of voice. She knew he would be back. "That would be just fine. I'll look forward to it."

Bowing to her quickly, Christian collected the pails he had used to bring in the bath water. Phaedra hugged herself. There had to be a way to escape. With Christian's help, she was sure to find it.

Phaedra winced at the verbal assault. She grasped her lower lip
ween her teeth and fought to keep it from trembling.

Zephir rolled his eyes away from her and headed for the door
ean up this mess and be dressed for dinner by the time I return…o
"

The hot bath soothed away all the tension of the past few days.
Phaedra submersed her entire body in the invigorating water. An enormous bar of softly scented soap had been provided as well. In minutes,
the cabin was filled with the smell of the soap and the tub was teeming
with bubbles.

The bath was so relaxing, Phaedra drifted off to sleep. In the midst
of her light slumber, another dream ensued. This time, the unsettling
visions appeared with crystal clarity.

"My God," she whispered, upon awakening. Her wide eyes stared
blankly into space for several moments. Finally, she looked toward the
front of the cabin and saw Zephir. His deep-set slanting charcoal gaze
practically bored into her.

"What are you doing in here?!" she snapped, angry and a bit
embarrassed after all that had happened between them.

Zephir did not appear to be in the mood for talking. He ignored
her question, walking slowly toward her and kneeling beside the tub.

Phaedra looked away. She was determined to put a cap on the
unease she felt in his presence. Zephir's hands treading the soapy water,
however, made it almost impossible for her to remain calm. His hand
delved deeper in the water, his long fingers brushing the undersides of
her breasts. Her lashes fluttered close against his touch, and she inhaled
sharply. His searching fingers journeyed lower until he brushed the sensitive spot at the joining of her thighs. Phaedra squeezed her eyes shut.

Slowly, Zephir's fingers probed her womanhood. He felt the muscles contract around his finger as she adjusted to the unfamiliar intrusion. He did not end the caress, but waited until he felt her relax. Then,
at a snail's pace, his middle finger slid further inside her. A whisper soft
cry passed Phaedra's lips and her legs shifted apart. The feelings she
experienced from the single touch were indescribable.

Zephir loved hearing the soft gasps Phaedra uttered and the look
of immense satisfaction on her exquisite face. He lowered his mouth to
the side of her neck and pressed tiny, wet kisses against her damp scented skin. His fingers probed deeper, stroking the velvety softness of her
body.

"Zephir…" Phaedra moaned. She never wanted him to stop.

A curt knock sounded upon the door and Phaedra jumped.

Zephir pulled his head from her shoulder and slowly pulled his hand from the water. Phaedra watched him walk over to open the door. Outside, two deck hands waited with the trunk.

"I'll take it." He said, easily lifting the trunk that had to be carried by the two men. After closing the door, he brought the monstrous piece of luggage to the center of the room.

"What's in that?" Phaedra called from the tub. She thought the trunk looked awfully familiar.

Zephir did not answer, prompting Phaedra to take a closer look. She had nothing to cover her nude body and Zephir certainly wasn't going anywhere.

Phaedra tapped her fingers against the tub in a clearly impatient fashion. "Would you mind leaving?"

Zephir shrugged one wide shoulder. "Why?"

"So, I can get out of this damned tub!"

Standing back on his strong legs, Zephir crossed his arms over his chest. "I've already seen you naked…several times."

Phaedra slapped her hands into the water. "Would you get out, so I can put something on?!"

The familiar, wicked white grin contrasted against his flawless blackberry complexion. He went over to the trunk, opened it and rummaged around inside for a moment. He headed to the tub after choosing an exquisite, ice blue silk dressing gown.

Phaedra studied the robe intently. As she reached for it, Zephir held it just out of her grasp. Each time she extended her reach, he held it further away.

"Dammit, will you please?!" she snapped, cringing when his hearty laughter filled the room. Finally, he ceased teasing and handed her the lovely garment.

Phaedra snatched it from him. Realizing she could not slip into the piece seated in the tub, she frowned up at him. He waited patiently, delighted when she disregarded her nude state and stood. She shook

the wrinkles from the robe and gasped, discovering that [...] to her. She pulled the piece over her body and stormed [...] to kneel beside the trunk.

"This is mine," she whispered, sifting through [...] Shaking from anger, she turned her stormy eyes on Z[...] say that you don't condone thievery."

Zephir's sleek, long brows rose. "Excuse me?"

"Do not play innocent with me, you jackass!" Ph[...] feet. "You broke into my home and took these thing[...]

"Phaedra…" Zephir sighed, surprised that it ha[...] her that her own family had betrayed her. "You ca[...] dense?"

"You're right. I'm not. So don't try lying your [...]

"You actually think I'd break into your home[...] clothing?" Zephir bellowed, coming to tower over [...]

"Of course not!" Phaedra spat. "I'm quite sur[...] to much more."

"You foolish little wench! How can you be s[...] on here?"

"Blind to what's going on here?" Phaedra r[...] the trunk. "I can very well see what is going o[...] in my very own hand!" she cried, throwing a [...] face.

Zephir lost his patience then and took ho[...] instantly began to ply his neck and face with [...] set into a harsh line. The delicate gown [...] Phaedra landed to the bed.

She knelt in the center of the bed and g[...] from her luminous dark gaze. Her long, w[...] her face and body like black snakes. Zeph[...] the delightful picture she made and raised [...]

"I knew you were spoiled, ill-manner[...] his chest heaving from the deep breaths [...] to be an idiot as well."

CHAPTER 7

The Venus had been at sea for several weeks. Phaedra had been going out of her mind with boredom. The initial tours of the ship had proven to be useless. There seemed to be no way off the vessel, unless she were to jump overboard and swim her way to freedom. She decided she would have to wait until they reached land, but when would that be? Since the awful fight with Zephir weeks ago, they had not spoken to one another. She could count the times he had taken her outside the cabin on one hand. Had it not been for Christian, the young deckhand, she would have surely lost her mind.

A soft knock filtered through the heavy wooden door. Phaedra stormed across the cabin, ready to blast Zephir for the way he had been treating her and waited for the door to open.

It was not Zephir, but Christian. Phaedra wiped the scowl from her face and replaced it with a pleasant look.

"Christian! How nice to see you."

The young man gushed, his thin face turning a bright red. "Thank you, Miss."

Phaedra slapped her hands to her sides. "What are you doing here?"

Christian took a moment to respond. His hazel eyes could not look away from Phaedra's captivating face. After a moment, he caught himself staring. "I'm sorry, Miss."

"Please won't you call me Phaedra? We are practically the same age."

"Phaedra," Christian repeated, his ease resurfacing. "Would you care to take a walk around the ship?"

Phaedra's arched brows rose at the offer. Folding her arms across the bodice of her sea blue gown, she debated. It certainly could not hurt to get out of the cabin for another secret excursion. Perhaps she would finally be successful in determining if the ship carried a dinghy that could assist in her escape. Turning back to Christian, she spread her arms wide. "It sounds like a wonderful idea."

Phaedra studied the ship with renewed interest. She still couldn't spot any other boats attached to the massive ship, unfortunately. It simply made her feel better to be working on a plan to return to Dominica.

She was so deeply in thought that she paid no attention to where they were heading. Though Christian had been more than happy to retrieve Phaedra from her cabin, this time he'd been acting under the orders of his Captain.

"Sir?" Christian called, waiting patiently for a response.

Zephir turned; Phaedra's mouth fell open. "What the—"

"Thank you, Chris," Zephir said, his hand curling around Phaedra's arm.

Christian nodded and watched Phaedra adoringly. Her eyes, however, were focused on her captor.

"What are you doing?" she politely asked through a tight look.

Zephir gestured to one of the mates at the ship's bow. He left the tall man at the wheel and pulled Phaedra along behind him.

"This ship isn't very large, Miss Toussaint. Word of your little walks with Christian was bound to reach me."

Phaedra watched him in surprise. "So? What is wrong with that?"

Zephir shrugged. Though he was fully aware of Phaedra's interest in the ship, he played the innocent. "You're my guest. I should've realized you would want out of that cabin. Phaedra, all you had to do was ask."

Phaedra knew she could not afford to have him learn that she was desperately seeking an escape. Therefore, she simply slipped her hand through the crook of his arm. "Thank you," she whispered.

As they strolled the deck, Zephir found himself more focused on Phaedra than on his fine ship. He could not help but be entranced by the way she appeared beneath the late evening sky. The setting sun shone against her black hair as the wind lifted the wavy locks around her face.

Phaedra held a pensive, far-away look. Taking notice, Zephir stopped walking and cupped her chin in his palm.

"Why do you drift off this way?" he softly asked, the wide pad of his thumb brushing her full lips.

"Drift off?" Phaedra asked.

"Mmm hmm…you do it quite a bit," he noted, a curious frown coming to his face.

"I guess I have been," she whispered, walking over to lean against the rails of the ship.

"What is it?" he asked, leaning against the rails as well. His fingers caught a flying tendril of her hair and he toyed with it.

"These dreams," Phaedra sighed, with a shake of her head. She glanced at Zephir and grimaced. "Silly, actually."

Zephir propped the side of his face against his palm. "To be silly, they certainly affect you deeply."

Phaedra nodded. "Yes." She breathed, bracing herself against the chill that touched her body. "The same one for months. Though now, it has changed somewhat," she said, unknowingly confiding in Zephir.

"How?"

"At first, it was cloudy…foggy. I could barely see what was happening inside my own head." She laughed. "The fog has faded now, and I see that I'm dreaming of my mother. I was in her arms when she died. Marquis, Carlos and Dante were there…so was their mother. Lucia. I have no idea what it all means."

"Maybe it means: beware of your cousins."

The far away, uneasy look in Phaedra's eyes, left to be replaced by an accusing glare. "You manipulating beast."

Zephir frowned, rising to his full height. "Excuse me?"

"There is no excuse for you! To think I could talk to you about something so private—"

"What the hell is wrong with you now?"

Phaedra poked her index finger against the crisp material of Zephir's gray shirt. "You trying to turn me against my family is what's wrong with me!" She raged. In her heart, she knew that Zephir was right. Still, to believe even they could be responsible for…she couldn't let herself accept it.

"Jesus," Zephir muttered, raking his hands through his hair, "if you'd open your eyes, you might find that I am right!"

"Mmm hmm," Phaedra replied, her lips twisted into a sour look. "You will burn for the things you have done. My cousins will see to that." She grimaced at how foolish of a possibility that was.

Zephir's efforts to control his short temper were only sucessful to a point. He managed not to explode there on the deck before his men. Taking Phaedra's upper arm in his iron grasp, he practically dragged her from the deck.

Phaedra's heart slammed against her chest as they left the cool loveliness of the upper level. The last thing she wanted was to be alone with Zephir in that cabin. Her cheeks burned as memories of what happened between them flooded her mind. When she recalled the things he had done, the places his hands and mouth had touched… The fact that she did not protest, made her even more uneasy.

Zephir wrenched the door open and pulled Phaedra inside behind him. As he shrugged out of his heavy, coat, she looked around the cabin and was amazed.

"What have you done?" she whispered, her eyes wider that usual.

Zephir did not turn to look at her. "I had the room cleaned."

"But this…" She walked over to the small round table in the corner of the cabin. It was elegantly set for two, with lighted candles, gleaming cutlery and silver dishes on a pristine white cloth. "What is this?"

Zephir warmed his hands before the fire then joined her at the table. "I know you feel like a captive here, but I thought you might appreciate a quiet dinner."

Phaedra gasped and took a small step backward. She couldn't believe he had committed such a sweet, thoughtful act. She remembered the beautiful painting he'd given on her birthday and recalled that the last thing she wanted was for him to become charming. She knew she would never be able to resist him.

"I'm not very hungry," she grumbled, going to the bed and reclining against the pillows.

Zephir congratulated himself on shocking and confusing her. He knew she was trying to determine his motives, and he laughed silently at the fact. With a deep breath, he lifted the silver covers that protected the food.

"You're not hungry, hmm?…I'm sorry to hear that. Chef outdid himself this night." He tore off a sliver of roasted duck and enjoyed the taste of the perfectly seasoned meat.

Phaedra turned her head away from the tempting aroma of the food. Meanwhile, Zephir tormented her by bragging over the delicious meal. He prepared himself a monstrous plate heaped with the tender duck, fresh corn, potatoes and crusty bread. Filling a polished tankard with wine, he took a seat at the table and began to wolf down the food.

Out of pure frustration, Phaedra pushed both hands through her hair. As starved as she was, there was no way she could resist helping herself to the fantastic meal. Moving off the bed, she stormed to the table and prepared her own plate.

Zephir stole a knowing glance in her direction as he took a sip of drink. Picking up the flask of wine, he offered it toward her. "You did tell me that your cousins allow you to drink?"

Phaedra reached for her tankard and held it out. "I do what I please." Her lovely eyes were stormy with frustration. The hard look grew softer when she noticed Zephir's eyes fall to her heaving chest. Her mind was quick and an idea quickly formed.

When the tankard was full, she downed the smooth, fragrant wine in one gulp. Walking around the table, she propped her hip against Zephir's shoulder. "More," she ordered, holding out the vessel.

Though her sweetness teased his senses, Zephir forced himself to ignore it. Instinct told him she was up to something. He decided to relax until she revealed herself.

The effect of the wine quickly took its toll. Phaedra bent low. "Thank you," she whispered next to his ear, her full bosom brushing his cheek.

Zephir cleared his throat and refilled his mug as well. Instead of sitting across the table, Phaedra pulled her chair close to his. During the course of the meal, she sent countless lingering looks his way. Zephir knew she had a plan in mind, but he could not help but be affected. All the weeks with her on his ship, he had counted on her coldness to keep him at bay. If she continued to toy with him…Heaven help her, for he would not be able to stop himself.

"Mmm…" she sighed, swirling the last corner of her bread in the duck's succulent juices. "That was delicious," she said, popping the bread into her mouth. Dabbing her lips with the linen napkin next to her plate, she fixed him with her dazzling eyes. "Thank you so much," she whispered, her fingers tracing the back of his hand with light circular motions.

Zephir looked to her small hand resting against his much larger one. "You're more than welcome." He finally replied.

Phaedra lowered her eyes to the table. "I only wish there were some way to thank you more properly." She sighed and pushed her chair away from the table.

Zephir's long, black brows rose a few notches as several wicked ideas came to mind. He remained silent though, tossing back the remainder of his wine as he watched her.

With a mischief curving her soft mouth, Phaedra returned to the monstrous bed in the middle of the cabin. She knelt to the center of the thick covers and faced him. "So… where will you sleep tonight?"

"Excuse me?" Zephir softly replied, his slanting eyes becoming more narrowed.

"Where will you sleep?" Phaedra repeated. The look in her eyes was soft and expectant.

Zephir stood, almost knocking his chair from its legs. "You know damn well where I sleep." He reminded her. Shortly after the voyage began, he had decided to sleep in another cabin. He did not trust himself

The hot bath soothed away all the tension of the past few days. Phaedra submersed her entire body in the invigorating water. An enormous bar of softly scented soap had been provided as well. In minutes, the cabin was filled with the smell of the soap and the tub was teeming with bubbles.

The bath was so relaxing, Phaedra drifted off to sleep. In the midst of her light slumber, another dream ensued. This time, the unsettling visions appeared with crystal clarity.

"My God," she whispered, upon awakening. Her wide eyes stared blankly into space for several moments. Finally, she looked toward the front of the cabin and saw Zephir. His deep-set slanting charcoal gaze practically bored into her.

"What are you doing in here?!" she snapped, angry and a bit embarrassed after all that had happened between them.

Zephir did not appear to be in the mood for talking. He ignored her question, walking slowly toward her and kneeling beside the tub.

Phaedra looked away. She was determined to put a cap on the unease she felt in his presense. Zephir's hands treading the soapy water, however, made it almost impossible for her to remain calm. His hand delved deeper in the water, his long fingers brushing the undersides of her breasts. Her lashes fluttered close against his touch, and she inhaled sharply. His searching fingers journeyed lower until he brushed the sensitive spot at the joining of her thighs. Phaedra squeezed her eyes shut.

Slowly, Zephir's fingers probed her womanhood. He felt the muscles contract around his finger as she adjusted to the unfamiliar intrusion. He did not end the caress, but waited until he felt her relax. Then, at a snail's pace, his middle finger slid further inside her. A whisper soft cry passed Phaedra's lips and her legs shifted apart. The feelings she experienced from the single touch were indescribable.

Zephir loved hearing the soft gasps Phaedra uttered and the look of immense satisfaction on her exquisite face. He lowered his mouth to the side of her neck and pressed tiny, wet kisses against her damp scented skin. His fingers probed deeper, stroking the velvety softness of her body.

"Zephir…" Phaedra moaned. She never wanted him to stop.

A curt knock sounded upon the door and Phaedra jumped.

Zephir pulled his head from her shoulder and slowly pulled his hand from the water. Phaedra watched him walk over to open the door. Outside, two deck hands waited with the trunk.

"I'll take it." He said, easily lifting the trunk that had to be carried by the two men. After closing the door, he brought the monstrous piece of luggage to the center of the room.

"What's in that?" Phaedra called from the tub. She thought the trunk looked awfully familiar.

Zephir did not answer, prompting Phaedra to take a closer look. She had nothing to cover her nude body and Zephir certainly wasn't going anywhere.

Phaedra tapped her fingers against the tub in a clearly impatient fashion. "Would you mind leaving?"

Zephir shrugged one wide shoulder. "Why?"

"So, I can get out of this damned tub!"

Standing back on his strong legs, Zephir crossed his arms over his chest. "I've already seen you naked…several times."

Phaedra slapped her hands into the water. "Would you get out, so I can put something on?!"

The familiar, wicked white grin contrasted against his flawless blackberry complexion. He went over to the trunk, opened it and rummaged around inside for a moment. He headed to the tub after choosing an exquisite, ice blue silk dressing gown.

Phaedra studied the robe intently. As she reached for it, Zephir held it just out of her grasp. Each time she extended her reach, he held it further away.

"Dammit, will you please?!" she snapped, cringing when his hearty laughter filled the room. Finally, he ceased teasing and handed her the lovely garment.

Phaedra snatched it from him. Realizing she could not slip into the piece seated in the tub, she frowned up at him. He waited patiently, delighted when she disregarded her nude state and stood. She shook the wrinkles from the robe and gasped, discovering that it did belong to her. She pulled the piece over her body and stormed out of the tub to kneel beside the trunk.

"This is mine," she whispered, sifting through her belongings. Shaking from anger, she turned her stormy eyes on Zephir. "You did say that you don't condone thievery."

Zephir's sleek, long brows rose. "Excuse me?"

"Do not play innocent with me, you jackass!" Phaedra rose to her feet. "You broke into my home and took these things!"

"Phaedra…" Zephir sighed, surprised that it had not occurred to her that her own family had betrayed her. "You can't possibly be this dense?"

"You're right. I'm not. So don't try lying your way out of this."

"You actually think I'd break into your home to steal a trunk of clothing?" Zephir bellowed, coming to tower over her.

"Of course not!" Phaedra spat. "I'm quite sure you helped yourself to much more."

"You foolish little wench! How can you be so blind to what's going on here?"

"Blind to what's going on here?" Phaedra replied, turning back to the trunk. "I can very well see what is going on here. I have the proof in my very own hand!" she cried, throwing a fistful of clothes in his face.

Zephir lost his patience then and took hold of Phaedra's wrist. She instantly began to ply his neck and face with vicious blows. His jaw was set into a harsh line. The delicate gown ripped noticeably when Phaedra landed to the bed.

She knelt in the center of the bed and glared at him, hate spewing from her luminous dark gaze. Her long, wet hair lay plastered across her face and body like black snakes. Zephir ordered himself to ignore the delightful picture she made and raised a finger toward her.

"I knew you were spoiled, ill-mannered and ill-tempered," he said, his chest heaving from the deep breaths he took. "I never figured you to be an idiot as well."

Phaedra winced at the verbal assault. She grasped her lower lip between her teeth and fought to keep it from trembling.

Zephir rolled his eyes away from her and headed for the door. "Clean up this mess and be dressed for dinner by the time I return...or else."

to keep his hands away from her. Besides, he knew he would never be able to rest peacefully with her next to him.

Phaedra watched Zephir grab his black coat. *If only I could get him to soften toward me, I might be able to reason with him!* she thought, moving to the edge of the bed. Curling her hands around the edge, she leaned forward. "Zephir, please don't go tonight."

Zephir had already wrenched the door open. "What?" he whispered, shocked by her words.

"There's plenty of room right here," she told him, managing to shield her exhilaration. Her heart slammed frantically in anticipation of his reaction.

He closed the door, rounded the bed then watched her for several moments. "What did you say?"

Phaedra tossed her thick hair across her shoulders and looked him squarely in the eye. "This is your cabin after all. You should sleep here."

Shaking his head, Zephir silently commended Phaedra's use of her…femininity. Her cunning had almost fooled him. Deciding to teach her a lesson for torturing his body and mind, he pulled the cloak from his wide frame.

"You're quite right," he growled, pulling Phaedra's hand from the bedpost as he hauled her against his unyielding frame.

Keeping a firm handle on her fear, Phaedra reminded herself that this was the reaction she sought. Zephir's hands spanned her small waist, and his lips trailed the silken line of her neck. She prayed for the will to remain unaffected and tentatively placed her hands upon his broad shoulders.

Overwhelmed by the feel of her in his arms again, after so many weeks, Zephir was like a man starved. His fingers brushed her breasts then expertly opened the buttons along the bodice of her gown. He nudged her back, and they both toppled onto the bed. He covered her lithe body with his massive weight, his mouth seeking the taste of her skin.

A shiver raced through Phaedra's body when she heard the material of her gown coming undone. Zephir's head was buried deep into her cleavage, forcing a soft moan from her lips. She realized that, once again, she was allowing him to control the situation and pulled his head away from her breasts.

"Zephir wait—"

"Why should I?" he grumbled, his wet kisses caressing the manilla birthmark below her ear."I have something to ask you."

The determined tone of her voice intrigued Zephir, and he slowly raised his head. "Yes?"

"If I allow you to do this—"

"Do what?"

"Whatever you want," she clarified.

"Mmm hmm…" He pulled his weight off her in order to relax at her side.

Phaedra tried to retain eye contact, but it was impossible. Zephir seemed to peer right into her soul. She averted her eyes and took a deep breath. "If I allow you to…do as you please with me, would you let me return home?" She quickly bargained. When silence met her question, she looked up. "Well?"

Zephir raked the length of her body, before coming to rest on her face. "Well what?"

Phaedra slammed her small fists to the bed and braced herself on her elbows. "I'm giving you permission to do whatever you want to me in exchange for my freedom. What's your response?"

The dangerous predatory gleam reappeared in Zephir's stunning gaze. He finished pulling away the front of Phaedra's gown. He ignored the blows that fell against his chest.

"Zephir, dammit! Answer me!" She roared, having little success in pushing him away.

Her breasts bared to his eyes, Zephir began to plant tiny kisses around one firming nipple. "Love, you seem to be forgetting your predicament."

"What are you saying?" Her lashes fluttered as she weakened beneath his caress.

Zephir suckled the stiff tip as he spoke. "If I wish, I could do whatever I want with or without your permission. I hate to inform you, but I'm afraid you have nothing to bargain with."

Phaedra was instantly outraged. She summoned all her strength and fought against him. "You devil! I swear you will pay for the hell you are putting me through!"

"Phaedra…" Zephir sighed, suddenly rolling onto his back. "Love, things are not always as they seem, you know?"

"Then clarify them for me." She urged, holding her gown together as she turned over and looked down into his face.

"You believe I'm holding you captive, stolen you from people who love you all because of gold."

"And you expect me to believe that's not the truth?"

His mouth curved into a humorless smirk. "To an extent it is. There's so much more."

"Dammit, Zephir," she raged, pounding her fist softly against his shoulder. "Why won't you tell me then?"

He supported his weight on an elbow. "You'd never believe me, and right now I couldn't handle seeing what the truth would do to you."

"Zephir—"

He pressed his index finger to her mouth and inhaled deeply. "I'd like for you to trust me. I know you can't, but just know that I'm not the evil one in all this."

His words held a meaning that thouroughly intrigued her, and her voice of reason told her to at least consider taking this man at his word. Zephir was becoming completely irresistable to her, and he knew it. When he finally pulled away from her and stood from the bed, she could not bear to look at him. The door to the cabin closed and she uttered a frustrated cry while beating the bed with clenched fists. If she didn't escape Zephir Mfume soon, she would lose her mind. Her mind and a few other things…

Morning arrived sooner than desired. Blinding white light filtered every cabin on the ship. The entire vessel was much cooler than usual, and the environment seemed extraordinarily peaceful.

Phaedra groaned against the insistent shoves upon her shoulder. "Hmm...."

"Wake up, Phaedra. Come on."

Slowly raising her head, Phaedra opened her eyes. She found herself level with Zephir's groin and frowned. "What?" She quickly inquired, her eyes roaming the incredible expanse of his thigh.

Zephir placed the tip of his finger beneath her chin. "Get dressed in something very warm. I will return in twenty minutes."

Phaedra waited until the door closed behind Zephir then whipped back the covers. The floor felt like ice beneath her feet, but she was far too curious to let that stop her. Peeking out of the porthole, her eyes widened and she gasped in amazement. A calm sea of white stretched as far as the eye could span. It appeared that the entire ship was floating on a cloud.

Eager to take a closer look, Phaedra tore open her trunk in search of warm attire. It didn't take her long to don her underthings, a burgundy velvet riding gown, black thigh boots and a white ermine wrap. Her thick hair cascaded from beneath the matching hat and tumbled down her back in a mass of waves. Against the white fur, her hair resembled a cloud of smoke.

Zephir returned in twenty minutes as promised. He was quite surprised to find Phaedra dressed and pacing in anticipation of his return. She whipped past him, anxious to view her new surroundings.

"Oh my Lord..." Phaedra sighed, once she had raced out to the deck. Her lovely eyes scanned the landscape. The ship did rest on a sea of ice, while the land in the distance was covered with the same white substance.

"Snow," she whispered, turning questioning eyes toward Zephir who had come to stand next to her.

"Mmm hmm," he confirmed.

"It's absolutely breathtaking." Phaedra said, entranced by the unfamiliar scene.

"It most certainly is," he agreed in the softest voice. Of course, his comment had nothing to do with the environment.

"Oh, Zephir, please say we can go riding?" Phaedra begged, her fingers curling around the lapels of the luxurious mink coat he wore.

Slowly, Zephir's hands rose to cover her much smaller ones. She would never know how much the tiny gesture meant to him.

"Zephir? Are you alright?" She arched brows drew together in concern.

"Mmm hmm." He shook his head in an attempt to dispel the tenderness of the moment. "I have already arranged it." He placed his arm around her shoulders as he escorted her from the ship.

Phaedra's expression brightened. "I can't wait. I've missed riding so."

Zephir squeezed her shoulder and they stopped walking. "I'm afraid you won't be able to do that."

"But, you just said—"

"We'll have to share the ride, love. The terrain is much too unstable for you to go galloping around on your own. Once you've gotten the feel of the land, perhaps you can ride out on your own."

Phaedra nodded and hugged herself. "I don't care. As long as I am out in it."

Nodding, Zephir beckoned Dubois. When his right hand man approached his side, he clapped his shoulder. "Have someone fetch our bags and take them to the house. We are heading there now."

Dubois nodded. "Should we unload the rest of the ship?"

Zephir glanced toward The Venus and shook his head. "No, you and the men deserve rest and a good meal. The ship can be tended later."

Phaedra had been frowning since Zephir announced they were heading to the house. The instant he finished speaking with Dubois, she stepped in front of him. "Could we please go riding before heading inside?"

Zephir grimaced and placed his wide palms against her stomach. "You must be hungry?"

"Mmm mmm," Phaedra replied, shaking her head.

Raking one hand through his thick, silky, black locks, Zephir frowned. "You will yearn for something warm in your belly once we're out riding in this."

The look in Phaedra's eyes was soft and pleading. "Zephir, I've been inside that ship for weeks. I'm not used to that. Surely, you can understand my being anxious to enjoy the outdoors?"

The frown clouding Zephir's face, vanished. How could he argue such a valid point? With a nod, he pulled her close. "Alright," he whispered then turned to Dubois, "tell Lijon that Phaedra and I will dine later this evening."

"Certainly." Dubois nodded, his green eyes brightened by amusement.

"Are you ready?" Zephir asked, giving her hands a gentle squeeze.

"Yes." Phaedra's eyes sparkled as she looked into his eyes.

For a moment, Zephir was so in awe of her that he could not move. His stupor lasted only a few moments. Then, he led the way around the snowy mountainside.

"Does this all belong to you?" Phaedra asked as they trudged through the heavy snow.

"It does," Zephir confirmed, tightening his hold about her waist.

Phaedra laughed suddenly and looked up at him. "One of the spoils from your countless treks around the world?"

Zephir's rich, masculine laughter echoed in the windy atmosphere. "This acquisition was a token of luck."

"Luck?" Phaedra repeated, squinting her eyes against the sun which reflected off the snow. "That sounds like an interesting, mysterious story."

"I may share it with you sometime," he whispered as they rounded the corner that led to a massive structure amidst towering spruce trees.

Phaedra shivered, but it had nothing to do with the cold. The attentive, charming facet to Zephir's personality was breaking down the wall of dislike she had placed between them.

Zephir pushed open the heavy wooden door with one shove of his shoulder. A serene look came to Phaedra's face when a rush of warm air surrounded her. From the outside, the stable appeared cold and impenetrable. Inside, it was just the opposite. Thick, golden hay covered the entire floor, while neat bales lined the walls and high shelves of the building. A grand, woodburning stove provided the comforting warmth that filled the structure.

From the shadows of the stable, a tiny old man emerged. He had been feeding the horses and was finishing with the last one, when he walked out of the stall.

Zephir watched his head caretaker and old friend, Josiah McPhereson. Zephir waited for the man to set down the bucket of feed, before he cleared his throat.

"Who's there?"

"One guess."

"Ha! Ha! I know that rough voice!" Josiah bellowed, a gleeful expression appearing on his red, weatherbeaten face. "Zephir? Is that you, my boy?"

"It is." He closed the distance between them. "How are you, Josiah?" he asked, embracing the old man for a few moments.

Josiah slapped Zephir's shoulder as he laughed. "We were not expectin' you 'til much later this evening." he said, his words tinged with a thick Irish brogue.

"We made good time." Zephir turned toward Phaedra. "Someone I want you to meet, Josiah." He beckoned her with a wave of his hand.

Josiah took the tail of his shirt and wiped the gold spectacles which dangled from a chain around his neck. His small, blue eyes widened when he saw the exquisite beauty standing before him. "My Lord…"

he whispered.

Zephir chuckled, nodding in understanding. "Josiah, this is Miss Phaedra Toussaint. Phaedra, this is Josiah McPhereson, my head care-taker and great friend."

Phaedra offered her hand, smiling brightly when Josiah enclosed it within both of his. "Very nice to meet you, Mr. McPhereson."

"Oh child," Josiah called in a hushed tone as he shook his head, "to have a such a lovely address me as Josiah, would be a great honor."

Flattered, Phaedra practically beamed at the compliment. Meanwhile, Zephir marvelled at the older man's way with women.

"Josiah, we'd like to ride about the grounds. Is Professor up for a run?"

"Is he?!" Josiah bellowed, already turning in the direction of the stalls. "The only time he gets any real work is when you're here!" He opened Professor's stall door. The impressive Clydesdale trotted around the hay as though he sensed something was about to happen.

Zephir followed Josiah to the horses's stall. When Professor heard his master's voice, he neighed and nudged his head against Zephir's chest.

"Time for a run, my boy," Zephir cooed, stroking the geldings beautiful golden mane. "You've been walking around looking pretty for too long."

Professor obviously agreed, for he neighed enthusiastically. Zephir laughed and pressed a kiss to the animal's head.

"He's so beautiful," Phaedra whispered. She had seen Clydesdales before, but never so close. Stepping past Zephir and Josiah, she patted Professor's lush mane. "He is almost too lovely to ride."

Josiah chuckled. "Do not tell him that Miss, please!"

"Could you saddle him up for us, Josiah?" Zephir asked.

"It'll take only a moment," Josiah promised, already collecting the polished saddle from the shelf in Professor's stall.

"Are you certain you would not rather eat first?" Zephir asked, tak-ing Phaedra's hand in his.

"I'm positive," she assured him, her eyes sparkling with excitement.

"Thank you," she added and squeezed his hand.

"Professor is all ready, you two!" Josiah called.

Phaedra rubbed her hands together and stepped past Zephir. As she stood across the barn petting Professor, Zephir stood watching her. His mesmerizing stare was guarded.

Zephir and Phaedra set out on Professor, a short while later. The air had turned even cooler while they had been inside the barn. The wind hit their faces in quick blasts, which were as exhilarating as they were icy.

Phaedra leaned back against Zephir's chest. Her eyes were wide as they feasted on the rugged landscape. She had never seen anything so entrancing. The entire area was covered in thick, white snow. Thin flakes drifted from the pale blue sky.

Zephir managed to keep a tight grip on Professor's reins, in spite of the fact that Phaedra was practically seated in his lap. Even though the heavy furs they both wore, Zephir was affected by her closeness. When Phaedra leaned into his chest a bit more, he dipped his head to inhale the soft fragrance clinging to her skin.

"Oh look at that!" she called suddenly. Her hand, which rested on Zephir's thigh, tightened against the hard surface. "What is that?"

"That's right, you've never seen water freeze before?" he said, reminding himself that Dominica like his own native Cuba did not grow cold enough for such a wonder of nature.

"Mmm mmm," Phaedra replied, with a slow shake of her head.

"Would you care to take a closer look?" he asked, the rough gravel tone of his voice turning whisper soft.

Phaedra turned to look into his eyes. "Could we please?" She was so anxious, that she was already moving off Professor's back.

"Whoa," Zephir called, his arms tightening around her. He easily slipped from the mammoth-sized horse and unhooked the reins.

"Alright." He caught Phaedra beneath her arms and brought her to the ground. He kept his hand curled around her upper arms as they walked.

"Is it an entire lake?" She stooped to smooth her gloved hand across the hard, translucent surface.

Zephir crossed his arms over his chest as he watched Phaedra marvel at the water. His striking, intense look was now soft and searching. It was as though he were seeing Phaedra in a new light, and he liked what he saw.

"How I wish we could spend the day here," she said, smiling up at him. "It's so lovely."

"It is at that." He bent to grasp the edge of Phaedra's wrap. "But I think it's time we head back."

"Not so soon."

Zephir chuckled. "Love, we have to eat."

Phaedra stomped her foot in the snow. "But I'm not hungry."

He slipped the reins he held around her waist. "Well, I am," he told her and dropped a kiss to her mouth.

It was intended to be a quick peck. When he tasted the cool softness of her full lips, that all changed. Phaedra gasped and allowed his tongue the entrance it sought. Immediately, the innocent kiss turned hot and lusty.

"Mmm…" she moaned as she tentatively mimicked the thrusting motions of his tongue.

This time, it was Zephir who was surprised. A deep grunt sounded within his chest as he pulled away. His long, black brows drew close as he watched Phaedra suspiciously. When her innocent gaze met his eyes, he turned away, pulling her along behind him.

The ride to the main house was tense and silent.

CHAPTER 8

Zephir spent what remained of that first day at his snowy mountaintop chalet, assisting his crew with the ship. The men worked excessively hard, having no desire to be caught in the bitter cold after dark.

Meanwhile, Phaedra had been left on her own at the main house. Though she would have loved to have been out riding the day away, the huge chalet was proving to be quite entertaining. She had expected the place to be similar to Zephir's home in Dominica; cold, dark and bare. The chalet was nothing like that. The massive stone structure sat amidst a sea of snow topped spruce trees. There was a candle in each window, making the house seem warm and inviting from the outside. Inside, was just as cozy and relaxing.

Phaedra could not count all the bedrooms she viewed on the upper levels. She did observe that they were all elegantly furnished and equipped with huge fireplaces. Large, furry rugs covered the floors, and the long staircase was located off the plush sitting room near the foyer. After satisfying her curiosity about the chalet, she realized that she had never had such a wonderful time indoors.

The men returned from the ship right at nightfall. With the exception of the top crew members, many stayed in the crew's quarters—a building just off from the chalet. It was just as warm and comfortable as the main house. Still, much of the crew had decided to venture into town for an evening of…companionship.

Zephir had instructed one of his housekeepers to show Phaedra to his bedchamber where she was to change for dinner. After a hot bath, she dressed in a dazzling black evening gown. The satin frock had capped sleeves, and a lace bodice which offered the illusion that it showed more of her body than it actually did.

Phaedra had taken extra time preparing herself for dinner that evening. Though she had tried to remain unaffected by Zephir's charm and sensuality, it had not worked. Each day she softened more toward him, aching for him to douse the flame he had kindled beneath her innocence.

Grimacing beneath the powerful sting of the whiskey, Zephir slammed his glass against the counter for a refill. He had hoped a day of work would quell the dull ache in his loins. It had not. There was only one thing that would relieve him, but he dared not turn to it. Clearly, Phaedra was softening. It was evident in her voice, her eyes and the way she leaned against him. Zephir knew he could take her whenever he desired and she would not put up much of a fight. Of course, it had

occurred to him that she could have been trying to win his trust in order to escape. Regardless of the motive, he could not allow her too close. He could not let her inside his heart.

"Zephir?" Phaedra called from the sitting room doorway.

Gradually, Zephir tuned into Phaedra calling him and he turned. She was a vision in the stunning black satin gown. Her thick, wavy hair was piled atop her head while several tendrils framed her face in a tumble of wild ringlets. He downed the remainder of his whiskey and uttered a soft, ragged groan.

"Zephir?…Are you alright?" she asked, gathering a bit of her gown in her hands and taking a small step forward. She admired the stunning breadth of his shoulders beneath the gray suit coat he wore.

"Mmm hmm, I'm fine," he assured her, setting his glass down. "Come here. I have something to show you."

A pleasant look on her face, Phaedra moved across the room. When she stood before Zephir, his eyes fell to the black lace covering her bosom.

"This is lovely," he complimented, trailing his index finger across the swell of her breast.

Unconscious of her actions, Phaedra pushed her shoulders back and lifted her chin. "Thank you."

"This way," he finally instructed. "Do you know what this is?" He gestured toward a huge round instrument on a wood stand.

Phaedra nodded. "A globe?"

"That's right," Zephir confirmed, nodding as he caressed her face with his eyes. Turning back to the globe, he twirled it slightly. "Look closer."

Phaedra watched Zephir point to the Newfoundland coast.

"We are here," he announced then slid his finger lower. "This is Dominica."

The sick look on Phaedra's face matched the nausea that flooded her body. All the contentment of the last several hours washed away as though it never existed. Pressing her hand next to her chest, she leaned against the tall stand supporting the globe. "Why did you do that?"

The hurt in her voice made Zephir want to kick himself, but he ignored it. "I thought you would like to see how far you are from home."

Phaedra shook her head, demanding the tears to remain at bay. "Everything was going so perfectly," she whispered.

Zephir toyed with one of the curls that had escaped the fantastic coiffure she wore. He watched it cling to his finger for a moment. "That is exactly why I did this," he whispered into her ear. "Because everything is going so perfectly. I wouldn't want you thinking about escape, now would I?" he asked.

He pressed a hard kiss against the beauty mark below her ear then walked toward the double doors leading out of the room. "Dinner should be ready now, love!" he called over his shoulder.

Phaedra felt as though she were burdened by a massive weight. She dragged herself out of the sitting room, her dislike of Zephir renewed.

The chalet had two dining rooms. The larger one was used for entertaining or when Zephir's top men joined him for dinner. The smaller room was the most used. It came in useful when Zephir entertained on a more intimate level. A small, square table was covered with a cream colored lace cloth. It was topped with a tureen of thick fish chowder, golden bread—piping hot from the oven—and a sweetcake for two. A sparkling wine was also provided.

Of course, Phaedra could not resist the delicious, meaty stew and soft bread. She ate heartily, but thoughts of Zephir's cruel act with the globe raced through her mind. She could not understand why he would do something so cold when things were finally civil between them. Clearing her throat, she looked across the table and froze. Zephir was glaring at her—his striking gaze was hard as coal.

"I'd like to be excused," she said, rising from her chair.

"Why?"

"It's been an eventful day." She laced her fingers together against the front of her gown. "If you'd tell me how to find my sleeping quarters, I'll be heading to bed."

"No need for that," he told her, downing the remainder of his wine. "I'll take you there myself."

Phaedra waited for Zephir to join her at the dining room door. His hand came to rest at the small of her back as he urged her forward. The tension was heavy between them, and Phaedra could almost feel Zephir's brooding stare upon her skin. She did an admirable job of remaining cool and detached, though the touch of his hand sent a surge of heat down her spine.

Phaedra stepped into the darkened bedchamber and turned to bid Zephir a good night. Her mouth fell open in surprise when she saw him follow her into the room and close the door. She waited silently, watching him light one of the lamps. Her eyes widened in surprise at the vaguely familiar surroundings.

"This is the room I dressed in earlier."

Zephir yawned and raked one hand through his thick hair. "It is."

"I was told this was your bedchamber." She propped one hand against her hip.

"You weren't misinformed." He pulled the heavy gray coat from his shoulders.

As Zephir undressed for bed, Phaedra watched him expectantly. He threw the shirt he wore to an arm chair in the corner and pulled off his boots then locked the door to the room. After placing the key in the drawer of the nightstand next to the bed, he pulled off his trousers.

Phaedra's lashes fluttered as she watched Zephir standing there completely nude. She had never seen a man fully unclothed in her life, but she knew none of them would compare to the one now before her eyes.

"What are you doing?"

"Getting into bed." He whipped back the heavy quilt.

"Well, if you recall, I asked to be shown to my room," she reminded him with a sigh, trying to dispel the shakiness in her voice.

Zephir looked around himself. "And here you are," he announced, watching the confusion in her eyes turn stormy.

"You can't expect me to believe this is the only bedroom in this chalet?!"

"No, I don't expect you to believe that."

"So, there must be at least one other room?"

Zephir shrugged. "There are plenty, but unfortunately, I won't be in any of them."

"Oh, sir, I assure you it would be most fortunate for me!" she snapped, clenching her fists.

Tired and ready for sleep, Zephir slammed his hand against the wall with such force, it rattled the portraits hanging on the walls. "Phaedra if you know what's best for you, you'll shut your mouth and get out of your clothes."

Exasperated, Phaedra ignored Zephir's warning and stomped over to the huge window that overlooked the rear of the estate. "You have me millions of miles away from my family. Tell me why you need me in your bed?!"

"Because I want you there," Zephir growled, suddenly right behind her. Easily aggravated when tired, he was in no mood to hear complaints from Phaedra. Taking her beneath his arm like a sack of potatoes, he carried her to the bed.

Phaedra was too shaken to fight. She couldn't believe a day which began to lovely, was ending so horribly. Watching Zephir glaring down as he removed the gown from her body, slowly turned her shock to anger.

"Now shut up, so I can rest," he commanded, tossing the tattered gown aside.

Phaedra sat up and removed the pins from her hair. Grimacing at the small rip in her chemise, she slipped beneath the bed's quilts. As soon as her head touched the pillow, Zephir's hand clamped over her wrist and pulled her arm across his chest.

I have got to get away from him! she vowed silently. If only she could get that key. Unfortunately, there was no escape from the bed with his iron hold around her wrist.

A few minutes later, she heard his steady breathing. She turned her head and saw him relaxed in sleep. For a moment, her eyes softened. His gorgeous features relaxed in sleep, were hard to look away from.

Phaedra shook her head and concentrated on grabbing the key. It would take a bit of doing since she could not risk waking Zephir, and she couldn't leave the bed. Very slowly, she pulled herself into a sitting position, careful not to tug against his grip. Biting her lower lip nervously, she moved across his frame to straddle his hips. She managed to get the nightstand drawer open and rummaged around for a key.

"Where the devil is it?!" she whispered frantically as she searched the cluttered drawer.

Zephir had followed Phaedra's every movement since she sat up in bed. "How many times must I tell you—"

"Dammit Zephir!" she cried, clutching her chest. "Are you trying to scare me to death?!"

Letting go of her wrist, Zephir sat up and Phaedra toppled off him. Turning the tables, he pinned her to the bed and held a clenched fist in her face. "If you cannot fall asleep on your own, I will be happy to assist you!" he warned, praying she'd believe his bluff.

Phaedra rolled her eyes away and pushed him away. Angry, but not in the mood to test his patience, she turned her back toward him in the bed.

In the hours before dawn, Zephir woke. His intentions were to get a drink from the stock of liquor he kept in the bedchamber. When he moved to leave the bed, he realized Phaedra was

sprawled across his body. In her sleep, she had wrapped herself around him. She was so close that her long hair was strewn across his neck. Gently, so he would not disturb her, he freed himself from the silken restraints then tucked her beneath the covers and watched her.

Sweet Heavens! I have become so captivated by her! Only to himself could he acknowledge his need—his desire to protect her from the dangers that awaited her at the home she was so desperate to return to.

When Phaedra woke later that morning, she was alone. The massive bed felt so warm and comforting, she hated to leave it. Unfortunately, the delicious aroma surging through the air was impossible to dismiss.

She sat up in bed and raised her nose in the air. The smell of the food was so powerful she knew it had to be close. Surely, when she opened her eyes, there was a table topped with breakfast set across the room.

Since she was alone, she did not bother to cover the dainty chemise she had slept in. Pushing back the covers, she hurried over to tha table and helped herself. The food was hot and seasoned to perfection. She was about to indulge in a little extra, when Zephir returned.

He removed a black cap from his hand and bounded across the room. Phaedra waited for him to speak, but he never did. He seemed much more interested in eating. There was hot ale, fresh

caplin and biscuits. He stood there wolfing down the food for several moments, before acknowledging Phaedra's presense.

"Did you sleep well?" he asked. The grumpy sound in his rough voice set Phaedra on edge. She was about to issue a snappy reply, but the look on Zephir's gorgeous face stopped her. Instead, she nodded.

Satisfied, Zephir nodded as well. He tossed back the last of his ale then left the room.

"Horse's ass," she muttered, massaging the tiny ache in her neck.

A moment later, there was a brief knock upon the door before it opened. A short, caucasion woman entered. Her head was wrapped in a dull brown scarf, and she wore a long white apron over a crisp, black dress. The woman nodded briefly in Phaedra's direction then began to tidy the room.

"Good morning," Phaedra called, watching the woman go about her work.

"Miss," the woman replied, her small blue eyes downcast.

Phaedra turned in her chair and watched the woman. "My name is Phaedra Toussaint. And your name is?"

The short housekeeper gave Phaedra a long stare. She could not believe the stunning young woman seated across the room was taking the time to speak with her. "My name is Lijon, Miss."

"Lijon? That's a lovely name."

Lijon bowed her head. "Thank you, Miss. So is yours."

"Why, thank you, Lijon. It's so nice to be talking with another woman. I've been surrounded by men for weeks now."

Lijon almost laughed. "I understand."

Phaedra leaned back in her chair and sighed. "Of course you do. Zephir and his men spend a lot of time here, I assume?"

"Oh no, Miss. Mr. Mfume has not been here at the chalet for almost a year."

"You mean you spend all that time alone here!"

A soft chuckle escaped Lijon as she made the bed. "Oh no, Miss. There are other servants, but I'm married with my own family. Like everyone else, my home is in town."

"Well I'm glad to hear that. It's quite lovely here, but I can't imagine any one being so far away from civilization by themselves," Phaedra stated, helping herself to more of the hot ale.

"There are neighbors, Miss," Lijon innocently replied, finishing up the bed.

Phaedra's ears perked up at the tiny piece of information. "Neighbors?"

"Mmm hmm."

"Well, where are they?" she pried, trying to keep her voice light.

Lijon stepped over to gather the breakfast dishes onto her tray. "They live on the other side of the mountain."

Phaedra let Lijon complete her work tidying the bedchamber, without interruption. It was not long before the woman bade her a good day and left the room. The moment the door closed behind Lijon, a devious expression appeared on Phaedra's face. She decided that it was time to go exploring.

Phaedra inhaled the crisp, clean scent of the freezing air as she stepped off the porch. Once she made the decision to find the neighbors Lijon had mentioned, she searched her trunk for a pair of dungarees. The pants, combined with two heavy wool shirts, black thigh boots and a thick cloak were perfect protection against the biting cold.

Though she had set out with a specific purpose in mind, the snow beckoned her attention. She could not resist spending a few minutes playing around in the frosty creation. Despite her situation, she had never felt so free. Rolling around in the powdery snow was so exhilarating she felt all her problems drift away.

Unfortunately, "play time" could not last forever. She reluctantly dusted snow from her clothes and prepared to set out on her exploration. Two steps into her journey, a hand fell upon her shoulder and turned her around.

"Where the devil are you going?" Zephir demanded.

"Damn you, Zephir, you have me out in the middle of nowhere and you still think I'm trying to escape?!" she lashed out, hands propped on her hips.

He noted the determination on her lovely face as she looked up at him. "Where are you off to?"

She cringed at the suspicion in his deep, gravely voice. "For a walk," she snapped.

Zephir grimaced and shifted his eyes out over the white landscape. He had a lurking suspicion that there was a plan churning in Phaedra's cunning mind. Instead of badgering her furher, he shrugged, rolled his eyes and walked away.

The first trip past the boundaries of the chalet, proved to be a disappointment. The powdery snow; once exhilarating and beautiful, was suddenly a hindrance. Phaedra only covered a short

distance before she was ready to give up. Wet, cold and discouraged, she reluctantly returned to the chalet.

She prayed that Zephir was not there when she walked through the heavy, wooden door. Lijon caught sight of her shuffling into the foyer and came rushing over.

"Good Lord, Miss. What happened to you?"

Pulling off the damp cloak, Phaedra sent Lijon a tired look. "The snow proved to be a bit much for my first day out."

Lijon shook her head and took the cloak from Phaedra. "Let's get you upstairs and out of these drenched clothes."

"Where is Zephir?" Phaedra slowly inquired. A wary look darkened her face.

"He mentioned something about chopping wood, Miss."

Sighing, Phaedra nodded and quickly followed Lijon up the staircase. Lijon helped Phaedra out of her heavy clothes and hung them close to the fire. She then went downstairs and returned with a large cup of steaming broth. Phaedra was so grateful, that at first, she simply held the hot cup between her hands. Wrapped in a thick, burgundy quilt, she snuggled in the armchair before the fire. She had almost drifted to sleep when a deep chuckle touched her ears.

"How was your walk?" Zephir asked.

"How do you think?" she grumbled, rolling her eyes toward the fire.

He pulled the wool gloves from his hands and tossed them aside. "From what I hear, it was quite wet."

"Did you come in here to make fun of me?" she snapped, pounding her fists against the quilt.

Zephir's lips twitched a bit, but he shrugged. "I didn't come to tease you, but to bathe you."

"Excuse me?"

"You could use a hot bath, don't you think?" he asked, leaving the room briefly. When he returned, he carried two silver buckets of water.

Phaedra watched him bring countless pails of the steaming water into the room. Soon, the porcelain tub, near the far corner of the fireplace, was filled.

Zephir's handsome face was brightened by a mischievous look. He noted the confusion on her face and wondered what was on her mind.

"Are you trying to kill yourself?" he asked.

Phaedra cringed at the amusement tinging his rough voice. "Why do you care?"

Zephir sat the last pail outside the bedroom door and turned. He pinned her with a look of mock surprise. "Have I treated you as though I don't care?"

"You've been ignoring me most of the day."

The frustration in Phaedra's voice did not go unnoticed by Zephir. He hid the knowing chuckle threatening to break free and turned his back to her. He checked the water, satisfied that it was a comfortable temperature.

Phaedra's eyes widened when she saw Zephir heading toward her. He leaned down and lifted her into his arms.

"What are you doing?" she gasped.

"Making sure I don't ignore you any longer," he murmured, carrying her to the tub.

The heavy quilt fell away from Phaedra's body. Her lashes fluttered madly as she watched his eyes cloud with passion.

Gently, he lowered her into the bath, smirking when he heard her gasp in response to the water touching her skin. He didn't comment, preferring to concentrate on bathing her. Zephir kept his slanting stare lowered as he worked the soap into a rich lather.

Phaedra's entire body jerked when Zephir's hands fell to her body. He slowly massaged the scented foam into her skin. His palms cupped her breasts, his thumbs grazing the firm nipples as a sculptor would mold an image.

The sweet, exquisite sensations stemming from the soft caress, forced a low moan past Phaedra's lips. Her head fell against the high back of the tub and her lashes drifted close. Zephir's smoldering gaze followed the path of his fingers. They slid beneath the surface of the water, dipping into her navel, then lower...

Stop him, dammit! Phaedra heard an angry voice scream inside her head. Squeezing her eyes shut more tightly, she ordered it silent. From the moment Zephir first touched her, she had ached for his caress. The feelings they stirred inside her had been unfamiliar and shocking. At first, she had been ashamed to be pleasured by them. Now, after the time they had spent together, she craved the sensations she experienced. She only wished she could find the courage to ask him to never stop touching her.

Zephir raised his eyes to Phaedra's face. A surge of male satisfaction swept through him to see her so relaxed. It was obvious that she enjoyed the feel of his fingers against her skin. Slowly, he leaned forward and brought his lips to the bright beauty mark below her ear.

"Zephir…" she sighed, tilting her head to allow his lips more room to explore. His mouth slid down the smooth length of her neck, then higher, pressing tiny kisses along the line of her jaw.

She tensed a bit as his fingers grazed the center of her body. At first, he toyed with the sensitive petals of her womanhood. Then, his touch became bolder. His fingers thrusted deep inside her, and he smiled when he heard her gasp. She didn't protest to the intimate touch, and he lost control. His mouth traced her collarbone as his fingers probed more deeply, causing Phaedra to sink deeper into the water.

"Zephir…" she gasped once more, just as his lips met hers. Water splashed outside the smooth porcelain tub as she arched closer to meet his kiss. Eagerly, she responded, mimicking the slow thrusts of his tongue. Her slender fingers delved into his thick, silky black hair, pulling him even closer.

"Mmm…" Zephir groaned. The white linen shirt and gray breeches he wore were practically soaked. His arms encircled Phaedra's waist like steel bands. He took a fistful of her hair and tugged her head back.

The sound Phaedra uttered in response was a mixture between pain and arousal. Her hands slid over Zephir's neck and shoulders to knead the taut muscle there. Her fingers curled around the neckline of his shirt and stroked the hard wall of his chest.

"Phaedra…" he moaned, his long silky brows drawing together. Suddenly, his hands closed over her arms, and he pulled her away.

The look in Phaedra's eyes relayed the confusion she felt. Their breathing came in short, rapid bursts as they assessed what happened between them.

"Stand up," Zephir gruffly ordered, rising to his feet.

Slowly, Phaedra complied. She watched Zephir dry his hands on a bath sheet. Then, he wrapped it around her shimmering body and lifted her from the tub. Phaedra's arms

curled around his shoulders. Her heart pounded with expectancy as they approached the bed. She remained silent, anticipating what might come next.

Zephir placed her lying back on the bed. His eyes never met hers; they were focused on the bath sheet covering her body. Determined to complete the task, he dried her. He pulled the thick sheet away and slowly rubbed it across her glistening skin. He followed the trail of the bath sheet intently.

Zephir could feel her captivating eyes trained on him. With great effort, he managed to keep his gaze averted. When he leaned over to dry her hair, he heard her voice.

"Why won't you complete what you've started?" she asked in the softest tone of voice.

The surprise Zephir felt at the question matched the look on Phaedra's face. Neither could believe she had asked such a thing. She pushed herself up on the bed and watched as Zephir throw down the bath sheet and bolt from the room.

CHAPTER 9

Phaedra spent the next couple of weeks practically on her own. Zephir had once again seen the need to pull away from her. After the night when Phaedra was so bold about her feelings, the tension between them became even stronger. Since Phaedra had so much time to herself, thoughts of escape multiplied and occurred more frequently.

Each day, she set out to explore the frosty land, with hopes of finding the mysterious neighbors she had heard about. Though she had no luck, the daily walks helped her become acclimated to the terrain. This made it possible to venture a little further each time. One afternoon, she had made it to the wooden fence that stretched across the land in a never ending line. Obviously, she had reached the end of Zephir's vast property. With a determined, anxious gleam in her eyes, she headed toward the fence. For a moment, she scanned the land before her.

Everything was covered in white, even the trees, which were small in number.

"They've got to be past this, Phaedra sighed, referring to the neighbors. She curled her gloved hands around the fence and tested its sturdiness. Satisfied, she climbed the five foot fence and jumped to the other side.

Surprisingly, the snow was not as deep on that side of the fence. Phaedra's steps were quick and sure while she looked straight ahead. There had to be someone out there who could help her escape…to get away from Zephir.

Suddenly, the ground beneath her feet gave way, causing her to lose her footing. She fell into a patch of thin ice then everything went black.

"Oooh…" Phaedra groaned, trying to force her eyes open. She found her surroundings to be blurred and dim. After a few moments, her vision cleared and she uttered a shocked gasp.

Once again, she found herself in a strange dismal room. She instantly realized it was not part of the chalet. The realization stood firm when she saw the room filled with at least a dozen grinning men. Adding to her horror, Phaedra saw ropes around her wrists—tying her to the bed.

In the center of the grizzly looking group was a dark man clothed in a multi-colored cap adorned with a plume and a matching cloak. He appeared to be older than his companions, but he was still well-built.

Phaedra flinched and backed away when the man reached out to touch her hair. The thick mass covered her bare breasts, but the rest of her body was completely exposed. The smiling man rubbed her hair between his fingers. When he reached over to stroke her skin, she tried to bite his hand. The entire room filled with laughter, but Phaedra found no comfort in the sound.

"My men, behold Zephir Mfume's newest toy. She is a feisty one, is she not?!"

Phaedra kicked out at the man, but was too far away to cause any damage. The laughter became louder. She rolled her eyes.

The older man placed his hand against his heart and tried to still his laughter. "I do apologize, my dear. Let me introduce myself. I am Cantone Lezard, Mr. Mfume's neighbor."

Phaedra shuddered beneath the wild look in the man's slightly cock-eyed brown gaze. Though his voice sounded pleasant and non-threatening, his eyes said something completely different.

Again, Cantone stroked Phaedra's hair. "And what is your name, lovely?"

"I was under the impression that you already knew that," Phaedra snapped.

Cantone bowed his head, acknowledging the fact. "It is true, I know quite a bit, yes. You are the extremely beautiful guest of Zephir Mfume. My men and I have been watching you for several weeks now."

Phaedra's eyes glared at Lezard with unmasked disgust. "And this is how you choose to introduce yourselves?"

Cantone Lezard laughed shortly. "Why, Miss, we could not leave you in those soaked clothes. You could have caught your death."

"I may do that regardless." She eyed her restraints.

"If that were the case, I would have left you to die in the cold," Cantone cooly assured her.

"Of course not. Better to gawk at a live woman, eh?"

Cantone's easy look faded somewhat at Phaedra's keen insight. "Tell me, my dear, how do you like the chalet?"

Phaedra's wide eyes narrowed a bit. "It's beautiful."

"It's mine, you know?"

"Yours?"

"I'm afraid your illustrious Mr. Mfume does not always practice honesty." Cantone sighed then took a seat on the edge of the bed where Phaedra lay. "He won that land and the chalet by cheating."

Phaedra watched him coldly. "Cheating? How?"

"Chess."

"It would seem that he capitalized on the weakness of his opponent."

An arrogant smirk tugged at Cantone Lezard's dry, lips. "What would you know about the game?"

"I know that the only way a person can be effectively *cheated* in Chess is if they are foolish enough to leave the board."

Cantone's arrogant smirk widened as his men laughed. He bowed his head, acknowledging the remark. Leaning over Phaedra, his fingers stroked her collarbone. "You are indeed a challenge," he whispered, his hot breath fanning the tendrils of her hair. "I wonder if you are as fiery between the sheets?"

"You fucking bastard!" Phaedra screamed, straining to break free of the ropes. Outraged, she spat into her captor's face.

Surprisingly, Cantone continued to laugh. He wiped the spittle from his cheek and winked at his men. "It will be such a pleasure bedding this fiesty beauty!" he roared. Turning back to Phaedra, he trailed one finger down her cheek. "My sweet, I realize I am considerably older than the dashing Mfume, but you will enjoy my lovemaking far more than you have ever enjoyed his."

Phaedra jerked away from his touch. "You cock-eyed son of a bitch! No man has ever had me and neither will you!"

Lezard appraised her with renewed interest. Even his men stepped closer to the bed. Phaedra groaned inwardly, realizing her mistake.

"Well, well…Mfume's charms are wearing thin. I suppose that means I am just the man to usher you into womanhood."

"I beg to differ, sir," she breathed, her voice heavy with hatred.

"Oh pretty," Cantone whispered, brushing his rough lips against Phaedra's cheek. "I will have you begging soon enough."

Laughter filled the room once again. The men's jokes were boisterous and crude. The room began to clear, and soon Phaedra was left alone. Again, she struggled against the ropes around her wrists. The restraints would not give, and soon she fell back against the bed. A defeated look crossed her lovely face as she looked to the frost covered window.

"Damn you, Zephir."

"What the hell do you mean, she's not here?!"

The servants filling the hallway shuddered beneath Zephir's roaring, raspy voice. They literally dropped everything when he raged over not being able to locate Phaedra.

Lijon clasped her hands together and took a small step forward. "Mr. Mfume, the Miss has not yet returned from her walk."

Zephir raked a hand through his thick, black hair. "When did she leave?"

"Quite a while ago, I'm afraid."

"Thank you, Lijon," Zephir whispered, managing a tiny nod. "You all are excused," he told the servants. When they were gone, a sound of pure frustration rose in his throat. His midnight stare was murderous as he glared at his men. "I want this place searched. Every inch of it, dammit!"

The men wasted no time setting out to look for Phaedra. They covered every square foot of the vast property. Unfortunately, their efforts went unrewarded. Phaedra seemed to have disappeared without a trace.

The night was becoming unbearably cold. The crew was ready to give up the search and resume at day break. Zephir, however, had no intentions of sleeping, until he found her.

"When I find her, I'll make her regret it. I swear it."

Dubois hid his humor when he heard Zephir's vicious, yet hollow, promise. Instead of commenting on it, he clapped Zephir's back. "Man, let's get some rest. We'll continue the search when it's morning."

Zephir pulled his heavy, black cloak tighter around his huge frame. "I can't sleep. She was my responsibility, and she's out there somewhere."

"You care for her very much, don't you?" Dubois inquired.

The cold, guarded look reappeared on Zephir's face. "She has been nothing but a constant irritation. When I get my hands on her, she will be very sorry."

Zephir walked away, leaving Dubois watching him with a knowing look. Poor man, Dubois thought, he has no idea how much he loves that woman.

Phaedra held her breath, her eyes widening as the knob twisted. Bracing herself, she prepared to see Cantone Lezard's ashen face appear inside.

To her surprise and delight, a woman entered. She was quite tall and robust. Her skin was pale and dry. Her eyes, however, held a calm, easy look that gave Phaedra hope for escape.

"Please, help me," she called from the bed. Her voice a frantic whisper, but she knew the woman could hear her. "You have to help me get out of here," she begged.

The woman did not respond. She carried a tray of food and began setting the small square table in the corner of the room.

"Please, I have money. I could get you out of this hell," Phaedra bartered, her eyes wide with worry.

The woman finished setting the table and turned. She headed to the bed and unfastened Phaedra's ties.

"Oh thank you, thank you." She massaged the sore skin around her wrists.

"There is a warm dressing robe on that chair. You should eat your breakfast while it is hot."

"But, I have to get out of this place."

"I cannot help you."

"But, I have money I could—"

"He would kill me a thousand times," the woman snapped, her green eyes filled with horror.

Phaedra pushed her thick hair away from her face. "I could help you. I would."

The woman shook her head regretfully. "Miss, my advice to you is to do as Cantone Lezard orders. He is an evil man."

The heavy wooden door shut behind the maid. Phaedra's clenched fists beat lightly against the sqeaky table.

In from another day of searching, Zephir stormed into the chalet. Wanting to be alone, he headed for his study. There, he located an unopened bottle of whiskey and proceeded to drink away his frustration.

Dubois had followed Zephir to the study and watched him down the contents of the bottle. Grimacing, he knocked lightly then stepped fully into the room.

"That will not help you at all," Dubois said, referring to the whiskey.

Zephir rolled his eyes toward the ceiling. "I disagree," he growled.

"I've never seen you this way."

"What way?"

"Upset...uneasy," Dubois cooly noted, drawing a furious glance from his friend.

"I am neither," Zephir assured the man, tilting back his bottle.

"I disagree," Dubois argued, challenging Zephir. "I've never seen you in such a state over a woman, my friend."

Zephir managed a shrug at his friend's words. Feeling a bit more relaxed, he lowered his tall form into an arm chair and set the whiskey bottle aside. "I don't know what it is about her. All we've done from the moment we met is argue."

"I'm aware of that," Dubois said, a teasing grin tugging at his mouth.

Zephir propped his index finger alongside his temple. "I tell you, I've never enjoyed arguing so much."

"So you do care for her?"

Zephir nodded. "I do. I have to. The girl has no idea how alone she truly is."

Dubois leaned against the oak cabinet where the liquor was stored. Crossing his arms over his wide chest, he eyed Zephir suspiciously. "Have you forgotten her family on Dominica?"

"I haven't," Zephir tiredly replied, massaging the bridge of his nose. "I'm sure they have forgotten about her."

Dubois shook his head. "I don't understand."

"To get their land. I had to agree to take her."

"Take her?"

"Mmm...on her twentieth birthday she is to inherit all of that plantation. To receive her inheritance, she must be there on Toussaints."

"They sold her?" Dubois asked, completely shocked.

"They sold her," Zephir confirmed. "And I...I took what they offered. Now..."

"Now?..."

"Dammit!" Zephir snapped, burying his face in his palms. "Now, I'm beginning to have...these feelings for her."

Dubois's grin brightened his caramel colored face. "That's certainly easy to understand. My God, just look at her."

Zephir acknowledged the fact. "There is more than that. Much more and it scares me. I'll kill you if you breathe a word of this."

Dubois raised his hands defensively. "You have my word, old friend. So what will you do when you see her?"

Zephir couldn't answer. His long, black lashes closed over his slanting stare as he slowly shook his head.

"Dammit, nailed shut," Phaedra whispered as she tried to force open the bedroom window. Even if it were open, she knew she would not last five minutes in the shabby dressing robe she wore.

"That is a chance I'll gladly take," she decided, trying to force one of the nails loose.

Suddenly, the heavy wooden door crashed open. Cantone Lezard strode inside, frowning when he did not see Phaedra on the bed. Spotting her before the window, he bounded across the room and jerked her around to face him.

"What the hell are you doing?!" he roared, lifting her against him. He threw her to the bed and fell on top of her.

Phaedra struggled only briefly. When the force of Cantone's body hit hers, she groaned beneath the pressure. Breathless, she could only lie there.

"You are a wild little thing, aren't you?" Cantone sneered, his hands venturing beneath the robe to slide across her bare thighs.

Phaedra tensed at the touch then began to struggle. Lezard ignored the frantic movements, his tongue stroking the softness of her throat, like a madman. He tried to gain entrance to her mouth, but Phaedra kept her lips sealed. Cruelly, he squeezed her buttocks, causing her to gasp in pain. Taking full advantage, he kissed her deeply.

Phaedra groaned, disgusted by the taste of whiskey and fish on his breath. Mistaking her groan of disgust for one of pleasure, Lezard's caresses became bolder. He released her mouth and his lips trailed the smooth column of her neck, stopping to suckle her earlobe. He moved on, bathing her collarbone with his leacherous tongue as he travelled down to the cleft between her breasts.

Suddenly, Phaedra found a strength she did not know she had. She pounded Cantone's chest, and her knee connected with his rigid arousal. A tight, shocked look crossed his face. His eyes practically bulged from their sockets.

"Bitch," he bit out, his voice sounding strained. He rolled off Phaedra, clutching his bruised manhood.

Phaedra jumped off the bed and stood wringing her hands. Tears filled her eyes as she cursed her helpless state. Cantone slowly recovered from his pain and pushed himself from the bed as well. A murderous glare added to the harsh look on his face as he stumbled over to Phaedra.

She tried to back away, but the room left few places to retreat. A tiny scream was torn from her lips as Lezard caught her arms.

"That was very foolish, Miss!" he raged, punishing her with a vicious backhand blow.

Phaedra would have fallen, but Lezard kept a tight grasp on the lapels of her robe. Fright kept her rooted to the spot, even as Lezard ripped the robe from her body.

"Sir! Sir!" an urgent cry came through the door.

Lezard grimaced and rolled his eyes. "What the devil is it?!"

"So sorry, sir, but we need you in the front room for a moment!"

Phaedra prayed the relief she felt did not show on her face. She remained still, waiting for Lezard's next move.

In an instant, he shoved her aside and headed to the door. He turned to leave her with a cold look. "I will have you this night."

When the dead bolt slid into place, Phaedra fell to her knees.

A heavy snow had fallen that day, making it impossible to do any searching. Rather than spend his time snapping at everyone who got in his way, Zephir closed himself off in his study. A bottle of Bourbon seemed to be the perfect companion. He helped himself to more than half of the fiery liquid, before setting the bottle aside.

Pushing himself from his chair by the fire, Zephir stood before the windows. *Lord, she is out there somewhere trying to get away from me*, he silently lamented. He could not count the amount of land they had covered in the search. There was no trace of Phaedra, and he was beginning to wonder if she was even alive.

A soft knock on the door pulled Zephir's attention away from the pitch blackness outside. Lijon entered the study with a tray set for tea.

"I thought this might make you feel better than that whiskey."

Zephir's features softened. "I doubt that will help."

Lijon leaned over and patted his hand. "She's safe. I know it."

Sighing, Zephir squeezed Lijon's hand. "I appreciate you saying that. At this point, I have to acknowledge she could be dead. She is not used to this climate and there is no one around for miles."

"The neighbors have not heard from her, I gather?" Lijon questioned, as she prepared a cup of the piping hot tea.

Zephir's glare narrowed to the thinnest slits. He took Lijon's hands in his and pulled her close. "What neighbors?"

"On the other side of the mountain," she explained. "I met the housewoman at the market a while back."

"My God…" Zephir sighed. Did he dare hope to find Phaedra

there? "Lijon, do you know who they are?"

"Let's see…I know I got the name," Lijon sighed, as she headed to the door of the study. Turning, she tapped her finger against her chin as she tried to remember. "Ah yes, Lezard. That's what she said. She was in the employment of a Cantone Lezard."

Lijon left the study and Zephir dropped to his chair. His hand covered his heart, which threatened to beat right out of his chest. "Lezard…" As badly as he wanted to find Phaedra, he prayed she had not come in contact with the notorious Moor. If she had, then he knew she was surely dead…or wishing she were.

Sick with worry over her fate, Phaedra had tried the window once again, knowing it was hopeless. There was no way out of the small, dank room, and she did not dare try the door. Lezard would return soon enough to fulfill his lewd promises. Phaedra ran shaking fingers through her hair as her ears caught the sounds downstairs. It seemed that Lezard and his men were in the midst of a fabulous party. The entire house was alive with loud music and foul language. Phaedra knew there would be no reasoning if she had to face the man in a drunken state.

Suddenly, the noise downstairs reached a fevered pitch. It sounded as though a herd of wild animals were bounding through the house. The thundering sound had even drowned out the music. Curious and frightened at once, Phaedra pressed her ear against the door. She could have sworn that she heard screaming.

The instant Zephir got over the shock of Phaedra being in the clutches of Cantone Lezard, he gathered his men. They had no idea anyone lived on the other side of the mountain. As a result, no searching had been done in that area. Everyone agreed that Phaedra could very well have been held captive there, and they wasted no time heading out.

It was not hard infiltrating Cantone Lezard's camp. The group was obviously in the midst of a great celebration. They never knew what hit them. Zephir and his crew invaded the party and slaughtered most of the guests. The scene was brutal-swords flew and guns fired.

Zephir found more satisfaction using his fists. All the frustration that had built inside him since Phaedra's disappearance, rushed forth. Of course, he wanted Cantone Lezard most. When he spotted his old enemy trying to escape through a door at the back of the sitting room, he followed.

Lezard's eyes widened when he saw Zephir Mfume storm toward him. Cantone could see the deadly hatred filling the man's eyes from across the room. Again, he turned to the door in an effort to escape. The knob would not twist between his sweating palms.

Zephir let out a bellow of rage when his hand clamped down on Lezard's shoulder. He jerked the man around and slammed him against the door. Splinters flew from the shabby wood, piercing Cantone's back.

Taking great satisfaction in hearing the man's screams, Zephir drove his knee into Cantone's belly. Then, he dragged the man to the floor and began to punish his face with vicious blows.

Zephir's mighty fists left Cantone Lezard's face a bloody mass. Still though, the injured man tried to speak.

"You savage fool! I'll see you burn for this," Lezard promised, blood splattering from between his busted lips.

"Where is she?" Zephir softly demanded, his rough voice filled with hate.

Lezard laughed. "The girl? You're here for the girl? She is a beauty, isn't she? And so tasty."

Zephir balled his fist and laid another blow to Lezard's face. "You son of a bitch! I said, where is she?!"

"You idiot! She's not your wife, you've not even taken her body. You have no claim, no right whatsoever to that beauty," Cantone drily noted, his ragged lips twisted into a smug smile.

Zephir tightened his grip on Lezard's lapels and jerked him from the floor. He was about to render a fatal blow, when a sharp pain pierced through the base of his skull. For a moment he was

unconscious on the floor, but not for long. He shook off the pain in his head fast enough to catch his gloating attacker. The man's eyes widened as he watched Zephir rise to his full height. Zephir's massive hand curled around the man's throat, and he hurled him into the roaring fireplace.

"Shit!" Zephir hissed, realizing Cantone Lezard had vanished. Forgetting that, he located the stairway and went in search of Phaedra.

"Lord, what is happening?" Phaedra whispered. She stood twirling a lock of hair around her fingers and watching the door. The wild roaring outside the room showed no signs of ceasing.

"Phaedra?! Phaedra! Answer me, dammit!"

Gasping sharply, Phaedra took a small step toward the door. Her long, arched brows drew close as she strained her ears to listen.

"Phaedra! Phaedra Toussaint!"

"Zephir?" She whispered, daring to hope that it was really him. "Zephir?" She repeated, pressing her ear against the door.

"Phaedra!"

"Zephir!" she called in her loudest voice. "Zephir, I'm in here!"

"Phaedra where the devil are you?!"

"I'm here! I'm right here, you fool!" she screamed, pounding her fists against the door.

Zephir found the room. Pressing his hand against the door, he uttered a brief prayer of thanks. "Move away from the door, I'll have to break it down!"

Phaedra did as he ordered and waited. A second later, the door crashed open beneath the force of Zephir's powerful shoulder. His , slanting eyes found her immediately, and he stormed across the room.

"I should whip you for this," he growled, hauling her shivering body against his chest.

Relief and anger flowing through her at once, Phaedra pounded her fists against his blood soaked shirt. "You jackass! I never would have had to do this if you had not kidnapped me!"

A soft growling sound began in Zephir's throat, and he pushed Phaedra away. He went out into the hall and she followed. Her eyes widened in horror as she watched him pull a cloak off the back of a man lying dead in the hallway. Zephir shook it once and wrapped it around her.

"What are you doing?" she gasped, trying to push the dead man's cloak from her shoulder.

Zephir caught her chin and forced her to look at him. "You will die if you dare walk outside in this," he promised, his eyes lowering to the tattered robe. For a moment, the hard look softened as the tan material offered tantalizing glimpses of chocolate toned skin.

"Come on," he rasped, hauling Phaedra across his massive shoulder. In moments, they were out of the house and headed into the cold, snowy night.

Every room in the chalet was lit that night. The place was in an uproar, with packing underway. There were men on the ship preparing the vessel to set sail. The houseservants set out food and drink for stocking the boat. In addition, the sitting room was being decorated and a huge dinner was nearing completion.

Zephir did not stop to investigate the chaos below, but headed right up the stairs with Phaedra.

"What's going on here?" she demanded, pounding against his wide back when he did not respond.

Zephir walked into the master bedchamber and let Phaedra slide from his shoulder. "Get dressed," he ordered.

"Not until you tell me what's going on here."

"Get dressed!" He cupped her chin harshly.

"Zephir—"

"Listen to me, I have no legal claim to you."

"Ha! You've got that right."

Zephir rolled his eyes and pushed Phaedra down to sit on the bed. He knelt before her and took a moment to explain the situation. "We must marry so that no one can take you from me.

Lezard is not dead, and, knowing him the way that I do, he will not rest until he has avenged this night. Anything could happen in a situation like this. Legally wed, you would be better protected."

"Why can't I just go home?"

Grimacing, Zephir debated on how to answer the question. They did not need a heated argument that night, but he knew it could not be helped. "You can't go home, Phaedra."

"Why not? I promise not to breathe a word of what has happened to my cousins. I'll think of something, some lie, they would—"

"Your cousins know the truth, my love."

"What are you saying?"

Zephir's wide, sensuous lips tightened into a thin line. "Your cousins offered to sell me the land with the condition that I take you from Dominica so you would be unable to claim your inheritance."

Phaedra laid a vicious slap to Zephir's face. Ignoring her burning palm, she pinned him with a scathing look. "You lying son of a bitch."

Zephir shrugged. "Just get dressed."

She ran her hands through her hair and turned on the bed. She saw a lovely white gown lying next to her and gasped at its beauty. "What is this?"

Zephir stripped the bloodied shirt from his back and tossed it aside. He walked to the bed and leaned over Phaedra. Her eyes were wide as they trailed the sleek, chiseled surface of his torso and muscular arms.

"We are to be married this night," he cooly informed her. "Refusal is not an option, and if you won't dress yourself, I'll do it for you."

He was right. She knew his revelation about her cousins was no lie. It was a shock to discover the lengths they would go to in keeping Toussaints, but she knew in her soul they were capable of much worse. Now, she was facing a marriage to Zephir. It was completely preposterous. He didn't love her and she…well, she was afraid to admit what she felt for him even to herself. Still, after what she'd been through with Cantone Lezard, she was more than willing to take Zephir at his word. He had saved her life that night and she knew she trusted him above all others.

Zephir had dressed on the other side of the room. By the time Phaedra slipped into the gown, he met her by the door. Dressed in a pair of black breeches, thigh boots, a fitted black suit coat and white shirt, he was even more devastating.

Phaedra had run a brush through her long, tangled locks but still grimaced at her reflection in the mirror. Zephir thought she looked ravishing, and he could not wait to make her his wife in every way.

The devastating couple descended the long staircase. Zephir led the way to the sitting room which was filled with his men and the houseservants.

Phaedra could not hide the shock on her face when she saw the minister at the front of the room. When Zephir found time to organize such a gathering, she would never know. Her responses to the minister were very soft. She felt as though she were listening to someone else's voice forming the words "I do." In a matter of moments, Zephir was being permitted to kiss his bride.

Shouts and whistles filled the room as Zephir pulled Phaedra close to him. Their kiss was long and deep. Phaedra felt herself responding enthusiastically to the lusty kiss and even curled her arms around Zephir's neck to draw him closer.

Too soon, they were being pulled apart. The women servants congratulated Phaedra, while Zephir's men bestowed their best wishes to him.

"Zephir, congratulations, my friend," Dubois said, enclosing his friend's hand in a hearty shake.

"It had to be done," Zephir sighed, though a smug smile touched his mouth.

"Mmm hmm," Dubois replied just as smuggly. "Listen, I hate to deprive you of the most enjoyable part of the evening, but we must be on our way."

"Dammit," Zephir groaned, thoughts of bedding his voluptuous bride already racing through his mind, "is the cabin all ready?"

"Mmm hmm. We need to move fast. Our lookouts have already spotted Lezard and his crew regrouping to head over here."

Nodding, Zephir clapped Dubois's shoulder. "Have someone make sure each servant gets on that boat to town," he ordered, turning to stare at Phaedra across the room. Soon, he promised

himself.

The chalet vacated a short time later. The place was sealed so tightly, it appeared that no one had ever been there. The servants headed out in their own boat, back to town. The crew, Zephir and Phaedra were set to board The Venus.

"I don't understand any of this. Some type of explanation would be greatly appreciated!" Phaedra bellowed, once they were back in the main cabin. She was so full of vinegar over all that had occurred, she paid no attention to the candlelit, cozy setting of the cabin.

Zephir remained silent, as he stripped away his boots and clothes.

"Will you at least be kind enough to tell me where we are going?"

Completely nude, Zephir turned. A knowing smile crossed his sensual mouth when he heard Phaedra's gasp. Her long lashes fluttered madly as her eyes scanned the devastating powerful build of his body. His flawless, blackberry toned skin stretched tightly across his chiseled body.

"Oh," she uttered in surprise as her eyes fell past his waist. She could not look away from the length of his maleness-erect with desire. Becoming weak and speechless at once, she began to back away.

Zephir did not rush, knowing he had all night to love her. The cool demeanor he exuded belied the need that raged through him. Phaedra was so beautiful standing next to the bed in her lovely gown, her almond-shaped stare was wide and expectant.

"Zephir…please, wait," she whispered, her words shaky and breathless. She continued to retreat from him until the backs of her knees touched the edge of the bed, and she tumbled back. "Wait." Though she had dreamed of him touching her again, she was horrified by the size and power of his sex.

Unfortunately, Zephir would not veer from his task. He straddled her body and pulled at the delicate ties of the gown's bodice.

She raised her hands to stop his fingers from tugging at her clothes. Taking both her wrists in one of his hands, Zephir pinned Phaedra to the bed. "The marriage is not real if it is not consummated," he told her, his striking black eyes seering into hers.

Phaedra closed her eyes in regret. "The marriage is not real anyway. You don't love me."

"Phaedra…" he whispered, lowering his lips to her ear. His strong, perfect teeth nipped at her lobe, before his tongue delved into the soft canal.

"Don't," she groaned; her small hands pressed weakly against his chest.

Zephir's lips slid down her neck. "Please don't tell me to stop. I've waited so long to have you."

The tortured tone of his raspy voice was Phaedra's undoing. She melted beneath his roaming fingers, deciding to experience the act that had filled her dreams.

Zephir's hands slid beneath her upper arms, and he cupped the sides of her breasts. His lips traced hers as his tongue sought entrance.

Phaedra instantly complied, moaning when his tongue filled her mouth. She arched into his hard frame, her hands sliding across his chest. The kiss deepened, becoming wetter, hotter. Phaedra's breathless cries mingled with Zephir's deep groans and filled the cabin.

Slowly, his hands caressed her body, which was still encased in the gown. He cupped her breasts, his thumbs brushing the nipples straining against the bodice. Needing to feel her silken body against his, he unfastened the front of the gown.

"Zephir…" Her fingers delved into his thick, black hair pulling him closer to her chest.

He didn't refuse her silent request. His lips slid across her collarbone, then dipped to the swell of her breast. For a moment, he inhaled the soft scent of her skin. When his lips closed around one hardened nipple, a wave of satisfaction rushed through him. Phaedra's tiny gasps only aroused him more.

After a moment, Zephir withdrew. A , worried frown clouded his very handsome face as he watched Phaedra. When she opened her eyes, his frown deepened.

"What is it?" she queried, her voice shaking.

Zephir braced himself on his elbows and ran one hand through his hand. "When you were…gone…"

"Yes?…Zephir? What is it? You're scaring me."

Clearing his throat, Zephir stroked the silky hair fringing her temples. "When you were with Lezard," he began again, "did he do anything? Did he…force you?"

Phaedra searched Zephir's eyes for a brief moment, before she realized what he meant. Quickly, she shook her head. "No, no. He tried, but he never…no, Zephir."

As though a tremendous weight had been lifted, Zephir let out a relieved sigh. He began to press fevered kisses to Phaedra's neck then trailed lower. Seconds later, he had pulled the gown off her body and discarded her underthings. The feel of her luscious form beneath his hard, muscular body was beyond thrilling.

His hands were everywhere, caressing her back, thighs and buttocks. When his fingers touched the soft, sensitive petals of her womanhood, she tensed. Zephir was not discouraged. He simply increased the pressure of his fingers.

The pleasurable sensations Phaedra started to crave during her time with Zephir, rose in her again. Slowly, her tension faded and she opened herself to his touch. Zephir was incredibly gentle, though every part of his body demanded he take what he wanted, how he wanted it. Still, he managed to restrain himself. The last thing he wanted was to make the loss of her virginity a frightening experience.

A tiny whimper escaped Phaedra's lips as Zephir's fingers probed. The strokes became more insistent and soon his fingers were slippery with her need.

"Phaedra..." he groaned, adding another finger to the caress.

Instinctively, Phaedra's hips ground against Zephir's fingers. Her hands tightened around his shoulders, her nails grazing the muscles rippling in his back.

The thick black locks of hair covering Zephir's head, teased Phaedra's skin. His lips closed around her nipple again, and he suckled madly. Phaedra thought she would lose her mind at the wondrous feel of the double caress.

"Mmm..." Zephir was lost in the softness of her body. He withdrew his thrusting fingers, smiling when he heard her disappointed moan. Slowly, his mouth traced the valley between her full breasts. His tongue outlined the undersides of each globe then tended to the flat plane of her stomach.

Phaedra's tiny cries grew louder the lower Zephir's kisses travelled. His lips brushed the tight, black curls shielding her womanhood then his tongue stroked the outside of the wet center. Settling between her thighs, he spread the silky petals of her femininity and kissed her there.

Gasping his name, Phaedra pushed her head deeper into the fluffy pillows. She was practically breathless as Zephir's tongue thrust deep inside, pleasuring her with repeated strokes. He was like a man hungry for the taste of her. His hands cupped her bottom to hold her in place while he feasted.

"Zephir please..." she breathed, knowing she could not possibly feel any better than she did at that moment.

Of course, there was so much more and Zephir could wait no longer. Slowly, he moved up and settled his body over hers again. With infinite gentleness, he kissed her. Tasting herself on his lips, Phaedra suckled his tongue and deepened the kiss.

The incredible mastery of his tongue kept her too preoccupied to notice much else. Zephir positioned the tip of his shaft against the entrance of her body. He cursed himself for having to hurt her, but knew it could not be avoided. His massive hands curled around her silken thighs and held them apart. Squeezing his eyes shut, he lunged forward.

Phaedra tore her lips away from Zephir's as her eyes stretched wildly. The pain engulfing her was so intense, she was unable to scream. Zephir winced at the feel of her nails digging into his shoulder. He could not turn back and continued the long, burning strokes. A moment later, he heard a piercing scream tear from her throat.

"Zephir please…please stop," Phaedra whispered, her words barely audible. She felt so overwhelmed, she actually thought she would break in two.

"Shhh…the pain will soon end. I promise," he assured her, his raspy voice deep and soothing.

The tears blurring her vision slid from the corners of her eyes and into her hair. Slowly, the pain faded. The indescribable pleasure that replaced it, forced a low ragged moan from her lips.

"You see?" he whispered next to her ear, his long lashes drifting shut as he became lost in the exquisite pleasure she gave him. Her tight, wet heat held his rigid length snuggly, making him breathless with desire.

Phaedra's hands slid from his back to slide through his hair. Her pleasure-filled cries filled the cabin each time he stroked the sensitive bud of her awakened femininity.

Although Zephir wanted the moment to last for hours, he knew he would not be able to control himself much longer. Soon, he was increasing the force behind the erotic strokes of his iron length. His seed erupted and spilled deep inside her.

The sound of their breathing filled the cabin. Phaedra could barely keep her eyes open and neither could Zephir. In a matter of minutes, they fell asleep in each other's arms.

CHAPTER 10

The next morning, Phaedra woke with a deep groan. Her entire body ached—especially her most private areas. With a sigh of relief, she noted that she was alone in the bed. Pushing thick strands of hair away from her face, she shoved the covers aside.

"Oh my God!" she cried, seeing the streaks of bright red staining the bed linens.

"It is natural to bleed your first time, love." Zephir assured, watching the scene from his place near the wardrobe.

Phaedra's wide stare crawled over Zephir distastefully. "You bastard," she breathed, turning her head away when she saw a smirk crossing his , face.

"That's no way to talk to your husband," he told her, selecting a pair of brown cotton breeches and a matching shirt from the wardrobe. "Especially, when we had such enjoyment last night."

Phaedra turned onto her back and glared at him. "Damn your black soul to hell for what you've done." Her angered renewed as all the events of the previous evening replayed themselves.

Forgetting his clothes, Zephir approached the bed. He braced his hands against his knees and leaned close to her. "You didn't curse me last night, did you? In fact, the only sounds I heard coming from that luscious mouth were soft sighs and breathless cries," he whispered, the look on his fiercely handsome face dared her to deny it.

Furious, Phaedra turned her back toward him. Zephir knew she'd been through an ordeal and hating that everything had been so rushed. He promised he would take time to show her just how enjoyable being his wife would be.

Late the next afternoon, Zephir walked into the cabin and found his wife sitting in the middle of the bed. She appeared to be in another world—her expression revealing nothing and her

gaze appearing blank. He closed the door softly and slowly closed the distance between them. He leaned across the bed and stroked her cheek with the back of his hand.

"What is it?" he asked as she looked up.

"Will I ever see my home again?"

"Of course you will," Zephir told her, folding his arms across his massive chest as he appeared uneasy.

"When?"

"Why?"

"Because it's my home."

"It's not safe for you to be there," he retorted, strolling to his desk, where he took a seat on the corner.

Phaedra moved to the foot of the bed. "What does that mean? It's not safe for me to be there? Because of what those bastards did to me? Home is exactly where I need to be."

Zephir hated the desperation he saw in her eyes, but steeled himself against softening. "We'll be dropping anchor soon and going ashore," he announced instead, glancing out the porthole.

"Damn you, Zephir, aren't you going to answer me?" she whispered in a fierce tone. Her heart raced a bit faster at the warning glare he sent her way, but she refused to back down. "When will you let me return?"

"You'll return when I decide, and I expect this to be the end of the discussion. Do you understand?"

"No!" She jumped off the bed, her tan gown whipping around her slender frame. "This is absurd. Who are you to issue orders and make decisions without consulting me?"

Zephir waited until she walked right up to him, then he caught her arms in his unyielding grasp. "In case you have forgotten, I am your husband. You are mine to do with as I see fit, anywhere and anytime I please," he growled, jerking her closer to his tall form. "I can see to it that you never return to that godforsaken island if I so choose."

Phaedra's opened her mouth to blast him, but never had the opportunity.

"Before you speak, I suggest that you also remember that as your husband, I also have the right to discipline you as I see fit."

Deep inside, Phaedra knew he was bluffing. However, a warning voice in the recesses of her mind told her it would be foolish to say so. She was so angry that she trembled. With a will she did not know she possessed, she managed to remain silent. When Zephir began to massage her arms where he had grabbed her, she wanted to kick him.

"Now, get your wrap. I'm taking you ashore."

Once the ship dropped anchor, the Mfumes set sail in a small boat and headed out. Phaedra was furious with her husband and offered no replies to his comments about the weather or the beauty of the land. She even refused to look at him, which was nearly impossible. The man was devastating when fully clothed, but without the cover of a shirt, he was magnificent. His massive biceps flexed as he rowed the boat. His blackberry skin glistened beneath the midday sun, enhancing the ripple of each sinewy muscle.

When the shoreline grew more defined, Phaedra's interest peaked. She wondered if there might be someone on that island who would be willing to help her. It mattered not, she told herself. To be away from Zephir, would be "help" enough. It was imperative that she return to Dominica and take her place at Toussaints. Clearly, her new husband didn't feel that way, and she knew he would be absolutely no help in getting her back. She would make her cousins pay, with or without Zephir's help.

While he secured the boat, Phaedra took in the lovely green expanse of the land. It was far too beautiful a place to be uninhabited, she thought.

"This way," he called, shrugging into a white, cotton shirt as he led the way.

Phaedra could feel the nerves twisting in her stomach as she debated on when to make her escape. She found her answer when they reached a fork in the path. Zephir ventured right, she went left. She broke into a frantic gait, unmindful of pine needles, cones, tree bark and other hazards littering her way.

Zephir watched her make a run for it. Though her previous attempt at escape had almost resulted in her being raped and murdered, she would not give up. He had to admire her for that. He followed her, but strolled instead of running. He saw her look back to see if he was gaining, and when she did, a slippery mudbank was her downfall.

"Oh nooo!" she cried, feeling the earth give beneath her slippered feet. Suddenly, mounds upon mounds of gooey brown mud oozed through her fingers and over her clothes. When she tried to pull herself out of the mess, it engulfed her more deeply.

"Mmm...you will definitely have to clean up before I make love to you."

Phaedra glared up at Zephir through the muddy tendrils of hair covering her eyes. "You buffoon, you will never do that to me again," she vowed, rolling her eyes when his dimpled grin appeared.

"Come," he ordered, without waiting for a reply. One hand curled beneath her armpit, and he pulled her from the mud like a sack of clothes. "I trust we won't have this problem again?" he queried, bringing his face close to her frowning one. "Unless you want this mess clinging to you indefinitely," he teased, then turned and retraced his steps.

They had not walked far, when Phaedra saw a charming clay cottage in the distance. She refused to show any interest, but was definitely intrigued. Zephir walked right up to the front door and unlocked it. Phaedra smothered a gasp when she saw that the place was even more charming on the inside. It was a spacious, one room dwelling complete with a well-stocked kitchen and dining space, cozy sitting area before a white stone fireplace and a grand, inviting bed in the far corner.

"Take off your clothes," Zephir ordered from across the room.

"Excuse me?" Phaedra retorted, a frown marring her face.

Zephir didn't bother to turn around. "Take off that gown before the mud begins to seep through to your skin."

Phaedra glanced around the room. "Where would you suggest I…undress?"

"My God, woman, I have seen you unclothed before. I am certain that I've seen parts of your body you've never even viewed."

"Imbecile."

"What was that?" Zephir called, pretending not to have heard the hissed insult. Finally, he turned to regard her with his unsettling pitch black gaze. "Well?"

Phaedra refused to let him see her unease. She stepped out of her slippers and began to unbutton the muddy gown without taking her eyes away from his. Even when Zephir folded his arms over his chest and leaned against the counter to enjoy the view, she remained undaunted. When the gown pooled at her feet, she kicked it away then stomped to the fireplace mantle wearing only her shift. She heard Zephir's footsteps and waited for him to pounce. When nothing happened, she turned to see that he had gathered her muddied things and was in the process of cleaning them. She knew that only Zephir Mfume could retain his overwhelming masculinity while undertaking such a chore.

When he left to hang the gown, Phaedra turned back to the mantle. She was studying the oil painting there, when suddenly, she was captive in an unrelenting embrace.

"What do you think you're doing?" she demanded.

"I've got to do something about this hair" He replied, glancing over the , tousled mass. "Can't have you dirtying my bed linens."

Phaedra tried to wrench herself out of his hold. "Conceited rogue. You don't have to worry about your bed linens, since I won't be sharing your bed!"

"Ah, Phaedra," he sighed, as he carried her toward the back of the cottage, "I always prided myself in possessing a superior will. Clearly, it's no match against yours."

Phaedra's fist unclenched a little. "I'm glad you have finally admitted that fact, sir."

They stepped outside and Zephir took a refreshing breath. "I suppose I'll just have to be content with possessing superior strength." His teased, his mouth crashing down upon hers.

"Mmm," Phaedra reacted, melting in his embrace.

His tongue stroked the ridge of her teeth, and then caressed the roof of her mouth. When she tentatively participated, his lips suckled her tongue, and he proceeded to kiss her all over again.

Suddenly, Phaedra found herself deposited on a hard chair. She leaned back and prayed to regain just a fraction of her dignity. A moment later, she felt water against her scalp.

"Stay still," Zephir softly requested. "I'll be done shortly."

Too exhausted to move, Phaedra closed her eyes and did as he asked. Zephir's strong fingers massaged away all the tension she had accumulated since their voyage began. The soothing, circular movements penetrated deep into her scalp, and she voiced a soft moan.

"I apologize for the crude soap," he told her softly as a rich lather formed.

Phaedra could not help but smile. "It's quite alright," she whispered.

Zephir's smirk triggered his dimples. He watched her long lashes flutter closed over her eyes and studied the breathtaking loveliness of her face. His onyx eyes moved to her hair, amass with rich, white foam. All the mud had been washed away long ago. He simply enjoyed the feel of the sleek locks between his fingers. *God, she is so beautiful*, he thought and realized that he was hopelessly in love with her.

"This is going to be cold." He poured a pitcher of water through her hair.

Phaedra savored the coolness drenching her scalp. Never had she felt so relaxed after having her hair washed. When Zephir told her she could sit up, she could not mask her disappointment.

He set the pitcher aside and watched her move from the chair. His eyes raked the shift which now clung to her curvaceous figure. "Dammit, now I've done it." he remarked.

Phaedra was wringing excess water from her hair. "What's wrong?"

She watched Zephir walk closer.

"You can't walk around in this, it's drenched." He hands went to the ties which secured the bodice.

Phaedra tried to slow her breathing, but could not. Her full breasts heaved in an unconsciously seductive manner and nudged his fingers as he unlaced the shift. Eventually, the garment fell away, and she stood naked before him.

Zephir's hands molded to her flawless chocolate skin with all the familiarity of an attentive lover. He cupped her breasts, his thumbs stroking the firming nipples before moving down to cup her hips. He pulled her up high against his chest and went back to the chair where he had her straddle his lap.

The intense determination on his face would have frightened Phaedra had she not been so aroused by his touch. Faintly, she snuggled her femininity against the unleashed power lying beneath his trousers. Slowly, her hands reached out to touch the seemingly chiseled expanse of his abdomen; visible beneath his open shirt.

Zephir nuzzled his face into the crook of her neck then suckled her soft earlobe. His hands rose once more to cup and weigh her breasts. He took turns favoring each one with the mastery of his lips and tongue. Finally, he reached down to free himself. He lifted Phaedra as though she were weightless and settled her slowly. A gasp caught in her throat as she felt his devastating length invade her body. His stunning girth stretched her tight inner walls, and he brought her to orgasm almost instantly.

Zephir commanded the movements of her body, squeezing her hips when he wanted her to slow or quicken. They made love beneath the afternoon sun, and then headed inside the cottage to continue the enjoyment.

"You've gotten no work done today," Phaedra purred, pressing a soft kiss to her husband's neck.

Zephir's eyes narrowed as they slid over her body. "I beg to differ with that."

The newlyweds had spent the entire day in the main cabin of the ship. After their day of lovemaking in the cozy cottage, Phaedra decided to stop denying her feelings for Zephir and to enjoy the pleasure he offered.

A knock on the door drew their attention.

"I'm sure that's our dinner," Phaedra said.

"I'm sure you're right," Zephir growled against her neck.

"Should we take advantage or send it away like the other two meals?"

Zephir raised his head and thought for a moment. "Mmm…I see with you, I'll need my strength, so we better eat."

Phaedra sat up in bed, while Zephir went to the door. He spoke briefly with the cook's assistant then brought the food laden tray into the room.

Phaedra lifted the silver cover to find greens, a thick beef stew, soft rolls and ale. "Ooooh, this looks wonderful."

Zephir slid beneath the covers and took a moment to watch Phaedra. He silently marvelled at her natural beauty and the refreshing wildness of her spirit. He never thought he would feel so deeply for one woman, but he did. He wanted her with him…always.

"Zephir, aren't you going to eat?" she asked, her expectant eyes wide as she bit into one of the soft rolls.

"Most definitely," he replied, pushing the tray aside and setting his wife onto his lap.

"We agreed to eat dinner," Phaedra sighed, gasping when his tongue stroked her breast.

"You have dinner, I prefer dessert," he growled against her skin.

Phaedra tossed her roll aside and decided to let dinner wait.

Over the next several weeks, Phaedra and Zephir became even closer. They fed each other from the same plate, shared long walks around the ship and long nights in each others arms. Though they had not put their feelings into words, it was obvious that they were completely in love with one another. Time seemed to pass in a blur and, soon, the trip had come to its end.

Phaedra snuggled deeper beneath the covers at the sound of her name being called. "Zephir…" she purred in response.

The dimples flashed in his cheeks. He tugged the covers down from her neck and pressed a kiss to the rise of her breast. "Love? Wake up," he whispered against her skin.

"Mmm…do I have to?" She turned onto her back to watch her gorgeous husband through narrowed eyes.

Zephir slid up over her and kissed her ear. "The ship has docked." He pulled her earlobe between his lips.

Phaedra gasped in response and smoothed her hands across the bare skin of his sleek chest still visible beneath the opening of his shirt. "The trip is over already?" she complained, hating to see the magic end.

"I am afraid so, love. We're here."

"And where is here?"

"Get dressed and I'll show you," he taunted, a mischievous gleam in his striking black eyes.

Phaedra dressed quickly in a cream colored gown that billowed about her like a fluffy cloud. She decided to pin her hair up in a tight ball, leaving wavy tendrils to dangle around her beautiful, oval face.

"Ready?" Zephir called, sticking his head just past the cabin door.

"Mmm hmm," she replied, bouncing to the door.

His stare instantly faltered to her full breasts, heaving enticingly against the gown's low neckline. His desire was immediately stimulated and he headed back into the cabin.

Her eyes widened when she saw the determined glint to Zephir's expression. "No, you promised to show me around."

"Later," he growled, pulling her against him.

Phaedra pounded against his chest. "Zephir…Zephir no, you'll ruin my dress!" she cried, when he sat on the bed and straddled her across his lap. In seconds, his massive hands were beneath her skirts.

"Shh…" he soothed, kissing the base of her neck softly. He caressed the satiny softness of her thighs then discarded her under-things. He smiled, when she gasped in response.

"Zephir…" Phaedra groaned, rotating her hips against his probing fingers.

"Would you like me to stop?" he teased, his fingers stroking her more deeply.

"No, damn you."

Chuckling softly, he pulled her head down to his. Their kiss was passionate and lengthy. She cupped his face in her palms as their tongues fought a furious duel. Meanwhile, he freed his stiff arousal from the confines of his breeches. He cupped Phaedra's hips firmly, and lifted her easily to set her down onto his throbbing length.

Phaedra's head fell back, as she screamed her delight from the pleasure surging through her body. Her arms encircled Zephir's neck as she arched closer to his body. In moments, the two lovers found a mutual seductive rhythm. Phaedra slid slowly, sensuously over Zephir's breathtaking maleness as he thrust up into her.

When their pleasure had spent itself, they rested against each other. Once their breathing had returned to normal, Zephir pulled Phaedra off his lap and forced her to stand.

"Do you need a few moments to put yourself together?" he asked, his gravely voice soft.

"Thank you," she whispered, knowing it would take much longer than a few moments to gather enough strength to walk.

When they finally stepped off the boat, Phaedra could not tear her eyes away from the sight greeting her. "My God, Zephir is it—"

"It's Cuba," he informed her cooly, before she could mistake the lush, green environment for the island of Dominica.

Phaedra only appeared disappointed for a moment. The incredible beauty surrounding her was so like her beloved homeland. There were lush banana trees everywhere, green grass and vibrant blue skies that matched the water surrounding them.

"This is unbelievable," she breathed, walking ahead of Zephir. The brilliant water beckoned her attention. She could almost feel the cool wetness touching her skin.

"Whoa…" Zephir called, taking her by the waist and pulling her small form back against his chest. A moment later, he had perched her atop a fierce looking black horse.

"Where are we going?" she questioned, watching him suspiciously.

Zephir did not answer and mounted the powerful Arabian easily.

"Zephir, where are you taking me?"

Gathering the reins, Zephir glanced across his shoulder at Phaedra. "Do you trust me?" he asked then urged the horse forward.

Phaedra smirked and pressed her face against his wide back. Sliding her arms about his waist, she silently admitted that she did trust him…with her life.

They rode through the fantastic countryside for what seemed an eternity. During the ride, Zephir pointed out so many interesting things that Phaedra was almost dizzy. There was such a peaceful aura in the air, she wished they could ride forever.

"Here we are," Zephir announced, spurring the horse into a fast gallop.

Phaedra shook her hair away from her eyes and feasted on the vision before her. Nestled amongst the trees and hills was an airy, white villa. The breathtaking structure sat beneath the vibrant blue skies like an enchanted castle. Off from the main house were healthy fields of sugar cane. Phaedra held a hand across her brow to shield her eyes from the sun. In the distance, she could see men toiling away in the fields, carrying the heavy sugar stalks to waiting wagons.

Zephir guided the sleek stallion to a wide clearing in front of the house. As soon as he slid from the horse's back, the double doors to the villa's entrance opened. A tiny woman with

round hips and a plump face came running down the curving clay steps.

"Zephir? Is that you, my love?"

Zephir's fierce, features softened as a devastating smile appeared on his face. He bent slightly and scooped the woman into his arms. "Mama…"

Carmelita Mfume relished the hug from her only child. She pressed dozens of kisses to his neck and face. "Oh, I have missed you so!" she cried.

"Me too, Mama," he whispered, holding the woman tightly against him.

Phaedra watched the touching scene in awe. She had never seen Zephir act so humble in all the time she had known him. He had called the woman Mama, but she believed she would have known the lady anyway. Zephir was practically the image of her. They had the same silky black hair and striking slanting obsidian eyes. Of course, his massive build and the flawless blackberry

complexion were still a mystery. Phaedra's wide eyes scanned the porch and yard to see if there was a father.

Surely, a few moments later, a tall powerful looking man emerged from the villa. It was obvious that Zephir had taken just as many genetic characteristics from his mother as he had from his father.

"Papa," Zephir called, setting his mother down and rushing over to hug the man.

Tumba Mfume produced a dazzling even white grin that sharply contrasted against his smooth, skin. "Boy, we had no idea you were headed home." He clapped his huge hands against his son's back.

"I didn't either, Papa. I hope it's alright?" Zephir asked in the same humble tone he had used before his mother.

Tumba waved his hand. "Don't talk foolish. You know your Mama always cooks enough to feed the masses," he teased.

Finally, Zephir turned and looked back at Phaedra still sitting atop his horse. "I have someone the two of you should meet." He pulled Phaedra down from the stallion's back and took her with him.

"Mama, Papa, this is Phaedra Toussaint. My wife," he announced, rubbing his hands reassuringly over Phaedra's arms.

Tumba and Carmelita exchanged surprised looks then rushed over to Phaedra. They both pulled her close and hugged her tightly. Of course, they knew what a brooding mood their son could possessed. The couple was overjoyed to meet the woman who had finally captured his heart.

"It's so very nice to meet the two of you," Phaedra said, smiling as her eyes twinkled.

"And likewise, my dear," Tumba Mfume said, patting Phaedra's hands softly.

Carmelita laughed. "Muy muy bonita," she sighed and glanced at her son. "Zephir, she is so beautiful. I can see the two of you compliment each other well."

Phaedra managed a smile at the suggestive compliment. Of course, she took no offense. The Mfume's welcomed her into their family and their home with unequalled enthusiasm. Phaedra felt as though she truly belonged.

Phaedra let me show you to your room," Carmelita offered while Zephir talked with his father.

Phaedra's eyes were focused on the lovely afternoon skies. The clouds were full and took turns shielding the bright sun. She was so entranced by the scene, it took a moment to pull her eyes away. When Phaedra saw Carmelita gazing at her in concern, she shook her head.

"I'm so sorry. I just drifted away for a moment."

Carmelita patted Phaedra's cheek. "Is there anything wrong, love?"

Phaedra sighed and looked back over the landscape. "I came from a place a lot like this."

"And you miss it?"

"Very much."

Carmelita's look of concern took on a more probing tinge, and she took her daughter-in-law's hands. "We should have a talk, dear. But first, you must rest for the feast."

"Feast?"

"To celebrate your marriage to my son. If I know Zephir, your wedding was probably harried with little or no festivities."

Phaedra's brows rose as she nodded in agreement.

"Well come," Carmelita ordered, heading up the long winding staircase. On the last carpeted step, she stopped and patted Phaedra's shoulder. "Take this stairway on the left to the next level. You will see three doors on the corridor. Take the one in the middle and get to bed."

"Thank you, ma'am."

"No. Carmelita," she urged. "I will arrange to have your things sent up in time for you to change for dinner."

Phaedra watched Carmelita descend the stairway. Then, she turned and followed the directions to the room.

"My Lord," she whispered, after pushing the double mahogany doors open. The spacious bedchamber was incredible. The room was decorated with tapestries which lined the walls and armchairs. Paintings of the vibrant countryside and thick rugs dyed in rich hues of purple, blue and green. Phaedra was in complete awe of her surroundings.

The most fabulous feature of the room though, had to be the bed. The massive four poster, had a polished mahogany head and foot board. It was covered by a thick quilt and pillows that matched the rugs over the floor. Phaedra decided to waste no more time and stripped out of her gown before hopping up onto the bed. She was about to slip between the covers, when the door flew open.

"You were expecting me?" Zephir asked, a devilish light twinkling in his eyes.

Phaedra managed to hide her delight. "Your mother told me to take a nap before our wedding feast. I don't want to disobey her."

"She won't mind," Zephir whispered, his deep voice filled with mischief.

Phaedra snuggled beneath the covers and watched Zephir come to stand before the bed. Her captivating eyes followed the direction of his hands as he pulled off his clothes. Her entire body tingled in response to his chiseled body.

A moment later, Zephir was covering Phaedra in the bed. He quickly ripped away her delicate shift and tossed it to the floor. As his mouth ravaged the satiny skin of her breasts, Phaedra pounded his chest.

"Your parents…"

"Are most likely doing the same thing," he whispered, his tongue dipping into her navel.

Phaedra could not suppress the urge to giggle. Soon, she and her husband were laughing uncontrollably. After a while, their attention returned to making love.

CHAPTER 11

Carmelita Mfume organized her son and daughter-in-law's wedding feast in record time. The fiesta was spectacular to say the very least. There were five tables filled with food. The buffets were located in various corners of the spacious patio, and each table was covered by a brightly colored cloth. It appeared that everyone in the village had been invited to the gathering: from the field women to the Mfume's closest friends. Though Phaedra knew none of the guests, they all made her feel welcome.

Zephir and Phaedra seemed to fall more in love that night. They ate, drank and shared several dances. The smooth, seductive melodies provided by the village band, filled the air with romance…and passion.

"I hope you are enjoying yourself, love?"

Phaedra turned to Carmelita. They were taking a walk along the beach outside the villa later that night. "Oh yes, I can't remember when I've had such a nice time. Thank you for doing this."

Carmelita nodded slightly. "You're more than welcome, child."

Phaedra folded her arms over her chest and tilted her head slightly. "Excuse me for saying this, Carmelita."

"What?"

"Well, earlier you asked me if there was something wrong. Now, I feel the need to ask you the same."

Carmelita leaned forward, taking Phaedra's hands into hers. "You're a very insightful young woman."

"So I've been told," Phaedra whispered, looking out at the darkened sky.

"Perhaps a better word would be, 'enlightened.'"

"What exactly are you trying to ask me?"

"Don't you know?"

Phaedra could not stop the knowing look from appearing on her lovely face. "I'm sure I do."

Carmelita clasped her small hands together. "I knew I sensed an enlightment in you, child."

"I've been told I have the gift of second sight. I inherited it from my mother, they say." Phaedra revealed, laughing at the delighted expression that showed on Carmelita's brown face.

"I knew it…but, I sense you are just discovering it?"

Phaedra bowed her head, acknowledging the fact. "I never would have realized it, had it not been for the dream…"

"What dream?"

Phaedra paused and stared into Carmelita's eyes. They were as dark as her son's, but there the similarity ended. While Zephir's striking black gaze was penetrating and unnerving, Carmelita's soothed and comforted. The lovely, onyx orbs coaxed Phaedra to confide.

"Since before my father passed away," she began, "I'd had these dreams. At first, they were so foggy…then, they became clearer. I could see my mother, who died when I was an infant, and there were other figures in the room."

"Who were they?" Carmelita asked, falling into step next to Phaedra as they continued their trek along the beach.

"At first, I could not determine. Then, as the dreams became clearer, I could tell they were my cousins—when they were small boys."

"What happens in the dream?"

"Well, that is what I had such problems with. You see, my mother died under very…mysterious circumstances. In my dream, I could always see a hand approaching me, but it wasn't my cousins. I could always see them standing close in the corner of the room."

"And what happened?"

"I know now, that in the dream, I was being held in my mother's arms. My father's sister, Lucia, was the other person in the room. It was her hand approaching me—or rather, my mother. There, the dream ends. I can't be sure if my aunt is helping or harming my mother. I believe I'll find my answer when I return home."

Carmelita stopped walking and took Phaedra's hand in hers. "If that is what you feel you must do, then God be with you. I urge you though, be careful of your cousins…and my son."

Phaedra's long brows drew close. "Zephir?"

"Sí," Carmelita affirmed, nodding briefly. "Like my husband, Zephir has a very negative view of the Voodoo religion. He only sees it as evil. He wants no one he loves to be a part of it."

"I can't hide who I am."

"I know, but Zephir feels he must control every aspect of his life. You're his wife, and he will do everything in his considerable power to keep you safe. If that includes keeping you from your cousins and your home, then I am afraid you will never find the answers to your questions."

Phaedra decided to continue her walk alone. Carmelita had returned to the party and tried to persuade her daughter-in-law to join her. Unfortunately, there was so much to think over; Phaedra knew she would be in no mood for more celebrating.

Her walk led her to a remote stretch of the beach. There, the water branched off into a small pond that was shielded by lush plants and towering palm trees. Gathering her skirts in one hand, Phaedra ventured into the greenery. When she spotted the calm water, a small delighted gasp escaped her.

"Oh, it's warm," she whispered, trailing her fingers along the surface of the water. Cupping her hands, she scooped out some of the water and splashed it into her face. Unable to deny the inviting pond any longer, she stood and looked around to see if anyone else was in sight. Then, quickly, she stripped away her gown and underthings. After making sure the pins that held her coiffure were secure, she submersed herself in the comforting water.

"Mmm…" she purred, floating in the water that was only waist deep. Standing, she raised her head and let the night air brush against her skin.

Zephir had been searching for his wife since his mother returned to the party without her. Knowing that Phaedra was walking along the beach, he simply assumed she would still be there.

It was not long before he found the intimate pond and his wife. Spotting her in the water, at first, Zephir could only stare. His smoldering midnight eyes traced the vision she made. His body instantly responded to the sight of her. Without taking his eyes away from Phaedra, he pulled the clothes from his body as he headed toward the water.

A tiny scream passed Phaedra's lips when she backed into an unyielding wall of flesh. Turning, her eyes widened when she saw Zephir standing behind her. Her legs weakened beneath the intense desire surging in his onyx glare. The moonlight streaming all around them was as vibrant as candlelight.

"What are you doing here?" she whispered, grasping his muscular forearms to maintain her balance.

"I could ask you the same," he slowly replied, his gaze faltering to look at her heaving breasts.

"I needed some time alone," she told him, her eyes trailing the wide, chiseled plane of his chest.

He shook his head, tendrils of his pitch black hair lifting against the breeze. "You know I can't leave you like this."

"Why not?"

"I would never sleep knowing I forfeited an opportunity to make love to you here."

The words, spoken in the raspy harsh voice, sent a shiver throughout Phaedra's body. When Zephir's hands encircled her waist and he cupped her buttocks, she melted. Their mouths met in a passionate kiss, and they both groaned from the intensity of it. Phaedra's arms wound about Zephir's neck as her fingers delved into his hair. He settled her against him so that the tip of his powerful erection brushed her womanhood. The delicious friction forced a sharp gasp from Phaedra's lips, allowing him to deepen the kiss.

Suddenly, he tore his lips away and brought both hands beneath her arms. Strong fingers tightened around her, and he lifted her easily.

Phaedra's head fell back as she marveled at the stars sparkling above. Her soft cries filled the night when Zephir's kisses touched her sensitive skin. His lips travelled across her collarbone and chest. His strong teeth grazed her nipple before his tongue swirled around it. Burying his handsome face in the valley between her breasts, he inhaled her sweet scent.

"Zephir..." she moaned, unable to find more words to communicate her need.

Zephir, however, understood her perfectly, for his own self control had reached its limit. He allowed Phaedra to slide back into the soothing water. She cried out when he turned her around and jerked her tiny frame back against him. His hands caressed her from neck to hip, trailing the warm water across her body. Slowly, they circled her thighs, separating them. In one fluid movement, he entered her from behind, groaning into her hair as his throbbing maleness met her femininity.

Phaedra let her hand fall back against his hard chest and pressed her bottom against his pulsing length. The increased sensation caused Zephir's huge form to shudder as his groans grew louder.

"Phaedra..." he whispered, bringing his hands up to cradle her full breasts. As the tips of his thumbs brushed her hardened nipples, he increased the force of his thrusts.

Soon, the night air was filled with soft cries and deep moans. Before their passion was completely spent, Zephir withdrew and carried Phaedra with him to the grassy bank. Dropping to his knees, he placed her on her back and covered her shimmering body with his own.

Phaedra raised her head to meet his kiss, moaning when his tongue thrust deeply into her mouth. Zephir draped her legs across his hips and sank his rigid arousal inside her. They resumed the rhythm, rocking against each other uncontrollably. When they were both satisfied and relaxed, Zephir gathered Phaedra in his arms. They lounged on the bank of the pond, and looked up at the stars.

"Zephir?"

"Yes, love."

She pulled her lower lip between her teeth and debated. She wanted to ask about returning home, but did not want to ruin the magic of the moment. Losing her nerve, she simply snuggled deeper into his embrace. "I love you," she finally whispered.

"I love you, too," he sighed, pressing his lips against her forehead.

The weeks spent in Cuba, turned to months. Phaedra never thought she would find such happiness with Zephir, but she had. She found herself wondering how she ever resisted him. All she wanted was to love him and to be everything he needed.

Sadly, nothing would ever be right until she settled her suspicions about the role her cousins and Lucia played in her mother's death. Her father had entrusted Toussaints to her care, and it was a task she tended to see through. Ridding the estate of Marquis, Carlos and Dante would have to be done before she could truly bask in the joy her new life promised.

"What do you think?"

Phaedra slowly shook her head. Her eyes were wide as she studied the scene before her. Zephir had taken her to a bull fight one afternoon. She could not tear her eyes from the spectacle of the matadors in their grand costumes. "I can't believe you grew up around this."

Zephir shrugged. He was actually having more fun watching his beautiful wife than the excitement in the arena. "In truth, the sport originated in Spain," he explained, turning his attention to the bull-fight. "Those who settled here brought the tradition with them."

"Goodness…" Phaedra whispered, following the graceful movements of the matador. He taunted the massive, ferocious bull; waving the billowing red cap in huge sweeping waves. When the vicious-looking animal charged toward the cape and the matador whipped the red cloak away, the crowd roared its approval.

Phaedra let out the breath she had been holding and sat back. "I have never seen anything so incredible."

"I'm glad to see you enjoying it."

Clasping her hands together, Phaedra sent Zephir a dreamy look. "I can't remember when I've had such a wonderful time."

Zephir leaned close to nuzzle her neck. "I can," he growled in her ear.

"Zephir?"

"Hmm?…"

Taking a deep breath, Phaedra gathered her courage. "When will I be able to return home?"

Zephir stopped his teasing kisses and pulled away. "I thought you said you were enjoying yourself?"

"I am, but—"

"Then why are you asking to go back?"

"Because it's my home, and I miss it."

"I don't believe this," Zephir muttered, rolling his eyes toward the sky.

"Why Is it so difficult for you to understand my wanting to go back? Zephir, the time we've spent here has been lovely, but… in truth, it has only made me miss Dominica that much more."

Zephir folded his arms across his chest and stared straight ahead. "It's not a good idea to take you back there."

Phaedra's sleek, arched brows drew close. "You are my husband, but I won't let you control me this way. Not about this!"

"You will lower your voice," Zephir fiercely whispered, his piercing black stare was murderous.

Phaedra's lashes brushed her skin when she looked down. "You never had any intentions of taking me back," she softly, but angrily accused.

Zephir's sensuous lips twisted into a grim smirk. "I never told you I'd take you back."

"Why are you doing this?"

Zephir's fingers closed around Phaedra's chin, and he forced her to look directly into his eyes. "We will discuss this at home. Do you understand me?"

Phaedra opened her mouth to issue a snappy response. Before she could utter one word, Zephir's mouth crashed down upon hers. She could hear whistles from onlookers witnessing the lusty, punishing kiss. Zephir's tongue thrust harshly past her lips, and she moaned helplessly.

Zephir broke the kiss then gave her a devilish wink and turned back to the bullfight. Phaedra held her fists clenched so tightly, her nails almost broke the skin of her palms. She did an admirable job of remaining silent for the rest of their outing.

"Ooooh, sometimes you can be such an overbearing, arrogant, insufferable ogre. It is so easy to hate you!"

Zephir slammed the front door to the villa then turned a murderous look on his wife. The two of them had burst into his parent's home, arguing viciously. Neither of them were willing to back down or meet in compromise.

Zephir stormed over to Phaedra and set her back against the clay wall. "Do you recall my telling you how your cousins tried to sell you to me?"

Phaedra searched his slanted eyes, but she was not put off by the anger she saw there. "I do remember," she assured him through clenched teeth, "don't you see? That's why I must go back. I have to find out what my dreams mean."

"Dreams?" Zephir replied with a harsh laugh.

"Yes, I've told you about them."

"Mmm hmm, and I still believe they are nonsense."

Phaedra winced at her husband's careless attitude about something which plagued her so. "They are not nonsense. I believe that more than ever after speaking with Carmelita."

Zephir tightened his grip around Phaedra's arm and pressed her against the wall again. "You went to my mother with this damn foolishness?"

The rough sound of Zephir's deep voice sent tremors down Phaedra's spine. "Yes, I talked with her, and she doesn't think it is nonsense."

Zephir raked one hand through his hair and grimaced. "She knows how I feel about this."

"And? "

"My mother has dabbled in voodoo for years against my father's wishes. If he knew—"

"Listen, Zephir, you are my husband, and I know I must respect your wishes. Unfortunately, I can't ignore who I am."

Zephir's hands closed around Phaedra's throat and he tilted her chin up with his thumbs. "Forget it."

Phaedra wrenched out of his grasp and slammed her hands against his chest. "Damn you! You're not my father!"

"Zephir? A moment of your time?"

Phaedra closed her eyes in relief upon hearing Dubois's voice. Zephir let her go, and she turned to bury her face in her hands.

"What is it?" Zephir growled, the look in his pitch black glare warning Dubois that there had better be a good reason for the disturbance.

Dubois cleared his throat and handed Zephir a folded sheet of paper. "One of your neighbors, Antonio Vallejo received this message from one of his ship's captains. The captain had an unfriendly encounter with Cantone Lezard several weeks ago."

Zephir scanned the note from the ship's captain to the owner Antonio Vallejo. The contents of the letter caused his heart to skip a beat.

Dubois could see the affect the note had on his friend. "As it states in the letter, Lezard has promised death to you and your new bride."

Looking back at Phaedra, Zephir muttered a vicious curse.

"Should you even take this rubbish to heart?"

Zephir clapped his hand to Dubois shoulder. "I have no choice, my friend. Lezard has wanted revenge since I took the chalet in Newfoundland. He has even more reason now with me killing half his men and taking Phaedra right out of his filthy hands."

"So, how do we deal with him?"

A grim smile teased Zephir's lips. "We deal with him face to face. He wants death—that is just what he will get." He turned his eyes on Phaedra once again. "Dubois, I need a favor."

Phaedra stiffened as she felt Zephir's hands close around her arm. He turned her around to face him, but did not speak until her eyes met his.

"You'll be on your way home tomorrow," he whispered.

The expression on Phaedra's face vanished to be replaced by a lovely smile. Tiptoeing, she pressed a hard kiss to Zephir's cheek. "Thank you, thank you so much."

Zephir returned the embrace, though he was sick inside. The last thing he wanted was to see her back in Dominica with her ruthless family. Still, he knew Phaedra. Where he was going, she could not follow. The moment he left, she would try to reach Dominica on her own.

He tightened his grip around her arms and pulled her away. "Would you mind joining me in our room?" he whispered, his deep voice soothing and seductive.

"I wouldn't mind at all," she replied, having no intentions of refusing such a delicious request.

They made love for hours, it seemed. When Zephir finally let Phaedra fall asleep, he promised himself that he would not be away for long.

Phaedra stretched like a satisfied kitten. A lazy smile crossed her full lips as she snuggled deeper beneath the covers. She felt happy, refreshed and very much in love. All she wanted was to spend the day in her husband's arms. Leaning across the huge bed, she reached for Zephir. When her fingers touched only cool sheets, her eyes snapped open.

"Zephir?" she called, silence answering her. Slowly, she pushed herself up in bed and looked around the room. *Zephir is gone*, she told herself-knowing it was true. Unwilling to believe her own words, she jumped out of the bed and raced out of the bedchamber.

Tumba Mfume was helping his wife into her chair when Phaedra flew out to the veranda.

"Good morning, child," Tumba greeted, his deep voice resounding in the morning air. Carmelita waved heartily.

"Good morning, where is Zephir?" Phaedra asked in the same breath. She headed over to the round iron table and was about to take a seat, when she saw Dubois at the far corner of the veranda.

"Dubois, have you seen Zephir this morning?" she asked, unconsciously wringing her hands.

Dubois's was regretful. He patted her hand and escorted her to the breakfast table. "Zephir had to leave on sudden business. He did ask that I see you home and watch over you in his absence."

"Business?" Phaedra parotted, her voice barely audible.

"Yes, it was quite sudden."

Phaedra pushed her thick tresses away from her face and pinned Dubois with her , eyes. "Quite sudden? This is what the two of you were discussing yesterday afternoon? He knew he was leaving and he didn't bother to tell me."

Dubois did not answer, but the look in his light green eyes confirmed Phaedra's suspicions.

Feeling as though she had been struck in the stomach, tears welled in her onyx eyes. Slapping the wetness from her cheeks, she ordered herself to be unaffected.

Carmelita rubbed Phaedra's bare arm briskly. "Shh, my sweet. This was something Zephir had to take care of. He loves you, very much."

Unfortunately, Phaedra found little comfort in the words.

CHAPTER 12

"My Heavens! Good Lord, please let this be real and not a vision!"

Phaedra was torn between wanting to laugh and wanting to cry. She stood in the doorway of the Toussaint mansion and watched Tisha clutching her heart.

"Phaedra, child is this you?" Tisha fiercely whispered.

Swallowing past the sizable lump in her throat, Phaedra nodded. "It is, Tisha. It is." She fell into the woman's arms as though a tremendous weight had just been removed from her shoulders.

"Oh, child," Tisha cried, her embrace tight and unyielding. "Love, I have missed you so."

Phaedra sighed and pressed a kiss to Tisha's shoulder. She inhaled the smell of fresh linens touched by the sun and crisp sea air. "I've missed you, too, Tisha…so much."

"I awoke one night and you were gone," Tisha said, after they had taken seats on the long staircase.

"I know," Phaedra breathed, remembering the awful night.

"Of course, the boys said they could not imagine what happened, at first," Tisha whispered, referring to the brothers. "Mr. Mfume was here, but only said that he had seen you. When he left, your cousins told everyone you had run off with the man. I never felt right about the story though."

Phaedra nodded slowly. She knew Tisha deserved to know everything, but at the moment, she could offer little more than a weak wave. A yawn welled inside her then and her eyelids grew heavy. Tisha patted her shoulder and left her sitting on the stairway, while she instructed the house servants to assist the crew with whatever they needed before setting sail again.

"Phaedra? Child, wake up now."

Phaedra's lashes fluttered open, and she smiled at Tisha. "Will you take me to my room?" she asked, sounding very much like a trusting little girl.

Tisha pulled Phaedra close and helped her up the plush stairway. "Yes, child, it is just as you left it." She relished the fact that Marquis, Carlos and Dante were out of the house that night. Dubois decided it would be best to watch over things from a far. His ship had been secured within the cover of the cliffs near the estate. Tisha was more at ease, that Zephir had sent his top man to watch over Phaedra, confident that the brothers would not discover him. She took time to have Phaedra's things secured in her bedchamber.

Phaedra awoke with a jerk, fearing that her return to Toussaints had been a dream. Clutching her pillow tightly, she studied her surroundings. A sigh of relief filled the room at the familiar, beloved sight of her own room. She sighed and was about to drift back to sleep when a brush stroked her hair.

"Tisha…"

"Shhh…go back to sleep, dear."

Phaedra sat up instead, turning around to face the woman. "I can't. I have so much to tell you. So many things have happened! I don't know where to begin."

Tisha sat the brush on the cherry dressing table. "I always like the beginning."

Sighing, Phaedra thought back over the course of the last ten months. "I had a dream that night. I awoke and knew I just had to get out of this house. I ran out in my shift, got Midnight and rode out. I came to the caves at the edge of the stable. There is gold in those caves, Tisha."

"My Lord…"

Phaedra nodded. "I caught the men and foolishly thought I could stop them on my own."

Tisha's expression became one of concern and she patted Phaedra's hand. "Did they hurt you, child?"

Phaedra shuddered, remembering how close she had come to being violated. "They tried, but…Zephir stopped them."

Tisha clasped her hands together. "Thank God for that man."

Mentioning Zephir's name caused Phaedra to drift away. For a long while, her eyes traveledd off into space.

"So why didn't Zephir bring you home that night?"

Phaedra sighed and grimaced as she shook her head. "He knew there was gold out there. When I discovered it, he knew I would expose him, so he took me with him."

"And?"

Phaedra pushed both hands through her thick hair, before propping her chin in her palm. "Tisha, to make a very long story short, we married. There were circumstances that made it necessary. Not to mention that we had…grown very close."

"You are a woman now." Tisha's eyes held a warm light. "You are a woman in love."

"Hmph, I thought I was in love," Phaedra snapped, her eyes narrowing with anger. "But, then Zephir just left. No word, no warning. He was just gone. He wasn't even decent enough to bring me back home. He left that to his first mate."

Tisha could hear the pain tinging Phaedra's voice, even as she tried to remain unaffected. She tugged on a lock of the girl's hair. "You know, I always thought he seemed quite taken by you."

"He took what he wanted from me, and now he is gone."

"What will you do?"

"Not worry myself over my fleeting husband." She pointed one finger in the air. "The most important thing now is taking care of my *loving cousins*."

Tisha's eyes widened as she listened to Phaedra's ranting. "You've never spoken this way before."

"I had no reason to. The dreams have come full circle, Tisha. I know that Marquis, Carlos and Dante were in the room with their mother…and mine. I don't know what they've done, but I intend to find out."

"And then?"

"Then, they will be out of this house and cast off Toussaints forever. Unfortunately, I can't do anything until I can be sure of what they are really up to—what they have done."

Tisha stood from the bed. "But how in the world would you find that out? Your cousins are the only ones who could tell you what you need to know."

"There's another way."

Tisha tilted her head to one side. "What other way?"

Phaedra did not reply, though the look in her eyes told Tisha exactly what she meant.

"To wealth and good living my brothers."

Marquis shook his head and grimaced toward his youngest brother. "Celebrating a tad early, aren't you Dante?"

"Bah!" Dante brushed off his brother's warning. "You know it and Carlos knows it. Soon, we will be the sole owners of this estate." He raised his glass to toast his words.

Carlos stood and refilled his wine glass. "Marquis is right. The deadline has not passed us yet."

"We have only a few months before Phaedra's twentieth birthday," Dante reminded them. "She has been gone almost a year. I don't think such a short period will change matters."

As if on cue, Phaedra appeared around the corner. She had taken great care with her appearance that night. Knowing she had to look nothing less than radiant, she chose a brilliant ocean blue evening gown. The dress had an empire waist and capped sleeves. The neckline called attention to the fullness of her breasts and tiny waist, while the color highlighted the rich tone of her skin. Matching satin slippers on her feet, a sparkling sapphire choker and the matching adornments in her hair, gave her a purely regal glow.

Marquis was the first to spot his beautiful cousin in the doorway of the sitting room. When his glass crashed to the polished wood floor, Dante and Carlos jumped to their feet.

"Good God, Marquis what! —" Carlos stopped talking and stared at the shocked expression on his brother's face. Slowly, he turned his head to look in the direction Marquis was staring. "Phaedra…"

Phaedra's humor was completely genuine, since her laughter was so very close to the surface. She rushed into the room, her dress floating around her. She gave each of them a sisterly kiss on the cheek then stood back to watch them. "Oh, I'm so happy to be home! I never thought I would see you all again!" she raved. "I know this is shocking, but it's me. I can imagine how worried the three of you must have been."

The three men were stunned speechless. The utter surprise on their faces said more than any words could have.

"Pha-Phaedra," Dante stammered, his eyes scanning every inch of her face.

"Yes, Dante?"

Dante finished the remainder of his drink and swallowed painfully. "My-my God. You-what…"

If Phaedra had any doubts about her cousins arranging her disappearance, they were wiped away in that moment. That only left her questioning Zephir's part in the scheme, did he accept their deal or was he really trying to protect her by keeping her away? The looks of shock that she had expected, instead of relief that she had hoped for, made it clear that her family had no wish to have her return home.

"Phaedra, my dear what-what happened to you?" Marquis asked, after the long moments of silence had passed.

"I was hoping someone could tell me," she whispered, hoping she sounded more confused than accusing.

Carlos came forward to take Phaedra by the arm. "My dear, Zephir

Mfume saw us on the night you disappeared. He said you...came to him and your innocence was compromised."

"That's right," Dante confirmed, "we thought you decided to run off with him."

"Mmm...I see," Phaedra sighed, her exquisite gaze remaining steady.

Marquis stepped over his broken glass and approached Phaedra. "We were just about to have dinner. Why don't you join us and tell us what has happened during the past year?"

Feigning a yawn, Phaedra walked away. "I'd like nothing more, but I've already eaten, and I'm still quite weary from the voyage. Perhaps another time. Goodnight."

Marquis, Carlos and Dante followed Phaedra out of the sitting room and watched her ascend the stairway. Their eyes followed her until she reached the top and turned the corner.

"Dammit to hell! I told you it was too soon to celebrate!" Carlos fiercely reprimanded.

"How the devil did she get back here?!" Dante cried, heading back to the liquor cabinet.

"There is a calmness about her," Marquis quietly noted, his brown eyes still focused on the stairway.

"And?"

"I don't like it."

"How do we handle this? She cannot be here when the deadline arrives."

Marquis turned away from the doorway and went to refill his glass once again. "The only way to ensure Phaedra's absense...is to kill her."

Phaedra headed right to Tisha's room after the reunion with Marquis and his brothers. The woman was working on a new quilt when the bedroom door flew open.

"I want them out! Do you hear me, Tisha? Out!"

"What happened, child?" Tisha whispered, ceasing her stitching.

"I want those bastards out of this house, off this land, off Dominica, out of my life!" Phaedra raged.

"But how?"

The look in Phaedra's onyx eyes reflected pure hate. "I want them out just as they wanted my mother out."

Tisha sat her quilt aside and rushed over to Phaedra. Taking the younger woman's hands in hers, she sought to calm her. "Now listen to me. I know you are confused and upset, but do not let this affect you for the worst. The dark side of voodoo is not something you want to toy with," she cautioned. "Your Aunt Lucia was a perfect example of how tragically it could affect your life."

Phaedra took several deep breaths and ordered herself to calm down. "I'll have to fight them on their terms if I expect to win."

"You'll have to fight, yes. You don't have to use their tactics."

"Tisha…" Phaedra wined, dropping to the bed.

"There are many ways to fight those deceitful boys."

"What ways?" Phaedra asked, eager to use any means to rid herself of her enemies. She stood then and lost her balance. "What ways, Tisha?" she repeated, laughing at herself.

Tisha laughed a bit as well. "I'm unsure of that, but we will think of something. Let your cousins use their evil tactics, they will only get them so far."

"Right." Phaedra leaned against the wooden table that supported a lamp in the room.

"Are you alright, my dear?" Tisha asked, stepping closer to Phaedra.

"Yes, I just need to get my mind away from the matter and rest."

"It'll be alright, child," Tisha promised, pulling Phaedra close for a hug.

"What's all this?"

"They belonged to your mother," Tisha explained as she brought an armload of books into Phaedra's room.

"What are they?"

"These books contain information on the religion—good and evil. There should also be writings about la prise des yeux."

"Second sight?"

"Come now, child. These contain many things you must be aware of."

Phaedra could not bring herself to leave the comfort of her bed. "Perhaps later, Tisha. I don't quite feel up to reading just now."

Tisha left the books on the desk in the corner. She pulled the covers neatly over Phaedra, tucking her in securely. "That's fine, love. You rest, the books will be here."

Phaedra had already drifted back to sleep before Tisha could leave the room. Smiling, Tisha pulled the bedroom door shut tightly and headed downstairs. As she approached the sitting room, the sounds of male voices rising in anger filtered out into the hall.

"…We don't have much longer."

"I know that, Dante."

"How do we get rid of her before the deadline, Marquis?"

"I have not decided yet, Carlos. But this time, we won't be plagued by her reappearance."

Just then, the sitting room door slammed shut and Tisha jumped as though she had been slapped. Closing her eyes, she took a seat on one of the cushioned highback chairs lining the hallway. Although she had hoped the cousins could be dealt with without delving into any dark dealings, she feared what she had just heard would make that impossible.

Later that afternoon, Phaedra thought she felt more like sitting up.

Unfortunately, once the book lay open in front of her, reading was the last thing she wanted to do. Sighing heavily, she tossed the book aside and fell back to the bed.

Lying there, studying the ceiling with blank eyes, Phaedra took a moment to reflect on everything that had happened. Though she knew in her heart that her cousins had betrayed her, she did not know what to make of their talk with Zephir. Why would he go see them and lie about a sexual encounter between them? Did he go there to assure them that he had received his "merchandise" and was satisfied? Did he go there with a false story to ease their minds about her? What? What was the truth? All she could be sure of was that someone knowingly set out to ruin her life. She prayed to God that it had not been Zephir.

Phaedra's inability to leave her bed was denounced as fatigue and renamed as sickness. It lasted for almost a week. She slept all night and most of the day. She could not eat or even sit up.

"Tishaaa! Oh my God! Tishaaaa! Please come quickly! Tishaaa!"

The entire house was awakened by Phaedra's screams that morning. When Tisha rushed from her bedroom, she saw most of the house servants waiting outside Phaedra's door. They all seemed paralyzed by fear at the sound of the high-pitched cries from the young woman of the house.

"What in heavens name?..." Tisha whispered as she opened the door. The sight that met her eyes shocked her speechless.

In her sleep, Phaedra had quite obviously vomited. When she woke and found the mess covering her sheets, her hair, nightclothes and the floor, she panicked.

"Tisha, what's happening to me?" she cried, using her sleeves to wipe the thick, yellow goo from her chin.

"Shh…shh now" Tisha comforted, rushing into the room and pulling Phaedra from the bed.

The house servants waiting outside the door, scurried when they saw the Toussaint brothers approaching their cousins room.

Phaedra could feel her stomach rumble the moment Tisha touched her arm. She pressed her lips together to hold back the flow of the liquid, but it was useless. In minutes, the nausea had her doubled over.

Marquis, Carlos and Dante were in the doorway watching their cousin. As she vomited violently, they stood there smirking. Once the powerful heaves ceased, they left Phaedra gasping for breath. Tisha hurried forward again with a wet cloth in hand. As Phaedra sat in the middle of the smelly, thick mess, she raised her eyes to her cousins's faces.

"Get out! Now!" she roared, her voice sounding surprisingly strong.

The brothers seemed startled by her words. They quickly did as they were told.

"I'm scared," Phaedra admitted in a small voice. As she sat in the tub watching Tisha change the soiled bed linens, she shuddered at the violent nausea that had overcome her.

Tisha did not respond at first. Her mind was racing with thoughts of what the brothers were truly capable of. She did not want to frighten Phaedra more, but she knew the girl had to be told.

"I know how this is weighing on you, love," Tisha whispered, kneeling beside the tub to soap Phaedra's back. "But sometimes, fear helps keep us alert and that is what you need to be right now."

Phaedra turned in the tub and pinned Tisha with an expectant glare. "What are you saying?"

Tisha focused on the bar of soap in her hands. "That night after you left your cousins in the sitting room, I overheard them talking. They want you gone, love. Permanently. I could not hear the particulars, but—"

"Dammit! If only I had the strength to fight them!" Phaedra cried, slamming her fists into the water. "Tisha, do you think they had something to do with what happened here today?"

"Quite possibly, child. Quite possibly."

After lathering Phaedra's thick black mane with the scented soap, Tisha wrapped her head in a linen scarf and helped her from the tub. Once Phaedra had donned a crisp, cotton gown, Tisha helped her back to bed.

"Now you get some rest, and I'll get you feeling better, I promise."

Phaedra nodded. Despite all that had happened, she was still glad to be home. Tisha opened the door to leave and found a visitor waiting outside.

"Kwesi!" Phaedra cried, delighted to see her father's great friend. "What are you doing here?"

Kwesi Berekua pressed a soft kiss to Phaedra's cheek and took a seat on the edge of her bed. "I had been told of your illness."

"I know I will be fine. Tisha's promised," Phaedra said, looking over at the woman who smiled before leaving the room.

"What happened to you, child?" Kwesi demanded, taking Phaedra's hands in his.

"Kwesi the story is very long, but it comes down to this: I believe Marquis, Carlos and Dante had a hand in my disappearance. If that is true, I need to know what they could be up to. What motive could they have for wanting to see me gone? I'm to inherit the land when I turn twenty. Besides killing me, nothing would prevent me from reaching the designated age."

Kwesi stood and warmed his hands before the flames in the stone fireplace. "When we last spoke, and I told you about your father's will. I did not tell you everything."

Phaedra drew her knees up and propped her chin on them. "I'm listening."

Kwesi turned, the look in his twinkling eyes becoming hard. "There was a stipulation to you gaining control of Toussaints. I never thought Fredericks should have included it. He had always been so overrought with guilt about those boys... I suppose it was his way of giving them a chance."

"What do you mean?"

"At first, your father wanted you to run the estate jointly with your cousins. With your spirit and goodness and their…lack thereof, I didn't think that would be a… fruitful union."

Phaedra gave him a stale grin. "I agree."

Kwesi stroked the thick, gray beard covering his chin and sighed. "Within two months of his death, Fredericks changed the will to state that you would be the sole heir to Toussaints on your twentieth birthday. However, to claim your inheritance, you would have to be here, on this land, by the stroke of midnight that day."

Frustrated, Phaedra pushed her hands through her hair and sighed. "I don't understand. The stroke of midnight? My father had to know I would be here."

"He did know."

"Well, why would you keep something so trivial hidden? And what does that have to do with—" Phaedra stopped in mid sentence, her eyes growing impossibly wider. "Kwesi? You don't think?…Did my cousins know about this stipulation?"

"I didn't think it mattered, you'd never been off the island. The boys went crazy when Fredericks told him he had changed the will. He informed them of the stipulation with hopes of easing their minds. But his first obligation was always to you."

"I know," Phaedra sighed, smiling as she remembered her father. "Kwesi, is this why you told me to be careful that day when we talked?"

Kwesi nodded and walked back to the bed. "I've known your family many years, Phaedra. I witnessed your birth, and I watched you and your cousins grow into adults. But those boys have always set me on edge. When Fredericks changed the will, I couldn't help but think he was making an even larger mistake."

Phaedra felt her nausea returning and leaned back against the pillows. "What lengths do you think they would go to for this land?"

Kwesi was obviously unnerved by the question, for he turned away from Phaedra's concerned expression. "I don't want to frighten you."

"Tisha says fear keeps us alert."

"Hmph. Tisha is a smart woman." Kwesi looked worried. "I believe those boys would do anything to keep Toussaints."

"I've never been this sick before, Kwesi." She rubbed her arms briskly. "Do you think they would…"

Kwesi knew what Phaedra was asking. He squeezed her hands tightly. "Love, I think those boys would try anything—including murder—to get what they want."

The long, thick white drapes in Tisha's room had been drawn to block the afternoon sun. Flaming candles had been arranged throughout the spacious bedchamber. Tisha sat upon a , woven rug in the center of the floor. Her hands were folded in prayer as she braced on her knees. Before her, on the run, was a clay dish filled with a clear liquid. Leaves, stems and flower petals floated in the steaming mixture.

Tisha's lips moved as she silently chanted her prayer for health. Afterwards, she looked down at the herbal potion and appeared pleased by her creation.

CHAPTER 13

"Tisha? Good heavens, where are you going with that?"

Tisha managed to hide her grimace when she met Dante in the hall that evening. She had just left her room with the potion. It was her intention to get to Phaedra's room and have her drink the mixture without the brother's awareness.

"What is that?" Dante asked, looking into the dish and sniffing the contents.

"Just something to remove a stain," Tisha quickly replied, brushing past Dante to continue down the hall.

Dante's eyes narrowed in suspicion.

"Phaedra? Dear? Wake up, sweetness."

"Tisha please…" Phaedra groaned, refusing to open her eyes.

"Sit up and drink this." She slid her arms beneath Phaedra's shoulders in order to prop her up.

Slowly, Phaedra opened her eyes and frowned. "What is this?" she asked, staring distastefully into the dish.

"Something to help you, now drink." Tisha pressed the edge of the bowl to Phaedra's lips.

The hot liquid had a tangy, grainy taste that burned a path down Phaedra's throat. She pushed the dish away as she sat up in bed, choking on the drink. "I can't."

Tisha would not accept a refusal. Her fingers closed around Phaedra's chin, and she poured the liquid down her throat. "Drink it and go back to sleep."

"Aaaagh…Dammit, Tisha!" Phaedra hissed, struggling weakly against the iron grip around her face.

Tisha wiped away the liquid that had dripped from the cup. She tucked Phaedra beneath the covers, ignoring the girl's grumbling. Five minutes had not passed, before Phaedra had fallen asleep. Tisha prayed over her briefly, then left the room.

"How long has she been this way?"

Tisha looked up at the tall, rotund man walking ahead of her. After calming Dubois about Phaedra's health, she sent the man off to fetch the family doctor. "She's been like this over a week," she informed the man.

Dr. Julius Claudius, who lived on the other side of the island, checked his bag. "What are her symptoms?"

Tisha released her skirts as she took the last step leading to the second floor. "She sleeps all day and night. She is nauseous and moody."

"Hmm…anything else?"

Tisha, suspicious about the brothers, rendered herself speechless for a moment. Shaking her head, she decided not to share her ideas with the doctor regarding black magic working its evil hand. "This is all. You can check her yourself. This way."

Dr. Claudius's eyes narrowed as they adjusted to the dimness of the bedroom. He slowly approached the bed where Phaedra was sleeping peacefully. "Let's have a look," he whispered, taking a seat on the bed. "Phaedra? Phaedra dear, can you hear me, love?"

A few moments of the doctor's soft calls pulled Phaedra from her deep slumber. "Mmm…" she moaned, trying to force her eyes open.

"Phaedra, it's Doctor Claudius. Can you hear me, child?"

"Doctor…Claudius?" Phaedra whispered, recognizing the doctor's smiling honey-complexioned face.

"That's right. How are you, child?"

Phaedra cleared her throat softly. "Somewhat better. Tisha has been helping."

Dr. Claudius nodded. "Well let's see if we can determine what the problem is." He stood from the bed and turned to Tisha. "I'm going to open the drapes for light. If you would remove her gown."

Tisha nodded and hurried to do as the man asked. When Dr. Claudius was satisfied with the amount of light in the room, he began the examination. Once the procedure was complete, he instructed Tisha to dress Phaedra. Then, he resumed his seat on the edge of the bed.

"You are no longer a virgin?" he knowingly inquired.

Phaedra's head moved slowly across the pillow. "No."

Dr. Claudius nodded, his brown eyes gazing steadily into her darker ones. "When was your last monthly flow?" He asked.

Phaedra's gaze faltered as she tried to remember. Finally, she looked up. "I'm not certain."

The doctor covered both Phaedra's hands beneath one of his. "My dear, " he said with a smile, "you are about to become a mother."

Tisha uttered a tiny scream of delight. Knowing Phaedra's illness was not the work of the brothers, filled her with relief and joy.

"A mother?" Phaedra whispered, her eyes lowering to her belly.

Dr. Claudius nodded. "The weakness and nausea are common symptoms. The fact that you have not had your monthly flow in what I determine to be at least eight weeks, and other changes in your body, enabled me to make the dianosis."

"My God." Phaedra caressed her flat stomach with both her hands. "A baby? I'm going to have a baby? Zephir… Zephir is going to be a father?"

"Zephir?" Dr. Claudius questioned, turning his eyes to Tisha.

"Phaedra's husband."

"Well, my goodness. Where is he? We must congratulate him!"

"No!" Phaedra snapped, her gaze turning stormy. "I want no one to know of this. No one. You both must give me your word that you will not speak of this."

Dr. Claudius and Tisha exchanged uneasy glances, but finally nodded.

A baby…A baby and Zephir is going to be a father! Phaedra recanted over and over in her head. The nausea and dizziness that had plagued her for so long, left and was replaced by anxiety and happiness.

That evening, Phaedra made her first appearance at the dinner table since she had arrived at Toussaints. When she practically glided into the dining room, Marquis, Carlos and Dante could not help but acknowledge how radiant she appeared.

"This is quite a surprise." Marquis noted, leaning back in his chair located at the head of the long table.

Phaedra shrugged her shoulders, while a serene look crossed her face. "It's quite a surprise to me as well. I feel wonderful."

"You're positively glowing," Dante noted lightly, as he cut into the baked chicken on his plate.

"I believe you're right," she agreed. "In fact, Dante, I feel so wonderful, I think I may organize a ball."

"A ball?!" The brothers simultaneously exclaimed.

"Mmm hmm." Phaedra pushed herself away from the table. "I'll be twenty in almost one month. I think a ball would be the perfect way to celebrate." She added two more pieces of chicken to her heaping plate.

"Well…this is a bit sudden, Phaedra," Carlos said, his brown eyes narrowing slightly.

"I think I'm entitled. Especially since my nineteenth birthday was such a disaster."

The brothers exchanged guarded looks across the table. When Phaedra returned with her plate, they all watched her-stupefied. Within twenty minutes, the girl had wolfed down three heaping portions of the dinner. They had never witnessed her eat so much and looked on in stunned amazement.

"Well…that was quite delicious." She dabbed her lips with a linen napkin. "That should give me more than enough energy to get started on arranging this ball."

"Are you sure about this?" Carlos asked.

"Positive. I'll keep you all informed of the plans," she sang as she bounced out of the room.

Dante waited until Phaedra left the room then leaned forward to pin his brother's with a stony expression. "I thought everything was under control. Now it's an even bigger mess than before," he whispered.

"I agree," Marquis added.

"You agree," Carlos repeated, watching his brother strangely. Marquis was always the one who kept a positive outlook on the darkest situations. If he was discouraged, where would that leave them?

Marquis pushed his chair back and stood at the head of the table. "This has turned into an even bigger mess. We need to devise a plan that will allow for no mistakes."

Dante cleared his throat. "Well Marq, in all fairness, our plan was perfect. If only Phaedra hadn't come back."

"That still could have worked to our advantage when she fell ill," Marquis reminded his brother.

"That damn Tisha. Cleaning potion, bah! I'd wager everything it was for that little wench!" Carlos snapped, pounding his fists against the table.

"My brothers, we will not leave this table until we organize a plan," Marquis stated, resuming his seat.

Dante nodded and rubbed his palms together. "A foolproof plan."

"A deadly plan," Marquis corrected.

Phaedra emersed herself in the planning of her twentieth birthday celebration. There was so much to do in such a short period of time, that it took the assistance of Tisha and most of the household staff. Of course, no one minded. Having such a gay mood settle over the estate was good for everyone. Besides, it would keep her cousin's preoccupied until they were enough off kilter for her put her own plan into affect.

Tisha was especially pleased by the transformation that had taken place in Phaedra's personality. Though none of the other servants were aware that their mistress was with child, they all commented on the brightness of her mood and the excitement welling in her eyes.

"You're not overdoing things, are you, love?"

Phaedra finished stuffing the brown leather satchel with the last of the telegrams and smiled. "No, I feel just fine."

"Have you felt any movement from the baby" Tisha asked, leaning back to study the floral arrangement on the black piano at the rear of the ballroom.

Setting the satchel to the armchair, Phaedra stood. "Not yet. I keep praying for a sign that it is actually in there." She patted her stomach.

Tisha turned and studied Phaedra. Her thin brows rose when she took in the minute plumpness of the young woman's face and the small bulge of her belly. "Oh, it is actually in there."

"Mmm hmm," Phaedra pointedly replied, hearing the teasing tone in her friend's voice.

"Is that the last of the telegrams?" Tisha asked, getting up to stroll across the ballroom.

"This is it. I'll have one of the girls take it out to the coachman later."

"Is there one in there for Zephir?"

The smile instantly vanished from Phaedra's lips, and she looked down. "I already had one sent out to his parents Carmelita and Tumba Mfume," She whispered.

"Will you try to contact him?"

"How Tisha?" Phaedra snapped. "I don't know where he is. He left without one word to me, dammit!"

Tisha folded her arms across her chest. She was undaunted by

Phaedra's temper. "Don't you think he should know that you are carrying his child?"

Phaedra shook her head. The long heavy braid she sported, slapped her bottom. "That's something he will never know."

"Phaedra—"

"Never, Tisha. It would be best if I never saw Zephir Mfume again."

CHAPTER 14

Two weeks later, guests began to arrive for the celebration. The beach began to resemble a loading dock. There were ships dotting the shore and cove.

Toussaints Plantation began to resemble an inn. Extra house servants were needed to assist with showing guests to their rooms, unloading ships and preparing the food. The guest list consisted of friends as well as family who had not visited in years. It seemed that everyone decided to attend the birthday ball and Phaedra could not have been happier. She was elated to see her beloved home return to the lovely, loving place it had once been. There were so many people, some feared everyone would not fit into the huge house. However, the party had been planned to perfection and everyone was comfortable.

"Phaedra, child?" Carmelita Mfume called when she spotted her daughter-in-law rushing toward her.

"Oh, it's so good to see you," Phaedra whispered, drawing the woman into a close hug. When Tumba Mfume patted her shoulder, she looked up. "Papa." She fell into her

father-in-law's strong arms. The embrace was so assuring, for a moment, she imagined she was actually in Zephir's arms.

Carmelita, with her keen intuition, could sense Phaedra's mood. She could tell the girl was trying hard not to ask about her son. "Come walk with me a moment, child."

Phaedra looked up into Tumba's handsome, face and pulled away. "Your room has already been prepared, so just tell the servants who you are, and they will take you there."

Tumba pressed a kiss to Phaedra's cheek then glanced at his wife. "Don't wear the girl out with talk, Carmel. Planning this ball has worn her out, I can tell."

"I won't wear her out with talk, my love. I promise." Carmelita clasped her hands together as she savored the kiss Tumba planted on her lips. When she and Phaedra were alone, Carmelita smiled knowingly. "We've had no word from Zephir, bonita."

"Did I ask about him?" Phaedra curtly retorted, turning away so Carmelita could not see the tears sparkling in her eyes.

"It is quite clear that you miss him."

"After what he did? I have to disagree with you there."

"That did not end your love for him."

"How would you know?!" Phaedra snapped, whirling around to face her mother-in-law. "You have no idea how much Zephir hurt me with this disappearance of his!"

Silence settled between the two women for a long while. Soon, tiny sobs rose in Phaedra's throat. She tried to stifle them, but that was useless. Carmelita rushed forward to draw her close as a flood of tears broke free.

"Why did he do this, Carmelita? Why did he leave when we were so happy?"

"Shh…my love. I'm sure this was something he had to do."

"But, why couldn't he tell me? We've been so close…"

"Child, sometimes men…well, they do things that we women do not understand. Many times, they will not share their deepest thoughts—thinking they are protecting us. Now you can either question him—which he may not approve of—or you can accept his decision to handle whatever it is, on his own."

Phaedra pulled away and pinned Carmelita with her gaze. "He could have at least told me that he was going."

"That is true, I agree. Perhaps you'll want to discuss that with him when he returns."

"Ha! Returns? I doubt Zephir will be returning here."

Carmelita shook her head. Her dark eyes twinkled as she took in the exquisite young woman before her. There was no way her son would ever let the beauty go. "I would have to disagree with you there, my dear. My son will reappear in your life sooner than you expect it."

"I must admit, I don't think this ball would be a good idea. But it just may be the answer to our prayers."

Dante and Carlos exchanged glances, before looking at their brother.

"Meaning?" Dante asked.

Marquis looked out the window of his study. His brown eyes scanned the crowded back lawn, which teemed with people and luggage. "The distraction of the party will allow us to go forth with our plan. Once it is put into effect, Phaedra will be far too frightened to remain. Besides, she will have her pick of family to leave with."

"And the land will be ours," Carlos predicted.

"Exactly." Marquis turned away from the windows. "Will we be able to depend on your assistance, Margantis?"

The tall figure lurking at the edge of the study stepped forward. His long, black cloak fell well past his ankles to shroud the heavy black boots he wore. A hood covered his head and face, giving him a look that was clearly sinister.

Margantis nodded, but did not issue a verbal reply. The reputed witchdoctor was a man of few words, but his knowledge of the occult was infinite.

Marquis rubbed his hands together and nodded. "Well, let's get this meeting underway, shall we?"

The brothers began their secret meeting with their accomplice. Though the plan they had concocted would have fatal consequences, none of them held any reservations. In fact, they were eager to put their deadly scheme into motion.

"Phaedra, the house is so beautiful. How you ever manage to keep such a huge estate is beyond me."

"Well, I do have a lot of help," Phaedra laughingly replied. Jasmine Toussaint's wide grin brightened her lovely, honey-toned face. Jasmine had demanded that her first cousin take her on a tour of the mansion the instant she arrived. Of course, Phaedra was happy to oblige.

"What's in here?" Jasmine asked, pointing to one of the double mahogany doors down the corridor they were about to leave.

"This is Marquis's study. Dante and Carlos each have one just like it," Phaedra explained, pulling the doors open.

Marquis bolted from his chair the instant the doors opened. "Phaedra!" he barked.

"I'm sorry," she whispered, grinning sheepishly. She was about to leave and close the doors when she noticed the hooded figure seated amidst her cousins. "I wasn't aware you all were having a meeting today."

"This is not a meeting," Carlos quickly corrected.

Phaedra asssessed that her cousins were definitely up to something, and she walked into the study. "Then this must be a member of the family I have yet to meet?"

"Phaedra, this is an old friend of ours and we were right in the middle of a conversation, so—"

"Well, I'm Phaedra Toussaint, and I like to know who all my guests are, so—"

"Phaedra please, we were right in the middle of something," Marquis said.

"And you can't take a moment to introduce your two cousins to your friend?" Phaedra snapped, her eyes narrowing dangerously.

Tiring of the bantering and nervous as well, Dante dropped an arm around Phaedra and Jasmine's shoulders. "We will be happy to introduce everyone later." He quickly hustled the two young women out of the room.

"My word!" Jasmine gasped as the doors slammed shut before her face. Her small, light eyes widened as she looked at her cousin. "What in the world is going on in there?"

"Nothing good," Phaedra softly replied.

The great dining hall had to be rearranged for the birthday gathering. Instead of one long table in the center of the room, there were now four. Each one had been elegantly set with white, embroidered tablecloths, silver candleabras, fragrant flowers and the best silverware and china. In the middle of each table, sat a robust succulent turkey that was baked to a golden brown. Flavorful juices oozed from the bird, boasting its tastiness. Surrounding the fowl were bowls of dressing, fresh vegetables, oven baked breads, hearty casseroles and gravies. On the cherry hutch at the rear of the dininghall sat five different cakes, plates of cookies and several pies.

For a while, the only sounds in the grand room were those of clattering silverware and glasses. Everyone enjoyed the delicious feast courtesy of the cooks—who enjoyed the meal along with the rest of the housestaff.

Carmelita Mfume had been playfully admonishing her husband about the amount of food he planned to eat. When she turned toward Phaedra, her mouth fell open in surprise. The portions on Phaedra's plate clearly outweighed Tumba Mfume's, and Carmelita was stunned. Besides having enough food on her plate to feed four adults, Phaedra seemed famished enough to eat more after she finished.

"Phaedra? Dear, haven't you been eating?" Carmelita finally asked, watching the shapely young woman devouring a massive leg quarter.

"Hmm?" Phaedra absently replied, dipping a corner of soft white bread into her giblet gravy.

"You look as though you haven't eaten in weeks," Carmelita noted.

Phaedra laughed and waved off her mother-in-law's observation. "Oh, I've been eating, but it's not everyday the cooks prepare a feast like this."

"I see," Carmelita whispered, leaning back in her chair. *Good Lord, she looks like she's eating for…for two!* The silent thought repeated itself over again. Suddenly, the look in her eyes turned questioning.

Tisha felt a headache coming after dinner and decided to retire to her bedchamber. She was just about to turn the doorknob when her name was called. A small woman with deep skin, hair and eyes was hurrying toward her.

"Tisha?"

"Yes…I am Tisha Tou."

"I'm sorry if I startled you. My name is Carmelita Mfume."

The guarded look in Tisha's brown stare was replaced by a softer one. "Yes, my Phaedra's mother-in-law."

Carmelita acknowledged the statement. "That's right."

"She speaks very highly of you and your husband." Tisha clasped her hands together before her waist.

"Well, we love her very much, and may I compliment you on raising such a lovely young woman."

Tisha nodded. "Thank you and may I compliment you on your son. He is a very handsome young man, and very much in love with Phaedra."

A worried frown brought Carmelita's arched brows closer. "I agree, but I get the feeling that no one is aware that Phaedra and Zephir have married."

"Unfortunately, she's decided to keep that hidden."

"But, why?"

Tisha sighed and looked away. "Phaedra has seen the need to keep many things secret as of late."

"Including the child she is carrying?"

Tisha's wide eyes snapped to Carmelita's face."How did you—"

"Besides the fact that she is eating like a bear, I have a

certain…insight when it comes to people and secrets."

Tisha's lashes closed slowly, and then she looked upon Carmelita Mfume with renewed interest. "I seem to have that same ability…as does Phaedra."

"I'm aware."

The two women exchanged knowing smiles and joined hands.

"Oh Tisha! This is such wonderful news!" Carmelita sang, her face glowing with happiness.

Tisha was overjoyed. "It truly is!"

"But, why won't she tell anyone? This is not something to keep hidden."

"I agree. She especially wants Zephir left out of it."

Carmelita's stare faltered as she nodded. "I am sure. After the way he left."

"Why did he leave her that way?"

"Oh Tisha, I learned long ago not to try analyzing my son's spontaneous character. I believe that it was something of great importance, though. He may think he is acting in his wife's best interest, trying to protect her."

"As true as that may be, Carmelita, I hope that he returns. Soon."

The next afternoon, while most of the guests had adjourned to their bedchambers, Phaedra went for a walk. She realized that she had not ventured out since returning home. Her steps took her to the cliffs overlooking the ocean—her favorite place. Though she planned not to be away from the house for long, that changed the moment she began to walk.

The incredible trees stood firm as their leaves danced wildly overhead. The high wind whipped through her hair, causing it to swirl in a black cloud around her , oval face. Pulling the long, green wrap from her shoulders, she spread it on the high grass and sat down. For a moment, she lookd blankly out over the ocean—her thoughts on Zephir. Lord, she missed him so!

"No!" she whispered in a fierce tone and shook her head to ward off the image of her incredibly handsome husband. *No, he made his choice…and I've made mine.*

The crashng waves captured Phaedra's attention. She inhaled the clean sea air. Everything was so peaceful, she could almost forget her troubles…

"Phaedra?"

Turning at the sound of a woman's voice calling to her, Phaedra saw her Aunt Saeeda, her father's eldest sister.

"Is something the matter, Auntie?" Phaedra quickly asked, brushing leaves from her skirts as she stood.

"No, no , child. There is something I need to give to you," Saeeda whispered, stopping a few feet in front of her niece.

Phaedra's wide, eyes lowered. "A book?"

Saeeda glanced toward the bound hardback in her hands. "It belonged to Fredericks."

"My father? This is my father's? Why wouldn't he have kept it?"

"There were things here that he did not want certain people to discover."

Phaedra pushed her windblown hair out of her face and held it back with her hand. "What things?"

"Suspicions."

"About?"

"The family. More specifically—Marquis, Dante and Carlos."

"Oh," Phaedra groaned, turning away from her aunt.

Saeeda grimaced. "He always believed their minds had been corrupted by their mother. Still, he felt he had to take care of them after what happened to Duvalier, their father."

"But what did that have to do with me? Why would he trust those devils to watch over me? Protect me?"

"My love—"

"Do you have any idea what they have put me through?!" Phaedra cried, her pulse racing with anger.

Saeeda rushed forward to take Phaedra's hands. "Child, listen to me. Your father felt guilty about those boys from the moment they lost Duvalier. When Lucia died, he felt even more pity for them. In many ways he was so blind to their ways; blinding by his own feelings of responsibility for what happened to their father."

Suddenly, losing the strength to stand, Phaedra dropped to the ground. "Why did you all leave me?" she whispered.

Saeeda clasped her hands together and turned away. "We never really understood why Fredericks entrusted them with your safety. We sent correspondences. Fredericks knew any of us would have happily taken you."

"My father…my father was dying. You could have come for me."

"Phaedra—"

"You could have taken me. I would have gladly left then."

Saeeda dropped to the ground beside Phaedra. "Love, no one wanted a confrontation with those boys."

"I don't believe this! You sound as though you are afraid of them!"

"We were!" Saeeda cried, pushing herself off the ground. "Lucia was evil, and she passed the trait onto her sons. They were willing students."

"I can't believe this. Marquis, Carlos and Dante are children beneath you. How could you give them that sort of power over your minds?"

Remembering her reason for being there, Saeeda retrieved the thick book from the tall grass. "Perhaps this can explain your father's reasoning."

"What's in this?" Phaedra thumbed through the crisp pages.

"Fredericks kept a journal. He began it when we left Haiti. Perhaps it will give you more insight into your cousins and all that happened when you were much younger."

"I already know my cousins are evil!" Phaedra spat, crossing her arms over her chest.

Saeeda looked out over the ocean and the shore dotted with ships.

"Maybe it will help you understand why we were reluctant to interfere."

"What could this tell me that I don't already know?"

Saeeda shrugged her rounded shoulders. "If you are anything like your mother, I am sure you have had...I am sure you have seen things that have confused or frightened you. Perhaps this will give you answers. If anything, it should draw you closer to your father and mother."

Phaedra watched her aunt for a moment then nodded. Saeeda pressed a soft kiss to her cheek then headed back toward the main house. The book rested in Phaedra's hands like a heavy weight filled with secrets. She decided not to waste time and carried the journal up to her room. There, she set the book in the middle of her bed and began to read from the first page.

June 18, 1860
From the Journal of Fredericks Toussaint

Chapel wasted no time getting the family out of Haiti. It is the only home any of us has ever known. None of us know what to expect.

We are sailing to Dominica, a very small island in the Carribean. There, we are to meet our father's brother Jurel Toussaint. Our uncle was a slave freed by his master just before the slave revolt of 1791. Jurel's master owned a vast plantation on the island, but died without any family to aquire the land. Uncle Jurel was the man's one loyal companion, and he was rewarded for that. The plantation was given to him, and it flourished beneath his hand. Now, dying from extreme old age, Jurel wants the land passed to his family. He sent word long ago of this matter and, at last, we are responding.

Though we are all apprehensive about this relocation, I believe it will be best for us all. Especially, my Marguerite. She is with child, and a change of environment will certainly be good for her and the baby.

I do not know how I could have survived this long without her. She is my life, and now we are to share a child. Marguerite has already decided to name the child Phaedra. Her extraordinary gift of sight has told her the baby will be a girl. Of course, we have had our spats about the name. From the Greek mythology, Phaedra married Theseus, then fell in love with her own stepson-Hippolytes. I did not think such a name was appropriate for our child. Marguerite, however, assured me she chose the name because of its beauty. It struck something in her. She has told me that while her visions have not let her glimpse our babe's face, she knows in her heart that our daughter will be a great beauty. I can only pray my Phaedra will possess the inner beauty and spirit of my beloved Marquerite...

The words grew blurred and Phaedra realized that her eyes were filled with tears. Unable to continue reading her father's beautiful words, she skimmed the pages for later passages. From an insertion written on March 20, 1861, she read...

...It sickens me to even think such a thing, but in my deepest heart, I know it is true. Lucia has hated Marguerite and I since Duvalier's death—perhaps long before...Still, to think my own sister could have murdered my wife, it is just too unreal. I suppose it was the way she and the boys behaved at the funeral. There was a calm, almost confident, aura about them. I always knew Marguerite suspected them of great evil. Perhaps she had more than suspicions. There may have been more, but now I will never know. I keep a picture of our family with me. It is the only thing I have to remind me of the entire family together. Though it was a portrait of happier times, Lucia and the boys have that same detached, calm, unaffected look on their faces. It was as if they knew the family would flee Haiti just one week after it was taken.

"Papa knew…" Phaedra sighed, as her fingers brushed the words on the page. Her father had suspicions, as did she. If only she could be positive that the same figure in the dream was her aunt…From behind the page she had just read, she discovered the picture her father had mentioned in his writings. It was extremely old and wrinkled, yet she could make out each figure. A light smile touched her lips as her eyes lingered on her father and mother—who held a small baby. Phaedra brushed their images then moved on to other people in the picture. When she looked upon her Aunt Lucia, she froze. Phaedra pulled her hand away as though it burned to touch the portrait. Her thoughts immediately returned to her dreams. There was always one thing she could clearly see—the hand with the charm dangling from the wrist. In the picture around Lucia's wrist, was the exact charm bracelet!

"My God…" she breathed, brushing the charm in the photo. She set the book aside and jumped off the bed. Racing out of the room and down the hall, her intentions were to find Tisha. Her room door was open, but the woman was nowhere in sight.

"I need you…" Phaedra sighed, brushing her hands across her arms to ward off the sudden chill that had overcome her. The change in temperature was so noticible that Phaedra went to check the windows for cracks. They were sealed tight, and she stood there for a moment deep in thought. Looking out of the windows, she saw the stables and decided to look for Tisha there.

"Monroe, have you seen Tisha today?"

Monroe Denault scratched his thick bush of hair and squinted against the sun. "Sorry, Miss Phaedra, I have not. I have been trying to find her myself."

"And she hasn't been in the stables any today?"

"I am sorry, Miss."

Phaedra patted Monroe's shoulder and gave him a rueful look. "I'll just take another look in her room. Thank you, Monroe."

Instead of heading straight back upstairs, Phaedra searched the bottom level of the house. None of the houseservants had seen Tisha, and it was not like the woman not to check on the house. Phaedra's slow steps eventually lead her back to Tisha's room. As soon as she cleared the doorway, an intense wave of dizziness washed over her. Careful, so she would not fall, she made it over to the bed. Phaedra curled her hand around the bedpost and took several deep breaths. She could not shake the errie sense of foreboding that filled the room.

Phaedra wound up falling asleep on Tisha's bed. When she awoke, Tisha had not returned. The room seemed even colder. Phaedra left quickly and got ready for that evening's dinner.

"Have you seen Tisha?"

Marquis stroked his smooth, cheek and frowned. "No, why?"

"I haven't seen her all day."

"There are a lot of people here, Phaedra. Perhaps she had found a friend."

Phaedra's head tilted, and she fixed him with a suspicious glare. "Friend or no, she would not ignore her household duties."

"She is a grown woman, Phaedra. I'm sure she will report to you soon." He sneered then bowed low before his cousin and stepped away.

Phaedra's captivating onyx glare followed him out of the room.

Tisha's absense from dinner was missed by everyone. The vibrant, older woman had captured each guests' heart, and they all looked forward to colorful stories of her life in her homeland of Barbados. Phaedra was so worried, she could barely eat. When she adjourned to her bedchamber, later than night, a terribly confusing dream contributed to a restless nights sleep.

CHAPTER 15

Phaedra took a deep breath as she stared up at the high ceiling. Today was her twentieth birthday. In twelve hours she would be a twenty year old woman and the stipulation would be met. .The smug smile slowly vanished from her lovely face as her thoughts returned to Tisha. How she wished that she could dismiss her suspicions that the brothers had initiated her disappearance. Talking to Marquis the night before, only intensified her suspicions.

All thoughts of celebrating gone from her mind, Phaedra whipped the covers back and ran from the room. Just as she had done the day before, she ran to Tisha's bedchamber. There was no sign of Tisha having returned. The chamber seemed even colder than the day before. There was no doubt in Phaedra's mind that something terrible had happened to her dear friend.

The entire plantation was alerted to Tisha's disappearance that morning. Many of the men took off on searching expeditions while the women searched closer to the main house.

Phaedra tried to keep her spirits up in light of the ball that was to take place that evening. Though the arrangements for the party had already been confirmed, Phaedra still doublechecked. She made sure the ballroom was in pristine condition, that there was more than enough food and that her dress was pressed and ready. In all the confusion, Phaedra realized that she had not had time to dwell on the greatest aspect of her life—her baby. She could do nothing to jeopardize its well being. Zephir's disappearance and now Tisha, Phaedra knew she would die if she lost her child.

"Phaedra? Dear, are you okay in there?"

Looking up from the shiny ballroom floor, Phaedra saw Carmelita Mfume standing in the doorway. "I'm fine." She headed over to her mother-in-law. "Just making sure everything is in order for tonight."

Carmelita glanced around the ballroom. "It will be a lovely event."

"Yes…" Phaedra sighed, closing her eyes.

"Oh my love, Tisha will return. I know it."

"But, are you sure?"

Carmelita could not admit that and simply came forward to envelope Phaedra in a tight embrace.

"Where is she?"

Carmelita turned Phaedra around and stared deeply into the young woman's eyes. "Listen to me, we may not know what has happened to Tisha, but I know she would not want to see you this way. Upset and worried over her, especially in your condition."

Phaedra's eyes flashed with surprise as she tilted her head to one side. "What condition?"

"The baby."

"Dammit! I told—"

"No one told me. I figured it out, and Tisha could not deny it."

Phaedra pulled away from Carmelita and walked off. "I don't want anyone to know," she said, thankful that she was still not showing overmuch.

"Especially Zephir?"

"Carmelita…"

"Phaedra, dear, I don't understand your reasoning, but it's not the important thing now. Tisha would not want you upset on your birthday. Not when you have managed to reunite your family for the celebration."

Shaking her head, Phaedra walked to the double glass doors at the rear of the balcony. The doors led out to the western side of the estate. Carmelita followed and watched Phaedra stand out amidst the flowery trail leading to the stables.

"It's so difficult keeping a smile on my face, knowing she's somewhere out there!" she cried, waving her hands in the air.

Carmelita descended the steps that led outdoors. "I know, child, but you have a responsibility to your guests and yourself to enjoy this night."

Before Phaedra could answer, she felt a hard nudge in back of her head. Turning, she found Midnight standing behind her. Laughter escaping her lips, she pressed a hard kiss to the black Arabian's nose and patted his neck.

"Perhaps you're right, Carmelita." She hoisted herself onto Midnight's bare back. "I think I'll take a ride."

Carmelita rushed forward, waving her hands. "You cannot in your condition!"

"We'll keep it down to a trot or a brisk walk, I promise, but I cannot go back inside. Not now."

Grateful to see some light in Phaedra's eyes, Carmelita did not argue further. She watched the great horse trot away and shook her head.

"Zephir Carlito Mfume, you idiot. Get back here to your wife and child," she whispered.

The instant Phaedra set foot in the ballroom, everyone turned. The conductor instructed the band to lower the volume on the enchanting piece they played. The music graudally faded into another tune, and the guests began to sing a song in Phaedra's honor.

A soft, genuine smile touched her lips as she gazed around the room. Carmelita was right; Tisha would want her to enjoy the night.

So much family filling the room with their love and laughter was certainly cause to celebrate. Everyone rushed forward to greet her then. They were so full of best wishes, she could not help but smile.

The evening was filled with eating, drinking and dancing. Every man at the ball wanted a dance; and Phaedra was happy to comply. In addition to all the offers to dance, she received just as many proposals of marriage. Phaedra turned them down easy and tried not to let the offers turn her thoughts to Zephir.

After several dances, her appetite was reawakened. The fact that she had not been eating heartily, had come back to haunt her. Luckily, the ballroom had been set with three tables filled with food. It did not take Phaedra long to wield her way through the guests and fill a plate.

"This is wonderful," she said, adding three cream puffs to her crowded dish. She popped one of the soft puffs into her mouth and closed her eyes to savor its sweet taste.

"You know, you are far too lovely to stand here wasting your time alone at this table."

Phaedra choked a bit on the cream puff as her eyes snapped open. It took quite an effort to swallow the morsel, but she managed to do so. She whirled around, her onyx stare blazing when she saw Zephir Mfume's gorgeous face.

"You…" she whispered, her long lashes fluttering close as her legs weakened.

Zephir's reflexes were quick. "Whoa…" he whispered, catching her and the plate before it fell to the floor.

Phaedra did not notice the plate, her eyes were trained on her husband. For a moment, she took in the incredible, missed sight of him. His striking features were marked so clearly in her mind, she would never be able to forget him. It was as though she had seen him only yesterday.

Unfortunately, that was far from true, and the reality of what happened came back like a slap in the face.

Phaedra felt her palm ache with the need to strike him. Before she could make any moves though, Zephir had slid his hands around her waist and was pulling her close.

"You're not smiling," he cooly said.

Phaedra's lashes fluttered from the surge of anger racing through her. "You horse's ass. If we were not in a room full of people, I would slap you."

The grin tugging at Zephir's mouth was knowing and exuded an unmistakeable wickedness. His fingers rose to stroke the line of her neck then dipped to brush across the swell of her cleavage. "I don't think you mean that."

"I'm not going to cause a scene before my guests," she whispered.

Zephir's intense expression seemed to grow more fixed. "I'm afraid we've already done that, love."

Phaedra took a moment to glance around the room. Sure enough, almost every eye was on them. She could just imagine what thoughts raced through their minds. The men were wondering who Zephir was and why she was allowing him to hold and touch her so deliberately. The women were thinking how magnificent Zephir was and cursing Phaedra for having all his

attention.

"Damn you to hell, Zephir Mfume. How dare you come here like this?" she furiously whispered.

"Like what?" Zephir challenged, his sleek brows drawing close over his slanting gaze. "Like your husband? Because, in case you have forgotten, that's who I am."

"In case I've forgottem?!" Phaedra cried, desperately trying to keep her words to a whisper. "You were the one who ran off without a word!"

"There were reasons—"

"Ha!"

Zephir's hands tightened around Phaedra's waist and caused her to gasp. "Listen to me, we need to talk. I prefer not to do it now, though."

"If you think that you can come back into my life like nothing's happened—"

"That's exactly what I think, and I'm damned well entitled."

"Entitled?" Phaedra retorted as she struggled in the embrace. "You bastard, let me go."

Zephir's grin was not humorous. "Now, love, remember our guests. Dance with me."

"You go to hell."

Zephir leaned back on his long legs, his eyes searching hers. "I have watched you for the last hour, twirling around this floor with every man here and you cannot grant me one dance?"

Phaedra's chin rose in defiance. "That's exactly right."

Zephir did not bother to waste time with more words. He kept one arm around Phaedra's waist and escorted her to the dance floor. He knew she was confused and hurt, and he could not blame her. The last two months were perhaps the most difficult in his entire life. Not having her around and not knowing what she was doing or how she was, almost drove him mad.

Though the dance floor was practically full, onlookers cleared the way when they saw Zephir. He stopped in the middle of the floor and pulled his wife close. Phaedra wanted to melt in his arms the moment they began swaying to the music. Praying for some sort of control over her emotions, she placed her hands over the bulging muscles in his arms. She hoped the ingenuine smile on her lips had the guests convinced.

"I've missed you," Zephir whispered, bowing his head low to rest his face in the crook of Phaedra's neck. His sensuous lips smoothed across the base of her throat, while his hands massaged her bare back. As he inhaled the sweet, soft scent of her, he could feel his manhood lengthen and firm in response to having her so close.

Phaedra shivered, not from the cold, but from the rush of incredible pleasure she felt at the man's touch. His massive hands glided across her bare back then rose to brush the sides of her breasts.

"Zephir, stop this."

"What?"

"You know exactly what," she said through a tight lips.

Zephir chuckled as his lips tugged on her earlobe.

"Stop!" she gasped, feeling his even teeth fasten to the soft flesh.

Zephir rose to his full height and looked down at her. "What is it, Phaedra? Afraid you may lose control?"

"Never!"

"Or maybe," he began, glancing around the ballroom, "maybe you're afraid of upsetting one of the poor fools in this room."

"What are you talking about?" she snapped, her lovely features twisted into a frown.

Zephir shrugged. "I've been away a long time."

"So?"

Bringing his index finger beneath her chin, Zephir forced her to look directly at him. "I would hate to discover that another has tried to take my place."

Phaedra slapped his finger away. "You filthy ogre. No one has tried to take your place, as you say. No one even knows we are married."

Zephir did not appear offended. "Keeping secrets?"

"I have my reasons." She lowered her gaze to the floor.

"As did I, when I left."

"Without a word?" Phaedra reminded him, her body stiffening in his arms once more.

Zephir uttered a heavy sigh and pulled his wife closer. She smelled of sweet peaches and her body was so voluptuous and soft...it was all he could do not to take her upstairs and bed her.

"My love," he whispered after several moments of silence, "have you gained weight?"

The innocent question was like a dash of cold water in Phaedra's face. Her hands curled into tiny fists, which she pounded against his hard chest. "You jackass!" she cried in a furious whisper.

"What?" Zephir questioned, his slanted charcoal gaze widening in confusion.

"Excuse us, Phaedra?"

The married couple turned to find two men standing behind them. One of the men was Phaedra's cousin, Devin Toussaint. The other was a field hand.

"What is it, Dev?" Phaedra asked, a small frown coming to her face.

Devin stepped forward and took her hand. "Where are Marquis, Carlos and Dante?"

"I haven't seen them. What is it?" Phaedra asked again, her voice sounding more firm.

Devin glanced around the room. "I need to talk with them."

"About?"

"Phaedra..." Devin trailed away. He glanced at Zephir, who towered above them all.

Phaedra grabbed the lapel of Devin's jacket and forced him to look at her. "If there is something wrong, Devin, I have a right to know. I am the overseer of this estate."

Zephir liked the confident, authoritative tone in his wife's voice. Unfortunately, it looked as though Devin was uneasy speaking with her about the matter. Sensing something was terribly wrong and believing the Toussaint brothers were behind it all, Zephir stepped forward.

"My name is Zephir Mfume. I'm Phaedra's husband and you are?"

Devin's mouth fell open at the news. His wide gaze shifted between his cousin and the , man at her side. "Oh...I-I had no idea—"

"Zephir, this is my cousin, Devin Toussaint," Phaedra interrupted. "Now, Devin, will you please tell me what is going on?!"

Instead, Devin stepped closer and pulled Zephir aside. "Mr. Mfume, we should speak privately."

"You will not speak privately, unless I'm right there to hear it," Phaedra haughtily informed them.

Devin bowed his head momentarily then turned his black stare toward Zephir. "She does not need to hear this," he whispered.

Zephir nodded and was about to usher Devin aside, when Phaedra caught both their arms.

"Look Devin, if there is some sort of problem, you are wasting time by being so secretive," she cooly informed him, though her gaze was stormy.

Devin cleared his throat, but did not argue the point further. He took both Phaedra's hands in his and held them tightly. "We found

Tisha, love. I am afraid the news is not good."

Zephir caught Phaedra, who had crumpled like a paperdoll at the mention of Tisha's name. Holding his wife securely against his chest, he caught Devin's eye. "What do you mean, you found her?" he asked.

"Tisha's been missing for several days now," Devin explained, letting go of Phaedra's hands. "Without a word, she simply vanished. There have been many search attempts, but—"

"Where?"

Devin and Zephir looked down at Phaedra, who had spoken.

"What, my love?" Zephir softly queried.

Phaedra stood straight and pinned Devin with her eyes. "Where is she?"

Devin was silent for a moment. Then, he turned to the tall, stout man behind them. "Carver?"

"We found her in the caves, Miss Phaedra," Carver stated, his deep voice resounding like a drum.

"I've got to go to her," Phaedra whispered, trying to pull out of Zephir's grasp, which had suddenly grown tighter around her upper arms.

"There is no chance in hell I'll let you out there," he growled against her ear.

"Zephir is right, Phaedra. This is not something you should see," Devin cautioned.

Phaedra continued to struggle against her husband's unbreakable hold. "Damn you both to hell. I'm not about to stay put here while Tisha's…"

Suddenly, Zephir turned her around to face him. His piercing midnight eyes bored into hers as he jerked her close. "Phaedra, we don't know what condition we'll find Tisha in out there. I will not have you exposed to that."

"I've been exposed to much worse, Zephir. Or have you forgotten? Now, in order to get me to stay here, you will have to knock me out."

Zephir signed and turned to Devin. "What's out there?" he asked.

Devin blinked rapidly and shook his head. "I can't-I can't describe,

You have to see…what they…did to her."

Zephir's mouth tightened to a thin line. "Go fetch your cloak," he finally said to his wife.

Marquis, Carlos and Dante had been located and they joined Zephir, Phaedra, Devin and Carver. Powerful Arabian stallions carried them across the plantation to the edge of the estate. When the riding party arrived at the caves, the area was lit with torches. Several workers who knew Tisha had discovered her in the cave and alerted Carver, the chief field hand.

The moment Phaedra spotted the grim scene before the caves, she tugged sharply on Midnight's reins. Before she could swing off the tall horse, Zephir was off his. He caught her around the waist and helped her down. As soon as her feet touched the ground, she was off running.

"Phaedra!" Zephir bellowed, watching her speed away as though the devil were at her heels. Instead of following, he turned to Devin. "What will she find in there?" he asked, not wanting to breech the subject earlier in his wife's presence.

Devin took a deep breath. "Some sort of ritual took place from what we can tell."

Zephir's frown deepened. "Ritual? What the hell are you talking about?"

"Nooooo! Agggggggh Tishaaaaa! Tishaaaaa…."

Phaedra's piercing cries halted all conversation. The men broke into breakneck sprints, all of them headed to the cave. Inside, hanging spread eagled on one of the cold stone walls was Tisha. Her face had been painted white and she had either been stabbed or pecked by the beak of a large bird, until she bled to death.

Phaedra was on her knees at the woman's feet. Her deafening cries tore at everyone's hearts. Zephir was by her side in an instant. He knelt and pulled her back against his solid, wide chest.

"Shhh…my love, shhhh…" he whispered against her ear as he rocked her slowly.

Phaedra squeezed her eyes shut tight and turned her face into his chest. "Why?" she cried. "Why?"

Zephir had never found himself on the verge of tears before. Hearing the helpless tiny sound of Phaedra's voice took his emotions into overdrive. His long lashes closed over his eyes, and he shook his head. "I don't know, love. I don't know." He sighed, pressing a hard kiss to the top of her head. He held her for the longest time, until her loud cries, became soft whimpers. After a while, he scooped her into his arms and took her out of the cave.

"Take the lady down from that damned wall," he demanded, pinning the field hands with a murderous glare.

CHAPTER 16

"Tisha…" Phaedra whispered her dear friend's name repeatedly as she sat rocking back and forth. The lovely, white gown she had worn for the ball, was now blackened with mud. Phaedra would not go far from the cave, where Tisha's body had been discovered. She sat on a cold, muddy boulder and cried. Her cheeks were wet with tears, and her eyes were red.

Zephir stood a few feet away. He leaned against the trunk of one of the great trees hovering about the mouth of the cave. He knew sitting on the cold stone could not be good for Phaedra, but he did not have the heart to intrude on her mourning. *Dammit!* he silently raged, he knew he had made a huge mistake in allowing her to come back to the island. As upset as he was over Tisha's death, he thanked God that it was not Phaedra hanging on the wall of that cave. He decided from that moment on, nothing would keep him away from his wife. He would know where she was at all times. It was clear that Tisha had been murdered, but why? His every instinct told him that Marquis, Carlos and Dante Toussaint were responsible.

"Phaedra?"

Hearing her cousin mutter her name, filled Phaedra with rage. "What?" she spat.

Marquis cleared his throat, before glancing back at his brothers. "We are all devastated by Tisha's death. It is a terrible shock."

"Mmmm…" she replied, the sorrow leaving her eyes to be replaced by hate.

Dante knelt beside Phaedra and patted her knee. "Perhaps you should leave with Zephir in light of what has happened?"

"Leave?" Phaedra asked, leaning back to watch him curiously.

Carlos took a step closer. "For your own well-being."

"My well-being?"

"Of course." Marquis kneelt next to her as well. "What has happened to Tisha will be on your mind day and night if you stay here. Besides, until we find out who did this—"

"Who did this?" she snapped, jumping to her feet. "We all know who did this!"

"Phaedra," Carlos called in a warning tone.

Phaedra, however, was too far gone to care about what else she said. "I know how much you three bastards want Toussaints."

"You will not speak to us this way, Phaedra!" Marquis ordered.

"I'll speak to you any way I desire! The three of you have done everything you can think of to get this land under your filthy thumbs!"

"How in hell can you say something like that after the way we've taken care of you?"

"Correction Dante, Tisha took care of me! And now she's gone because of you!"

"What the hell are you saying, cousin?" Marquis whispered, his brown gaze stormy.

Phaedra's expression was cold; her black eyes unwavering. "I'm saying that I know you killed her."

"You little bitch!" Dante hissed, taking a step closer to Phaedra. When he heard Zephir clear his throat, he reconsidered moving any closer.

"You have no proof." Carlos stated, straightening his shortwaist linen coat.

"I don't need any. I know you did it. All of this just to get me off this land and leave it to you. I suppose the three of you began to plot when I came back home."

Suddenly, Marquis laughed. "You're grasping at straws, little cousin. You are right about one thing, though, we do want this land. It should be ours. It's the least your father could do after he murdered ours."

"Ha! Your crazy mother told you that to protect herself!"

Dante's wide eyes narrowed. "What are you talking about?"

"Aunt Saeeda presented me with my father's journal. He would have no reason to enter falsehoods in it. There is a detailed account of your father's…murder? Unfortunately, the crime was committed by your own mother who, in a wild rage, pushed him into a roaring fire amidst a Voodoo ceremony she attended!"

"You stop this, Phaedra!"

"No!"

"You have no right to speak of this!"

Phaedra shook her head, loving the murderous looks on her cousins' faces. "I have every right! Why my father ever felt he owed you three anything, is beyond me. Perhaps he felt sorry for you because your father was dead and you had a lunatic for a mother!"

Marquis rushed toward Phaedra with a clenched fist. He halted the moment Zephir moved away from the tree. "I order you to stop this!" he whispered, his fist still raised.

"And I order you off my property!"

"What?" Carlos asked, completely surprised by the roaring demand.

Phaedra had already turned her back. "You heard me. I want all of you out!" She whirled around and pinned them all with a vicious look. Her black, wavy mane whipped around her, giving her a beautiful, yet sinister aura.

"This is just as much our home as it is yours!"

"Not anymore."

"You can't do this to us!" Carlos cried.

Phaedra stopped a few feet away from Midnight and turned. "I can't do this to you? After what you three did to me? You tried to sell me!"

"Tried?" Marquis replied, his eyes shifting to Zephir, whose eyes were focused on Phaedra.

"…then you killed Tisha or, had her killed, I know it," Phaedra continued, not noticing the questioning look on Marquis's face. "So the three of you can just get the hell off Toussaints. Tonight, dammit!"

Marquis saw his brothers about to follow their cousin, but he stopped them.

Carlos glared at his older brother with murderous intent. "What the devil are you doing? We can't just allow her to do this."

"She doesn't know everything. Maybe we can still salvage something." Marquis whispered, watching Phaedra mount her horse and ride away.

Zephir watched Phaedra until she was almost out of view. Snapping his fingers once, he summoned one of the field men to follow her and make sure she returned to the main house. Then, he turned to face the brothers.

Marquis headed over to Zephir, with his brother's following him closely. "Get her out of here, Mr. Mfume."

"Excuse me?" Zephir questioned, his slanting onyx stare narrowing further.

Marquis massaged the back of his neck. "You know how badly we want this land. You, more than anyone, should understand the lengths we will go to to keep it."

"You son of a bitch, I would snap your necks myself if I thought you were worth the trouble." Zephir growled, not bothering to hide his dislike of the men. "I suggest you stay away from my wife or I will not hesitate to provide you three with the most painful deaths I can conjure."

The rough, gravel tone of Zephir's words added an even more sinister element to his fatal promise. Carlos and Dante shuddered beneath the murderous gleam on the man's face. Marquis, however, was more interested in something else.

"You and Phaedra have married?" he asked.

"That's right, and I couldn't have done it without all of your assistance," Zephir sarcastically replied. Leaving the three brothers, he turned and walked over to his horse.

Marquis, Carlos and Dante watched him in silence. Their tempers raged as the reality of their wealth slipping away hit them like a dash of cold water.

The ball ended soon after the word spread about Tisha. Most of the guests retired to their bedchambers, while others talked downstairs in the sitting room.

Once Phaedra secured Midnight in his stall, she dropped to the hay covered floor and cried. *Lord, why Tisha? Why did they have to take her?* If it was the last thing she did, she swore she would make her cousins pay.

A gust of cool air stirred the hay and whisked against Phaedra's back. She turned to see Zephir entering the stable with his horse. In all the madness, she had little time to dwell on the fact that he had returned. If possible, he seemed even more incredible than she remembered. No! No, she would not be taken in by him again! She vowed. If she were to open her heart and he left...

A pair of heavy, black boots appeared beneath her downcast gaze. After a moment, Phaedra looked up the devastating length of Zephir's powerful body. When she stared into his fabulous eyes, she gasped at the intensity of his gaze.

"Are you alright?" he asked as he knelt before her.

Phaedra's words caught in her throat. Her eyes wandered over his magnificent, dark features and she was entranced. Finally, she nodded her head and sighed. "I'm fine."

His eyes narrowed, and he lifted her chin with the tip of his index finger. "Are you sure?" he whispered.

"No," she admitted, feeling the tears pressure her eyes again. Forcing them to remain at bay, she cleared her throat. "I will be fine when I see my cousins pay for what they did."

Zephir brushed away a lone tear that had escaped the corner of Phaedra's eye. "I think you have said everything you need to."

"Mmm mmm," Phaedra disagreed, rising to her feet. "I can't rest until I see them…hurting. Hurting the way they hurt Tisha."

Zephir took a deep breath then stood as well. "Phaedra, I forbid you to see them again."

Phaedra uttered a short laugh in response and watched him in disbelief. "That is something I can't do."

"Phaedra," Zephir called, his tone clearly warning.

Phaedra had already turned and was heading out of the stables. "No!" she shouted across her shoulder.

Back at the main house, Phaedra burst in through the kitchen door and rushed upstairs to prepare for bed. Zephir walked in only minutes behind her and found his way to the bedroom.

"Don't ever turn your back and walk away from me again," he cooly ordered, though his dark eyes glistened with anger.

Phaedra sent him a warning glance and shrugged her shoulders.

Zephir bounded across the room and caught her shoulders in an unbreakable hold. "Do you understand me?"

Stubborness prevented Phaedra from issuing a verbal response. "I understand," she finally whispered when it was clear he wouldn't relent.

"And you will not see your cousins again?"

"I told you I can't do that, Zephir!" she cried.

Zephir cut his eyes away from her and turned. He was so frightened for her and she refused to see how dangerous the situation was. The bed groaned beneath his great weight when he fell against it. "I refuse to argue about this, Phaedra."

"You can't understand this, Zephir," she whispered in an absent tone. "You still have both your parents," she said while removing her jewels then went to work on the gown. "Tisha was all I had. Now she is gone."

Zephir remained silent. His pitch black eyes following her every move. He shook his head, ordering his raging hormones to soothe themselves. He wanted to finish the conversation at hand. "I understand the way you feel, love. But if anyone is to handle your cousins, it will be me."

"You?" Phaedra replied, with a short laugh. "I'm not interested in having them pulverized...well not yet. I have my own ways of avenging Tisha's death."

A furrow formed between Zephir's long brows. "What ways?"

Phaedra took a seat on the satin covered stool before her dressing table and removed her shoes. "It's time I started fighting my cousins using their game. Obviously, Lucia taught her boys the dark magic she practiced. I can use it, too." she muttered. Her anger over Tisha's death caused her to momentarily forget how her husband felt about the supernatural art.

"No!" Zephir raged, leaving the bed as though it burned him to lie upon it. "I won't have you dabbling in that nonsense!"

Phaedra removed her other shoe and threw it to the floor. She stood with her hands propped on her hips and glared at him. "Who the hell are you to give me orders?!"

Zephir wasted no time storming across the room. His fingers curled into the low neckline of her gown. "I'm your husband." He reminded her softly before his mouth crashed down upon hers.

Phaedra moaned as her small hands curved around the biceps that bulged beneath the black velvet suit coat he wore. Her lips parted instantly amidst the onslaught of the lusty kiss.

Zephir uttered a soft helpless sound as he tasted the sweetness of her mouth. Painfully aroused, his tongue thrust repeatedly, parting her lips. The wet strokes deepened each time, filling them both with an indescribable need.

"I'm your husband..." he growled again and pulled her up against him. The need to feel her beneath his body, throbbed within him.

Phaedra curled her arms around his neck and let her slim fingers play in his gorgeous, black hair. Kissing passionately, they approached the bed and fell atop the heavy, green quilt. Zephir pulled away and began to cover her neck with harsh, wet kisses.

"I love you…" he whispered against her skin.

"Then, why did you leave?" she asked, her voice extremely soft as a sob rose in her throat. She felt his breath against her skin as he uttered a heavy sigh.

"I had to deal with Lezard, my love."

"Lezard? Cantone Lezard is the reason that you left me in Cuba without a word?" she whispered, her midnight stare was accusing as she looked up into his handsome face.

Zephir planted his face in the crook of her neck and inhaled her scent. "I knew you would be safe there. Unfortunately, I knew you would either follow me or try to get back here on your own. I couldn't chance that. You were so determined…I asked Dubois to bring you."

Her aggravation renewed, Phaedra pushed Zephir away and moved off the bed. "You talk to me about letting matters rest with my cousins and you can't even stop chasing after Cantone Lezard."

"I had no choice."

"Hmph." She unfastened the hooks and snaps on her gown. "We were well away from him. There was no reason for you to go back to look for him, love."

Zephir rested his head in his hands and watched Phaedra with intense longing in his eyes. "He threatened to kill us."

Phaedra turned, her eyes wide. "What?"

"That's right." He confirmed. "I suppose you made more of an impression on him than you realized. He was upset after losing that chalet, but it was nothing compared to this."

"Well, is he-is he…dead?"

Zephir's expression hardened. "Unfortunately, not. Our last encounter was bloody, but he was being sheltered by friends, and I was unable to get to him and finish the job."

As Zephir recounted his adventure, Phaedra continued to undress. She never realized how much she tortured her husband with the unconsciously seductive removal of her clothing. Zephir's words soon trailed off, and he simply watched her. When the dress, hoopskirt and pantaloons were removed, she stepped behind the changing curtain at the rear of the room and donned a short, white shift.

"Take that off, too," Zephir requested from the bed.

Phaedra glanced over her shoulder to find him frowning. She shook her head and ignored the command as she resumed her place at the dressing table. If she stripped completely, they would surely make love, and she could not risk becoming attached to him that way again. Besides, he had

already commented on her slight weight gain. He was certain to notice the small, but noticeable

increase in her size if she were nude. Forcing her eyes to the looking glass, she began to remove the pins from her coiffure.

A surprised gasp filled the room a moment later, when she felt delicious, moist kisses covering her back. Zephir was kneeling behind her, his hands cupping her hips. He had brushed away the straps of her shift and was caressing her cocoa skin with his lips.

"Zephir," she whispered, her voice shaky with need. She moved away and got into bed, pulling the covers around her chin.

Zephir was there in an instant. Determination beamed on his devastatingly handsome face. "We've been apart far too long. I know you feel that, too," he said, his voice deliciously rough in her ear.

Phaedra shut her eyes against the rush of pleasure surging through her. Zephir's hands slid along the satiny swell of her thigh and disappeared beneath the hem of her shift. "Zephir…" Phaedra sighed, her thighs trembling beneath the possessive caress of his massive hands. Unable to deny her need any longer, she turned onto her back and brought her lips to his.

Zephir squeezed his eyes shut tightly as Phaedra's mouth touched his. He eagerly responded, thrusting his tongue past her soft lips.

They moaned simultaeously, kissing madly. Phaedra wantonly threw her leg across Zephir's hip. In response, he encircled her tiny waist in his arms and caressed her back. Phaedra let all her desire for him rush forth in her kiss. Her head rose from the pillow as she grasped the collar of his white linen shirt.

Having Phaedra so willing beneath him, threatened to break down Zephir's self-control. Wanting the pleaure to last as long as possible, he pushed her to her back and pulled her hands away from his chest.

"What is it?" she asked, straining against his grip around her wrists.

"My love, this should last a while," he whispered, his perfect white grin appearing.

Phaedra's long lashes fluttered close as she arched herself into his hard frame. "I need you."

"I need you, too." He told her softly and released her wrists. "You have no idea how much I have missed the taste," he paused to trail his mouth along her collarbone, "the touch," his hands squeezed her buttocks gently, "and the sight of you." His strong teeth tugged at the ruffled neckline of her shift and pulled it away.

"The light…"

Zephir shook his head. "I have been refused the treat of seeing this luscious body for far too long as well. I won't be robbed of that tonight."

Phaedra opened her eyes and began to tremble just slightly. "Zephir…"

However, Zephir was determined to see what he touched. In a matter of seconds, he had removed the cotton shift she wore. Phaedra's wide gaze was expectant as she searched for any sign of displeasure on his gorgeous face. To her relief, the look in his expression held nothing but desire. The slanted gaze traced her body with undeniable intensity.

"My God," he breathed, his raspy voice sounding strained with emotion. Phaedra's added weight seemed to arouse him even more. He caressed her satiny skin, his hands fondling and

squeezing with infinite gentleness.

The obvious worship emmanating from his pitch black eyes had an incredible effect on Phaedra. More confident in her beauty than ever before, she arched her body and drew his eyes to her bosom. He lowered his head and took one of the rigid nipples between his lips.

Phaedra gasped from the sheer pleasure of his mouth on her body and his silky hair brushing her skin. Zephir suckled one of the firm peaks with merciless expertise, while his fingers manipulated the other. He had yet to remove his formal attire or even the heavy boots he wore. Phaedra experienced a wave of debauchery at the fact of being completely nude beneath him. She shuddered from the pleasure of it all and rested her hands above her head, allowing him to have his way.

Of course, Zephir took full advantage of the situation. He sat up and pulled off his suit coat and shirt. Phaedra actually moaned at the sight of his incredible chiseled torso. The smooth blackberry skin was flawless and stretched tautly across his bulging muscles. For a moment, Zephir simply stared down at Phaedra. Then, his hands followed the trail of his eyes as they caressed her body. He found the mound of silky curls which shielded her femininty. Phaedra moaned, when the tip of his middle finger probed her moistness. She slid her hands across the incredible expanse of his thighs and urged him to remove his trousers.

Zephir ignored her silent plea, pulling his fingers away from her womanhood as his head lowered. His tongue nuzzled into the sweetness of her body and he cupped her hips to hold her in place as he deepened the caress. Phaedra pushed her head into the pillows and cried out her satisfaction. Zephir only pleasured her there for a brief moment before he ended the delicious treat and slid his lips along her thigh. When he reached her ankle, he cupped her small foot in his hand and suckled each toe.

"Zephir please…"

"Not yet," he whispered, turning his attention to the other foot.

Phaedra's soft cries gained volume. She could feel the moisture increase between her thighs. It was as though Zephir were intent on requainting himself with every inch of her body. Instead of granting her the fulfillment she craved, he flipped her to her stomach. He continued to rain kisses across her skin, beginning with her calves and working his way up. He nipped at the swell of her buttocks, before his tongue traced her spine.

Phaedra's slender fingers curled around the edge of the pillows, and she thought she would die from the pleasure. The possessiveness in every kiss from his mouth sent a deeper shiver through her body. As his hands slid beneath her to cup and fondle her breasts, she moaned into the pillow top.

Zephir buried his face in the sweetly scented curls atop her head. He felt her nipples harden in his palms and thought his desire would rush forth at the unexpected surge of satisfaction it provided him. After a moment, one hand eased down her midriff, past the curls above her womanhood.

Phaedra shifted her legs apart as she felt Zephir's fingers slip over the velvety softness there. He teased her relentlessly, until she bucked beneath him and demanded a different form of satisfaction.

"Zephir, please…I can't stand this…"

This time, he granted her request. He entered two fingers and rotated them gently in her creamy need. Phaedra leaned her head back against his chest and gasped his name. After a while, Zephir's own arousal demanded to be sated. He moved away from the bed and stripped off his boots and trousers. Then, he was upon her again, flipping Phaedra to her back and settling over her.

Her breath came in tiny pants when he buried his long, wide length inside her. He filled her to overflowing, but there were no complaints. Soon, his hips moved in a deliciously wicked manner. He caressed the inner walls of her love with deep, masterful strokes.

The wondrous rhythm of their lovemaking lasted for what seemed an eternity. When they finally settled down to sleep, Phaedra thought their night of love was more exquisite than either of them could have imagined.

CHAPTER 17

Guests began to leave Toussaints within two days following the birthday gala. Many remained, though, eager to enjoy the home they had all missed. While Tisha's death had brought a storm cloud over the rest of the festivities, the family was happy to remain and offer their support and love.

The Mfume's had also remained. Tumba and Carmelita were happy to do so. Although Zephir had requested they visit a while longer, the distinguished couple had no intentions of leaving their daughter-in-law after all that had happened.

Of course, Phaedra could not have been more pleased. Ever since Cuba, she had felt a special connection to Zephir's mother. Carmelita had a peace surrounding her that could soothe anyone's mood. With Tisha gone, Phaedra knew she would need an older, wiser presense in her life. Especially now that she was with child. Phaedra had a feeling that her cousins would not be quick

to leave her be. Not to mention Zephir, who was still as overbearing and arrogant as he had always been.

"I think we should have breakfast outside tomorrow. The skies have been so lovely these last few days."

Carmelita nodded, agreeing with Phaedra. "That's a wonderful suggestion, dear. I will be sure to have Tumba out of bed, so he can join us," she replied, with a soft laughter following her words.

Phaedra shook her head. "You have such a wonderful marriage."

Carmelita leaned back and regarded Phaedra thoughfully. "I've been very lucky, unlike many of my sisters and other women I know."

"What do you mean?"

"Child, many women are not so lucky to wed a man they truly love. Marriages are arrangements of convenience—nothing more. As it happened, Tumba's father worked my father's sugar cane fields. The two became great friends, close as brothers you could say. When Tumba's father passed away, my father took him in as his very own. Can you believe that?"

Phaedra propped the side of her face in her hand and sighed. "So, you've known him all your life?"

Carmelita nodded. "I've known him all my life, and I loved him from the first moment I saw him."

"That must be a wonderful feeling."

Carmelita could hear the regret in Phaedra's soft voice. "It is. But, it matters not, whether you love from first sight or second, there is nothing more wonderful than being in love with the man you have married."

"Even if he is an overbearing, insufferable ass?"

"Yes!" Carmelita laughingly replied and leaned across the table to pat Phaedra's hand.

The two women laughed for several minutes. Eventually, an easy silence settled between them. Carmelita took a deep breath and watched Phaedra more closely. "He loves you very much, you know?"

"I know," Phaedra quietly acknowledged.

"So how long do you think you can hide the fact that you are carrying his child?"

Phaedra's shoulders tensed visibly, and she raked her slim brown fingers through her wild mane of wavy tresses. "Zephir was gone a long time. I am no stranger to being on my own and getting things done myself."

Carmelita frowned. "Meaning?"

"Meaning, I don't know if I want him involved!" she snapped, bolting from her chair.

Carmelita was stunned. "Why ever not, child?"

Phaedra glared across the room at her mother-in-law. "Do you recall that he just left me without a word? Besides, he'll probably be gone before I really begin to show."

Carmelita was not fazed by the scowl Phaedra wore. "Bonita, do you recall why he left? Do you recall how much in love the two of you were in Cuba? Think how much more wonderful things would be with a baby. Do you honestly want to miss that?"

"What if he leaves again?"

Carmelita shrugged. "I suppose you have to ask yourself if that possibility is enough to stop you from experiencing true happiness. Do you want to experience a lifetime of shutting him out of the child's life? Or worse, him never even knowing he has a child?"

Phaedra could not put her answer into words, but in her mind she screamed, "No!" There was nothing she wanted more than to have Zephir's help in raising their child.

"Phaedra?" Carmelita called, a worried look on her pretty, face. "Dear, I hope I have not upset you too much. I only want to see the two of you as happy as you were in Cuba."

Walking back to the long dining room table, Phaedra took Carmelita's hand in hers. "I want that, too."

"So…"

A bright smile appeared on Phaedra's face as a well of happiness began to spring inside her. "Sooo, I'm going out to the fields and tell my husband he is about to be a father."

Phaedra rushed upstairs and changed into her riding gear. Zephir had been out in the fields since dawn, so she decided to look for him there. She practically floated downstairs and was on her way outside, through the kitchen door, when a knock sounded on the front door. She decided to greet the visitor with a dazzling smile and whipped open the door. On the front porch, stood Kwesi Berekua with Marquis,

Carlos and Dante.

"We've come for our things, Phaedra!" Dante bellowed and brushed past Kwesi.

Phaedra stopped her cousin by placing a hand against his chest. "I'll have them sent to whatever dwelling you three have slithered your way into. You're not welcomed in my home."

"You little bitch," Dante sneered.

Carlos stepped forward as well. "How dare you presume to think you can keep us away from this house?"

"Since I have become its sole owner, I can presume anthing I please. That includes keeping murderers off this property!"

Carlos gasped. "Murderers?"

"You have no proof that we had anything to do with Tisha's passing!" Dante cried.

The look in Phaedra's black expression was purely hate-filled. "I have my suspicions and that's more than enough for me."

Kwesi uttered a heavy sigh, realizing the mistake he had made in bringing the brothers to see Phaedra. "I think it's time we leave." He pulled Carlos and Dante away from the door.

Marquis, who had been silent, suddenly stepped forward. He brushed past his brothers and Kwesi. Phaedra was almost knocked down as he stormed into the house.

"You get out!" she bellowed, following him into the house.

"There's something you need to see, first!" he called.

Everyone followed Marquis down the long hallway which led to the large sitting room. Marquis's eyes shone briefly with unease as he glanced around for any signs of Zephir. Then, he headed to the polished maple desk in the far corner of the room. Tearing through the middle compartment, he withdrew a crisp stack of papers.

"What the hell is that?" Phaedra demanded, watching him wave the documents in the air.

"These papers outline the transfer of property from the Toussaint Plantation to one Zephir Mfume." Marquis smuglly announced.

Phaedra's eyes narrowed. "What…property?"

"The property near the caves…you're familiar with that land, are you not?" Carlos asked, shoving his hands into the pockets of the long linen coat he wore.

Phaedra fixed them all with a hateful look. "I'm familiar with that land. And as far as Zephir goes, I saw him there on several ocassions as I tried to tell you. Why would he buy it from you if he were already getting away with trespassing?"

Marquis shrugged. "Perhaps there was something out there he wanted badly enough to pay for."

Phaedra remained silent as she remembered the gold.

"Unfortunately, we weren't about to let go of our property without a hefty price involved."

Kwesi stepped forward. "What does that mean?" he questioned, his pensive brown gaze boring into Marquis.

"To get his hands on one blade of grass out there, Mr. Mfume had to agree to our monetary price, and he had to take our cousin."

"What?!" Kwesi bellowed.

The brothers were gleeful. "Mfume could not have the land without agreeing to take Phaedra as well," Dante confirmed.

"You three bastards…" Kwesi whispered, his usual soothing voice now filled with loathing.

The three men retreated beneath the older man's cold glare. Of course, they were far from unsettled.

"If I had known you three were coming out here to accuse this poor girl's husband of something like this—"

"Please, Kwesi!" Marquis interrupted. "She knows it is true. Look at her!"

Phaedra's lashes fluttered madly as she fought to keep her tears at bay. "Zephir told me…long ago," she managed not wanting to give them the satisfaction of knowing how deeply shocked she was, "even after the way you jackasses have treated me…I didn't want to believe him. That you would actually sell me."

Kwesi walked over to comfort Phaedra. He smoothed one hand along her back and pressed a kiss to her cheek. "I suggest you three leave now," he whispered.

"And I suggest you take this dear man's advice," Phaedra warned, knowing her cousins would choose to continue the argument.

"Phaedra—"

"If you don't leave, your lives will be in even more danger than they already are."

"You haughty little bitch!" Marquis roared, bounding across the room. "How dare you threaten us?!"

Kwesi stepped between Marquis and Phaedra. "I think you should step down, son."

Marquis spat into Kwesi's face and received a stinging backhand in return.

"You vicious ingrates, leave here this instant!" Kwesi bellowed, a hateful gleam in his vibrant chocolate gaze.

Marquis, Carlos and Dante appeared to have an abundance of courage that day. They stepped right up to Kwesi and confronted the taller, more powerful man. Since the battle lines were clearly drawn, they saw no need to continue their polite charade.

Phaedra knew she had to have peace or lose her sanity. While the men argued, she left the room and went to the rifle cabinet just off from the sitting room. She selected one of the long, polished mahogany shotguns, found the shells and loaded the weapon.

As Phaedra filled her rifle, Zephir entered the house from the kitchen entrance. He was about to head upstairs when he heard raised voices around the corner. Wiping the sweat from his brown, he pushed his handkerchief to the back pocket of his denim trousers. In the sitting room, he discovered the Toussaint brothers in a heated argument with a man he did not recognize.

"What the hell is going on in here?!"

Silence fell over the room, when Zephir's heavy baritone voice called out.

"This is none of your concern, Mfume!"

Marquis grinned at his brother. "On the contrary, Carlos, I would have to say that Mr. Mfume is right in the center of it."

Zephir's slanted eyes narrowed even further. "What the devil are you talking about?" he demanded, folding his arms across his heaving chest.

"Phaedra knows it all, Zephir," Dante announced, brushing past his brothers. "She claims that you told her about our… arrangement, but that was probably to hide her embarrassment."

Knowing his temper had reached its most heated level, Zephir closed his eyes. "I swear that I told you three to stay away from her."

"Phaedra had to be made clear on the situation. She should know that her husband was a willing participant in our plans," Marquis replied in a cool, detached tone. "We did what we had to do."

Zephir was far from amused. "Well then," he sneered, walking forward with murderous intent flashing in his midnight eyes, "you three will understand my breaking your worthless necks is what I have to do."

For the first time, the brother's were truly horrified. Kwesi moved aside, knowing the huge young man approaching them, was not bluffing.

All action, however, ceased when Phaedra walked into the sitting room and fired the rifle into the air. She hit the impressive crystal chandelier that loomed above. The glittering object crashed to the floor, just inches from the brothers. Shards of crystal flew, slicing the three men who had come for revenge. Marquis clutched his bleeding arm, while Dante and Carlos gasped at the blood seeping from their ripped trouser legs.

"Get out or the next shots I fire will not be aimed at the ceiling," she whispered, shaking with the anger that threatened to consume her.

Facing the double threat from Zephir and Phaedra, the brothers were drained of all argument. They ran past the servants; who had rushed in to see to the confusion, and out of the house, grimacing at the pain stemming from their wounds.

Kwesi decided to follow, but stepped over to Zephir first. "Mr. Mfume, I am Kwesi Berekua." He clapped the younger man's shoulder. "I was advisor to Phaedra's father and now, to her."

"It's good to meet you, sir," Zephir said, extending his hand. "I regret the circumstances, though."

Kwesi nodded. "As do I. Take care of her." He glanced toward Phaedra who was inspecting her rifle.

Zephir looked toward his wife and sighed. "I will."

Kwesi left then. When the door front door slammed shut, Zephir approached Phaedra.

"Give me the rifle."

"I should kill you where you stand."

Zephir uttered a short laugh and tilted his head to one side. "May I ask why?"

"How could you do that? How could you accept such a ridiculous proposal from my cousins?"

"Why are you asking me?"

"What?" Phaedra cried, shocked by the question.

Zephir folded his arms over his chest and glared down at her. "You obviously believed whatever story your cousins just told you."

"I want to hear it from you."

"Why, Phaedra? If you recall, the last thing you wanted was to believe what I had to say about those fools."

Phaedra squeezed her eyes shut to ward off her frustration. "Damn you, Zephir. You had me captive on a ship in the middle of nowhere! You tell me my family gave me to you and expected me to believe it— no questions?!"

"You're damn right I expected you to believe it! Did you think that was something I would boast about? I wanted that land and what I agreed to made me sick. I couldn't tell you that. I don't have to cut deals for female companionship, Phaedra. It is something that I have never lacked. I wasn't proud of this, but I should have included my part in the deal, not only your cousins."

Sadly, Phaedra was beyond listening to reason. "As far as I am concerned, you are just as devious as they are," she sneered, "not only did you take part in their scheme, but you were even scandalous enough to scheme them out of the gold you had sniffed out."

The cool expression Zephir wore slowly turned into anger. "I'm about to lose my temper with you, woman."

"I don't give one damn about your temper, bastard. I want you out of my house and my life!" she commanded, even as she retreated from his advancing figure. Remembering the rifle, she aimed it at his chest.

The anger in Zephir's eyes was quickly replaced by shock. Though his temper was raging, he could not ignore the pain that tore at his heart.

"Get out," Phaedra whispered, clutching the weapon tightly. She tried to remain strong, but the emotion she saw in Zephir's unnerving gaze, weakened her entire body. The moment her stare faltered, he grabbed the barrel of the gun and ripped it out of her hands. He threw it to a nearby sofa, before turning back to her. The loathing glare he sent her way brought a quick terrified cry past her lips. Her back was inches away from the wall, but she lifted her chin in defiance.

"Zephir—"

"Shut your mouth," he ordered through clenched teeth. Taking her upper arm in an unbreakable hold, he shoved her back into the wall. "You dare to pull a gun on me?" he marveled masking the hurt in his voice with disgust. His hands squeezed around the soft flesh of her arms.

Phaedra bristled. "Let me go."

Zephir jerked her close. "Never. I'm your husband. By law, you are my property. You and your beloved Toussaints. No, my sweet, you will never be rid of me."

Feeling more frustrated than ever, she broke free of Zephir's grip and landed a resounding slap against his face then raced upstairs to the master bedchamber.

"Phaedra! Phaedra!"

Zephir's raspy voice thundered throughout the house, but Phaedra continued to run. She did not stop to breathe, until the heavy oak bedroom door was locked behind her. She stopped in the middle of the room and faced the door. Knowing it would not be long before the heavy wood splintered, she waited. Soon enough, Zephir's steps thundered up the stairwell as he opened the door with one mighty kick from his boot.

He stood there, looking evil as Lucifer. His massive chest heaved, and his hands clenched into fists. "Come here," he whispered.

Phaedra's heavy black locks flew wildly about her as she shook her head. Slowly, she retreated further into the room.

"Don't make me chase you, love," Zephir warned. The soft tone of his rough voice did little to comfort. He only wanted to calm her in hopes that he could get her to listen to him and hopefully to forgive him.

Still, Phaedra would not obey her husband's request. She mistook her husband's expression of weariness for something more menacing. He took one step forward and she rushed to the bed.

"You stay away from me!" she ordered, pointing down from where she stood in the center of the quilts.

Despite the circumstances, Zephir grinned. He believed she would always captivate him with her courageous demeanor.

The grin added a ruthless, yet sensual gleam to Zephir's magnificent features. Phaedra read it easily and mirrored the challenge she read in his eyes. Zephir moved quickly and caught her off guard. He pulled her legs out from beneath her, causing her to tumble to the bed.

"Get off me!" Phaedra screamed, using her small fists to pound at his neck and chest.

Zephir grunted when one of her punches caught him in the throat. Taking both her wrists in one of his hands, he sought to press them against the bed. Phaedra retaliated by sinking her teeth into the soft flesh of his hand. He released her and the back of her hand connected with the side of his cheek and the room echoed the sound of the slap. The murderous look in his deep set eyes, turned Phaedra's thoughts to the baby.

"Zephir...wait..."

"Oh? Are we done fighting now?" he breathed.

Knowing she had pushed him too far, Phaedra closed her eyes and instintively pressed her hands against his lean hips where they ground against hers. "Zephir...the baby...the baby."

The shaky words were whispered right into Zephir's ear. His head snapped up, the evil expression on his face left to be replaced by a blank look. "What?" he breathed.

Phaedra's eyes slid over to his face and she swallowed past the lump in her throat. "I'm going to have a baby...your baby."

"Jesus," Zephir whispered, his long lashes fluttering over his incredible eyes. He looked as though he were about to faint! "Are you positive, Phaedra?" he asked, watching her nod. "Why didn't you tell me?" he whispered, moving off her. His pitch black eyes raked her body, finally settling on her slightly swollen belly.

Phaedra sighed, relieved by the change in his mood. She watched his hands caress her raised tummy. "I was on my way to tell you," she began, smiling when his eyes rose to her face, "when my cousins arrived."

"How long have you known?" Zephir asked, looking back at her stomach.

"Several weeks."

"Why didn't you tell me before?"

"Zephir, you had been gone so long... I'd grown use to handling things on my own."

"Well, that's over." He dropped to kiss Phaedra's midriff. "From this moment on, I will handle everything. Everything, Phaedra, including the plantation and your cousins."

"Zephir—"

"Is that understood?"

Having no desire to argue, Phaedra nodded. "Zephir?"

"Hmm?..."

"Are you happy?"

The devastating grin broke through on Zephir's sinfully handsome face. "Love, I cannot begin to tell you how very happy you have made me."

Phaedra laughed and pressed a kiss against his lips. She would have moved back, but Zephir held her close. The deep groans rumbled in his chest as his tongue tasted the sweetness of her mouth.

"Zephir…" she gasped, amidst the kiss. She eagerly responded, pressing her bare breasts into his chest.

The kiss deepened, and Zephir pressed Phaedra back against the bed. His manhood returned to its aroused state, and he felt weakened by the intensity of it. Tearing his mouth away from her soft lips, he trailed the satiny column of her neck. As his thumbs brushed the hardened peaks of her nipples, her hand reached down to fondle his pulsing length.

"Will this harm the child?" Zephir whispered against the swell of her breasts.

Phaedra was lost in the pleasure she received. "If you are gentle, it should be fine."

Zephir seemed satisfied by the answer and continued his sensuous assault on her breasts. Unfortunately, when his fingers brushed her stomach, he pulled away. "I can't take that chance."

A small frown marred Phaedra's delicate features. "What chance?"

"If I do this and something happens to the baby—"

"Zephir—"

"We should wait."

"Six months? Zephir we have already been intimate several times since you've come back and nothing's happened yet."

Zephir closed his eyes and tried not to think of being away from her that long. Finally, he shook his head. "Let me get you into bed." He offered, trying to ignore the obvious disappointment on his wife's beautiful face.

Phaedra watched him move away. If she had not been there, she would never have believed that Zephir Mfume had just passed on the chance to make love with her.

"Dammit to hell, send him in, I said!" Cantone Lezard bellowed, his words followed by a dry hacking cough.

Julian Kazro nodded toward the armed guards at the doorway and inside the darkened bedchamber. His eyes narrowed toward the frail man nestled among the covers.

Cantone Lezard was but a shell of his former self. He had spent the last several weeks bed-ridden, unable to perform the most basic bodily functions without assistance.

"You have information for me?" he asked Julian, watching the tall, vanilla-complexioned young man pull a document from inside his cloak. He scanned the first two lines of the crisp page. "An announcement of a gala." His eyes seemed to bulge from his gaunt face when he looked up.

Julian stepped closer to the four poster bed. "Please read on, sir. See who the gala was for."

"Phaedra and...Zephir Mfume," Cantone recited, just as another bout of coughing claimed him. "When?" he asked, his voice muffled by the handkerchief covering his mouth.

"A week ago today, sir," Julian replied. "But it proves that Mfume is alive and living with his wife."

Cantone's weak gaze returned to the document. "Where is this Dominica?"

"It's my home, sir. That is how I happened upon this information."

"Well, in light of that, I'll place you in command." Cantone waved his hand to beckon Julian closer. "It appears that my business with Mr. Mfume is not over."

CHAPTER 18

"Zephir…" Phaedra moaned, snuggling close beneath the bed's heavy quilts.

Zephir ran one hand through his hair and muttered a curse. *How the hell am I going to survive this, when Phaedra is so willing and in love with me?.* His tortured thoughts had kept him awake for most of the night. He could envision the two of them making love so clearly…

No! He had made his decision, and it was a good one. There was no way he could let anything happen to either of them.

Phaedra had turned her face into his neck. In her sleep, she smoothed her hand across the chiseled surface of his bare chest. The unconsciously erotic caress moved below his waist.

Zephir felt his entire body weaken, when Phaedra's fingers grazed the soft hair surrounding his manhood. As she stroked his rigid shaft, he squeezed his eyes shut and prayed for self-control.

Phaedra had practically wrapped herself around him. Her soft lips brushed his neck when she murmured in her sleep. Suddenly, her lashes fluttered open. "Good morning," she whispered, her lovely eyes lowering to his mouth.

"Good morning," Zephir softly replied. "Did you sleep well?"

Nodding, Phaedra traced the curve of his mouth with the tip of one perfectly rounded nail. "I would have slept much better had my husband made love to me."

"Phaedra…"

"Zephir, why? We've made love many times since your return. Don't you remember?"

"I'm doing all I can to forget it!" he silently snapped. "It's better for the baby if we don't."

Phaedra tossed her hair over her shoulder. "Are you a doctor?" she asked, pinning him with her , expressive gaze.

"Love, you said it yourself."

"I said if you were gentle, it should be fine."

"Are you a doctor?"

"Would you have me beg you?" she crooned, trailing her mouth along the strong line of his jaw. Taking advantage of his tortured groan, she slid her tongue past his lips and stroked the even ridge of his teeth.

Zephir curled his hands around her upper arms and had every intention of pushing her away. Instead, he found himself pulling her close as the kiss deepened. Phaedra shivered at the sensations coursing through her body. Her fingers toyed in his gorgeous, pitch black hair as she pressed herself against his firm arousal. In response, Zephir cupped her bottom in his hands and mimicked slow, thrusting motions with his hips.

An instant later, he turned the tables and flipped Phaedra to her back. Burying his face in the crook of her neck, he groaned. "Phaedra, my decision is final," he said, raising his head to look into her eyes. "I won't change my mind on this."

He promised, then dropped a quick kiss to her cheek and left the bed.

"Good morning, child. I didn't think we would see you at break-fast."

Phaedra smiled at Carmelita then pressed a kiss to Tumba Mfume's cheek. "Good morning, Poppy," she whispered to her father-in-law. "It took me a while to get out of bed," she told Carmelita before glancing at Zephir.

"Are you alright?" he immediately questioned.

"Just fine, love," she snapped, settling to her chair.

Tumba and Carmelita exchanged knowing glances. Obviously, all was not well with the young couple.

"Are you hungry, bonita?" Carmelita asked as the housemaids set a place for Phaedra.

"Quite," she replied, helping herself to a stack of flapjacks and a few thick strips of steak. "At least this is one pleasure I won't have to worry about being denied."

Zephir grinned at the subtle, yet meaningful comment. He kept his gaze downcast, and concentrated on his food.

"Well, we already know Zephir plans to work in the fields today," Tumba shared, nodding toward his son, "what about you, Phaedra?"

"I thought I'd help the men in the stables. Perhaps I'll even take a ride later."

"The hell you will!"

Everyone turned to Zephir. Phaedra was quite pleased that her words had gotten a rise out of him.

"Is there a problem, husband?"

"Yes, there is a problem you little fool. There is no way in hell you'll be out on a horse in your condition."

Phaedra threw her fork to the table. "So you will refuse me this as well?"

"If it is for your well-being and that of my child's, yes!"

Roiling with anger, Phaedra stood with such force her chair teetered on three legs. "Pardon me, Your Greatness! I should have known that if you wouldn't even pleasure me in our bed, you certainly wouldn't allow me to ride a horse!" she bellowed, closing her eyes in regret the instant the words passed her lips. With a grimace, she turned to face Tumba and Carmelita. "I'm so sorry," she whispered, moving away from the table. "Excuse me," she muttered then ran from the dining room.

Everyone watched her leave. A second later, Zephir stormed out of the house.

"Boy, you know that I've raised you to lead your own life. I rarely interfere."

Zephir's frown relayed his confusion, but he nodded. "I know that, Papa."

Tumba nodded, casting his pitch black eyes out across the sea. He had requested his son join him for a walk along the beach the following afternoon. His serious expression and the tone of his words, said that he had something important on his mind.

"The welface of my grandchild is the most important thing to me," Tumba said, crossing his arms over his wide chest. "I want it to have a good life. A good family life," he clarified, stopping to face his son.

"What are you saying, Papa?"

Tumba took a deep breath before speaking. "Is your marriage well?" he asked, watching Zephir's gaze falter. "I take it there are problems between you and Phaedra?"

"Papa..." Zephir sighed, raking both hands through his hair. "I love her so."

"Then, what is the problem?"

"Keeping my distance."

Tumba frowned. "And why would you want to do this?"

"Because she is having a baby," Zephir replied, as though his father should have realized the answer. "Papa not...being with her is so painful. In more ways than one."

Tumba's deep laughter rumbled forth, earning him a sour look from his son. "You are refusing yourself the pleasures of your wife because she is to have a child?"

"Yes," Zephir whispered, his voice sounding hollow. "I have been so rough with her. I can't allow myself to do anything that would jeopardize the baby, regardless of what her doctor says."

"So you don't touch her?"

"I don't," Zephir confirmed, shaking his head. "Unfortunately, Phaedra has changed. Her... frustration has made her so um...sensual...so *aggressive* these last weeks. It's next to impossible turning away from a beautiful woman who wants you that way."

"That it is," Tumba agreed, a knowing smirk coming to his handsome, face. "You would be amazed how demanding a woman can become once she is introduced to, and then denied the pleasure of lovemaking."

"Well, I'll just have to ignore it."

Tumba nodded at his son's stubborn nature. "Zephir, if it helps to know this, I went through this very thing with your mother."

Zephir's slanting stare widened a bit. "Did you?"

"Mmm…I must commend your strength. I couldn't abide by my vow not to touch Carmelita for more than a few hours."

"Is that so?"

"It is," Tumba sighed, remembering the grand time as it if were yesterday. "Neither of us could resist."

Zephir grinned at the far away look in his father's eyes. "I take it everything turned out well?"

The devilish grin on Tumba's face was mirrored on Zephir's. Clapping his son's back, he pulled him close. "You're here, are you not?"

Phaedra enjoyed the feel of the brush through her hair and the luxurious bubbles surrounding her in the tub. "Carmelita, may I ask you something?"

"Of course, Dear." Carmelita whispered, setting the brush aside to gather Phaedra's hair into a thick braid.

"When you were carrying Zephir, did Papa…would he…touch you?"

"Touch me?"

"Make love to you?"

"Oh," Carmelita whispered, blushing beneath her caramel complexion.

"I know it is of a personal nature," Phaedra sighed, trailing the bath water along her skin. "It is just that…Zephir will not touch me.

He is afraid that he will hurt me or the baby."

Carmelita's airy laughter filled the bedroom. "My sweet, I am afraid I suffered a similar torture from my own husband."

Phaedra turned and looked up at the woman. "What did you do?"

"Well, thankfully, I didn't have long to ponder the situation. Tumba was not very committed to honoring his decision."

"What happened?"

Again, Carmelita laughed. "My dear, the agreement not to make love until the baby was born, was short-lived. In truth, it only lasted a few hours."

The two women dissolved into laughter and were still chuckling when Zephir walked into the room. Carmelita completed the loose braid, leaving several tendrils framing Phaedra's lovely, oval face. She pressed a kiss to her daughter-in-law's forehead then stood and walked over to her son. "Hello, love," she greeted.

Zephir lifted his mother against him and pressed a kiss to her lips. Then, his eyes focused on Phaedra; who watched him from the porcelain tub. When Carmelita left the room, he began to remove his clothes. Phaedra tried to continue her bathing, but she could not keep her eyes away from Zephir's massive, frame. Clearing her throat, she decided to make conversation.

"I had an interesting discussion with your mother."

"About?"

"About how your father treated her just as you are treating me now."

"Is that so?"

"Mmm...only your father realized how foolish he was being and changed his ways."

Zephir kicked off his heavy boots and pulled off his pants. "And why are you sharing this with me?"

"Because I—" Phaedra's words caught in her throat when she looked upon his powerful, nude body. "Because, I want you... to make love to me," she breathed, watching him cross the room.

Zephir stepped into the hot water and lowered himself into the bubbles. Leaning back, his charcoal gaze met and held hers. "Alright." He took her wrist and pulling her against him.

Their lips met with such passion, they both groaned from the fiery pleasure. His tongue delved deeply, forcing Phaedra's head back beneath the pressure. She met it eagerly, her tongue fighting an erotic duel with his.

Zephir's massive hands spanned Phaedra's waist then curved around her hips. In one smooth motion, he impaled her upon the throbbing sheath of his arousal.

Phaedra's head fell back, and her nails dug into Zephir's wide shoulders. He held her still for several moments, relishing the feel of her creamy tightness surrounding his manhood. When he urged her up and down over the steel length of his body, their cries filled the room.

Phaedra was so weakened by the pleasure that she could have fainted. Zephir would not allow that, though. Water sloshed outside the tub amidst the rocking of their bodies. Zephir's lips found the tips of Phaedra's full breasts, irresistible. He suckled mildly on one, while his fingers manipulated the other.

"Zephir…Zephir, please don't stop. Oh, don't stop." She gasped into his shoulder. Being granted the full pleasure of his body after so long, overwhelmed her. Her words were barely comprehensible. Soon in the clutches of an incredible orgasm, her inner walls constricted around his sex. His satisfaction rushed forth then, spewing deeply inside her.

Too exhausted, too pleasured to move, Phaedra and Zephir lounged in the tub until the steamy water turned cold.

"Phaedra? Love?"

Stretching like a lazy cat, Phaedra looked up into her husband's , face. "Yes," she sighed.

Zephir toyed with her hair, watching a tendril cling to his finger.

"You need to get dressed."

"Mmm…what for?" She traced his chest bared to her gaze by his open shirt.

Zephir kissed her hand. "For dinner."

"I'm not hungry just yet."

"Well, we are having guests tonight."

Phaedra frowned and propped herself on her elbows. "What guests?"

"Neighbors."

"Whatever for?"

Zephir grinned as he searched his wardrobe for suitable dinner attire. "Good Lord woman, don't you ever just entertain for the hell of it?"

Phaedra pursed her lips and gave him a sour look. "I rarely entertain unexpectedly," she haughtily informed him.

"Well, tonight will be different. Now, get dressed," Zephir ordered, choosing gray linen, matching coat and crisp, white shirt.

Phaedra offered a heavy sigh in response then whipped the covers back and headed to her wardrobe.

Of course, Zephir bathed and dressed more quickly than his wife. When she finally emerged from the bedchamber though, she was a vision. Her flowing burgundy satin gown had long sleeves which flared at the wrists. The bodice was snug across her chest, emphasizing the fullness of her breasts.

Phaedra smoothed her hands across the billowing skirt and uttered a sigh of relief. She had a feeling that soon, none of her things would fit. Dismissing the wave of uneasiness that coursed through her, she made her way down the spiral staircase.

The lower level seemed unusually quiet, and Phaedra wondered how many of the neighbors had decided to visit. Bringing a dazzling smile to her face, she took the last step down and rounded the corner leading to the great room.

Zephir met her just outside the door. The familiar gorgeous grin appeared on his face the instant he spotted Phaedra. "Incredible," he breathed.

"I appreciate you saying so," she whispered, placing her hands in Zephir's.

"Ready?"

Phaedra offered him a lazy shrug. "Of course," she sang, preceding her husband around the corner.

"Congratulations!"

The defeaning cry sent Phaedra's heart to her chest. The sitting room was filled with most of the island's citizens. Everyone arrived dressed in their finest evening attire with celebration on their minds. Phaedra's eyes searched the crowd, lingering on their smiling faces and raised champagne-filled glasses. Clearing her throat, she looked over her shoulder.

"Zephir?"

"I'm afraid my wife has been kept in the dark about tonight's affair," Zephir announced, pulling Phaedra back against his hard body. "Love, our guests have come to offer their best wishes for the birth of our baby."

Gasping, Phaedra turned in Zephir's arms. "You? You arranged this?"

"Is it so difficult to believe?" he questioned, his long brows rising slowly.

She smiled, focusing on the dimples at the corners of his mouth. "I just didn't think—"

"I love you," he interrupted, tracing her lovely face. "I want everyone to know how much."

Standing on the toes of her burgundy slippers, she pressed a quick peck to his jaw.

Laughter and applause filled the air once again.

The celebraton lasted well into the night. Dinner was the most enjoyable affair. The cooks had prepared an unbelievable amount of food. All sorts of delectable sweets, not to mention an assortment of vegetables, meats and breads, covered the buffet table. Zephir found Phaedra filling her plate. He watched her for several minutes, shaking his head at her increasing appetite.

"Will you come with me, please?"

Phaedra felt warm at the sound of her husband's voice, but did not raise her gaze from the table. "Where?"

"Out to the balcony."

"Why?"

"There's something I want to give you."

Intrigued, she set her plate aside and looked up at him. "A gift?"

"Of sorts."

Gathering her skirts in one hand, she slid the other through the crook of Zephir's arm. "Lead the way."

Zephir took Phaedra out to the spacious stone balcony and lowered his mouth to her neck. His sensuous lips nibbled along her satiny skin, while his hands cupped the sides of her breasts.

"Mmmm…is this what you wanted to give me?" Phaedra whispered, her lashes fluttering in response to his touch.

"Would you be disappointed?"

"Only if you stop."

A deep chuckle rose in his chest, and he raised his head. "I never imagined we would become so close."

She nodded in agreement. "I don't think either of us could have foreseen such a thing."

Zephir took Phaedra's hand and pressed his lips to her palm. "I pray things never change." She brushed her fingers across his cheek. She was mesmerized by the love flashing in his eyes. Suddenly, she felt the grip around her hand tighten, and she glanced down. Her eyes widened, and she gasped before looking up at Zephir.

"What is this?" she whispered.

Zephir kissed the gold wedding band encrusted with diamonds then pressed Phaedra's hand flat against his chest. "As I recall, our wedding was quite… hurried. I felt it was time I made you look more like

253

my wife."

Phaedra laughed. "I don't think there will be any mistake about that in a month or two," she said, patting her hand against her belly.

Zephir grinned at the joke then his expression became serious. If possible, his striking, onyx stare grew even darker. "I love you," he simply stated, his rough voice slightly shaky with emotion.

"And I love you," she whispered back, the emotion etched clearly on her face.

A lovely ballad floated out from the ballroom to the balcony. Zephir and Phaedra danced the rest of the night.

The lusty wailing of a new life fills the air with joy…and love.
~4 Months Later~

"My love, Doctor Claudius says you're almost there. Push, love, use all your strength."

Phaedra grimaced and turned angry eyes toward her husband. "Damn you, Zephir, what do you think I've been using these past ten hours?!"

"Come on, love," Zephir coaxed, ignoring her snappy comment. He could only imagine the pain she must be experiencing.

Unfortunately, Zephir could not imagine a fraction of what Phaedra was going through. The contractions had begun early that morning, and she had been in pain ever since. She actually felt as though she were being ripped in half. The pain was excruciating and throbbed all over her body. Rising to her elbows, she gave another mighty push. A defeaning scream tore from the back of her throat as a new wave of pain rushed through her.

"Here we are!" Dr. Claudius announced as the baby's head appeared. He guided it carefully and beckoned to his assistant. The young man hurried over to aid in cutting the unbilical cord. A swift slap to the baby's bottom brought forth an ear numbing wail. "It's a boy!" he cried.

Phaedra and Zephir's joyful laughter was mixed with tears. The screaming baby boy was as dark as a panther and as wrinkled as a prune. He was the most beautiful thing either of them had ever seen.

Zephir pressed his lips against Phaedra's soaked hair. "Thank you, love," he whispered, watching the doctor wrap the baby in a blanket.

Phaedra stroked Zephir's cheek. They were about to kiss when a piercing pain rippled through her side. Zephir frowned as his heart began to race with fear.

"What's wrong with her?!" Zephir demanded, watching the doctor examine Phaedra closely.

Dr. Claudius appeared to be stumped for a moment. Soon though, his brows rose in surprise. "Good Lord!"

Phaedra screamed again, and Zephir squeezed her hand. "Dammit, man, what the hell is wrong with her?!" he bellowed, coming to his feet.

Dr. Claudius grinned and looked up at Zephir. "Sir, you are about to become a father twice in one day!"

Zephir's long legs weakened beneath him. "She is having another baby?"

"She is," Dr. Claudius confirmed, settling to the foot of the bed once again. "Now get behind her and take her hand. Make her bear down and push."

Recovering from his shock, Zephir resumed his place and propped Phaedra back against his chest. "Come on, love," he gently coaxed, knowing her strength had almost completely deserted her.

Thankfully, the second birth turned out to be just a little easier than the first. The baby entered the world as robust and healthy as its brother.

"Another boy!" Dr. Claudius announced.

"Did you hear that, love?" Zephir whispered against Phaedra's ear.

A lazy smile touched her lips as her eyes closed from exhaustion. "I want to hold them," she sighed.

Dr. Claudius and his assistant placed the howling infants in

Phaedra's arms. The boys quieted the instant they settled next to their mother.

"Phaedra, I can't believe you did this." Zephir said, his massive hands squeezing the babies's feet gently. He was in complete awe of their tiny bodies, and inspected every inch of them.

"Would you like to hold your sons, Mr. Mfume?" Phaedra called, smiling at the expression on his handsome face.

He glanced at her before shaking his head. "They're quiet. I don't want to disturb them."

She looked down at her little men sleeping peacefully. "I'm sure they will be just as content in your arms. Doctor?"

Dr. Claudius ushered Zephir into the maple rocking chair next to the bed. "I fully agree, Zephir," he cheerfully stated.

Phaedra had never seen such unease on Zephir's face. Seeing him as a father would be very interesting, indeed.

Dr. Claudius and his assistant took the boys from Phaedra and placed them in their father's strong arms. Zephir appeared to be holding his breath as he watched his sons.

"My God." He swallowed the lump that had formed in his throat. "They are so small, I fear that I might break them."

The room filled with laughter at Zephir's nervousness. Dr. Claudius went to open the bedroom door and waved Tumba and Carmelita inside the room.

"Is everything alright?" Carmelita asked, gasping when she looked across the room. She and her husband were shocked to find their son holding two babies!

"Everything is in order," Dr. Claudius confirmed, as he shook Tumba's hand. "However, I do believe another celebration is in order."

Tumba laughed. "I fully agree, doctor!"

Dr. Claudius turned to Zephir; who finally felt comfortable enough to stand while holding the babies. "Of course, these men will need names." He took a seat next to his wife. "I think Tumba and Fredericks," he suggested, looking down at her. "What do you think, love?"

Pressing a kiss to the boy's tiny feet, Phaedra smiled up at her husband. "Perfect," she whispered.

"Any middle names?" Carmelita asked.

Phaedra looked up. "Their middle names will be Zephir, of course," she sighed then smiled at the father of her children.

Elated by the love in his wife's eyes, Zephir's gorgeous white grin appeared. "I love you more than I ever imagined I could."

Phaedra blinked back the tears of happiness that pressured her eyes. "I love you, too, and I will show you how much, each day."

Onlookers watched, waiting for the passionate kiss that was sure to follow. Unfortunately, Tumba Zephir Mfume and Fredericks Zephir Mfume had other ideas. Their throaty cries filled the air and mingled with the laughter that flowed throughout the room.

CHAPTER 19

Carmelita and Tumba left Toussaints a couple of months after the birth of their grandsons. Their concerns about Phaedra's cousins somewhat soothed, they decided to let their son and his wife begin their lives.

Phaedra didn't know how she would survive without Carmelita's guidance. She had no idea how to care for one baby, let alone two. She could only pray that a higher power would keep watch over her. She need not have worried. During the months after the Mfume's departure, Phaedra flourished. The high-spirited, independent young woman excelled as wife, mother and mistress of the Toussaint Plantation.

Zephir, like Phaedra, had just as many preliminary concerns. He wondered how he would manage overseeing the vast plantations while handling his other interests. Of course, he worried for nothing. The estate became more successful than ever before. It was run effectively and turned huge profits that further boasted its increasing power.

Again, the land was filled with laughter and love. Neither Phaedra or Zephir ever thought they could be so happy. Though they were having phenomenal financial success, it was their role as parents that made them most proud. The boys—Toumie and Ric for short—were still quite young, but they grew at an astonishing pace. It was very obvious that they would be just as strong, powerful and handsome as their father. Everyone who saw them, stood amazed by how quickly the twins had learned to walk. The parents boasted that their sons would be talking in no time.

Of course, the fact that Phaedra had two rambunctious sons and a demanding husband to care for, did not make her any less outgoing. She spent just as much time outdoors tending to the stables, working in the gardens or riding. All the horses in the stable received thourough workouts from their mistress. Phaedra rode the land practically every day.

"Excuse me, Miss Toussaint?!"

"Whoa, Lucinda," Phaedra called to the black Arabian mare she sat astride. "Toussaint-Mfume," she corrected the man who spoke to her.

The messenger tipped his hat. "My apologies, madam. The letter is addressed to a Miss Phaedra Toussaint."

"Whoa, Lucinda," Phaedra whispered again to the stunning horse that fidgeted beneath her. "Letter?"

"Yes," the man replied, going to the satchel that hung from his horse's saddle. "I was instructed to deliver an urgent letter to Miss Phaedra Toussaint." He held out the folded document.

Phaedra urged her horse closer and took the letter from its bearer. "Thank you," she whispered, tearing into the sealed correspondence. A sharp gasp passed her lips when she scanned the first line.

> *To the bitch who dares to call herself*
> *the Mistress of The Toussaint Plantation,*
> *you are approaching your last days as*
> *one of the living. You, your husband*
> *and your mongrel seeds will regret the*
> *day you crossed us! If you even hope*
> *to save yourself and your blasted*
> *family, you will relinquish your*
> *hold on Toussaints. NOW!*

"They are still on the island," Phaedra whispered, reading the note once more. She had thought, wished, prayed they were dead. Her cousins had simply retreated to plot their next move.

Now, they were threatening her children with death. She would let no harm come to them, even if it meant giving her own life.

"Miss?" The messenger called, eyeing her strangely. "Madam, are you ill?"

Phaedra managed a tense smile and shook her head. "I'm fine. Thank you for the letter," she said, watching the man tip his hat before he rode away. She didn't move until he disappeared around the corner of the gravel trail leading back to the main road. She folded the letter into fours

and shoved it deep into the bodice of her dress. She decided to contact Kwesi. She would need his help to determine her cousins' whereabouts.

Phaedra sighed in relief when she realized Zephir had not returned to the house. He must still be out in the fields, she silently noted. Rushing into the study, she leaned against the desk to draft a quick letter.

Zephir walked into the house a few moments after Phaedra. He entered through the front door and was headed upstairs. He passed the study and, spotting Phaedra. His lips curved into a mischievous smile as he approached her. She was clearly quite involved in whatever she was writing, he thought, for she did not raise her head. On silent footsteps, he stepped up behind her and slipped his long arms about her waist.

Phaedra gasped and pulled a blank sheet of paper over the letter. She decided it would be best to keep Zephir out of the business with her cousins. "You're in early." She pressed herself back against his hard body.

"I've been out all morning," he growled into her neck. His dirty hands reached up to cup her breasts gently.

She could feel the bulge of his arousal through the crisp linen of her crimson button down riding dress. She let her head fall back to his chest and sighed her satisfaction.

In one swift movement, Zephir turned Phaedra around to face him. Burying one hand in her thick hair, he pulled her head back to meet his kiss.

"Mmm…" she moaned as his tongue invaded her mouth. The intensity of the hard, deep kiss made her moist with desire. "Zephir…" She slid her hands along the dingy cotton work shirt he wore.

He continued to kiss her madly, even as he shoved everything from the mahogany desk behind him. Effortlessly, he sat Phaedra on the edge of the table and pulled her legs apart. His hands rose to the top buttons of her dress and slowly unfastened them.

She arched herself closer to his dexterous fingers. When the dress was unbuttoned to her waist, he pulled his lips from hers. Burying his handsome, face in her full bosom, he inhaled her scent. Seeking one, taut nipple, his lips closed over the firm peak and suckled softly.

Phaedra's long lashes fluttered from the maddening pleasure. Her slender fingers delved into Zephir's thick, black locks and enjoyed the silky strands brushing her skin. He fondled her breast, his thumb stroking the nipple. His lips continued to suckle the other, his tongue increasing the pleasure of the heated caress.

"Zephir, please…" Her hands slid from his hair, down his chest and past his waist to massage the throbbing ridge against his pants.

"What do you want?" he teased, his raspy voice muffled between her breasts.

Phaedra cupped his hips, urging him closer. "You know," she whispered.

Zephir took great enjoyment in the moment and chuckled. In response, Phaedra ripped his shirt apart and pushed it from his body. Her lips stroked his blackberry-toned skin that glistened with sweat. His grimy state was such an aphrodisiac to her that she quickly unfastened his trousers.

Losing control, Zephir pushed his hands beneath Phaedra's dress and he tore away her underthings. He positioned himself and thrust inside. A grunt of pleasure rose in his throat as he repeatedly stroked the tight, creamy center of her body. They rocked against each other for countless moments. The sturdy desk squeaked beneath the force of their coupling. Phaedra pulled her lower lip between her teeth to keep her ecstatic cries from the rest of the house.

"Damn," he groaned with every stroke of his iron shaft. Without breaking the rhythm of their lovemaking, he managed to push Phaedra back to the middle of the desk. His massive frame covered her voluptuous form as the movement of his hips became more rapid. Again, his sensuous mouth crossed the peak of one breast. Soon, the wet strokes of his tongue matched the speed of his thrusts.

A soft moan of disappointment escaped Phaedra's lips when she felt Zephir's warm seed flow inside her. His entire body shuddered as a powerful wave of satisfaction wracked his body.

"Zephir..." she called a few seconds later. Her hips nudged his insistently.

A wicked smile touched Zephir's mouth. He kissed his wife's ear, knowing she wanted more than he had just given her. Of course, he was more than willing to comply.

"I've sent word to Kwesi. He should be joining us for dinner tonight," Zephir said as he and Phaedra lounged on the desk a long while later.

Phaedra supported herself on one elbow and looked down into Zephir's face. "What made you do that?" she slowly asked, thinking that he might know of the letter.

Zephir shrugged. "I know he's been away for a while and that you haven't seen as much of him as you would like."

Relieved and touched by her husband's thoughtfulness, Phaedra smiled. She began to drop tiny, wet kisses to his neck and chest, gasping when he grabbed her hips.

"If you're trying to thank me," he growled, setting Phaedra astride his hips, "I know a better way."

Later that afternoon, Zephir relaxed on the long front porch. As he read over some correspondence, he was delighted to find a letter from Dubois. A smile came to his face when he discovered that his first mate and great friend would be visiting soon.

The nursemaids had set Toumie and Ric on the front porch with their father. The twins were to play on the heavy quilt spread out for them. Of course, they preferred to stumble over to Zephir. Dropping to their knees, the boys found more enjoyment playing around their father's boots.

"What have we here?" Zephir sighed, spotting his sons at his feet. Unable to ignore the little ones, he pulled Toumie and Ric close and kissed their plump cheeks. Lifting the laughing boys under each arm, he headed back to the quilt. In minutes, the three men were emersed in play.

Unbeknownst to the happy father and sons, three brothers watched them intently. From across the lawn in a patch of thick bushes and trees, Marquis, Carlos and Dante Toussaint spied. Their eyes gleamed with triple emotions of anger, hate, and jealousy.

They had wandered aimlessly for almost a year. What money they had, was squandered—carelessly spent on liquor and women. Now, they were back to reclaim what was taken. They only needed to sieze the opportunity at the right moment.

Phaedra walked out onto the porch and laughed at the scene before her eyes. She would never get used to seeing Zephir Mfume rolling around and playing like a child. She wished she could freeze the moment in time.

"Zephir, Kwesi will be here soon," she called, clapping her hands together. "You should come in to wash up and sample tonight's dinner."

Instead of rising from the quilt, Zephir stopped playing with the boys and stared up at his wife. A devious grin appeared on his face, and he pulled Phaedra down to the porch.

"Zephir!" she cried, tripping over the long folds of her satiny, powder blue gown.

Lying flat on the cushiony, multi-colored quilt, Phaedra was at the mercy of her husband and sons.

"I think we have a few moments to spare," Zephir said, his hands sliding down her arms.

"I assure you we don't," she replied, her breasts heaving from the obvious desire in her husband's eyes.

A look of disappointment clouded Zephir's face. "There should always be time to offer our sons useful instruction."

Phaedra's expression was suspicious. "What type of... instruction?"

Zephir glanced over at his sons, who were rolling around in the folds of their mother's gown. "Well, as men, who will undoubtedly have more than their share of female companionship, they should know how to make a woman laugh."

"And how do you propose we teach them to do that?" Phaedra asked. Her voice shook as she watched Zephir straddle her body.

Staring at her with wicked intent, he brought his face close. "I think the best way to make a woman laugh...is to tickle her!"

"No!" Phaedra cried, gasping as tears of laughter formed in her eyes.

Zephir ignored her pleas for mercy. He continued to tickle her belly, beneath her chin and under her arms. The boys gleefully watched their mother laugh uncontrollably. Of course, Zephir's play was mingled with desire. His fingers stopped moving, and he began to press soft kisses to Phaedra's jaw and neck.

"Zephir...the boys."

"Are paying us no mind." He assured her, as his mouth travelled across the luscious swell of her breasts that peaked out over the edge of the gown's bodice.

Phaedra sighed and gave in to the expertise of Zephir's touch. When he cupped her chin in his fingers and kissed her, she pressed her hands to his chest and eagerly participated.

Unfortunately, Toumie and Ric grew bored playing in the vibrant fabric of Phaedra's gown. They crawled over to their parents and watched them for several moments. Then, they each pressed a soft, innocent kiss to the mother's cheek.

Zephir and Phaedra broke apart as though they had been burned. The parents were speechless as they realized their sons needed no lessons just yet on how to treat the fairer sex.

"I think it's time we go inside," Zephir whispered. He moved away from Phaedra and ushered the boys off the porch.

Phaedra stood from the quilt and brushed the dust from her gown. "I agree."

Across the lawn, Marquis, Carlos and Dante watched the delightful scene with growing disgust.

"I feel nauseous," Dante groaned, turning away from the house.

Carlos grimaced. "So do I."

"Phaedra and Zephir do not act like two people who received threats today, Carlos." Marquis noted. His voice held an accusing tone.

Raising his hands, Carlos bowed his head. "I swear to you she received it. I placed the letter in her hand myself."

"Do you think she recognized you as the messenger?"

Carlos glanced at Dante then turned back to Marquis. "The disguise was perfect. She had no idea it was me."

While Zephir bathed for dinner, Phaedra chose yet another stunning gown for the evening. This one was of a shimmery pearl color and seemed to give her flawless, molasses-colored skin an unearthly glow. The long sleeves were made of lace, while the hoop skirt bodice and collar were satin. Matching satin shoes, a pearl choker and pearl earrings completed the breathtaking outfit. Satisfied with the change, she returned to the front porch to watch for Kwesi.

"God, I'm so happy," she whispered. "Please let me remain this way."

From the massive gates which stood at the very edge of the plantation, Phaedra saw a carriage approach. Rushing off the porch, she walked out to the middle of the yard and waited.

Kwesi had been travelling abroad for quite a while. He missed his home and friends greatly. Unmistakeable joy brightened his brown face when he stepped from the carriage and saw Phaedra.

"My sweet," Kwesi pulled her close for a hug. "I can't tell you how happy I am to see you."

"Kwesi," Phaedra sighed, inhaling the crisp scent of mint and leaves that always seemed to surround him, "I hadn't realized how much I'd missed you."

He kissed Phaedra's cheek then glanced around the yard. "Don't tell me my Godsons have already been sent to bed? I expected to see them racing around getting into some mischief."

Phaedra laughed. "Oh, Kwesi, I assure you those two have seen enough mischief this day," she said, remembering the scene on the porch.

Eyeing her strangely, Kwesi placed his arm around her shoulder. "I have the feeling there is a story there."

"Oh there is, believe me!" Zephir bellowed, smiling when Kwesi and Phaedra turned at the sound of his voice.

"Zephir!" Kwesi greeted, walking across the lawn to meet him.

"How are you, man?" Zephir asked, taking Kwesis's hand in a hearty shake.

Kwesi grinned and glanced at Phaedra. "I am even better now that I see how happy you two seem."

Zephir pulled Phaedra close and rubbed his hand along her arm. "We are that, my friend," he said, his eyes filled with desire as he gazed down at his wife.

Before Phaedra became lost in the gorgeous midnight depths of Zephir's eyes, she shook her head and walked over to Kwesi. "Why don't we all have a drink?" she suggested.

Kwesi smiled down at her then looked out over the landscape. "Something warm to fill my insides does sound good. Has the climate turned considerably cooler in my absense?"

Zephir crossed his arms over the beige quarter-length wool dinner jacket he wore. He looked over the lush estate. "It has, Kwesi. Strange for it to be quite so cool in this part of the world."

"I think another hard rain is in store," Phaedra predicted, gazing up at the cloudy sky.

"No matter," Kwesi said, clapping his hands. "I'd still like to take a walk around the land."

"I think that can be arranged," Phaedra told him, rubbing her hands over her arms in an effort to ward off the chill in the air. "Zephir, would you ask one of the maids to fetch my wrap?"

Zephir pressed a kiss to Phaedra's palm. "I'll fetch it myself." He headed back inside.

"It is good to see you so happy."

Smiling, Phaedra turned and hugged Kwesi. "Oh, I am. I can only pray nothing happens to jeopardize it."

A frown tugged at Kwesi's bushy, gray black eyebrows. "Why would you say such a thing, child?"

Phaedra cast a quick glance over her shoulder, before speaking. "Earlier today, I received a letter from my cousins."

"What sort of letter?" Kwesi asked, instantly suspicious.

"A death threat."

"Have you told Zephir?"

"No."

"Phaedra—"

"Kwesi, those bastards are only trying to scare me into giving them Toussaints. You know I won't do that."

"And I'm not suggesting that you should," Kwesi told her, pulling her hands into a tight grip, "but you should not keep this from your husband."

"There's no need to worry him unnecessarily."

"Unnecessarily?"

With a wave of her hand, Phaedra dismissed all concern for her cousins. "My cousins need to be handled in a certain way. Besides, Zephir has enough on his mind. Marquis, Carlos and Dante know I would kill them in an instant if they come anywhere near me or my family. They think that I have wronged them by casting them out. Revenge is their motivation, but they can't forget what has been done to me—by their hands. I assure you, Kwesi; they don't want to draw any more of my anger."

When Zephir stepped into the bedchamber he shared with Phaedra, there was a blank look on his handsome face. He realized he hadn't the faintest idea of where the wrap could be. Instead of asking one of the maids, he looked through Phaedra's dresser drawers. The top drawer overflowed with lingerie. Frilly shifts, chemises, stockings and negliges cluttered the space. Smiling at the dainty articles, he lifted several pieces and inhaled the light fragrance clinging to the material. Stopping himself, before he became too fargone, he pushed the articles back where he had found them. Before he pushed the drawer closed, something in the corner caught his eye. Withdrawing a crisp, folded sheet of paper, Zephir scanned the contents. It was a letter—unsigned, but there was no doubt where it came from.

Zephir read the vicious words twice. His content expression slowly turned sinister and dark.

"Dammit." He slipped the note into the pocket of his dinner jacket and stormed out of the room.

"What are those boys eating? They are far too sizable to just be a few months shy of one year old."

Phaedra laughed. "I think they'll take after Zepir in size…and looks." She sliced the succulent roast chicken that had been prepared for dinner.

Kwesi leaned back in the high-backed, cushioned chair. "You must be a proud man?"

Zephir nodded, his eyes slid away from Phaedra, and he smiled at Kwesi. "I'm a very proud man. I'll do anything to ensure they continue to grow healthy and strong."

"My goodness, Zephir. You make it sound so morbid," Phaedra noted, laughing softly.

Again, Zephir pinned his wife with an unwavering, stare. "You, my love, should not have to be reminded of all the dangers waiting right outside our door."

Kwesi shifted his stare between Zephir and Phaedra. He noticed the unease in Phaedra's eyes. He cleared his throat and clapped his hands. "Have I told you two about my travels?" he asked, effectively changing the subject.

Dinner was followed by drinks in the sitting room. Zephir and

Kwesi talked, while Phaedra went upstairs to help the nursemaids prepare the boys for bed.

"Is Cognac alright, Kwesi?" Zephir asked, pulling two goblets from the cabinet above the bar.

"It's fine." Kwesi settled in a cushiony arm chair. When he heard the glasses and bottle slap against the bar, he frowned and looked up. "Zephir, excuse me for saying this, but you don't appear to be pleased this evening."

"I'm not pleased, Kwesi." He passed the man a goblet of Cognac.

"Your mood was changed when you came back outside for our walk."

Zephir pulled the letter from his pocket. "That's because I found this."

Kwesi took the folded page and opened it. He began to nod when he scanned the words. "Ah…the letter."

"You knew about it?" Zephir questioned, his long brows drawn together.

"I knew. I advised your wife to tell you, but…well…"

Zephir grimaced. "She is unconcerned."

"Even after all that has happened, she thinks she can handle this on her own."

"She's fearless and overconfident—a foolish combination!" Zephir snapped, pounding his fist to his palm. "She constantly underestimates those bastards."

"What will you do?"

Zephir drank the Cognac in one swallow and went to refill his glass. "First, I'll have a talk with my wife."

Phaedra walked into the sitting room just then. She was smiling brightly and rushed over to Kwesi. "The boys love the ships you gave them."

Kwesi forced a smile to his face. "I knew they would."

Phaedra looked from Kwesi to Zephir. "Is something the matter?"

Kwesi took Phaedra's hands in his. "Walk me to my carriage?"

"You're leaving?" Phaedra cried.

"It is getting late, and I don't want my coachman trying to maneuver the horses through any storm that might arise."

Nodding, Phaedra managed a smile. "I can understand that."

"Good," Kwesi said, offering her his arm. "A good night to you, Zephir."

Zephir gave the man a curt nod. "Good night, my friend."

"Phaedra, I implore you. Keep nothing from your husband regarding your cousins."

" I can take care of myself."

Kwesi shook his head and cupped Phaedra's chin. "This time I'd like for you to try letting someone else take care of you." He pressed a light kiss to her cheek.

Phaedra was silent as she watched Kwesi settle into his carriage and ride away.

"These drinks mark the last of our funds, and that frumpy innkeeper just informed Carlos that unless we pay her more money tomorrow, we lose our rooms!"

"Dante, calm yourself."

"He's right, Marq," Carlos interjected. "Our funds are depleted. We were hoping this master plan of yours would have gone into effect by now."

Marquis sipped on his mug of rancid ale. "These things take time and certain resources."

Dante sighed. "Dammit man, we have no resources!"

"I know that!" Marquis hissed.

"Excuse me, gentlemen?"

The brothers turned toward the average-looking man who had spoken. They watched him step closer to the bar, taking in the worsted fabric of his overcoat, with unmasked envy.

"I hope I have the honor of addressing the Toussaint brothers?"

"You do," Marquis slowly replied.

The man smiled and reached out to shake hands with each brother. "My name is Julian Kazro. I have a home on the island. I am a native and I work for a man named Cantone Lezard. Have you heard that name before?"

Dante leaned forward. "We have, if it will get us a decent meal."

Julian chuckled. "I will take that as a no. However, a decent meal is in your future if you all agree to be guests in my home tonight?"

"What's this all about?" Marquis inquired. "Who is this Cantone Lezard and what does he want with us?"

"I believe you share a mutual aquaintance with my employer."

"Mutual aquaintance?" Carlos asked. "Who?"

"Zephir Mfume."

"Zephir?" Marquis snapped, his eyes flashing with devilish intent. "What is this about?"

"This is about revenge, Mr. Toussaint," Julian promptly explained. "My Mr. Lezard has business of that sort with Zephir Mfume. Judging from your present state, I assume you have similiar interests with the man."

"That black mongrel will pay for what he's done!" Dante vowed.

"He and his slut wife," Marquis added.

Julian's smile was satisfaction personified. "I assure you then, gentlemen, your wishes run parallel to those of Mr. Lezard's."

CHAPTER 20

Phaedra decided to dress for bed after Kwesi left the house. Once inside the bedchamber, she headed to her lingerie drawer for a gown. She chose a lacy peach neglige, then tossed it aside and decided to scan her cousin's letter once again. After a few moments of searching the cluttered drawer, her eyes narrowed.

"Dammit, where the hell is it?" she whispered, shuffling through the drawer at a frantic pace.

Zephir had been leaning against the door for several moments. He watched Phaedra select the gown then waited for her to realize the letter was missing. Pulling the note from his pocket, he walked up behind her and thrust the page in the line of her view. "Are you looking for this?"

Stunned by her husband's deep voice and the letter he held, Phaedra whirled around to face him. Her angry expression was matched by his. Of course, she was not intimidated. "What the hell are you doing rifling through my things?" she blasted.

"What the hell are you doing keeping something like this from me?" he challenged, his bellow far outweighing hers.

Phaedra's angry glare faltered. "I didn't want you upset over this piece of—of nothing!"

"Nothing?" Zephir whispered, his eyes dropping to the letter. "'…you are approaching your last days as one of the living. Does that sound like nothing to you, Phaedra?"

With a cry of pure frustration, Phaedra pushed past Zephir. "I'm not becoming unraveled over this nonsense, so why are you?"

"How can you ask such a thing?"

Phaedra massaged her neck and tried to think of a way to make him understand. "Zephir, do you remember when you left me in Cuba to go after Cantone Lezard?"

The question caught Zephir off guard. "Yes," he slowly replied.

"I didn't understand it at the time. You had to go after the man. He had wronged you, threatened you. For your own sanity and peace of mind, you had to handle it your way."

Zephir sent Phaedra a knowing look then rolled his eyes toward the ceiling. "If you are trying to convince me to step aside and let you face those insane jackasses on your own, stop. "

"You know I will not do that."

Phaedra buried her face in her hands and groaned. In the next instant, she was running from the room. She ignored Zephir when he shouted her name and did not stop running until she was outside the house. There, she took a few deep breaths and had a seat on the back porch step. "Calm yourself, Phaedra," she whispered several times until her heartbeat slowed. Enjoying the solitude, she leaned back on her elbows and gazed up into the black sky.

"Miss Phaedra?… Miss Phaedra?"

Several minutes passed before Phaedra even tuned in to the sound of her name being called. She opened her eyes to find three of the stablemen standing in front of the porch. "Something wrong, Hammie?" she asked the first man she looked at.

The young man in the middle of the group twisted his hat in his hands. "Sorry to bother you, Miss Phaedra."

With a wave of her hand, Phaedra stood. "What is it?"

Hammie cleared his throat and glanced at the boys next to him. "Miss Phaedra, we can't stay on with you."

"You can't stay on? Why?" she questioned, her eyes darting to the other two men.

Dezard, the taller, stockier boy to Hammie's left, stepped forward. "We hate to do this to you, Miss Phaedra, but we just can't stay."

"But why?" she repeated, raising her hands in a pleading gesture. She watched the young men give each other uneasy looks, and sighed. "It's Zephir, isn't it? He can be so demanding."

"Oh no, Miss Phaedra," Corel, the third stableboy, spoke up. "Mr.

Zephir is a good man."

Phadra dropped her hands to her sides. "Then, I'm afraid I don't understand. Have you all received better offers to work elsewhere?"

"Miss Phaedra, maybe we should talk to Mr. Zephir."

Phaedra sent Dezard a knowing smile. "So you have received better offers? I'm willing to match them, you know?"

"Miss Phaedra, it's not that."

"Then what?"

"We don't want to upset you."

"But you three are upsetting me by not telling me what's happening!"

"I would like to know that myself."

Everyone turned at the sound of Zephir's voice. He had decided to give Phaedra a few moments before going to find her.

"Hammie, Corel and Dezard say they cannot stay on with us, and they won't tell me why." Phaedra explained, running a hand through her wavy tresses.

"You men care to explain yourselves?" Zephir asked, crossing his arms over his wide chest.

Hammie swallowed. "Not in front of Miss Phaedra, sir."

Zephir grinned. He glanced at his lovely wife, who stood fuming at his side. "Boys, I'm afraid she will not have it any other way."

Corel and Dezard looked at Hammie, urging him to step forward and explain their actions. "We are dead men if we stay here," he blurted.

The slight frowns on Zephir's and Phaedra's faces deepened, and they both stepped forward.

"Has someone threatened you?" Zephir asked.

"Oh no, sir!" Hammie said, looking back at Corel and Dezard who also shook their heads.

"Then why would you say such a thing?" Phaedra questioned, propping her hands on her hips.

"We just have a bad feeling, Miss Phaedra. It's tellin' us to leave."

Phaedra only nodded. She could very well understand the effect "bad feelings" could have on one's mind. Still, in her bones, she knew her cousins had done something to provoke their outlook; but why? Unfortunately, she could not share her realization with Zephir. Knowing how he felt about it all, she felt it best to keep her suspicions to herself.

"Well, if you three feel so strongly about leaving, I'll not stop you," Zephir said, turning toward the wide-screened wooden door. "Come inside for your severance pay."

The young men stepped up to the porch and stopped before Phaedra. "We're sorry about this, Miss," they all muttered.

When the men disappeared into the house, Phaedra rubbed her hands across her lace covered arms and looked out over the darkened landscape. "Dear God, please let me see what they are planning before it is too late."

The next day began sunny, with only a slight wind blowing. By late afternoon, heavy clouds had moved in and the wind had picked up a bit.

Lulani Obu, Kwesi Berekua's daughter, had stopped by to have tea and chat with Phaedra. The two young women often visited one another. Lulani had a son almost the same age as Phaedra's two children. As the three rambunctious boys played on a huge quilt in the front yard, their mothers had tea and cookies on the porch.

Lulani crossed her arms over the high-necked bodice of her blue linen dress and smiled. "Oh, Phaedra, can you believe our boys are approaching their first birthdays?"

Phaedra broke a crisp ginger cookie in half and popped it into her mouth. "I have to pinch myself everyday to make certain this is real," she replied, while munching on the sweet treat.

Toying with a lock of her shoulder-length light brown hair, Lulani closed her eyes and enjoyed the breeze. "How will you celebrate?"

"Oh we are planning a great celebration," Phaedra raved, having begun to prepare the event long before the threatening letter she'd received. "I only hope it will take place," She still worried, knowing it would be a terrible chore to postpone.

The dismal tone in Phaedra's words was impossible to miss. Lulani's lashes fluttered open, and her light eyes filled with confusion. "What is it?"

"Nothing." Phaedra pushed a crumb off her cream colored straight skirt.

Lulani turned in her chair. Her beautiful, round face was a picture of concern. "Nothing. But it still has you worried?"

The wind had loosened a curl of Phaedra's hair from the lovely coiffure she wore. Suddenly, needing something to occupy her hands, she tried to fix it. "Three of our stablemen left us last night. They said they were dead men if they remained here."

Lulani gasped, her hands brushing the exquisite broach pinned at her neck. "Had they been threatened?"

"They said they had a bad feeling about staying here. I couldn't fault them for wanting to go."

"What do you think it is?"

Phaedra shook her head. "Whatever it is, their leaving has put us in a bit of a state. Losing them now, with the boys' celebration upon us, we'll need good people to replace them."

The moment the words passed Phaedra's lips, the wind began to howl. The light breeze turned fierce and freezing cold. Phaedra and Lulani gathered their boys and rushed inside the house.

A few hours after the furious windstorm began, Zephir burst into the house. His face was darkened by a frown as he brushed away the leaves that clung to his overcoat.

"This place is beginning to resemble Newfoundland," he muttered, eyeing the heavy tree limbs that swayed in the wind.

Slamming the door shut, he shrugged out of the heavy brown coat and headed through the foyer. He followed the delicious smells wafting through the air, until he reached the kitchen. There, he found his wife toiling away at the stove along with their staff of cooks.

"What's going on in here?" he asked as he stood behind Phaedra.

"The cooks and I thought we should prepare soups for you men in the fields," she explained, trying to ignore Zephir's massive, hard frame against her. "What would you like to have?" she whispered as she stirred a tall pot of broth. "We have beef stew, fish chowder, vegetable, chicken…"

"I prefer you," Zephir whispered against her ear then pressed a kiss against it.

Phaedra poked her elbow into his ribs and smiled when he grunted. "Well, the soup will have to do for now. Go to the dining room and I'll bring you a bowl of the stew."

Zephir gave her bottom a playful swat then walked off. "No bother, I'll have it right here at the kitchen table."

The cooks were working diligently, but cleared a nice spot for Zephir at the , oval table. In the time that Zephir had taken over Toussaints, he had charmed every woman there. From the cleaning women to the headcooks-everyone felt at ease in the presense of the handsome giant.

"What do you make of this weather, Zephir?"

Zephir shook his head at Elsa, the chief cook. The short, rotund dark-complexioned lady had taken an instant liking to Zephir. Likewise, Zephir could not get over how much the woman reminded him of his own mother.

"I can't make much sense of it, Miss Elsa." He took a bite of the hearty stew. "I do believe it will turn worse before getting any better."

Everyone, including Phaedra, nodded in agreement with Zephir's prediction. Soon, though, conversation filled the kitchen as the cooking resumed. A heavy knock on the back door, caught Zephir's ear. He went to answer and found two, haggard looking men standing on the top step.

"Good day," he greeted.

The men huddled close together to ward off the chill of the wind. "Sir, if you could spare just a bit of food, we would be most thankful."

"Where are you men from?" Zephir asked, eyeing their torn over-coats and ragged beards.

One of the men pulled his dusty cap down a bit further over his eyes and shuddered. "Sir, my name is James and this is my friend William. Our village is on the far side of the island."

"It was torn apart by this storm that seems to be visiting you all now," the other traveller replied, bowing his head when Zephir looked his way. "It's a beast, sir. My friend and I have been travelling for weeks."

Phaedra walked over to Zephir and squeezed his arm. "Love, let them inside."

Zephir stood aside and held the door open for the two men. Their steps were slow, as though it hurt them to walk. The two bedraggled men appeared so stiffened by the cold that they kept their arms wrapped tightly around their bodies and shuffled into the house on the torn soles of their shoes.

"You men take the seats next to the fire," Zephir ordered as the cooks cleared two more places at the table.

Phaedra prepared two heaping bowls of the hearty beef stew along with crusty bread and hot ale. The men wolfed down the meal as though it was their first in ages.

"You say the storm ravaged your village?" Zephir questioned, resuming his seat at the table.

Both men nodded. "It tore right through, sir. Many homes…and lives were lost," one of them said, his voice barely audible.

"Where are you men headed?" Phaedra asked, coming to stand behind Zephir's chair. Her eyes narrowed as she tried to get a better look at their faces. Unfortunately, the long dusty beards and oversized caps made it impossible to judge their features.

The travellers exchanged weary looks. "For now, we are wandering,

Miss. Since we left our village, we have been taking work along the way, in exchange for a meal or even a few scraps."

"Could you tell that the storm touched any village besides your own?" Zephir asked, his long black brows drawn together over his eyes. He had never heard of such a lengthy storm.

"Not with as much power," one of the men explained. "It completely destroyed our community."

Everyone in the kitchen shook their head. They all felt the utmost sympathy for the two unfortunate strangers. Suddenly, an idea came to Phaedra's mind, and she bent to whisper in Zephir's ear.

"Are you sure?" he asked, an expectant look on his face.

"I can't think of a better idea."

Zephir cleared his throat and leaned forward. "We have recently lost three of out best stablemen. Would the two of you be interested in the position?"

Expressions of hope erased the drawn, weary looks on each man's face. Immediately, they began to nod.

"Thank you, sir. Miss. Thank you both."

"This is indeed a blessing."

"Then it's settled." Phaedra clapped her hands together. "You men will find your quarters in the stable." She smiled, watching the men clasp their hands to pray. Obviously the two were stunned by the blessings that had visited them that day.

Zephir was reclining in the , wooden chair farthest from the stone hearth. He crossed his arms over his chest as he eyed each man speculatively. "It's nothing fancy, but at least you will be warm."

The men appeared quite grateful. They could barely finish their meals for thanking Zephir and Phaedra for their kindness. Afterwards, Zephir offered to show them to the stables.

"The two of you will be responsible for the upkeep of the horses. I assume you have had experience with animals?"

Both James and William nodded as they glanced around the building.

Zephir turned and headed further inside the cozy structure. "You'll find everything you need in those sheds along the far side of that wall. In the very back, you'll see your quarters.

There are blankets for the bunks and wood for the stove as well. Of course, you must exercize great caution if you build a fire."

"Of course, sir," the men agreed, eyeing their new surroundings.

Zephir sighed and rubbed his hands together. "Well, that should get you men started," he said as he headed back to the front of the stable. "Breakfast is at dawn, the noonday bell will announce lunch and supper is at dusk."

"Thank you, sir," the men called.

Zephir nodded then opened one of the heavy stable doors. "A good night to you both," he bade them over his shoulder.

The new stablemen watched the closed stable door for a couple of minutes. Then, one of them shrugged out of his torn overcoat and slammed it down to the hay covered floor.

"That black son of a bitch."

"I fully agree."

Dante Toussaint pulled the oversized cap from his head and threw it next to his tattered coat on the floor. "Can you believe that little bitch Phaedra has us sleeping out here like animals? We are actually servants in our own home," he marvelled, his once clean-shaved, round face, now thin and covered by a long, rough beard.

Carlos shook his head. If possible, he looked even more haggard than his brother. "This will never work. There is no way in hell I can take orders from that traitor Mfume!"

"It will be worth it in the end, my brothers."

Carlos and Dante turned to see their older brother emerge from the depths of the stable. He stopped near Midnight's stall and patted the Stallion's head.

"Marq, between the three of us, are you sure of this plan that you and Lezard have concocted?" Carlos inquired.

Marquis' smile was smug and wicked at once. "You forget that it was my plan, Carlos. Lezard's interest are in revenge against Mfume. I want something a bit more… sustaining. Soon, Phaedra and Zephir will be begging us to take Toussaints."

Dante and Carlos exchanged guarded looks. Before either of them could say another word, a few tufts of hay fell from the loft. Each of the men were quite shocked by the simple occurrence and focused their uneasy eyess on Marquis.

"Brother, do you really believe this will prompt them to relinquish their hold on Toussaints?" Dante asked.

Marquis' smile was grim, but confident. "When this all goes into effect, they will give us anything we desire."

Phaedra found Zephir in the boys' room later that night. Though his sons were fast asleep, Zephir simply sat on the bed and watched over them.

"Love? Is everything alright?" Phaedra asked, tightening the belt around her emerald green silk dressing gown.

Zephir reached out to Phaedra, and she did not hesitate to take his hand. She sat close to him on their son's bed and propped her chin on his shoulder. "What is it?" she asked.

"I just wanted to check on them," he whispered.

Phaedra smoothed her fingers against his close-cut hair and inhaled the crisp scent of outdoors still clinging to his clothing. Zephir pressed her hand to his mouth.

"Are all the invitations out?" he asked.

Phaedra smiled at his mention of the party. "All the invitations were sent out weeks ago."

"I can't believe these two will be one year old so soon," he said, his penetrating gaze soft as he brushed the silky hair curling over the boys's heads.

"It's quite unbelievable, isn't it?" she whispered.

He took a deep breath. "I pray all their days will be happy."

She nodded in agreement. "I swear they will be, despite my cousins attempts to cause havoc."

He turned and pressed a hard kiss against her lips. "I pray nothing will come of that letter, love."

"Words on paper do not worry me."

"I don't like the way you say that," Zephir seemed to growl, his expression turning hard.

Phaedra's body stiffened against Zephir's, her eyes narrowing. "Those bastards are not above using what they have been taught, for evil. They used it to take my mother... then Tisha. I won't let them do it again. I know how to fight that way, too."

Talk of black magic roused Zephir's anger. He watched Phaedra, bringing his face close to hers. "I told you once before that I did not want you involved with them or with that voodoo nonsense. Now, get it out of your mind."

"I can't."

Zephir's full lips thinned with anger, and he stood. Curling one huge hand around Phaedra's upper arm, he pulled her from their children's bedchamber. When he reached their own room, he closed the door with a vicious slam. The murderous expression on his sinfully, handsome face, should have convinced Phaedra to submit. Of course, it did not.

"Do you know how sick I am of trying to protect you?" Zephir asked, as he leaned against the door.

Phaedra tossed her thick hair across her shoulder and pinned him with a fierce look. "You can't be half as sick of it as I am."

Zephir stormed across the room and towered over her. "You say you know how evil those ingrates are. You have two children to consider and are putting yourself at war with them instead of concentrating on your sons!" he fiercely whispered.

"Oooooh!" Phaedra stewed. She could barely stand still, she was so angry. "I have always thought you to be a halfway intelligent man, Zephir Mfume. But you are truly causing me to question my judgement. I am thinking of my sons, dammit! I can't show cowardice or back down and let them take control by using what I know their mother taught them. I'm sorry if you do not or cannot approve, but asking me to step away from this is out of the question."

Suddenly, in a manner completely uncharacteristic of him, Zephir raised his hands in defeat. Phaedra watched him in disbelief. Slowly, she closed the distance between them. When she stood right before her husband, she gently rubbed her hand across his warm chest.

"I only ask that you listen to me, love," she whispered. " If I should become…aware of their plots, you should listen."

Though he said nothing, the look on his face spoke volumes. Clearly, Zephir Mfume had finally decided to submit to Phaedra Toussaint's strong will—for a while.

CHAPTER 21

The storm raged on. It had graduated from a heavy wind to include hard rain. The two elements combined with the ususual biting cold, made it impossible for any work to be done out of doors. Fortunately, the rain was not constant. Still, the terrain was slippery, treacherous and; in many places, iced over.

Zephir and Phaedra had no further disagreements concerning Marquis, Carlos and Dante. The letter and the threats it contained were forgotten. The couple concentrated on loving one another and taking care of their home and family. As a result, the intense cold outside made the inside more cozy.

The birthday gala for Toumie and Ric occurred as planned. Even though the wind and rain made travelling fierce, all the guests braved the weather. Since everyone invited lived on the island, almost the entire backyard was filled with carriages and wagons.

The two handsome guests of honor descended the curving staircase holding their father's hand. Instantly, the lower level, which was filled with well wishers, became alive with sounds of applause and laughter.

Zephir and Phaedra made a stunning pair. Zephir appeared the proud father—a wide confident grin brightening his face. He wore a three-quarter length gray wool suitcoat over a crisp, white linen shirt. A gray silk necktie matched the suit coat as did the wool trousers that draped impressively over his long legs. A pair of heavy gray boots, polished to a high shine, completed the ruggedly formal ensemble.

Phaedra was no less devastating. Her thick wavy hair was brushed back and wound into a loose knot atop her head. Tendrils fell from the ball to frame her beautiful face. The wine-colored gown she had chosen complimented her dark coloring and emphasized her tiny waist. The oval neckline was fringed with black lace and drew attention to the smooth, graceful line of her neck and full breasts. The only adornments she wore were a pair of diamond earrings and her husband's dazzling wedding ring. Delicate satin shoes complimented the gown perfectly, though they were partially hidden beneath the hem of the dress as it swept the polished wooden floors.

Once the little family joined the festivities downstairs, the string quartet resumed its music. Toumie and Ric appeared to be in awe of all the people and fancy dress. Soon, however, their attention was drawn to all the children playing in a area in the far corner of the ballroom.

"Papa!" the boys called up to their father.

Zephir was speaking to a few of the guests and could not hear his sons. A moment later, sharp tugs upon his trouser legs caught his attention. Kneeling, Zephir drew his sons close and pressed kisses to their smooth cheeks. "What is it, you two?"

Toumie and Ric pointed in the direction of the children before they looked back at him. Zephir smiled knowingly and took the boys across the sitting room. Every woman watched the tall, powerful male who had commanded attention without uttering a word. Every female in attendance, was in awe of his looks, build and the undeniable sensuality that followed him like a shroud.

Of course, Phaedra was no exception; she found it hard to take her eyes off the man as well.

Because the weather had turned so fierce, Zephir and Phaedra suggested their guests bring sleeping attire and a change of clothing. The fact that the gathering would include an overnight stay, made the night that much more enjoyable.

"After we cut the cake, I would like you two to get the boys settled to bed first. Then, instruct the other housemaids to the sleeping quarters for the other children."

Desiree and Nelia nodded. "Yes, Miss Phaedra," they replied in unison.

Giving the nursemaids a quick smile, Phaedra left them. She was about to rejoin her group of friends in the den, when two arms slid around her waist.

"I need your assistance." A deep rough voice growled.

Phaedra gasped and tried to turn in Zephir's arms, but he would not allow her to do so. "Well, what is it?" she inquired.

Zephir kept his lips pressed against her earlobe. "It's urgent," he replied, releasing her waist and taking her arm.

Phaedra grabbed her heavy skirts and had to run a little to keep up with him. Her confused frown deepened, when she noticed they were heading to the bedroom.

"What the hell is so urgent in here?" Phaedra demanded once Zephir had ushered her into the room and slammed the door behind them. "Zephir?"

Before she could say anything more, he came to tower over her. He continued to move forward until she lost her footing and tumbled back onto the bed.

"Zephir, this is not the time," she argued, recognizing the desire in his black eyes. She tried to push herself up, but he had already settled over her. "We have a house filled with people." She groaned, gasping when he lowered his head to her chest and stroked the swell of her breasts with his mouth. "Zephir…" she sighed, melting against the thick quilts covering the bed.

A wicked grin appeared on Zephir's mouth when he glanced up and saw the relaxed expression on Phaedra's face. His attention returned to the bodice of her gown; the rapid rise and fall of her breasts held his stare captive. As his lips traced the luscious curve, his fingers tugged at the delicate lace neckline.

"Zephir, please don't tear it," Phaedra moaned, feeling his breath upon her skin.

"Shh…" He pulled gently at the material until one full breast was exposed to his gaze. His lips captured the firm tip, soothing it with his tongue. The sound of Phaedra's soft cries in his ear increased his arousal. Slowly, possessively, his hands slid down her body and disappeared beneath the heavy skirts of her gown. He removed her underthings with such expertise, Phaedra did not realize he had done so.

A low moan passed her lips when his fingers thrust deeply inside her. The caress made her breathless with arousal. Zephir buried his face in Phaedra's neck, his tongue stroking the base of her throat. He added two more fingers to the caress and groaned at the increased rush of creaminess against his skin. Unable to control the urges of his body, he unbuttoned his trousers and freed himself.

Phaedra threw her arms above her head when he cupped her bosom in his hands and eased his throbbing length inside her. She had to pull her lower lip between her teeth to keep from screaming her pleasure. Zephir kept his hold tight as he increased the force of his thrusts. Soon, the room was filled with sounds of deep moans and breathless cries.

"Phaedra…Phaedra…" he repeatedly groaned as he approached complete satisfaction.

Phaedra was unable to say anything; she was too absorbed with the man who held her in his arms.

"Stop fidgeting, love."

Phaedra clasped her hands together and sent Zephir a sour look. "You could have waited, you know?" she whispered, as they descended the long staircase.

Zephir trailed his fingers along the nape of her neck. "Aren't you glad that I didn't?" He asked, using his most wicked tone of voice.

"I can just imagine the way I look."

"You're glowing."

"That's what I am afraid of!" she snapped, her eyes spewing fire. "Everyone will know what we've been doing the instant we are back downstairs."

A look of mock concern settled over Zephir's gorgeous face. "I must agree, love. I do hate to make our guests jealous, but it could not be helped."

Phaedra pressed her lips together, but was unable to resist the urge to laugh. When she and Zephir returned to the party, there was indeed no mistaking what they had been up to.

A five tiered lemon cake decorated with sweet white icing, had been prepared for the celebration. Once it was cut, served and partially devoured, the children's birthday party turned

into an "adults only" affair.

Phaedra endured countless jibes regarding her lengthy absense from the party. But it was all in good humor. Zephir was cursing himself for even letting her out of bed. Since the guests were also spending the night on the estate, many had journeyed upstairs to their respective rooms. Phaedra found her husband in the den before the fire. He was seated on the floor and leaning back against the sofa. She watched him for the longest time, entranced by the devastating appeal of his profile. Clearing her throat, she shut the den door and stepped into the room.

"Everything alright?" Zephir asked when he turned and saw her approaching.

"Mmm hmm…" She trailed her fingers along the back of the sofa then took a seat next to him in front of the long, burgundy and green upholstered seat.

Zephir followed her every move. "Would you like a drink?"

Phaedra pressed her hand against his arm, urging him to remain seated. "I'll just drink from yours," she whispered, glancing at his Brandy filled crystal goblet.

Zephir shrugged and offered her the glass. He watched her sip the dark liquid, looking towards her lips where a drop of the drink glistened. Groaning, he cupped the side of her face and kissed her deeply.

Phaedra allowed his tongue further into her mouth. The empty glass tumbled from her weak fingers, and it landed with a dull thud against the rug. She met the tremendous force of his kiss with a fire of her own. Zephir's hands cupped the soft mound of her breast, his thumb brushing the nipple straining against the bodice.

"Make love to me, Zephir."

"Don't worry, love."

Winding her arms about his neck, Phaedra pressed herself against his wide chest. They were kissing passionately, until Zephir pushed her to the rug and trailed his lips across her chest. Seconds later, a quick knock fell upon the den door.

"What?!" Zephir bellowed, sending a fierce glance toward the door.

"So sorry to interrupt, sir. There are two men awaiting you in the foyer."

Zephir sighed and raked one hand through his hair. "Tell them I'll be out shortly, Melin."

"Yes, sir."

"No…" Phaedra groaned, tugging at the loosened tie around Zephir's neck.

"I'll make this up. I promise," he growled, giving her a tight hug.

"I know." She pressed a kiss to the back of his hand.

"James, William," Zephir called, recognizing the two stable hands. "What can I do for you?"

James—Carlos Toussaint—stepped forward. "Please forgive us, sir, for disturbing your home at such a late hour."

"What is it?" Zephir asked, eyeing the men's drenched attire.

"Sir, the terrible rains have worn a hole in the roof of our sleeping quarters. The room is so bitterly cold. We ask your permission to request extra blankets."

Zephir waved his hand in the air. "Nonsense. It is far too treacherous out there to have you men sleeping in a place like that."

William—Dante Toussaint—came to stand next to his brother. "Sir, we do not mind sleeping in the stable. It is only our room that is drafty and wet."

"The animals can sustain weather like this out in the stables, but not men. We'll find you quarters inside," Zephir said.

The men exchanged uneasy looks then nodded. "Thank you, sir…thank you."

"Melin," Zephir called, waving to the housemaid, "show these gentlemen to one of the vacant rooms off from the kitchen."

The clouds darkening the sky made it seem more like evening than early morning. Of course, inside the house, the aura was cozy and relaxed. A few guests had awakened early to enjoy the huge breakfast buffet in the main dining hall.

Since the guests would be leaving that day, Zephir rose early as well. He had planned to assist the stablehands and the dockworkers in the send off. Phaedra had slept soundly after a long night of lovemaking. Zephir watched her snuggled beneath the heavy quilts. The moment he turned his back, her eyes snapped open and she bolted up in the middle of the bed.

"What is it?" he asked, watching his wife shove the covers back and jump to the floor. Shock registered on his face as she raced from the room.

Covered in nothing but a thin sheet, Phaedra flew down the hall which lead to her sons's room. Her long, black hair followed her like a storm cloud. When she pushed the door open, a tortured scream ripped from her throat.

The sound woke the entire house. Zephir thundered down the hall and into his boys's room. "What the hell is going on with you?" he roared.

Phaedra could not speak. She simply sat crouched on the floor and rocked herself back and forth. She stared straight ahead and Zephir followed suit. When he noticed Toumie's and Ric's bed, his heart dropped to his stomach. An instant later, he was gone from the room. With the assistance of several friends who had attended the party, the entire house was searched. Prayers swirled throughout Zephir's mind in hopes of finding the boys somewhere…anywhere.

Phaedra managed to make it half way down the staircase before she dropped to one of the steps and hugged herself. Though she was covered only by a sheet, she shivered from fear instead of the cold.

The boys were nowhere to be found, and Zephir could not stop the feeling of dread that washed over him. When he walked into the foyer and saw Phaedra on the staircase, he stormed over to her.

"Where are my sons?" he demanded, through clenched teeth. If possible, his harsh deep voice sounded even rougher.

"I swear I don't know. I wish to God that I did." Tears blurred her vision.

The low growl in Zephir's chest sent shivers down Phaedra's spine. In an instant, his hands gasped her upper arms, and he jerked her from the stairs. "Where are they?" he repeated, his eyes glaring down at her with murderous intent.

Phaedra tried to struggle out of the powerful grip. "I don't know!"

"Why not use your great powers to find them?!"

"Damn you to hell, Zephir," Phaedra whispered, using all her strength to shove against his chest. "How can you be so cruel?" she cried.

Zephir lifted her to face him eye to eye. "Madam, if my boys have been harmed in any way, you will see true cruelty."

"You black devil. They are mine, too!"

"And a fine job you have done in protecting them!"

"Remember, Zephir, it was you who told me to forget my cousins—to have nothing to do with them!"

"How dare you push this off as my fault?" he raged, his slanting midnight eyes narrowing to tiny slits.

Phaedra tossed her hair away from her eyes. "You hypocrite, you are doing the very same thing!"

Dubois had arrived that morning and was horrified by the scene which greeted him.

"Zephir, man, stop this!" He urged, hoping to douse the rising argument.

Zephir whirled around to face the man with nerve enough to step between he and his wife. Seeing Dubois's face, a smile almost crossed his mouth. "It is good to see you, friend," he whispered, laying a hand to the man's shoulder.

"What in the hell is going on here, Zephir?" Dubois questioned, frowning fiercely.

The hard glint returned to Zephir's eyes and he grimaced. "She lost my boys," he mumbled.

"You horses's ass, I did no such thing."

Dubois raised his hands in an effort to quell the couple's anger. "Phaedra—"

"What the hell would you call it?"

"How can you accuse me of something like this? Hell, Zephir, I was in your bed all night or have your forgotten?" she raged.

Zephir pointed a finger at Phaedra. "Don't play coy with me, woman. You know damn well what I mean."

"Oooooh!"

"Will one of you please tell me what all this is about?" Dubois demanded.

Phaedra cleared her throat and rolled her eyes away from Zephir. "The boys are missing. I went to their rooms this morning, and they were gone. I… should have seen it, before it was too late."

"Hmph," Zephir grunted, leaving Dubois and Phaedra standing on the stairway.

"My God…" Dubois whispered, stroking his smooth light jaw. "Are you certain they are gone? Have the house and the grounds been searched?"

Phaedra nodded, using the corner of the bed sheet to wipe her nose. "Zephir and some of the other guests did… earlier. The boys are gone."

"Man," Dubois called to Zephir, who leaned against the porcelain console table next to the front door. "Zephir, what will you do next?"

"I have no idea," Zephir groaned, massaging his temples with shaking fingers.

Phaedra could stand no more. Her legs weakened beneath her and she wanted to drop to the staircase again. When her gaze clashed with Zephir's, she stifled the urge. Lord, she had never seen him appear more threatening. He raked the length of her body in one cold stroke then he looked away and shook his head. A moment later, he stormed out of the foyer. Like a wilted flower, Phaedra succumbed to her weakness. Dubois was by her side in an instant.

"Come now," he whispered, pulling her close, "you must be strong for your sons." He carried her back up the staircase.

Phaedra could only rest her head against his shoulder. At that moment, she felt like giving up completely. Her boys were gone, perhaps for good, and Zephir...Zephir hated her.

Dubois secured Phaedra in the bedroom and went to check on Zephir. He searched the entire house before locating his friend near the icy cliffs at the edge of the plantation.

Zephir appeared to be in deep concentration, but noticed Dubois appearing from the corner of his eye. He turned to face his friend, the question on his face was unmistakeable.

"She's alright, my friend. She's resting," Dubois assured him. "The cooks are preparing a bit of soup for her."

Zephir turned back toward the cliffs. "Thank you," he muttered, though his deep voice carried amidst the heavy winds.

"This is not time for the two of you to be at odds."

"Don't you think I know that?!" Zephir hissed, turning his head just slightly. "My children are gone. Snatched from their beds in the middle of the night, and I have no idea where in this world they could be. The only place I want to be is with Phaedra, but I can't coddle her right now."

"Coddle? Man, she is hurting and confused just as you are. The last thing she needs is you blaming her for what has happened."

Zephir buried his face in his hands and uttered a tortured groan. "Where are they, Dubois?"

Dubois walked over and clapped Zephir's shoulder. "I wish to God I knew, my friend."

Zephir pulled his hands down and decided to stop wallowing in sorrow. He turned to Dubois and fixed him with a wicked look. "What brings you to these parts, my friend?"

"Actually, I'm as surprised to be here as you are to see me."

"I don't understand," Zephir replied, folding his arms over his chest. "What's this all about?"

Dubois's expression seemed to cloud. "Cantone Lezard."

"Lezard," Zephir breathed, a foul bile rising in his throat at the mere mention of the man's name. "He should be dead now or in his deathbed, at the very least," he remarked, recalling the bloody events of their last encounter.

Dubois cleared his throat. "He returned to his home on Wesleyville for a brief time before heading back to Africa. Afterwhich, he set sail for parts that were unknown to us. We have been paying a few of his guards to keep us informed."

"And?"

"It seems that he has a man in his employ that lives on this island. Lezard was livid when he discovered you and Phaedra were here living in bliss."

Zephir's jaw set into a grim line and his features took on an even more menacing appearance. "Lezard …Cantone Lezard on this island."

"Zephir, we don't know—"

"Oh, he's here. He's somehow involved in this. He and those maniacal brothers."

Dubois's brown brows drew closer. "What do you mean? The boys? You think—"

"I know."

"How do you want to handle it?"

Zephir was already headed back across the field. "We'll scour this entire island if need be. Once that bastard tells me where my boys are, I'll make sure that the next trip he takes will be in a coffin."

CHAPTER 22

"Love, please forgive me for what I said before. Everything will be fine, I promise," Zephir whispered against the soft hair feathering Phaedra's temple. He spoke the words with such conviction, he almost believed them.

By the time Dubois arrived upstairs, Zephir had joined Phaedra on the bed and was rocking her back against his chest. Dubois smiled and took a seat in a cushiony arm chair next to the fire. "Now, what are we going to do about getting your boys back?"

"Other than organizing a massive search, I cannot think of another way. We certainly cannot rely on my wife's…visions to assist us."

Phaedra appeared to be dozing. When she heard Zephir's comment, she landed a soft punch in his chest.

"I am only teasing, love," he whispered, rubbing one hand across her bare arm as he pressed a kiss to her forehead.

"I will inform the men. We can be ready to set out before noon," Dubois said, enjoying the warmth radiating from the huge stone fireplace.

Just then, Melin walked into the room. She carried a tray laden with a bowl of vegetable soup and honey buttered toast.

"Phaedra," Zephir called, shaking his wife from her light slumber, "let's get something into your stomach, love."

Dubois cast a thoughtful stare toward Melin as she set the tray before Phaedra. When she turned to leave the room, he stood. "Miss?"

Melin trembled and cast an uneasy look at the tall, attractive, vanilla-complexioned stranger. "Sir?" she whispered.

"My name is Dubois. I am an old friend of Mr. Mfume's."

Melin nodded, trying to force a smile to her lips. "I'm Melin."

"It's very nice to meet you, Melin," Dubois whispered. "Tell me, did you notice anything out of the ordinary last night during the party?"

"I saw nothing." Melin quickly replied, with a curt shake of her head.

Phaedra looked up from her soup and watched Melin closely. She had known the girl many years and could hear the terror in her light voice.

"Thank you, Melin," Dubois said, about to see the young woman out of the room.

"Melin?"

"Yes, Miss?" Melin replied, hearing Phaedra call her name. She kept her back turned, unable to face her with panic in her eyes.

"Melin…if you know anything, I beg you to please speak with us. I'll die if I lose my babies."

A mother herself, Melin's heart ached at the helpless tone she heard in Phaedra's usually strong voice. "Oh Miss…" she shuddered, her voice cracking as a sob rose in her throat, "they will kill my family if I say."

Zephir and Dubois exchanged glances across the room. Gently, Dubois took Melin's shoulders and turned her away from the closed bedroom door.

"Who will kill your family?" Zephir asked as he stood before Melin. Taking her hands, he squeezed them reassuringly. "I promise you, no harm will come to you or them, Melin."

"They are evil, so evil," Melin whispered, through tears and sniffles.

"My cousins?" Phaedra asked, already knowing the answer.

Melin nodded. "They came disguised as the two stablemen. I didn't know who they were until I showed them to their quarters. When they removed their hats and coats…they threatened my family," she cried. "I'm so sorry."

"Damn!" Zephir thundered, pounding his fist against his thigh. "Dubois, let's get that search party organized."

"And we had better find three sturdy ropes for the Toussaint brother's necks," Dubois suggested, falling in step next to his friend.

Zephir grimaced, his pitch black eyes becoming more narrowed. "There will be no need for a lynching. I'll break those necks myself."

"I was a day away from booting their worthless arses out of here, but they left on their own."

Dubois stepped closer to the bar. "Did they say where they were headed?"

Junie Somers scratched the colorful scarf that covered her bushy hair. "No, sir, they did not. In fact, for three men in such a dire state, they seemed especially haughty."

"Did they mention having any prospects for obtaining more money?"

Junie's eyes widened as she looked upon the huge, man who had spoken. "I am sorry, sir. They did not."

"Dammit," Zephir hissed.

"However," Junie said, raising one plump index finger in the air, "there was a man."

Zephir's hand curled into a massive fist. "What man?"

"He met with them the night before they left here. I don't think they knew him, but whatever they discussed was very intense."

"Ms. Somers, did you know this man?" Dubois asked, already setting a small bag of gold to the bar.

Junie nodded. "Kazro. Julian Kazro. He has or, had, a lovely place on the island. It's been deserted for some time, though you know?"

Zephir was grinning. "No, Ms. Somers, we didn't know. Why don't you tell us all about it?"

"Did they ever talk about their plans after leaving here?"

Several field and stable hands who had worked with the two phony stablemen gathered around Phaedra and shook their heads.

"We're sorry, Miss Phaedra. They kept to themselves and never mentioned movin' on once they got here," Corin Jes told her.

Phaedra pushed her hands into her cloak's deep pockets and bowed her head. *Why would they? Everything they want is right here.*

"It would help if she could speak with the boy."

Phaedra looked up at the man who had spoken. "What boy?"

"He's been living in the stable for weeks now. We only discovered him during the search this morning," Mitchell Gray explained.

"In the stable?"

"The loft actually, Miss," Mitchell clarified. He nodded toward a young man seated alone at the long wooden tables outside the barn.

The instant Phaedra set eyes on the boy, she raced over to him.

"Miss Phaedra, wait!" Corin called, but it was no use.

"Hello?" Phaedra called, stopping a few feet away from the young boy. When he turned and gave her a bright smile, she sat next to him. "You must be new to the plantation?"

Still smiling, the boy nodded.

"Could you see the men who were in the stable with you?"

Again, the young man nodded.

A tiny frown came to Phaedra's face, but she continued her questioning. "Did you ever hear them talking? Making plans?" She watched the boy nod continuously. She placed her hand across his and leaned forward. "What did they talk about?"

Finally, the bright smile on the boy's long, brown face, faded. Slowly, his hand rose and he tapped his fingers against his mouth.

"He's a mute, Miss," Corin explained. He and the other hands had witnessed the pityful scene between the boy and Phaedra.

Phaedra felt a momentary pang of defeat. She patted the boy's cheek. "Would you come with me?" she asked him softly, watching the child's smile return. She moved off the wooden bench and waited for him to join her. Arm in arm, they headed into the stables.

"You men wait here. I do not want us disturbed," She closed the door.

Inside, she guided the boy to a high stack of hay. When he was seated, she took his hands in hers. "Now, I want you to trust me, alright? I want you to see the men that were in this stable, hear their voices. Can you do that?" she whispered, watching him nod.

The boy was very cooperative. He did not shy away when she approached him. His lashes fluttered closed over his wide, deep-brown eyes when Phaedra placed her hand upon his brow.

A veil of mist clouded the vision. Then, the scene cleared. There, in a dank,

dark room, that resembled a cabin, were the brothers. They were staring down at Toumie

and Ric. The children sat upon a dirty quilt on the floor in the center of the room…

Phaedra snatched her hand away from the boy's head. Never before had she done such a thing. While she was elated by the ability, it was rather unsettling to know she could actually see

another person's thoughts. Clearing her throat, she forced her attention back to the situation. She still needed to know where the babies were being held…

The vision of the boys had vanished. It appeared that the scene had turned to the stable. In the center of the floor stood Marquis, Carlos and Dante. Marquis held a crisp, tan document in his hand. It was a map. A map showing the location of the ship where they held the boys.

Judging from the drawing on the page, the ship was docked in a hidden cove between the cliffs. It was the perfect spot…

Phaedra expelled a sigh of relief and patted the boy's shoulder. When he opened his eyes, she urged him to stand. Together, they headed to the massive double doors of the stable. Outside, the men waited as they had been instructed. Phaedra waved Corin over and glanced at the boy.

"See that he has a hearty meal. As much as he can stand. Then, find him clothes and more suitable sleeping quarters."

Julian Kazro's home was situated on the western bank of the island. The place was overgrown and resembled a decaying fortress. To a passing traveller, it would seem deserted, but Zephir and his men were eager for a closer look. Sadly, their move had been anticipated. Zephir was moments away from instructing his men on where to take position, when they were ambushed.

A monstrous net was thrown across Zephir and his horse, while Lezard's men aimed and cocked their weapons toward their adversaries.

"Cooperate, or your fearless leader is a dead man," Julian Kazro warned, then waved toward the men who were holding onto Zephir.

Of course, Zephir knew he could have broken free of the hold anytime he chose. Instead, he nodded, urging his men to remain calm. He hoped to be taken to Cantone Lezard.

The captors were instructed to do just that. They escorted Zephir up a long, creaking staircase and through a maze of corridors which led to a set of double doors. Inside a dim, musty room, lay Cantone Lezard in a bed covered by tattered linens.

"A fitting venue for your last days, Lezard," Zephir remarked, his eyes blazing with fury.

Cantone Lezard managed a weary smirk. "This isn't the sort of greeting I expected. Gentlemen," he instructed, and the men holding Zephir kneed his midsection with sharp blows. Their eyes registered surprise when their victim stood tall and uttered little more than a soft grunt.

Cantone Lezard even appeared mildly surprised. "I want to thank you for being so predictable."

"Where are my sons?" Zephir growled.

"Ah yes, the little Mfumes. Quite handsome."

"If you have so much as breathed upon them—"

"What? You'll kill me?" Lezard challenged, dismissing the possibility with a flippant wave.

Zephir was not fazed by the man's sarcasm. "I would torture you in ways not even you could imagine. Then I would kill you. If they are unharmed, and you tell me where they are. I will forgo the torture and simply kill you."

For a brief instant, Cantone Lezard appeared shaken. He laughed to mask his unease. "I do commend you, Mfume. Even in the face of unavoidable death, you fight as though victory is at hand."

"Where are they?" Zephir growled.

"Safe. For now."

"What do you want?"

"From you, your life. From your delicious wife… something a bit more… satisfying."

Zephir's expression grew more menacing. "You leave her out of this."

Cantone appeared shocked. "Now how can I do that? When it was she who rekindled our rivalry."

Zephir ordered himself to keep his distance. "Decrepit jackass, you took her from me," he whispered.

"Took her from you?" Cantone Lezard inquired, his voice shaking a bit before a terrible coughing spell set upon him. "She was on my land, and I took her from you. She was fleeing from you, and I saved her life!"

"Whatever fantasies you have wielded in that rotting brain of yours are of no concern to me. I want my sons."

"Ah, the boys…" Cantone sighed, trying to retain his cool demeanor despite the pain ravaging his body. "I must say, Mfume, you do play the role of the doting father quite realistically. However, I feel it is time to tell you what will be."

Zephir bowed his head. His hands were clenched into massive fists.

"My men are going to strip you bare and take you down to Kazro's rank, rodent infested cellar. Your men will be slayed and placed their as well. This house will be boarded and abandoned and you will have the joy of anticipating how death will visit you. Will you die of starvation and cold or will you simply go mad listening to those hungry rodents devour the flesh of your men before they begin to feast on you?"

"Your men would never be victorious over mine," Zephir growled.

Cantone's bony shoulder rose beneath his brown, linen smock. "I suppose we will never know, considering your men have been relieved of their weapons. No time for a fair fight, you understand?"

Zephir managed a smirk. "Of course."

"Moving on," Cantone sighed, praying he could perpetuate the image of a man at ease for just a while longer, "we will be off to the Toussaint plantation where I will begin to collect on several nights of promised ecstacy from your luscious Phaedra."

Zephir felt his stomach roil at the image. "You will not touch her."

"Not only will I touch her, Mfume, I will have her every way that I can think of. Perhaps, I'll even invent a few new ways."

Suddenly, Zephir laughed. The sound filled the room and unnerved all who heard it. "You decaying fool, look at you. I doubt you could shit on your own, much less produce enough of an erection to bed a woman."

"Never fear, my virile friend!" Cantone snapped, eager to remove the grin from Zephir's face. "Should I not be able to carry out my duties, I assure you my men would be most eager for the pleasure. There is a certain enjoyment in watching, you know? I think I may let them have a go at her. I'll even have your handsome sons watch their mother being taken by a hoard of sex-starved men." He managed a weak laugh.

Zephir waited until Lezard's men had joined their leader in laughter. The two men next to him had slackened their hold on his arms, and he siezed the opportunity. In a split second, his arms rose and he swung them inward, causing the men to butt faces. Their noses broke and blood spewed in a gush of fiery red. By the time Lezard realized what had happened, Zephir had already killed another guard and was now armed with a sword and gun. He moved a rickety bureau before the door, while fighting at least four attackers. Incredibly, Zephir was the victor. Cantone Lezard lay helpless and watched his guards lose their lives, one by one.

At last, Zephir stood less than a foot away from Lezard's bed. He was drenched in blood and entrails and looked as evil as Lucifer. Cantone Lezard let out a curdling scream and tried to leave the bed. Zephir was upon him then, one massive hand curled around the throat of his adversary.

"Where are my sons?"

Lezard coughed raggedly. "Not here. Not here, I swear."

"Where then?!"

Though he feared for his life, Lezard would not submit. "As I told you, they are safe. For now."

Zephir brought his face closer to Lezard's. "Do you realize that I am about to kill you?"

Lezard's gaze faltered for a moment. "Go ahead. As you said, my body is decaying. I am but a hair's breathe away from the other world. Do it, Mfume. But understand that by killing me, you will never know where your children are, and I will die a happy man."

Lezard's smug certainty assured Zephir that the man would never reveal what he knew. Keeping one hand around Cantone Lezard's throat, Zephir placed the other over the man's nose and mouth.

Lezard's brown eyes widened suddenly, when his breathing was stifled. He began to claw the the monstrous hand covering his face, but could not budge it an inch. Though weakened, he thrashed about like a wild animal. Zephir was oblivious to everything, intent on extinguishing the life of the man who threatened the welfare of his family.

Lezard's thrashing ceased and, at last, he lay dead. Zephir's hands did not move from their murderous position. It was not until Dubois voice sounded through the door, warning Lezard's men to surrender, that Zephir broke free of his trancelike state.

Dubois's green eyes widened when the door opened. "My friend, are you—"

"I'm alright." Zephir\ leaned against the doorjamb.

"What happened?" Dubois inquired as he and their men filled the room.

Zephir turned to take in the bloody sight. "What does it look like?"

"The rest of Lezard's men are dead." Dubois stared down at the Lezard's lifeless body. "Did he tell you anything?"

Zephir massaged the bridge of his nose and fought the pressure of tears behind his eyes. "He knew, but he would not say."

Dubois could only imagine how distraught his friend was. While the men inspected the scene for any live bodies, Dubois crossed the room and patted Zephir's back in hopes of reassuring him. The strokes had the desired affect. Zephir straightened and fixed his friend with a determined glare.

"Let's get back to Toussaints, regroup and resume our search."

Dubois nodded. "Men, burn this godforsaken stack of boards to the ground and get back to the plantation."

When Phaedra returned to the house, the entire lower level was filled with men rushing about. Some were loading guns, while others were bundling up for the cold. Phaedra saw Zephir in the far corner of the foyer. He was studying maps showing the outlay of the island, and he did not notice his wife standing a few feet away. It was just as well for Phaedra. She wanted to speak with Dubois. She found him pulling on a heavy cloak and rushed over.

"Dubois? A moment of your time?" she whispered, pulling the hood of her wrap from her head.

A small furrow formed between Dubois brows and he took her by the arm. "What is it?" He asked.

Phaedra placed her small hands against his chest. "Don't tell Zephir where you learned of this."

"Phaedra what—"

"Listen! A mute boy living above the stables witnessed my cousins plotting the abduction of the babies. I know where they are."

"How could you, my dear, if the child is a mute?"

Phaedra braced herself. "I could see his thoughts. Now, I know Zephir thinks that is nonsense, but I swear to you. My sons are being held in a ship that is hidden in a cove between the cliffs."

Slowly, Dubois nodded. "Since we do not know where to begin our search. The cliffs will be as good a place as any."

"Thank you," Phaedra sighed, her eyes sparkling with relief.

"We'll bring them back." He headed out with the other men.

Phaedra watched everyone head out and prayed that her sons would return…alive.

"Are you sure about this, man?"

Dubois only nodded at Zephir's question. They travelled along the rocky bottom near the cliffs. Though the terrain was treacherous, given the harsh weather of the past weeks, Dubois had insisted they begin the search there.

The group of armed men located the cove. It was sheathed by a heavy fog, which made it impossible to see beyond the opening.

"My God," Zephir breathed when the fog lifted, and he made out a ship in the distance. "What the devil?" he whispered, following the path along the wall of the cliff.

The men forged ahead. When they reached the boat, they rushed aboard—on the look out for any hidden attackers. There were none to be found. Fortunately, Toumie and Ric were in a small cabin playing together on a dingy quilt. They were alone, but content.

The moment the two small boys spotted their father, their cute, dark faces lit up. They both raised their arms to Zephir and he wasted no time going to them.

"Thank you God," he whispered, pressing hard kisses to Toumie and Ric's wavy, hair. Taking a boy in each arm, he headed out of the dismal cabin. "Burn this contraption to the ground. I want nothing left but ashes."

"How did you know where to find them?" Zephir asked Dubois as they headed off the ship.

The man shrugged. "A field hand thought he saw something."

"He'll never know how indebted I am," Zephir whispered, squeezing his sons against his chest.

Hiding behind a deep crack in the cliff's stone wall, Marquis, Carlos and Dante watched their home burn.

"If Zephir is alive, Lezard is dead," Carlos said. "Whatever will we use to bargain with now?"

"Damnation! How in hell did they find them so quickly?!" Dante whispered.

"It had to be Phaedra," Marquis growled, his deep-set brown eyes shining with hate.

"Where can we go now?" Carlos cried.

Marquis was silent for a moment. "I have an idea."

CHAPTER 23

"They have returned, Miss Phaedra! Miss Phaedra, they are here!"

Phaedra ran from the den to the kitchen. From the back door, she watched the men return from the search. The moment she saw Zephir with their sons, she raced out to meet them.

"Thank you, God," she whispered, her hands cradling Toumie and Ric's heads as she pressed fevered kisses to their baby soft cheeks. She turned from Zephir, who held the boys, and took Dubois's hands in hers. "Thank you," she whispered, pulling him close, "thank you so very much."

Dubois nodded. He glanced toward Zephir and took note of the curiosity on the man's face. Clearing his throat, he smiled at Phaedra before stepping away.

Phaedra had no words for her husband. She simply relieved him of their heavy sons and carried them inside the house.

"I thought I gave the nursemaids permission to take you two outside," Phaedra whispered to Toumie and Ric. She found the twins at play in Zephir's study. Surprisngly, they were quite content in spite of their father's rough, deep voice filling the air. Phaedra could hear him barking orders to his men about the changes he wanted made to the house. Phaedra listened in horror and realized that Zephir actually wanted to have a brick wall constructed to shield the house from view.

Phaedra was seething with anger, but waited until Zephir finished his meeting before she intervened. "What the hell are you doing?" she demanded to know, pushing thick tresses away from her face as she stepped closer to him.

Zephir's black eyes raked his wife's voluptuous form encased in a long, red, riding crop. He shook his head and pushed away the erotic thoughts which filled his mind. "I am trying to protect my family."

Phaedra propped one hand on the curve of her hip and met the comment with a short laugh. "I can't believe you are contemplating the construction of a brick wall."

"I'm not contemplating. I have already decided to have the wall erected."

"You'd actually deprive your children of sunlight. They need it to grow, in case you have forgotten."

"Well, luckily, the wall will not shield the sky," he cooly replied.

She uttered a long, frustrated sigh. "Are you afraid of my cousins?"

Zephir slammed his fist against the desk with such force, it creaked. Even Toumie and Ric ceased their play to look up at their father. "That is not the case," he assured her, trying to keep his

tone light, "but I do plan to hunt those devils down and kill them. While I'm about that business, I do not want to be concerned with anything further happening to my boys."

Knowing it was useless to try changing Zephir's mind, Phaedra searched for a better solution. She tapped her index finger to her mouth and pondered. Finally, the perfect idea came to mind. "Why don't we send them to Cuba?"

The idea struck Zephir's interest. "You think?"

"It would be perfect. Your parents would love to see their grandsons. Besides, the letter Carmelita sent with the boys's birthday gifts said she and your father would love to have them for a while."

"It would be good for them." He stroked the side of his jaw.

She looked back at her little men who had resumed their play. "Yes, I agree."

Suddenly, he grinned. "That place can certainly do a world of good for a growing boy's body."

Phaedra's wide, expressive eyes slid across the impressive expanse of her husband's powerful form. "That is quite obvious."

Obviously, Zephir was a bit shocked by her blatantly suggestive comment. He cleared his throat and looked toward Toumie and Ric. "Cuba will be the best place for the boys. Especially, until things change around here. I'll put Dubois in charge of getting them there."

Sending her husband a dazzling look, Phaedra clasped her hands together. "That is a wonderful idea. Dubois would be perfect for the job."

His wife's wholehearted endorsement for his first mate and best friend roused Zephir's suspicion. "Love," he sighed, massaging the bridge of his nose, "is there anything I should know?"

Phaedra fixed him with a confused look and tilted her head to one side. "Such as?" she asked, only to have Zephir stare at her in response. Finally the confusion cleared from her eyes. "Zephir, you know Dubois did save the boys?"

"Hell, woman, I was there, too!" he bellowed, the look in his eyes a mixture of hurt and disbelief.

Phaedra pressed her hand against her chest to still her pounding heart. "Zephir…are you jealous?" she whispered.

"Nonsense," he denied with a wave of his hand, "you act as though I had nothing to do with my sons's rescue."

Frustrated, Phaedra buried her face in her hands. Before Zephir's mood could cause him to really lose his temper, she decided to soothe his concerns. "Listen to me, you men wouldn't have found those boys so quickly had it not been for me."

"You?" Zephir replied, his laughter close to the surface.

"That is correct, Zephir Mfume. Little, insignificant me! A mute boy living above my cousins in the stables, overheard their plot. I was able to see his thoughts, just as though I had been there myself. I confided in Dubois, because I knew you would never believe me. Of course, Dubois had a difficult time accepting what I was telling him, but he listened. Had it not been for me, my sweet, you would most certainly still be searching for our sons!"

Zephir was far too stunned to speak. Of course, he knew it was true. He stood completely still while Phaedra stormed out of the room.

A few days passed before the boys were able to leave for their grandparents' home in Cuba. The ship was thouroughly checked from bow to stern. Each deck was scoured for any trace of the Toussaint brothers or any other threat. Phaedra and Zephir had not spoken to one another since the day they had decided to send the children to his parents. Of course, with all the preparations in progress for Toumie and Ric's departure, quiet moments alone were practically non-existent. Unfortunately, this only pulled the couple further apart.

Finally, The Enchantment, Dubois's impressive ship, was ready to cast off. Neither Phaedra nor Zephir could believe they were actually about to say goodbye to their babies. Still, they both knew it was for the best that Toumie and Ric leave the island.

Phaedra hugged herself, rubbing her arms briskly to ward off the chill in the air. As her eyes followed the ship that carried her sons away, she wondered what was to happen next.

"Now, I hunt down those sons of bitches," Zephir growled, as though he were reading her mind.

"Where will you begin to look?" Phaedra asked, her eyes still focused on The Enchantment.

Zephir's slanted eyes slid down to Phaedra, and he smirked. "I was hoping you could tell me, love."

Phaedra didn't know if Zephir was serious or being sarcastic, so she kept her eyes on the sea and her mouth shut. Of course, she had her own helpful ideas, but in light of her husband's mood, she would keep them to herself.

Zephir was up before dawn the next morning. He was to be gone several days before returning home and had spent much of the previous night packing. He and Phaedra had yet to settle their differences and there was no time for that then. As he pulled on a pair of heavy black boots, his onyx stare stole secret glances on his wife, who still slumbered. Lord, how he ached for her, he thought. The entire situation had affected the two of them far more than he had anticipated. The path his thoughts had taken caused him to shake his head. With his mouth set into a grim line, he decided that they would most certainly talk upon his return.

Phaedra waited until the bedroom door shut behind Zephir then opened her eyes. Then, she was up in a flash. She quickly changed into a pair of navy, blue riding breeches, matching coats and boots. After shoving her long, thick hair beneath a cap, she headed out. She saddled Midnight and the two rode all the way to Berekua to see Kwesi.

"Sir? Sir, a moment of your time, please!?"

Kwesi set the papers he held on the desk and fixed the young man standing in the doorway of the study, with a confused expression. "Good heavens, Jules, what is it?"

Jules clutched his beige cap tightly in one hand while waving Kwesi forward with the other. "A young woman to see you, sir," he whispered.

Kwesi frowned and pushed the , leather chair away from the desk. "Where?" he inquired, his long strides bringing him across the office.

Instead of answering, Jules took Kwesi by the arm and pulled him through the house. Outside, propped against one of the massive columns that lined the front porch, was Phaedra.

"Good Lord, child," Kwesi whispered, dropping to his knees next to her. "What are you doing here? Does Zephir know about this?"

Phaedra offered Kwesi a weak smile and curled her fingers around the lapel of his forest green suit coat. "He doesn't know…please don't send word to him."

Kwesi patted her hand and nodded. "Love, what ever possessed you to ride all this way on your own?"

Phaedra was far too exhausted to offer any answers to Kwesi's questions. When her long lashes fluttered over her eyes, Kwesi pulled her into his arms and put her to bed.

"Feeling better?" Kwesi asked later that evening when Phaedra stepped into the sitting room.

"Much better. Thank you." She took a seat on one of the upholstered white armchairs before the fire.

He handed her a cup of steaming tea then took a seat in the opposite chair. "Love, what forced you to do this? Why would you not want Zephir to be informed of your whereabouts?"

Realization dawned on Phaedra's face. "You didn't send word to Toussaints, did you?"

"No, no. I'm waiting for you to offer me some sort of explanation."

"Well, Zephir isn't home. He's out searching for Marquis, Carlos and Dante."

"I see, and you've decided to offer your…assistance without his knowledge?" Kwesi guessed.

Phaedra leaned forward in her chair and pounded her fist against the arm. "Those bastards took my children. They disguised themselves as stablehands and worked the land for weeks. On the night of Toumie and Ric's birthday celebration, the storm was so terrible we allowed them shelter in the house. The next morning the boys were gone."

"My Lord." Kwesi pressed one hand against his face.

"Thankfully, I was able to see the thoughts of a stableboy who overheard them plotting. He was a mute, and it was the only way I could find out anything."

"Did you tell Zephir about this?" Kwesi asked, watching Phaedra nod. "I know he didn't approve."

She shrugged. "He didn't like it, but he would have sought the devil's assistance to find Toumie and Ric then."

"So why didn't the two of you join forces?"

"Zephir wants me to stay at home, Kwesi. He does not want my assistance in this, no matter how helpful it may be. I refuse to sit by and do nothing. I want my cousins dead—preferably by my own hand."

Leaning back in his chair, Kwesi braced his fingers together. "So, what can I do?"

"I know where they are."

"How?"

Phaedra fixed him with a pointed look. "How else? I need your help in getting to them."

"Of course. Let me round up some men, and we can set out. Where exactly are we heading?"

Phaedra propped her chin on her fists and stared into the fire. "My cousins are with Margantis."

"Margantis?" Kwesi repeated, rising from the armchair. "Margantis, the witchdoctor?"

"That is the one," Phaedra said, standing as well. "I can see them all together so clearly now. If only I could've seen it before," she lamented.

"Good Lord, child. If they join forces with the likes of that man—"

"They already have." She turned back to the fire. "At least once that I know of… when they murdered Tisha," she said, cursing herself for not realizing it was Margantis meeting with her cousins then.

Kwesi was silent for several minutes. Then, he patted Phaedra's shoulder and headed out of the room.

Phaedra continued to look into the roaring fire. *Marquis, Carlos and Dante Toussaint, your time upon this planet is quickly approaching its end.*

Margantis lived in a remote village located at the northern tip of Dominica. The trip took several days, but it was well worth it.

"Alright men, we must be certain that they are inside," Kwesi cautioned the group. "We will wait… silently."

The wait proved to be a lengthy one. Just as the group turned bored and restless, the front door opened. Indeed, there were Marquis, Carlos and Dante.

"Those devils," Kwesi whispered. "Alright, men, we want them dead."

The group, including Phaedra, stormed Margantis's fortress. Kwesi lost several of his men, as did Margantis—who died at the tip of Phaedra's knife. Somehow, Marquis, Carlos and Dante evaded death. They escaped, but not before seeing Phaedra. They each acknowledged the force of her gift. The brothers realized the time for plotting had come to an end. It was time for their cousin to die.

Phaedra breathed a relieved sigh when Midnight galloped into the front yard of Toussaints. She could not wait to get out of the grimy riding clothes and soak in a hot bath. Zephir would most likely be returning any day, and she wanted to be well-rested when she faced him.

"Miss Phaedra! Lord, we did not know what happened to you!"

Phaedra leaned forward on Midnight's back. She grabbed Melin's hand and held it tightly. "I'm alright. Just cold and very tired."

Melin's hazel stare was filled with worry. "Mr. Zephir almost went mad when he found out you were—"

"Zephir is back?" Phaedra asked, her heart beginning to flutter.

Melin nodded. "Yes, he returned last evening."

Phaedra grimaced and looked back at Kwesi, who had seen her home. Before she could dwell on it all, the front door opened and Zephir stormed outside.

"Where the devil have you been?!" he demanded to know, his long strides bringing him across the yard quickly.

She raised her hands. "Zephir, wait!"

"Not until you explain this to me, Phaedra, and it damn well better be good!" In one swift movement, his massive hands encircled her waist, and he lifted her from Midnight's back. "Start talking."

She could understand how livid her husband must have been, yet she was in no state to talk to him just then. Her eyes dropped, and she lost the strength in her legs. Zephir watched his tiny wife slump against her horse for support and he immediately pulled her into his arms.

"What is this? What's wrong with her?" he whispered, his deep voice holding a trace of fear.

"She needs rest, Zephir," Kwesi explained as he jumped from his own horse. "I'll explain what has happened."

Zephir nodded and beckoned Melin and another housemaid. He instructed them to carry Phaedra upstairs for a bath and put her to bed. Then, he nodded toward Kwesi. "We'll get the horses and your men settled. Then, you tell me everything."

"I haven't wanted to admit that I believe she has some...power. I suppose her visions are not nonsense after all."

Kwesi chuckled and shook his head. "No, my boy. This is not nonsense."

Zephir reclined in a burgundy armchair in his study. His fingers massaged his forehead as he listened to Kwesi recount the events of the last few days. "She actually killed this Margantis?" he asked, undoubtedly amazed.

"She did," Kwesi confirmed. "Unfortunately, he wasn't the one she truly wanted."

Zephir nodded. "I know... Jesus, Kwesi. In wanting to keep her save, I've been so hard on her."

"I understand. Phaedra's father, Fredericks, felt the same way about

Marguerite, Phaedra's mother. using her gift. Perhaps, you could try accepting it. Besides, it seems she only uses it when her family is in danger."

Slowly, Zephir nodded. "You're right, my friend. I should speak with her." He glanced toward the ceiling. "Will you be staying?"

Kwesi shook his head. "We must get back after we've eaten."

"Thank you, Kwesi."

Kwesi waved one hand. "No need for thanks. I'm only glad that I could be of some assistance. Take care of her."

Zephir stood and shook hands with the older man. "I will. I will."

Zephir saw Kwesi and his men off that evening. Then, he headed upstairs. When he stepped into the bedroom, the drapes had been drawn and the chamber was in semi darkness. Making his way to the huge four poster maple canopy bed. Zephir took a seat on the edge. He toyed with Phaedra's hair for a moment then pulled her close.

"Zephir…" she murmured in her sleep and snuggled her head deeper into his lap.

No other words were spoken. The two held each other through the night.

Zephir woke long before daybreak, wanting to get an early start on the hunt for the Toussaint brothers. So he would not disturb his wife, he began to ease his way out from beneath the covers. He had not moved far when her arms tightened around his waist.

"Please don't leave me just yet," she moaned.

Zephir slid back beneath the covers and pressed a soft peck to her cheek. "Love, I have to get an early start if I hope to catch up to your cousins. That is, if they are still on the island."

"They—" Phaedra began, and then cut herself short. She could feel them near and wanted to share the information with her husband. Knowing how he felt about her "gift," she decided to keep quiet.

"It's all right, love," he whispered against her ear.

"What?"

"I don't want you to feel the need to hide this from me anymore. Anything to do with your cousins, or the visions you have about them, I want you to tell me."

Phaedra propped herself on her elbows and looked down at him. "What changed your feelings?"

"Something Kwesi said." He toyed with a wavy strand of her hair. "I've always had a problem accepting things I couldn't understand or control."

"Most people do, love," she whispered, running her lips along the smooth surface of his cheek.

"Promise me one thing, though?" he whispered, waiting for her to look in to his eyes again.

"Yes?"

"Promise me you won't have this house filled with herds of people seeking to have their fortunes told?"

When Phaedra saw her husband's dazzling white grin in the semi-darkened room, she burst into laughter. "I promise." She pressed her mouth against his.

After so many nights away from her, the simple kiss was not enough. Zephir's wide hands took Phaedra's upper arms in an unbreakable hold, and he lifted her to straddle his hips.

Phaedra's sharp intake of breath was clearly audible in the silent room. She threw her head back and groaned as Zephir's fingers ventured beneath the hem of her short nightgown. Beads of moisture slid down her thigh in anticipation of his touch. "Zephir…" she gasped as he stroked the soft, wet center of her body.

Zephir teased her mercilessly, not stopping even when she begged him to take her. Instead of giving her the treat she craved, he ended the caress in order to unbutton her gown. The soft material slipped from her shoulders, falling to the bedcovers without making a sound.

Phaedra raked her fingers through her silky hair and the mass tumbled against her back. Daylight was beginning to fight past the drapes, touching the room with faint streams of light. Zephir's eyes narrowed as they traced every inch of her body. He would never get past how incredibly beautiful she was.

The same was true for Phaedra as she looked down at her husband's magnificent form. With his smooth blackberry-toned skin and taunt, rigid muscles, he was her every desire come alive. She trailed her fingers over the wide surface of his chest, down his flat belly and past the waistband of his lounging pants. Her hips began to rock against his in a manner that was purely erotic.

Zephir could not ignore her need, or his, any longer. Without pulling the pants completely away from his body, he untied the fastening and freed his stiff arousal. Easily, he lifted her and settled her down upon his pulsing, devastaing length. When the creamy heat sheathed his manhood, his deep groans filled the room.

Phaedra was speechless as she slid up and down above his hips. She was too pleasured to even moan as his fingers trailed the length of her thighs before they teased the satiny swell of her buttocks. When her desire rushed forth, she wanted to fall against his chest and catch her breath.

He would not allow her to do so and tightened his hold on her waist. He thrust upwards, drawing a ragged, helpless moan past her lips. Then, wanting more control, he kicked the pants from his long legs and flipped Phaedra onto her back. The powerful lunges deepened as he increased the speed of his thrusts. Soon, the room was filled with breathless cries as Phaedra experienced another strong orgasm.

Zephir buried his face in the crook of her neck and cupped the sides of her breasts in his hands. His fingers brushed the soft nipples until they hardened beneath his touch. His lips closed around one rigid peak, and he suckled it harshly, alternating between grazing it with his perfect teeth and soothing it with slow strokes of his tongue. The effect was incredible and, within minutes, his seed spilled deep inside her.

"I love you," they whispered in unison moments later and held each other tightly.

Zephir and his men had already been gone several hours when Phaedra finally emerged from the bedroom. As she strolled through the elegant rooms of her home, she was amazed. She

and Zephir had decided to give much of the staff time off after the boys birthday. With only a staff of four or five, the house took on a tranquil aura that was quite appealing.

A thunderous pounding on the front door shattered the peacefulness, and Phaedra hurried downstairs. The knocking was so incessant, she gathered the heavy skirts of her gray button-down riding gown, and ran the rest of the way. When she opened the massive maple door to her cousins, a startled cry escaped her lips.

Marquis stood there with his brothers. They were all soaked by the pelting rain. Each man appeared ragged and miserable, though their deep eyes burned with murderous intent.

Phaedra tried to push the door close, but it was no use. The brothers shoved against the heavy maple and whipped it from her grasp. A piercing scream sounded from her throat, and soon the foyer was filled with the few remaining servants.

"Stay back!" Dante ordered, grabbing Phaedra by her hair and jerking her back against his musty form. He held a jagged knife next to her throat.

Melin and two of the other housemaids tried to stifle their cries, while the butler attempted to inch closer to the maniacal brothers. Of course, Marquis, Carlos and Dante would now allow anyone to interfere with what they had come to do.

"You son of a bitch! Get the hell back or you will damn well be cleaning up your mistress's blood sooner than you expect," Marquis sneered, his voice hoarse.

Horace, the butler, moved away.

Carlos grinned at his brothers. He and Marquis secured the servants and then headed out to the sitting room. Dante tightened his hold around Phaedra's waist as they walked forward.

"Sign it!" Marquis ordered, shoving a sheet of paper in front of her.

Phaedra spat onto the document then raised her eyes to her older cousin's face. "I curse you three rank bastards to hell. Get the hell out of my house, this instant dammit!"

"Haughty bitch!" Dante roared. He pressed the grizzly-looking edge of the knife to her throat and drew a few drops of blood. "Your pretty face will be next."

Phaedra pushed away the fear and helplessness which threatened to overtake her. She gathered all her strength and stabbed Dante's ribs with her elbow and smirked when he howled in agony. As his arms fell away from her, she bolted from the room.

"You fools! Get her!" Marquis roared, storming out after his cousin.

Phaedra did not stop running when she reached the foyer. Deciding she would feel safer outside the house, she raced out the front door. The rain was falling in blinding, heavy sheets and running across the land was quite hazardous. The day had become almost as dark as night. Though she knew the land by hand, the utter blackness made it quite difficult to see more than two feet before her face. Still, she continued to run . She used the brief illumination of the sharp lightning to forge ahead. She never looked back and ran until she could make out the cliffs.

Stopping just as she approached the edge, Phaedra searched frantically for any escape. There was no way out, and she realized this was the way it would have to be. This was where it would end. She braced herself and turned to face her cousins.

Dante caught her and held her back against him. He pinned her arms behind her back, while Carlos landed a vicious blow to the side of her face. Phaedra retaliated with an angry bellow and was able to use both her boots to place a quick kick to his midsection. Carlos moaned and fell to his knees. Phaedra did not have long to enjoy the small victory. Marquis landed a blow just as vicious to her belly and followed it up with a stinging backhand to her face.

"Oh thank the Lord you have returned, Mr. Zephir!"

Zephir had returned and found the servants bound. "Where is she?" He asked Melin once she was freed.

Melin pointed. "She ran past us and out the door, off into the storm!"

Filled with an indescribable rage, Zephir turned in the direction of the cliffs. Somehow he knew she would be there. Of course, his men followed only to be stopped. "They are mine." He growled and raced into the night.

The scene meeting Zephir's eyes almost stopped his heart. The lightning was steady now. He could see clearly and watched, stunned as his tiny wife was attacked by her own flesh and blood.

"Toussaints!" he bellowed, bringing a halt to the assault.

"I want him first," Dante whispered, spotting Zephir's imposing form in the distance. He shoved Phaedra to Carlos then handed him the knife. Nodding at Marquis, the two silently decided it would be more prudent to double team their powerful adversary.

"All right," Zephir whispered, his voice holding just a trace of humor. He held his arms away from his body and flexed his fingers. His frame was haunched and resembled a grizzly bear about to attack.

Dante and Marquis pounced in unison. They landed several vicious blows against Zephir's neck and face. Their knees simultaneously punished the man's abdomen with heavy hits. Their triumph was short lived. Sneering like a wild bull, Zephir first knocked Marquis to the muddied ground with one swing of his elbow; the man lay stunned and unable to move.

The youngest Toussaint continued to fight, only to have Zephir pull him away like an annoying insect. Dante shrieked his pain when Zephir slammed him across one powerful thigh. The smaller man's back bone shattered, and he was paralyzed.

Phaedra and Carlos watched the bloody fight with wide eyes. A high pitched scream flew past Carlos's lips when Zephir turned back to Marquis and effortlessly pitched him over the side of the cliff.

Marquis had managed to grab the edge of a sharp rock and pinned himself against the ragged wall of the cliff. He looked up when Carlos screamed again. This time, Zephir had thrown Dante across the edge.

"Danteeee!" Marquis cried, watching his baby brother fall to his death.

"Zephir!" Phaedra screamed, only to have Carlos press the knife closer to the base of her neck.

"Shut up !" he ordered in a high, shaking voice.

"Toussaint!" Zephir called

Phaedra used the sharp heel of her boot to stab her cousin in the shin. Carlos gave an agonizing scream and was about to shove the knife's grimy blade into her throat.

"Let her go, Carlos," Zephir prompted. His raspy voice was low and calm as he took note of how close they were to the edge of the cliffs.

"Stay the hell away from us, Mfume! I will see to you after I carve this proud slut!"

Phaedra used all her strength to struggle out of Carlos's arms. "You mad son of a bitch!" Landing another blow to his shin, she managed to pull the knife away from her neck. "Join your brothers!" she commanded and turned in his arms. She grabbed the lapels of his tattered coat and jerked him close. Before Carlos could react, she rammed her knee into his groin and shoved him over the rocky edge.

"Aaaaagh!" Carlos's cry sounding high pitched and piercing then turned faint as he crashed into the raging sea far below.

Phaedra's gaze narrowed as she stood there staring over the side of the jagged edge. Marquis, still pinned against the side of the cliff, was able to reach up and grasp her ankle. With one sharp tug, he managed to bring her over the edge.

"Phaedraaaa!" Zephir roared, watching helplessly as his wife disappeared off the cliff. For a moment, he was shocked motionless. He covered his face in his huge hands and uttered a ragged, painful cry.

After several moment, Zephir thought he heard his name in the distance. Slowly, his feet moved in the direction of the cliff's edge. Relief brightened his face and surged throughout his body when he discovered his wife alive and balancing herself on a decaying rock.

"Phaedra!"

Her head snapped up, her eyes brightening as they widened. "Zephir!" She raised one hand to her husband.

Zephir lay flat on his stomach and curled one of his massive hands around her upper arm. Then, he easily pulled her to safety. "Thank you, God," he whispered as he stood and took her with him. With his wife in his arms, he buried his handsome face in her neck and inhaled her scent.

Marquis still pressed himself against the cliff wall. Though he was slipping inevitably toward his death, his eyes still possessed the look of hate. "I curse your filthy souls to hell!" he growled, glaring up at the couple. "I promise you both, this is not over! I will come back. We will all come back for you and your sons!"

Zephir and Phaedra exchanged knowing glances then looked at Marquis once more.

"We will await your return, Toussaint!" Zephir grimly replied. The tip of one boot swung out and landed squarely in Marquis's upturned face.

Phaedra shuddered when her cousin's screams filled her ears. As Marquis plummeted to his death, she turned her face into Zephir's neck and sighed.

324

EPILOGUE

~The end of a nightmare, brings a new era of happiness~

The Toussaint plantation was filled with people and laughter once again. Zephir and Phaedra were celebrating five years of marriage with family, friends and neighbors. The adults enjoyed dancing and singing inside the cozy interior of the lovely main house. Meanwhile, the children played in the huge backyard. Toumie and Ric Mfume were growing taller and more handsome with each passing day. They both ate like children more than twice their ages. Of course, they were just as confident and courageous as their parents.

"What's this?" Zephir called, finding his beautiful wife alone on the balcony which overlooked the front yard.

Phaedra enjoyed the feel of her husband's arms encircling her waist. "I'm just appreciating all of this." She stared out across the estate that had changed greatly during the past five years.

News of the Marquis, Carlos and Dante's deaths spread like a wildfire across Dominica and further. As a result, much of the family returned to build their homes on lands surrounding the plantation.

Zephir settled his gorgeous face in the softness of Phaedra's wavy locks and breathed in the coconut scent of the billowing onyx mass. "Have you seen them yet?" he whispered, brushing his lips against her ear.

Phaedra took a deep breath and looked up at the darkening evening skies. "Who's reading minds now?" she teased, knowing he was referring to the three black ravens that always appeared on the plantation whenever a party was in progress.

"There," she whispered, pointing to a tree across the yard.

Zephir's piercing midnight eyes narrowed a bit more as he looked high into the tree. "We should get our rifles."

Phaedra poked his stomach at the playful suggestion. "They must adore parties."

"Still," Zephir sighed, becoming slightly serious, "they're rare in this part of the world."

"I like to think they are my Mother, Father and Tisha enjoying the sights and sounds of family filling the land again."

Zephir smoothed his hands across the lavender satin of Phaedra's gown then turned her to face him. He lowered his head and thrust his tongue into the fragrant softness of her mouth. She uttered a tiny moan and arched her small frame against Zephir. Her slender fingers grasped the soft tweed of the three quarter length suit coat he wore. His hands cupped her breast beneath the lacy bodice of her gown. She pushed her hands into his silky hair and deepened the kiss.

He raised his head. "Do you suppose we could slip away from this celebration for a while?"

Phaedra offered her most wicked look. "I think it could be arranged." she whispered.

Suddenly, Phaedra's laughter bubbled inside her and rose to the surface. Soon, both she and Zephir were laughing heartily. Arm in arm, they disappeared into their home.

From the towering tree, the three wild ravens sang their passionate cry into the cool evening breeze.

ABOUT THE AUTHOR

AlTonya Washington published her first novel *Remember Love* in April 2003. The novel received a 4 star rating from *Romantic Times Magazine* and went on to be nominated by the magazine as the Best First Multicultural Romance for 2003. Her second novel "Guarded Love" was released in December 2003 and was granted a 4 1/2 star rating from *Romantic Times Magazine*. She has signed with Genesis Press to release her first Historical Romance, *Wild Ravens*. AlTonya has been acknowledged by South Carolina Congressman Jim Clyburn following the publication of South Carolina's *Community Times* newspaper's "31 Leaders Under 35," a cover story for her accomplishments. In April 2004, *Shades of Romance Magazine* readers chose AlTonya as the Best New Multicultural Romance Author of 2003.

AlTonya Washington is a South Carolina native. She lives in North Carolina where she works as a Senior Library Assistant.

BLOODLUST

BY

J.M. JEFFRIES

Release Date: September 2005

PROLOGUE

Martinique—1745

"You sold my children!" Mignon curled her hands around the edge of the blanket covering her nakedness, fighting the impotent fury inside her. Candles lit the opulent bedroom, casting flickers of flames over his face, highlighting the evil twist of his lips and the shadow of his eyes.

Charles Rabelais seemed to gloat. "Your brats were mine to dispose of as I chose." He stroked her cheek with long, pale fingers.

She tried not to turn away as he traced her bottom lip with his thumb. Instead, she concentrated on his white skin showing stark against her duskiness. "Please give them back."

Because he was her children's father, she had hoped they'd be safe from the slave blocks. Charles felt had no kinship despite the fact his seed, planted deep within her, had given them life.

"*Non,*" he said.

Agonizing pain knifed through her as his chilled fingers slid across her light brown cheek. She steeled herself not to draw away no matter how she loathed his touch. Once before, she'd been foolish enough to defy him. The bite of the whip still echoed in her mind, as well as the piercing pain that had raced across her back. His amused laughter had frightened her most of all.

"Why?" she asked, dreading his answer. Lace curtains billowed in the breeze, bringing a hint of fragrant wisteria inside the room.

Leaning over, he kissed her earlobe. "So that you will be mine for eternity."

She trembled as he slid his hand down the side of her throat to the curve of her breast. "Master, they are so little." Her darlings were gone. Helplessness filled her. They had been the only reason she had not taken her own life as her mother had. She would not leave her babies at his mercy.

Charles chuckled. "I brokered a deal with the devil and your whelps were the price."

Her lips trembled. A tear slid down her cheek. "Angeline is only eleven years old and Simon is but seven. They are your children, too."

Charles waved his hand. The soft light of the candles illuminated his pale skin. "Be happy I didn't kill them. My love for you is what kept them alive. What should concern you now is an appropriate means of showing your gratitude." He moved over her, parting her knees with his leg.

Gratitude for what? For her living hell? For her children's lives? What were her choices. She was a woman. A slave with no recourse.

If she complied with his demands, she might find out who he'd sold the children to. Perhaps then she could…she couldn't finish the thought. She had no means of finding them or obtaining their free-dom. Mignon closed her eyes and forced out the words he wanted to hear. "Thank you for letting them live."

"Very pretty." He kissed her lips. "Now I must finish what I start-ed."

He had talked about that before. What did he mean? "I don"t understand."

"Do you want to live forever? By my side? Warming my bed?"

What choice did she have? He already owned her flesh, her blood, everything but her soul. "What are you saying?"

He scraped his thumbnail along the throbbing pulse in her neck. "Say yes and I will give you eternal life. Eternal beauty. My heart for-ever. Everything any woman could ever want."

She only wanted her children back. A dark pit formed in her heart, and an icy shell seemed to surround it. "What must I do to please you?"

"Say yes." He kissed her again, forcing his tongue between her lips.

Whatever Charles wanted, he had only to take. He'd already taken her virtue. Her mother, once a household servant, had been put to work in the cane fields when she'd objected to him taking Mignon as his whore. She had died soon after. Of her own father, Mignon had no knowledge, only that her mother had warmed the bed of another planter before being sold to Charles. Now Charles had sold her children. Nothing was left for him to take. The years stretched out before her bleak and dismal, all joy removed. "Yes."

"I knew you would." His hand tightened around her neck. He forced her head to one side.

Squeezing her eyes tight, she willed the pain rippling through her to end. Endless years, endless nothing. With her children gone, what did she have to live for?

"Look at me," Charles commanded in a guttural tone.

Mignon opened her eyes and stared at his mouth. Was she mistaken, or were his teeth growing? The pearly white tips rested on his colorless bottom lip. Fear surged through her. She wanted to pull back, but his grip was so strong, she feared he might snap her neck.

Charles licked her neck, starting at her ear and slowly moving down toward the beating pulse. The seconds, measured by the ticking of the clock on the mantle, passed slowly.

She couldn't look away from the evil in his face. Suddenly his mouth opened. Sharp fangs gleamed at her. No sound came out of her mouth as she tried to scream. He gripped her hair in a tight fist, pulling, bringing tears to her eyes.

He smiled at her, enjoying her distress, her fear. He sniffed at her mouth as though her fear were a palpable object to be fondled and enjoyed.

Her body froze. She couldn't close her eyes. His mouth neared her neck. After a long moment, he bit and sighed, as though savoring the trembling of her body. Pain seared into her flesh. Her blood seemed to run like fire in her veins. Death, she hoped, she prayed. Let him give her death.

WILD RAVENS

2005 Publication Schedule

January

A Heart's Awakening
Veronica Parker
$9.95
1-58571-143-8

Falling
Natalie Dunbar
$9.95
1-58571-121-7

February

Echoes of Yesterday
Beverly Clark
$9.95
1-58571-131-4

A Love of Her Own
Cheris F. Hodges
$9.95
1-58571-136-5

Higher Ground
Leah Latimer
$19.95
1-58571-157-8

March

Misconceptions
Pamela Leigh Starr
$9.95
1-58571-117-9

I'll Paint a Sun
A.J. Garrotto
$9.95
1-58571-165-9

Peace Be Still
Colette Haywood
$12.95
1-58571-129-2

April

Intentional Mistakes
Michele Sudler
$9.95
1-58571-152-7

Conquering Dr. Wexler's Heart
Kimberley White
$9.95
1-58571-126-8

Song in the Park
Martin Brant
$15.95
1-58571-125-X

May

The Color Line
Lizzette Grayson Carter
$9.95
1-58571-163-2

Unconditional
A.C. Arthur
$9.95
1-58571-142-X

Last Train to Memphis
Elsa Cook
$12.95
1-58571-146-2

June

Angel's Paradise
Janice Angelique
$9.95
1-58571-107-1

Suddenly You
Crystal Hubbard
$9.95
1-58571-158-6

Matters of Life and
    Death
Lesego Malepe, Ph.D.
$15.95
1-58571-124-1

2005 Publication Schedule (continued)

July

Class Reunion
Irma Jenkins/John
  Brown
$12.95
1-58571-123-3

Wild Ravens
Altonya Washington
$9.95
1-58571-164-0

August

Path of Thorns
Annetta P. Lee
$9.95
1-58571-145-4

Timeless Devotion
Bella McFarland
$9.95
1-58571-148-9

Life Is Never As It Seems
J.J. Michael
$12.95
1-58571-153-5

September

Beyond the Rapture
Beverly Clark
$9.95
1-58571-131-4

Blood Lust
J. M. Jeffries
$9.95
1-58571-138-1

Rough on Rats and
  Tough on Cats
Chris Parker
$12.95
1-58571-154-3

October

A Will to Love
Angie Daniels
$9.95
1-58571-141-1

Taken by You
Dorothy Elizabeth Love
$9.95
1-58571-162-4

Soul Eyes
Wayne L. Wilson
$12.95
1-58571-147-0

November

A Drummer's Beat to
  Mend
Kay Swanson
$9.95

Sweet Reprecussions
Kimberley White
$9.95
1-58571-159-4

Red Polka Dot in a
  Worldof Plaid
Varian Johnson
$12.95
1-58571-140-3

December

Hand in Glove
Andrea Jackson
$9.95
1-58571-166-7

Blaze
Barbara Keaton
$9.95

Across
Carol Payne
$12.95
1-58571-149-7

WILD RAVENS

Other Genesis Press, Inc. Titles

Acquisitions	Kimberley White	$8.95
A Dangerous Deception	J.M. Jeffries	$8.95
A Dangerous Love	J.M. Jeffries	$8.95
A Dangerous Obsession	J.M. Jeffries	$8.95
After the Vows	Leslie Esdaile	$10.95
(Summer Anthology)	T.T. Henderson	
	Jacqueline Thomas	
Again My Love	Kayla Perrin	$10.95
Against the Wind	Gwynne Forster	$8.95
A Lark on the Wing	Phyliss Hamilton	$8.95
A Lighter Shade of Brown	Vicki Andrews	$8.95
All I Ask	Barbara Keaton	$8.95
A Love to Cherish	Beverly Clark	$8.95
Ambrosia	T.T. Henderson	$8.95
And Then Came You	Dorothy Elizabeth Love	$8.95
Angel's Paradise	Janice Angelique	$8.95
A Risk of Rain	Dar Tomlinson	$8.95
At Last	Lisa G. Riley	$8.95
Best of Friends	Natalie Dunbar	$8.95
Bound by Love	Beverly Clark	$8.95
Breeze	Robin Hampton Allen	$10.95
Brown Sugar Diaries &	Delores Bundy &	$10.95
Other Sexy Tales	Cole Riley	
By Design	Barbara Keaton	$8.95
Cajun Heat	Charlene Berry	$8.95
Careless Whispers	Rochelle Alers	$8.95
Caught in a Trap	Andre Michelle	$8.95
Chances	Pamela Leigh Starr	$8.95
Dark Embrace	Crystal Wilson Harris	$8.95
Dark Storm Rising	Chinelu Moore	$10.95
Designer Passion	Dar Tomlinson	$8.95
Ebony Butterfly II	Delilah Dawson	$14.95

Erotic Anthology	Assorted	$8.95
Eve's Prescription	Edwina Martin Arnold	$8.95
Everlastin' Love	Gay G. Gunn	$8.95
Fate	Pamela Leigh Starr	$8.95
Forbidden Quest	Dar Tomlinson	$10.95
Fragment in the Sand	Annetta P. Lee	$8.95
From the Ashes	Kathleen Suzanne	$8.95
	Jeanne Sumerix	
Gentle Yearning	Rochelle Alers	$10.95
Glory of Love	Sinclair LeBeau	$10.95
Hart & Soul	Angie Daniels	$8.95
Heartbeat	Stephanie Bedwell-Grime	$8.95
I'll Be Your Shelter	Giselle Carmichael	$8.95
Illusions	Pamela Leigh Starr	$8.95
Indiscretions	Donna Hill	$8.95
Interlude	Donna Hill	$8.95
Intimate Intentions	Angie Daniels	$8.95
Just an Affair	Eugenia O'Neal	$8.95
Kiss or Keep	Debra Phillips	$8.95
Love Always	Mildred E. Riley	$10.95
Love Unveiled	Gloria Greene	$10.95
Love's Deception	Charlene Berry	$10.95
Mae's Promise	Melody Walcott	$8.95
Meant to Be	Jeanne Sumerix	$8.95
Midnight Clear	Leslie Esdaile	$10.95
(Anthology)	Gwynne Forster	
	Carmen Green	
	Monica Jackson	
Midnight Magic	Gwynne Forster	$8.95
Midnight Peril	Vicki Andrews	$10.95
My Buffalo Soldier	Barbara B. K. Reeves	$8.95
Naked Soul	Gwynne Forster	$8.95
No Regrets	Mildred E. Riley	$8.95
Nowhere to Run	Gay G. Gunn	$10.95

Object of His Desire	A. C. Arthur	$8.95
One Day at a Time	Bella McFarland	$8.95
Passion	T.T. Henderson	$10.95
Past Promises	Jahmel West	$8.95
Path of Fire	T.T. Henderson	$8.95
Picture Perfect	Reon Carter	$8.95
Pride & Joi	Gay G. Gunn	$8.95
Quiet Storm	Donna Hill	$8.95
Reckless Surrender	Rochelle Alers	$8.95
Rendezvous with Fate	Jeanne Sumerix	$8.95
Revelations	Cheris F. Hodges	$8.95
Rivers of the Soul	Leslie Esdaile	$8.95
Rooms of the Heart	Donna Hill	$8.95
Shades of Brown	Denise Becker	$8.95
Shades of Desire	Monica White	$8.95
Sin	Crystal Rhodes	$8.95
So Amazing	Sinclair LeBeau	$8.95
Somebody's Someone	Sinclair LeBeau	$8.95
Someone to Love	Alicia Wiggins	$8.95
Soul to Soul	Donna Hill	$8.95
Still Waters Run Deep	Leslie Esdaile	$8.95
Subtle Secrets	Wanda Y. Thomas	$8.95
Sweet Tomorrows	Kimberly White	$8.95
The Color of Trouble	Dyanne Davis	$8.95
The Price of Love	Sinclair LeBeau	$8.95
The Reluctant Captive	Joyce Jackson	$8.95
The Missing Link	Charlyne Dickerson	$8.95
Three Wishes	Seressia Glass	$8.95
Tomorrow's Promise	Leslie Esdaile	$8.95
Truly Inseperable	Wanda Y. Thomas	$8.95
Twist of Fate	Beverly Clark	$8.95
Unbreak My Heart	Dar Tomlinson	$8.95
Unconditional Love	Alicia Wiggins	$8.95
When Dreams A Float	Dorothy Elizabeth Love	$8.95

Whispers in the Night	Dorothy Elizabeth Love	$8.95
Whispers in the Sand	LaFlorya Gauthier	$10.95
Yesterday is Gone	Beverly Clark	$8.95
Yesterday's Dreams, Tomorrow's Promises	Reon Laudat	$8.95
Your Precious Love	Sinclair LeBeau	$8.95

Order Form

Mail to: Genesis Press, Inc.
P.O. Box 101
Columbus, MS 39703

Name _____
Address _____
City/State _____ Zip _____
Telephone _____

Ship to (if different from above)
Name _____
Address _____
City/State _____ Zip _____
Telephone _____

Credit Card Information

Credit Card # _____ ☐ Visa ☐ Mastercard

Expiration Date (mm/yy) _____ ☐ AmEx ☐ Discover

Qty.	Author	Title	Price	Total

Use this order form, or call 1-888-INDIGO-1	Total for books _____
	Shipping and handling:
	  $5 first two books,
	  $1 each additional book _____
	Total S & H _____
	Total amount enclosed _____
	Mississippi residents add 7% sales tax

Visit www.genesis-press.com for latest releases and excerpts.